CORA

A. L. HAWKE

PHANTOM HEART, LLC

ISBN: 978-1-7329563-3-9 (paperback)

ISBN: 978-1-7329563-2-2 (ebook)

Library of Congress Control Number: 2019912915

This is a work of fiction. It all comes directly from the imagination of the author's mind. This includes names, characters, places, and incidents. Any public names are used solely for creative purposes. Any resemblance to actual people, living or dead, or to companies, institutions or locales is entirely coincidental or accidental.

Developmentally edited by Maya Rock

Line edited and proofread by Eliza Dee of Clio Editing Services

Cover Design © 2019 by: Regina Wamba of MaeIDesign.com

Published by Phantom Heart, LLC

27702 Crown Valley Pkwy D-4, #201

Ladera Ranch, CA 92694, USA

Printed and bound in the United States of America

First printing October, 2019

Learn more about A.L. Hawke at www.alhawke.com

Correspondence: contact@alhawke.com

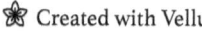 Created with Vellum

1

MS. CORA AREGARD

Cora sunbathed in shades on her deck overlooking the shore while occasionally gazing up at the fluffy white pillows among the cerulean Southern Californian sky, trying her very best to forget all about Danny. She wasn't in the best of moods. It wasn't about Danny—he was dead.

Earlier that very morning, she and Hashan, her stiff butler, had traveled to downtown LA to visit their family lawyer. Danny was giving her back her things in his will. They were all her things, anyway. Cora often put most of her possessions with her husband's in order to claim them again after he passed, avoiding suspicion over her wealth. He'd left a very expensive abstract painting to his cousin in Madrid. He'd willed his gold Rolex to Hashan. Next, he had arranged for her mother-in-law to keep their chateau in Madrid. All of that had been expected and rather boring, but then, at the end of the meeting, Danny had done something no one had ever done before—he bequeathed her a name.

Of course, she had always changed her name with the death of a husband. She had to change her identity so people wouldn't be suspicious over her immortal damned soul. But this time, the recently deceased had forced her to change her name immediately in order to reacquire her things. *Her* things. No one had ever forced change on her so quickly before. He'd shut the door on her heartlessly, but that was Danny—he was always hurting her when trying to do something nice.

Forthwith, the goddess Persephone would be known as Ms. Cora Aregard. And so Mrs. Cora Anastra was lost and forgotten.

You bastard! You want me to forget you? 'Kay.

She opened her eyes, readjusted her tight red bikini top, ran her fingers through her long deep red hair, and looked down at the shore. Below her cliff was a little boy digging his hands in the sand. He was wet and muddy, getting sand all over his chest, arms and face. He had a little plastic play shovel and made two mounds of dirt, likely trying to build a sandcastle. It was far below, but Cora's vision was sharp. A wave came and washed the boy and all his work away. The poor kid tumbled over and over until landing by his mommy's feet. She quickly picked him up. Cora laughed. *Poor thing.*

You don't mind if I empty your closet tonight, dear? Since you want me to forget you. I was going to wait a month, but why wait? I'm Ms. Cora Aregard now, after all. Right, fucker?

But she did like the sound of the name. *Aregard.* It sounded so elegant. So regal. She and Danny had agreed on it years ago.

A group of teenagers played volleyball on the sand next to the tumbling boy. The ball was hit into the water and rose with the waves, the water rising high today. There were a lot of surfers behind the floating ball.

First, I'll gather up your house shirts, the stupid ones covered in paint I kept telling you to get rid of, or maybe the shirt you loved that I cut into pieces. Remember? Or maybe I'll donate that one to a museum and people can wonder why it has holes in it. We can display it next to one of your abstract works. No one will ever know the difference.

I never liked your choice of pants, by the way. You always wanted to wear sweatpants with suit jackets. Why did I have to marry an artist? You were so weird.

Oh wait, what do I care? I'm Ms. Aregard now. Right? I don't even know who the hell you are, you fucking bastard!

Two couples, both young, walked along the sand hand in hand. They looked *so* in love. *Bastards!*

That was when she heard her butler Hashan talking to a guest inside her house.

Ah, here comes the new young man from Platinum Properties.

She had already heard the car circle around her driveway from her backyard deck. Her hearing was sharper than any human's, and she was aware of everything from the inside of her house to everyone along the beach down below. She had been waiting for him to meet her outside.

I think I'm going to fuck him. How does that sound, Danny? If I'm lucky, your spirit can watch us. You wanted me to change my name. 'Kay. So, I, Ms. Cora Aregard, will fuck Mr. Gabriel Cartwright right under the tip of your goddamn nose in honor of your dead decaying body, you motherfucking bastard! How dare you tell me when ...

The sliding glass door opened. She turned and tipped her sunglasses down.

Hashan, looking odd as usual with his olive-skinned crow-shaped face, jet-black suit and shades, stood under a tall, very handsome late-twenties man with short, wavy black hair. The guest looked too young for the dark gray suit he wore.

"A Mr. Gabriel Cartwright, madam," Hashan announced.

Gabriel walked slowly around the swimming pool with Hashan and then stood over Cora. Cora turned and faced him, still with her shades tilted down, on the chaise lounge.

"Uh, would you happen to know where I can find Mrs. Anastra, miss?" the stranger asked her rudely. "I'm very late. My flight was delayed."

Cora smiled. Then she quickly gestured for Hashan not to say a word.

"She'll be here shortly, Mr. Cartwright. In the meantime, have a seat. We have a lovely view of the sea, don't you think?"

"Yes, very nice," the man said impatiently. She sat up straighter, admiring the curves of his broad shoulders and legs.

"I'm sorry," he apologized. "It was a long flight. I'm supposed to meet Mrs. Anastra. Are you her granddaughter?"

Granddaughter? Granddaughter! Priceless.

"No." Cora got up with a nod. "I'm her niece. My name's ... Percy. Percy Aregard." Hashan looked over disapprovingly. Cora smiled at Hashan when Gabriel wasn't looking. "Auntie Anastra is away at the moment." Hashan rolled his eyes. "But she'll be here soon. Why not sit? Relax and enjoy the scenery. It is lovely, isn't it?" She looked up, right into his brilliant blue eyes. He moved back nervously. "Have a seat."

He looked exhausted, poor thing.

"Will you be needing me any longer, madam?" interrupted a perturbed Hashan.

"No." *Shoo. Shoo. Go away.*

Gabriel sat down uncomfortably on the lounge chair beside her. Cora lay back in hers. She heard him rustle in a pocket. "Do you know how much longer she'll be, Percy?"

"Oh, I don't think much longer." She cocked her head. He was staring at his cell phone. She reclined and resumed sunbathing. "If you'd like, I can get you a bathing suit and you can have a swim. Such a lovely day."

"No, that's okay," he said, sounding annoyed.

"'Kay." She scooted up and closed her eyes. "Enjoy the view. The sun is setting. She'll be here soon." She waited for him to speak. He didn't, so she rattled on. "You know, when I was a little girl, Mr. Cartwright, I used to stand before a view just like this one overlooking the ocean. I used to stand out on a cliffside looking out at the water of the Aegean. There's so much out there, you know. That's always amazed me. I just love looking out at the waves. It's so lovely, isn't it? You can imagine all the fishies, all the boats, all the world, for that matter, out along the horizon. It's mind-boggling considering all the fishies under the water. Sharks. Manta rays. Octopuses. Kelp. It's like another world. I just love the beach. And the sand. And it's fun, you know, looking down and people watching."

"It's very nice, Percy. So, you live here with Mrs. Anastra?"

"Um-hmm. Do you like it?"

"The view?"

"Yes. And my home."

"Of course."

"What do you like about it?" she asked.

"The Doric columns and statues around the driveway and gardens are impressive. I've never seen anything like it before." He was still staring at his phone.

"You have a keen eye, sir. Doric columns, eh? Of course, when I was very young in Greece, much younger than now, I lived in the fields. We had columns there in Hellena too. Are you from the country, Mr. Cartwright?"

"No," he said absentmindedly, heaving a deep sigh. He seemed to have no interest in talking to her. "Jersey."

"Ah, but you don't have a Jersey accent. It sounds Southern."

"As a boy, I lived in Missouri."

"The show-me state. I like a confident, honest man. It's refreshing in a world full of bullshit and lies."

"Uh-huh." He fiddled more with his phone again. "Well, your aunt has a beautiful home, Percy." He took a deep breath, getting more impatient. "I also noticed the polished brass along the floor molding and under the windows. It's unique and very classy."

"I suggest you relax, sir. Here you are in the loveliest home you've ever seen, beside a fabulous view, and yet all you want to do is assess my molding."

He coughed. "I—"

"Anyway, I'm very pleased that you like my home."

"Your aunt's," he corrected.

"The molding isn't brass, by the way. It's gold."

"Gold?" He laughed. "Covering the floor molding? It can't be."

"Solid gold," she said, shrugging. Then she dipped her shades down over her nose and stared at him. "You want me to get you some swim trunks? Perhaps you'd like a swim. You look really weird by my pool in a suit."

"Your aunt's pool."

"Come again?"

"Your aunt's pool."

"Oh, yeah." She bit her lower lip. "Actually, I'm just messing with you, Mr. Cartwright. I'm Cora."

She stuck out her hand. He was taken aback. He didn't seem to believe her, keeping his hand down.

"Percy, I have a meeting with Mrs. Anastra."

"I know. You need to be patient. The sun hasn't set yet."

"Can you go get her for me?"

"No."

"Why?"

"Because it's rather difficult to get yourself."

"You're joking?"

"No, I'm quite serious."

He looked perplexed.

She jumped up from the chair. "Fuck the sunset. Come inside, since you're so impatient. We can do business indoors."

Then she swayed her hips around the pool to the sliding glass doors as he ran to catch up to her. From an outdoor wooden dining table near the sliding doors, she grabbed a short white satin dressing gown and draped it over her bikini, untied, then opened the sliding door, gesturing for him to follow.

"Is this a joke?" he repeated, trailing behind her. "I was expecting someone—"

"Older?" she asked laughing. "I get that a lot."

Hashan met them by the hallway. He was carrying a small

handbag and keys. "Snacks for your guest are under the warmer upstairs, madam. If you are in need of anything else, please call."

"Don't worry about it, Hashan."

Mr. Cartwright looked at her in shock. She laughed.

"Good day, Mr. Cartwright," Hashan said with a bow.

"You're leaving?" he stammered.

"Yes. Madam Cora wanted to meet with you alone in her bedroom upstairs."

"Oh ... all right," he said.

She sensed a hint of anxiety in his voice. She adored that.

"Follow me, Mr. Cartwright. To my room."

They walked up a stairway wide enough to accommodate six people. There was more "brass" along the rail. She watched him run his finger over it in awe. Although they were only two stories, the steps seemed to extend to a height of three or four. It also became darker as they ascended. Towards the top were a group of lit antique candlesticks, creating a nineteenth-century feel. He seemed to admire the tiled dome ceiling vaulted above them and sporadic small white marble statues in recesses on the wall. Over the rail glowed the downstairs, brightly lit from windows, but the upstairs was dark apart from the shimmering candlelight.

"An odd choice of décor," he commented, looking at the candles.

"I thought you liked it?"

"I ... of course I like it, but it's completely different from the entrance. It's bright and inviting outside, but very dark up here."

They entered a giant open space that filled the entire second floor. It was dark up here too, lit by a dozen candles along the walls. Behind the candles were closed burgundy velvet curtains that stretched from one wall to the other. Light came in between and under the curtains, which obscured the floor-to-ceiling windows. She headed to the center of the room, walking up three marble steps and sitting on a raised swivel chair. She reclined and gazed down on him with a smile, allowing her robe to open over her pale white legs. Then, to complete the impression, she raised her arm and a majestic black bird landed on her forearm—it looked like a giant raven, but with bright blue eyes and rainbow-tipped wings. Cora petted the bird without turning her gaze from him.

She threw her hand up and the bird took off to the opposite side of the room.

"Hi," she said.

"Mrs. Anastra?" he asked, still unsure.

He looked around the room in awe.

He was a very handsome man. She liked the stubble on his face. He probably hadn't had time to shave. He had a hard chin and thin lips. She would love to touch those soft lips to hers—lightly, just play and bite at his hard upper lip and then lick across the rough stubble of his cheek. His body was hard, cut and yummy too. A few more tosses of her red hair, perhaps, a couple stray glances, and maybe a stray finger along her chest might make the young stag horny enough to want to lie with her tonight. That would be her message to Danny. *Fuck you, hubby, I'm moving on exactly like you wanted me to, 'kay?* After all, her extra-large bed was just a handful of steps away, still open with dark silk sheets, not made from the morning.

Hashan had reprimanded her like a child for arranging the meeting upstairs, but she needed a good fuck—for Danny. Fucking could help her forget her pain. She always used sex to do that. And maybe, if she was lucky, Danny's spirit would watch them from above as retribution.

She liked Gabriel. He was reserved. Danny had been reserved. Of course, it was his eyes she liked the most—azure like her own.

She laid her pale fingers over the naked parts of her skin along her legs, turned her head down, and looked down on him with a sly grin.

"Hi."

"Cora?" he repeated, still not believing her.

"How do you like Los Angeles, Gabe?"

"I haven't seen much of it," he muttered.

"Your flight was delayed?" she asked. "Sorry. I hate flying. It's so miserable—even first class. There's no fucking leg room, right?"

He nodded. Then he sat down on one of two simple black leather chairs below her.

"Where did I leave it?" she asked, putting her finger to her chin.

"I'm sorry for mistaking you for someone else," he said very formally.

"That's *my* game, mister." He looked uncomfortable and she laughed. Then she threw a hand in the air. "I like having fun. So, tell me, how long have you been working for Platinum Properties?"

"One year."

"A year? And I'm supposed to trust you with selling the place?"

"It's already sold, Mrs. Anastra. You have a buyer."

"From China?"

"Yeah."

"Right. After I sign the papers, how long before I have to vacate?"

"One week. But, from what I've heard, the buyer isn't going to move in right away. We could ask for more time if you need it."

"Why isn't he moving in? Does he intend to bulldoze it down?"

"No, Mrs. Anastra," he said with a laugh.

"Call me Cora. I wouldn't altogether mind, you know. I intend to bulldoze the property in Toronto. I don't intend to live in a log cabin."

"It's up to you, but the property in Toronto is no *log cabin*. It's a mansion overlooking a lake. You should see it before you

... bulldoze it. You might want to keep it. It's a stunning mansion."

"But it snows."

"Yeah ... it's *Toronto*."

"Right. Tell me, Gabe, how long have you been a realtor?"

"Five years."

"So you worked in other jobs?"

"Quite a few. I'm not so young, Cora."

"Oh, are you offended by being thought of as young?"

He laughed. "You got me there."

"Did you always want to be a realtor?"

"Yes." He looked uncomfortable at the question. "Once I wanted to be a nurse. I even studied for it."

"Health care? How noble."

"I couldn't stand studying," he added with a laugh. She laughed too.

She liked how he answered her questions. He was a nervous fellow. Had someone been watching them, she mused, they would have marveled at the contrast. She had her body sprawled half-naked before him, sitting on a pedestal and looking down on him, exuding confidence, while he sat looking up like a frightened little boy. He was prim and proper, and despite his baby face, he looked older than her. He was almost thirty.

I stayed away too long. Too partial to his Napean sister, Lilly. Damn. I like him.

She leapt down the steps and bounded to a glass table between two white fabric-covered chairs all the way across the room. It took some time, as the large room spanned the entire second floor.

"Why didn't you become a nurse?" she hollered back to him.

"I wanted to make money."

She laughed. "Oh, is there a lot of money in the realty business?"

"Yes, Cora, there is. Particularly with clients like you."

There were some magazines along the small glass table. She leaned down and flipped through them. She felt her robe fall to her side and knew that the thong of her tight bikini bottoms was pressing inside her butt, perfectly delineating the crack of her ass. He could probably make out the curvature perfectly. She took advantage of the view, swaying her ass back and forth a little as she crouched forward, searching the magazines.

She liked playing with men. And she liked this one. Quiet and demure. She liked shy men. And handsome.

She wanted him. It wouldn't be so difficult. She had caught him looking at her chest outside by the pool. He might be shy, but she was sure she could find a way to get into his pants tonight.

When she looked back at him, he quickly looked the other way.

"What are you looking for?" he asked, staring at the curtains.

"The contract. That is why you're here, isn't it, Mr. Cartwright?"

"Of course."

She stood still and cupped her chin again, tapping her finger on her cheek. "Shit. Where did I leave it?"

"Your"—he cleared his throat—"your home is very beautiful."

"Elegant," she said with a chuckle. "Elegant. Not beautiful, Gabriel. Elegant."

She bent down over the mounds of magazines again, but then whirled around suddenly.

"Hey, would you like a drink? I'm being so rude. I've got a full bar. Anything you want. What's your taste?"

"Whiskey."

"Ummm, yummy. But I like vodka."

She quickly turned and walked to the bar, where her large majestic bird perched atop the marble counter. Cora went behind the bar and petted the bird again. "I'm sure I've got whiskey somewhere."

"Whatever, Cora. Vodka's fine."

She leaned over the bird and whispered into his ear. "You like him? Nice, huh? He's Napean." She caught him looking over at her oddly. The bird nodded his majestic head. Cora giggled. "I like him too."

Cora's bar was a full bar indeed. She had bottles decorating a mirrored back wall, and a metallic table faced the front. She grabbed two martini glasses and a cocktail shaker, then walked near the entrance to the counter and bent down. She had her back turned as she opened a refrigerator. She looked back as she pulled out a jar of olives. Gabriel suddenly squirmed and looked away yet again as she flashed him a lascivious smile.

What's his deal? Relax.

Then she turned and reached up high to grab two bottles, placing them on the counter, and turned from him for a second, adjusting the top of her bathing suit over her breasts.

"If we're going to continue to talk, perhaps you should put on something warmer," he said.

"Fuck you. I wear whatever the hell I want."

"Sorry, Cora." He jumped at her language, looking disturbed for a moment. "I wasn't trying to be offensive."

"You weren't. I just don't like guys telling me what to wear."

"Oh."

"You like my bird? He's named Mainax."

She opened the two bottles.

"I've never seen a bird like that. Never in a house. Is that why the room is so big?"

She laughed at his sarcasm. "No. He's a phoenix. Legend says that he never dies. An awful legend. Why would anyone want to live forever?"

"Where does the bird sleep? I don't see a cage."

She expertly mixed the drinks and then shook the shaker, looking at him. It made him squirm.

"He's very well trained. Been in the family for generations. Would you like to pet him?"

"Sure." He got up.

Sure?

The minute she heard the word, she slammed the shaker down, closed her eyes and leaned her head in her hands for a moment. Her eyes started to burn and there was a red glow along the white marble counter.

"Shit," she said quietly, rubbing her forehead.

Sure.

"Are you all right?"

Sure.

"Did I say something wrong?" he asked.

"No." She took a deep breath and shook her head. "Sometimes my migraines act up. That's all. Sorry."

"No, I'm sorry." Gabe jumped up. "Perhaps I can help—"

"No," Cora said, sticking her hand out. "No. No. Just stand back for a second. You had a long flight. The pain comes in waves."

Her eyes shone red on her hands as she leaned her head against the counter, waiting for it to pass. She had forgotten to put her shades on when she had come back inside.

Finally, she felt the warmth fade. She was surprised to find him standing beside her. When she turned and looked into those azure eyes, she felt unsteady for a moment. His eyes weren't only familiar, they were hypnotic. He had the bright, almost glowing, blue eyes from his distant ancestors thousands of years in Napea. Only the gods and goddesses of Greece and the Ambrosia nymphs had such brilliant azure blue eyes.

She had never met a Napean man. Nymph men were nearly as rare as Greek Goddesses. Even after centuries, she had never been acquainted with one. Was there ever another? She was drawn by the chance of getting to know one, protect one, and ... become close to one.

She took a deep breath. She felt lost looking into his eyes, and his look of concern made it worse.

"You okay?" he asked.

"Fine." She forced a fake smile. "Fine." She handed his drink to him. "Here. Taste it. It's my favorite, a vodka martini—dirty."

He sipped the drink. Then she sipped hers.

"Is it yummy?"

"It's very good, Cora."

She clinked her glass against his.

"Aha." Then she sipped it again with a laugh but shook her head. "No. Too much vermouth." She almost spat it out. "Fuck."

"What sort of—"

"Fuck ... what?"

He coughed again and then tried a smile. He looked at her, perplexed.

"Here," she said with a gaping grin, holding the large bird. It spanned her entire arm, standing majestic like a hawk. "Pet him. He loves it."

Gabe obliged.

"Isn't he wonderful?"

"Yes," he said. "I've never seen such a bird. He's like an eagle or hawk. Very well mannered."

"You like birds?"

"Not really."

"Neither do I," she said with a laugh. Then she downed half her drink. "But Mainax ... Mainax is one of a kind. A family heirloom, you could say. Very old. I can tell he likes you."

And indeed, the bird seemed to snuggle up near the man's arm.

Gabriel seemed to examine the bird's multicolored wingtip feathers and the azure chest.

"A strange bird," he said. "But magnificent."

"Elegant, Gabe. Elegant."

"Sure."

Fuck!

She angrily leaned down on the counter again, but he didn't

seem to notice this time. He was too mesmerized by the bird. *His* bird, Nephrea's bird, had he known the truth.

"Can you do me a favor?" Cora said, looking down at the white marble.

"Hmm?"

"Stop saying that word. I know it's a little weird, but it was a favorite of my recently deceased husband."

"What word?"

She took a deep breath, avoided his gaze and gesticulated with her hand, reluctantly uttering, "*Sure.*"

He turned from the bird and chuckled. "Oh, all right. Sorry."

She took a deep breath and nodded.

Oh, how you haunt me, Danny. Is it because I invited a virile young boy to our bedroom tonight?

"He's magnificent," Gabriel said, transfixed by the bird.

"Huh? Oh, yeah. Look, I have a proposal."

"What?" he asked, still petting the bird's feathers.

"An idea. An offer you can't refuse."

"What is it?" He turned to her, finally looking relaxed after petting the ancient bird.

"The contract will take time to be fully reviewed," she said, throwing her deep red hair back. "I'd really like it if you met with me again for dinner in a few weeks."

"I was hoping we could finalize all that today," he said, disappointed.

"I know, but I need time. I've lived in Los Angeles a very long time and I have some very important family business to attend to before I move. You can imagine, with everything that's happened, that I need a little bit more time to sort things out."

"I understand, Cora," he said, "but the sooner the better. I have known clients to renege on the deal if they have to wait too long. But, if you wish, I can try to extend the escrow."

Cora downed the rest of her martini. "You said they won't be rushing to move in. Do it for me, please. I can sign in a month ... I also was hoping we could meet for dinner when you return, Mr. Cartwright." She smiled big and sultry. It made him look uncomfortable again.

"Thanks, Cora, but I'm not sure I can make it back to Los Angeles. I wasn't expecting to return. But, you are a very important client to us. I'll talk it over with my wife."

Wife? Wife! Married!

You've gotta be kidding. You're not wearing a ring. Is that what the coy act was all about? Shit!

Funny, I don't recall MARRIED in his dossier, husband. Was that omission on purpose?

There was an uncomfortable silence. She lifted her drink up but realized the glass was empty. Then she giggled nervously.

"Tell me about her," she blurted out.

She really didn't want to know.

2

THE WATCHER

Long ago along the burning sand of the desert under an endless horizon where there was nothing for many miles except dust, a man appeared like a mirage in the midst of absolute emptiness, walking alone with a black cloak and cane. He roamed the desert at a time a thousand years before any Spaniard or American had yet stepped foot there. The natives thought he was a ghost or vapor, and few believed he was actually real. They saw his three tracks and kept their distance. Those lucky enough to catch a glimpse of him reported that the black-clothed hooded figure would disappear as quickly as he'd appeared. He had no belongings, and yet he seemed to roam where there was no food or water. Native Americans called him the Watcher.

The Watcher was no ghost. He was the ancient Greek god of the underworld, Orcus—also once named Hades and Pluto. He had once been Cora's husband, and the Americas had been Orcus's home long before it had been Cora's.

Today, Orcus was stroking his goatee and thinking of these wanderings as he walked the same trails again. He wore similar dark clothes, this time a formal black suit, and as he approached the base, he had to flash a government ID badge for further passage beyond a mechanical fence and a white pickup truck. He walked past Army barracks, some nearly half a century old. To his far right along the horizon, he could see the raised dirt of a caldera from an explosion he had witnessed decades before. There were many calderas at the base from past nuclear explosions.

A soldier met him by a modern glass-windowed building, an attractive woman wearing a beige camouflage uniform. She was young, with long blond hair in a ponytail, a complexion reddened by too much sun, and a hard expression.

She opened the door for him.

"Sir," she said with a smile. "General Matson is expecting you."

"I know," he said.

"Do you need assistance to the lift?" she asked, keeping an amused smile. She gestured towards his cane.

"How 'bout I lend it to you?" he asked, tossing it to her.

He strolled with her without difficulty to a metal gate at the end of a dark hallway. There they were stopped by a guard, a young man in thin glasses and a formal beige uniform, who jumped up, checking her papers. Then the guard turned and opened the creaky gate.

"May I ask you a question, sir?" she asked as they walked on.

"You already have. And a pretty girl can ask me anything she'd like."

"Why do you use a cane?"

He didn't answer.

She followed him down the lift. The motor whirred and the chains clanged loudly as they descended. It was dark with the exception of the flicker of light from an overhead fluorescent light in the ceiling above. They went many floors down under the earth. At times, he shot her a glance.

"Why do you tie your hair in a ponytail?" he asked about

halfway down, nearly having to shout to be heard over the noise. She turned, surprised.

"Pardon me?"

"You asked me about my stick, I'm asking about your hair," he said, leaning closer.

"I ... don't like my hair getting in the way of my eyes," she said, brushing her bangs back from her forehead. "And ... it's accepted regulation. And, you never answered *my* question."

"Ah, I get it," he chuckled. "You wouldn't want to cover those eyes, love."

"Here's your cane back," she said, throwing it to him with a smile as the elevator stopped. "It's a long walk across the hall. An old man like you may need it."

"Thank you."

He let his eyes wander over her athletic figure for a moment as she led the way. She was pretty, other than the uniform. She had shapely hips.

He considered how to get her alone tonight. Yes, tonight. Just the two of them. That would be nice. Perhaps they could watch the sunset beside one of the old caldera remnants of the Cold War.

The walk was indeed long. The prisoner's cell was at the very end. There were windows with bars to the sides of him, lit by hanging lights. If it wasn't for the various dim lights above, it would be pitch black. The air was musty and thin. He liked it. It reminded him of his ancient home in the underworld.

The last door opened up to a large empty bright white room with a desk and four chairs at the center, the walls decorated with framed pictures of war—planes, missiles, bombs of a bygone era. He walked alongside the wall, ignoring the men by the desk.

"Welcome. I take it you had a nice flight, Orcus?" It was General Joe Matson. Just like his new companion, the general was wearing a beige camouflage uniform, only he had medals displayed along his chest. Orcus had met with the general in Langley only two months before.

Sitting beside him was a man in an orange prison jumpsuit with his hands bound, a coil of chains thick enough to anchor a boat behind him.

"I walked," Orcus answered, still browsing some World War II photographs. He ran a sharp fingernail along one particular frame. It was a black-and-white picture of a mushroom cloud in New Mexico, circa 1945. "Savagery, Joe," he said, tapping the glass covering the photo with his sharp nails. "Absolute savagery."

Flashing the general a big sardonic smile, Orcus walked slowly over to a seat opposite the general and prisoner and sat down.

"We are recording this, gentlemen." The general nodded and flashed a smile of his own. Orcus's female companion placed a large leather bag on the desk, sat down next to Orcus, and took out a computer from the bag. Smiling at him, she arranged her keyboard in front of her and a few files to her side and then began typing.

"Oh, I'm graced with someone lovely for our interrogation?" Orcus asked, addressing her.

"I'm your stenographer, sir," she said, introducing herself formally. "Lieutenant Harris."

"Pretty," he said, nodding to her.

"Yes," General Matson said with a cough. "Well, can we get on with this, Orcus?"

"How long do you think you can keep me here, Hades?" asked the prisoner. He had a Spanish accent.

Orcus lost his smile. He had done everything he could to ignore the god's presence. He turned to the prisoner.

The prisoner was a large lanky man with long flowing golden-blond hair, bright blue eyes, and soft, almost feminine features.

"Oh, how the mighty fall," Orcus said. "But you've always

been a messenger boy, haven't you? Well, now you went too far. You murdered my wife's husband and tried to kill the next one."

"Do you have any idea how idiotic that sounds?" asked the prisoner. "Your *wife* still, is she?"

"If you would," interrupted Lieutenant Harris, looking at the prisoner, "please state your name for the record, sir."

"He is Hermes," Orcus answered for him. "Or Mercury, and just as slippery. He once gifted mortals language and safe swift travel. He was also the god of fertility." Orcus winked at her. She quickly looked down at her keyboard. "And he once worked for me. He moved from Spain to Los Angeles a couple years ago—no doubt to keep an eye on Cora."

"Your innocent wife was tracking me for years in Madrid, Hades," Hermes replied. "She was after all of us. That's where she met her dead husband."

"Hermes was once a friend of mine," continued Orcus. "He worked the gate at Mount Ambitus, towards the entrance to what you mortals once called Mount Olympus. But when Persephone challenged our family, he didn't have the guts to face them."

"You are traitors to Imada!" he shouted. "That's why Zeus kept you underground. You're snakes and not real members of our family."

"And now you, my dear Mercury, are an enemy of the United States of America. And, therefore, of me."

"State your name," Lieutenant Harris repeated, addressing Hermes.

"He already did," Hermes replied, dropping his head.

"What is your name *now*?" asked General Matson.

"Horace. Fernando Horace."

"And you, sir?" she asked, turning to Orcus with a sweet smile.

"I am Orcus."

"Last name."

"I have none. Never did. But, my pretty, you can type down whatever you'd like."

"We found him on the streets, Orcus," the general added, turning to him. "He was around Persephone's house at the time of her husband's death—Mr. Daniel Anastra. He was arrested drunk that same evening after running his car into a department store. And he was seen again a year earlier in Times Square during an attempt on Mr. Gabriel Cartwright's life. You said Mr. Cartwright was important to Cora too, right?"

Orcus nodded.

"We do not have direct proof of the connections, but Mr. Horace's whereabouts are certainly suspicious. And there are certain people, not scrupulous, law-abiding people, that Mr. Horace likes hanging around. One of them killed Cora's husband."

Orcus nodded again.

"How long do you think you can keep me here, Hades?"

"I don't know," Orcus said, looking around at the empty room. "You know, this room was built out of an empty silo. It's not all that different from home. Perhaps you'd be happy here."

"Your bitch wife destroyed your home!" Hermes said, gnashing his teeth. "She flooded Greece and became an enemy of all of Imada! You once helped us. Why you still hold any loyalty to her is beyond me and the rest of Imada. It can't be love. She's married a hundred times over since she loved you—that is, if she ever loved you."

"Who sent you?" asked Orcus. "Who had you loiter around Persephone's home?"

"We suspect Minerva," the general said.

"Let him tell me," Orcus said, not turning his eyes from the prisoner.

"How do you know it wasn't my own plan?"

"You're too stupid for that," Orcus replied. "You're a messenger. You've always been a messenger. You never had it in you to do anything on your own, even when you worked for me. So, I repeat, who sent you to hurt Persephone?"

"The feud has to stop," interrupted the general. "I can't have your family spilling more blood on American soil."

Orcus did not turn. He simply lifted a hand in front of the general's face and, still staring at Hermes, repeated, "Who?"

"Why should I tell you?"

"You're the messenger god," Orcus said with a shrug. "Give us their message. Tell me who sent you and I might be kind to you. If you don't, I will show the same savagery you showed my wife. In fact, I intend much worse."

"She's not your wife!" he exclaimed. "If she is, you ... you certainly don't mind infidelity!" Then he burst into nervous laughter, his eyes opening inappropriately wide. For the first time, Orcus considered that Hermes might have become mad.

"You're a bum, a vagrant," Orcus said. "You all are. All of you have no power left in this world. And now you're a criminal. I suggest you tell me who sent you."

"He's been here for years, Orcus," replied the general. "It's still possible no one sent him."

Orcus finally turned to the general.

"Joe, Imada could have planted him years ago. Your concept of time is quite different from ours. Decades fly like years for us."

"I understand. But he could have been acting alone."

"I don't think so."

"Even if they didn't send for me, you know how much Hera and Dellon don't like her," said Hermes. He laughed inappropriately again. "Perhaps you should question them."

"Is that a hint?" asked Orcus.

Hermes shrugged.

"Do not give me hints." Orcus leaned forward wagging a finger. "Tell me directly who sent you."

But the prisoner remained silent.

"Has it been so long, Hermes, that you have forgotten who I am? Do you doubt what I am capable of doing to you?"

Orcus caught Lieutenant Harris looking up from her keyboard while still typing away the notes of the meeting.

"You're a snake," Hermes said, but he shook a little. "You've always been a snake. But I don't understand why you care for her anymore."

"Can you reconcile this, Orcus?" asked the general. "I can't have your family fighting."

"On American soil, General?" asked Orcus, amused.

"Yes, exactly."

Orcus turned to the stenographer. "Read back what Hermes said a moment ago, love." Then, steepling his fingers, Orcus closed his eyes for a moment. Then he said, "You know ... *how much Hera and ...*"

"The prisoner said, 'Even if they didn't send for me, you know how much Hera and Dellon can't stand her. Perhaps you should question them.'

"And," Lieutenant Harris added, "I would appreciate if you stopped calling me 'love.'"

Orcus chuckled. "Tell me, *Mr. Horace*, when is the last time you communicated with our family?"

"I don't think I have to answer that," he stammered, then he turned to the general. "I ... I would very much like to speak with a lawyer. What right do you have questioning me?"

Orcus burst into laughter. No one else laughed.

"You think this is a trial, *Mr. Horace*?" asked Orcus. He could not stop laughing. "You're twenty stories down under a top-secret military facility in Nevada. How do you think a lawyer is going to help you here? But," Orcus added, raising a finger to the general, "it proves how moronic he is and that he couldn't possibly have been acting alone."

"Who are Hera and Dellon?" the general asked Orcus. "I've spoken to Minerva, but who are Hera and Dellon, Orcus?"

"Hera was Zeus's wife. To my knowledge, she never changed her name. Delian is now *Dellon*. Born from the city of Delos. Dellon is Apollo, Joe. Anyway, whatever we get out of this pitiful weasel, I've already contacted Minerva. I'm well aware of her hatred for Cora."

"I won't tell you anything else," Hermes said with a confident smirk. "Get me a lawyer ... and"— he looked hopelessly around the empty white room—"get me out of here."

Orcus leaned over the desk again, forming a sly smile. "Oh yes, you will."

"I will not," he replied arrogantly with a nervous laugh.

"You are Hermes, the messenger god. I am Hades. Give me your message. Who?"

"I ... I don't know of any contacts, Hades. I swear."

"We shall see." Orcus cocked his head at the stenographer. "Enough of this. Leave. I would like a word alone with my nephew."

The stenographer lifted her fingers from the keyboard and furrowed her brow. "I'm recording minutes, sir."

"I don't want you to witness this, love," Orcus said. "This is family business that you might find rather unpleasant. Please leave."

Lieutenant Harris looked at the general, who nodded. She closed her computer and haughtily headed for the door. The three of them waited as her boots echoed across the room. Then Orcus addressed the general. "I need you to leave too."

"Orcus, I am here—"

"You're here, Joe," Orcus replied, closing his eyes, "because I asked you to be here. Now I'm asking you to leave. I will take care of the rat. Leave my family to me and I will see to it that no more American blood is shed over our little family squabbles. Isn't that what you asked of me?"

The general sat at the desk for a moment, then sighed and got up.

"Do not disturb us," Orcus added, raising a finger. "Whatever you hear from inside this room, do not open the door until I am finished. Do you understand, Joe?"

"As you wish, Orcus," said the general. "Have it—"

"Keep him away from me!" screamed Hermes. "He's insane! He's a sadistic snake! He takes pleasure in inflicting pain!"

But the general walked out and the door slammed shut.

Orcus turned back to Hermes. The messenger god looked terrified, shaking in fear. Orcus made his tremor worse by pulling out a long curved knife from his pocket. "Certainly, you know that I can't kill you, nephew. No god can die. That is why I chained your father and grandfather to the earth in Tartarus. But I can inflict pain. I am very good at that." Orcus ran a finger along the tip of his knife. A small drop of blood dripped down the blade. "You know, the natives who lived on these lands, before the white man, scalped their enemies as war trophies. I once lived among them. True savagery. I studied and learned their techniques. They used to—"

"I know no one!" he said, desperate. "You must believe me. I haven't spoken to any of them in decades." His eyes were wide and glowed a bright red, sweat dripping down his forehead. He couldn't wipe his eyes, for his hands were bound by the thick chains behind him.

"They used to hang the scalps on their walls in honor of their victory," Orcus continued, cutting deeper along his left index finger, withstanding the sharp pain all for the satisfaction of instilling horror in his prisoner. "They used tomahawks, but I can use the more traditional Hellenistic curved blades of ceremony and sacrifice from our brethren. Consider yourself a sacrifice, if you don't tell me what I ask you. Far be it from me to be averse to such effective uses of savagery."

"You're on the wrong side. Persephone wants everything destroyed, including you!"

"And you have sunk so low that you and Imada have resorted to terrorism. There was a time when I respected you. What I'll do

—if you don't tell me, nephew—is slowly cut underneath that lovely long blond mane of yours. I will—if you don't answer me, nephew—cut each strand as you squirm. Then, when your lovely mane is left red and sticky from your warm blood, fallen to the floor, I will move on to skinning you alive. You, as a god, can survive even this—even if all that is left of you is muscle and sinew. But I have all night to cut you, old friend."

"Why do you still care about her!" he asked, fighting back tears. "Why are you protecting her?"

Orcus laughed a sinister laugh. "Has it ever occurred to you that I might be protecting you from her?"

3

IMADA

Cora's living room was the brightest room of the house. It was her favorite. The windows surrounded the room and afforded a beautiful view of the shore. There was a white grand piano at the center and, when relaxing, she loved to play while looking out the windows. This was precisely what she intended to do now. She opened the lid and ran her hand along the ivory, playing a tune with a few fingers. Hashan walked beside her. She turned and giggled. Then she sat down on the bench and started playing with more vigor.

Cora had taken a break from more sunbathing. It was another lovely day. She wore the same tight red bikini she had worn when she'd first met Gabriel.

"Why don't you change into a bathing suit and relax?" she asked Hashan. "You're gonna regret it when we move to cloudsville."

"No, thank you, madam."

"When will they take the piano?" Cora asked while still playing.

"I don't know. I wish they were taking more."

She played something terribly depressing, but she played the dismal tune with a bright smile. There was something about that, where she could turn misery into fun. It seemed she was always trying to do that. Hashan smiled in spite of himself.

She played flawlessly.

"Relax, Hashan."

The best he could do was sit straight in a nearby white leather chair with his hands folded and listen to her. Boxes surrounded the grand piano too. He kept looking at them.

"You know, I met him once."

"Who, madam?"

"Rachmaninoff. I met him in LA. He was old and gray at the time." All the while she played as if she was the composer herself. "It was in the 1930s. He reminded me a little of you. A bit stiff. I never saw him laugh. But he smiled a lot. A lot more than you anyway, Hashan."

"Thank you, madam."

"Don't mention it."

She ran her fingers quickly down some high notes and then turned.

"Hashan, we're moving to the country," she emphasized, still rolling her hands down the keys. "You need a change of scenery. It's gonna be fun." She kept touching the keys mindlessly and sighed. "Still, I'll miss the shore. I love the ocean. The birds. The sunsets. The smell of the sea. I'll miss it."

"I'm glad to see you are in better spirits, madam."

"Aha."

Hashan didn't smile. The dismal music being played with a joyful flair did seem to perk him up, though. She never could really read him, though she had known him all her life, but she knew when she was reaching that cold heart. She adored him.

Then the doorbell rang and she frowned. She was in no mood for guests. Whoever it was rang the doorbell out of courtesy. The front doors had been left ajar in order to move more belongings.

Hashan jumped up and ran to the door.

"Who is it, Hashan?" Cora called out.

"A Mr. Orcus, madam. Shall I let him in?"

Cora's heart sank. She threw her sunglasses on but continued to play the piano. In another moment, the guest was standing three steps above the living room in the hallway, looking down at her. She cocked her head.

The very tall, broad-shouldered man was dressed formally in black with long, wavy yellow hair and a short perfectly groomed goatee. The hair was fake and didn't precisely match his darker beard. His skin was tanned, almost reddish-brown. He didn't wear a shirt under the sport jacket, so his chest and abs, which were extremely well developed, could be seen. He wore sunglasses, which looked silly, being large and dark on him.

She switched her piano tune to Chopin's "Funeral March."

"It's been too long, Cora," he said.

She said nothing, just kept tapping the dreadful notes as he walked down and stood towering over her.

"Really, Cora?"

She looked up at him, striking the notes as if she meant to hurt him. "I'm playing our fucking song."

"Sorry, madam," said Hashan, rushing in. "He didn't wait."

"He never does. Here's the part few people know about." And she played with more zeal and enthusiasm. Just as before, she smiled, feigning having a great time. Orcus laughed. "It's really quite beautiful. It's just the beginning that's so well known as to seem silly, eh, husband? Kind of like your outfit."

"You play lovely."

"I know."

"Are you here for a swim? Such a lovely day. But I'm afraid there are boxes everywhere. You see, I'm moving. But you probably already knew that. And you'll need swim trunks. I can't have you jumping into the pool in a suit."

When she got back to playing the familiar part again, she laughed. The funeral song did sound silly. Finally, she brushed her fingers down all the keys with one abrupt stroke and slammed the lid down. She jumped up. "Well, I'm going for a swim."

She heard them follow her as she swayed her hips through a large living room and kitchen and then down some steps, through a glass door, and onto her brick patio.

"Have you had intercourse with her yet?" she heard the bastard ask Hashan behind her back as they followed. "Intercourse? You know, *sexual* intercourse?"

"No, sir!" Hashan answered. "Of course not."

"That's too bad. She is ravishing, isn't she? She's perfectly perfect. Always has been. But her attitude, you see, her attitude spoils it all. Or maybe it makes her more irresistible. I don't know. I could never tell. What do you think?"

"Do you know Ms. Aregard?"

"Oh, yes. I'd say we've met."

Cora walked up to the edge of the pool, threw her shades on the pavement, and dived in. She let the water wash over her, providing a brief respite from the world. The water rushed her ears, and all she could feel was the cold water as it soothed her from the heat of the sun. She didn't want to see or hear anyone anymore. Especially not Orcus. He was a demon—Orcus, or Pluto, or Hades, the god of the underworld. Why was it that Danny had to die but this fucker haunted her for eons? When she had married him, he had been her jailer. Her "husband," long since figuratively divorced, but she was never fortunate enough for him to be lost and forgotten.

She remained underwater for an unnaturally long time, sitting in the deep end.

It was her fault. She had summoned the beast. What had she expected? But she still never wanted to see his face.

The pressure hurt her ears as she watched her butler and the jerk converse with each other through the water. Probably over fucking her again, the sick bastard. Of course, they knew she'd be fine. She bore the pain in her lungs and stubbornly remained under. After another minute, she saw the bastard's bearded face looking over the pool. She finally rose to the surface.

"Are you all right, madam?" Hashan asked with concern.

She violently coughed out water. Hashan grabbed her a towel. She threw her wet red hair back under the towel and then dried her ears. Walking over to her nearby chaise lounge, she coughed more water out from her chest, then laid her towel down, put her shades back on and plopped down. She reclined and looked down at the sea again, ignoring her guest. He stood over her.

"You look stunning as always, Cora."

"And you look like a whale," she said. "The wig doesn't match your beard. The glasses are typical. And the suit makes you look fatter." Hashan brought over a martini. She raised it in a toast to him. "To deadbeat government assholes."

She coughed out more water, then drank her fill of the martini. Orcus sipped his own cocktail. "Umm. This is quite good."

"Hashan has a lot of practice," she said with a giggle.

"I'm not here to swim, my dear," Orcus said. "Or to drink."

She drank more of her martini.

"May I excuse myself, madam?" asked Hashan. "I have a lot of work to do."

Her silence was enough. Hashan bowed to both of them and went inside.

"Have you screwed him too?" Orcus asked.

"All you think about is sex. There's more to life than fucking, you know."

"This from you?" he asked with a laugh.

"But you do miss me, don't you?" she asked, tipping her shades and leaning towards him with a wink. "You sick bastard." She leaned back. "But you'll never—"

"Why are you moving, Mrs. Anastra ... or is it Ms. Aregard?"

"None of your business."

"I think you owe me. I gave you the information on Gabriel. Are you planning on having sex with him too?"

"You didn't tell me he was married."

He shook his head with a sly smile. "I have no interest in your affairs, Cora. I gave you what you asked of me. Why did you want to know about him now?"

"Nothing suspicious. I just don't want what happened to Danny to happen to Gabriel."

"Sure."

Uttering that word was nasty. And judging by his mischievous grin, he knew it too.

Sure. Orcus smiled a sly grin, looking at her from the corner of his eye, then sipped more of his drink, facing the shore. *Sure.* She had hoped never to hear that stupid word again. It seemed it was the only thing that ever came from Danny's damn Spanish-accented lips.

She struggled to control her rage. Heat and a red light shone through her sunglasses.

"Fucker," she said under her breath.

He sat down beside her.

"Who killed him?" she snapped.

"How should I know?" He shrugged. "I'm just a deadbeat government asshole."

"Did you do it?"

"I love you, Cora. Why would I want to make your life more miserable?"

"You're very good at that."

"Why are you seeing a psychiatrist?" asked Orcus. He lifted his eyes in thought for a moment. "A ... Dr. Tenor. You planning on screwing him too? He's married, by the way."

Cora felt the warmth from her eyes fade. She giggled. "I'm simply crazy." She scooted back in the chaise lounge and closed her eyes.

"Imada, Cora. Imada. They're watching. I warn you, you need to stay away from Lilly and Gabriel."

"They're the ones stirring up trouble, not me, husband."

"Cora," he said, wagging a finger, "they can't kill you, but they can make you miserable—imprison you or take away all the things you love. Instead of hunkering down and protecting them, you should let them go. Go find other mortals to play with. Not the Ambrosia family."

"I think I'm going for another swim."

She jumped up from her lounge chair, but as she passed him, he grabbed her wrist. Something snapped when she felt that steel grip. It wiped the smile off her face. She lost all her playfulness and yanked her arm back.

"Let go of me!" Her shout echoed throughout the valley, and birds along the beach took off in fright. She glared at him. Her eyes shone like fiery lasers through her shades, a red haze reflecting back on her.

The sound of thunder cracked from the clear sky. Orcus put his hands up in a gesture of surrender.

"We had an agreement!" she shouted, waving a fist right up to his face. "You don't touch me! Why are you here? I asked for information, and you gave it to me. Thanks. Now go away!"

"You summoned me. Answer my questions, Cora. I might be able to help you. Otherwise ... another lover might end up dead on your doorstep."

"You already know. Nephrea's special to me. I'm protecting them."

"A nymph man. How interesting. Knowing your love for Nephrea's Ambrosia family, Gabriel sounds irresistible."

She laughed and felt the tension finally escape her.

Yeah, Gabe might just be irresistible.

She plopped back down on the chaise lounge, grabbed her martini glass from the brick deck, nearly spilling it, and took deep breaths. She hadn't seen Orcus in years, and he was already getting her worked up. Something about him always took her over the edge.

"I like LA," she said with a smile, "if you must know. I'm not looking forward to leaving. I hate snow. I don't belong in the cold, unlike you, you icy bastard."

"Then stay here. Love a human instead. It would be safer for you—and them."

"Anything the matter, madam?" hollered Hashan from the house.

He must have run out at the sound of her yell. Every neighbor within five square miles had probably heard her. She gestured for him to go back inside.

"Such a lovely day," she said, scooting back and looking down at the shore. "I really do adore it here. Always have. The salty air and the wind. The sand between my toes." She giggled and looked at him. He had that same sly expression on his face, still waiting impatiently for her to answer. Then she flashed a dark expression. "I remember what I did to your brother on the sands of Aigai, Hades. Do you? I used the sea god's own trident and your weapon. Such a long time ago. I was close to burying him. I think I should have."

"No one doubts your power, Cora."

"You do." She turned back to gaze at the waves. "You just dared touch me."

"I'm on your side. But you can't stop our family."

"Don't ever call them *our* family! They hate you and me. Why do you help them?"

"Business, Cora."

"Did they kill him?" She was surprised at how quiet her voice suddenly became. Part of her didn't want to know.

He took a deep breath and looked down. "Yes."

Of course they did. But somehow, she'd wanted him to confirm it.

"Why do you associate with them! After all they've done?"

"Cora, they don't like you."

"You're a coward. If you want to help me, fight them."

"Come on, Cora. You destroyed their home. Wasn't that enough? They're the ones taking vengeance on you. Once they kill Lilly and Gabriel, the feud's over. You made an agreement. No more protecting Napeans. Let Imada cleanse them."

"The feud's just starting. Danny wasn't Napean."

"Oh, Cora," he said with a sigh. "I know. That was wrong. But you know their hatred and—"

"Did they give Lilly her cancer?"

"Jesus, Cora."

"Answer the question. Did they or not?"

"Your interest in Ambrosia nymph blood is putting those you love in danger," he said, wagging his finger. "Forget 'em. Forget the realtor and Lilly. It would please Imada to no end to hurt you, and you're giving them a really good way to do it."

"Did they plant the cancer or not?"

"I don't know." She didn't believe him. "Truly, I don't."

"I don't care about anything but the Ambrosia family. They're my people. I should never have let them do what they've done to the Ambrosia line. It's because we never stand our ground that they have slowly achieved what they wanted all along. Their genocide disgusts me. And so it should you."

"The nymphs are an alien race," he said, rubbing his eyes and shaking his head. "Imada's job is to live with humans, not nymphs. Both Lilly and Gabriel have alien blood. And they're not *your people*."

"We, husband, *Imada*, are an alien race. Perhaps the family should spend their energy figuring out a way of destroying ourselves and leaving everybody else alone."

"Cora, I understand your anger, but I can't protect them. I can only protect you."

"You failed at protecting me. As usual."

"If you only knew the things I do for you!" he snapped, finally losing his temper. His eyes glowed red.

She could imagine, but she didn't want to know.

They were interrupted, just in time, by the footsteps of the butler again. He carried a large tray in his arms, which he laid on a small glass table beside them. "I've brought snacks."

"Thanks, Hashan, but that won't be necessary," Cora said. "He's leaving."

Hashan nodded and was about to take the tray, but Orcus quickly snatched a cracker and some caviar. Cora rolled her eyes.

She lay down on her back again and decided to close her eyes. Perhaps, if she was lucky, he'd be gone when she opened them.

"Your involvement will not help them," he said with his mouth full. "I'm warning you. You're better off staying clear."

"I don't think so. I should have been there that morning for Danny."

After a long silence, she looked at him. Then he did something Cora rarely saw—he looked genuinely pained for her. "I'm sorry it happened," he said. "I'm sorry. Be assured, I had nothing to do with it. I did what I could to prevent it."

"I know."

"They didn't leave a trace," he said, sitting back down. "As far as I know, the killer was a hired man. There are no leads to Imada."

She nodded.

"Of course, you're lying, Cora—you, who has the power of prophecy. Obviously, he was terminal and there was nothing you could do to save him."

She shrugged. "And you're lying about no leads."

He laughed. "Oh, this is fun. I should visit more often. Perhaps if you offer us your gift, I can help you better."

"Imada just killed my husband! You told me you'd take care of them. Just get out! I don't want to talk anymore. Is that why you're here? To ask for my gift?"

"No, Cora. I'm here to convey my condolences. Truly, I'm sorry for what happened to Danny."

"Right."

She took a deep breath, then coughed some more water, now mixed with vodka, still lingering in her lungs. She thought of sitting on the bottom of the pool again until he left.

But, after a long silence, he got up again.

Thank God.

"Prophecy is a curse, not a luxury, dick," Cora remarked. "Just like your ugly face. Don't ask me for that ever again. Just do your fucking job, or I'll do it for you. I'm very close to taking things into my own hands again."

"Don't do anything stupid, Cora. Be warned: stupid government assholes like myself can always intervene in your habits instead of turning a blind eye. Watch yourself. I'll take care of the family."

"I think I could do better."

"Possibly. We could both do a lot better ... together. Especially with your gift."

"When you find the balls to take my side, I might just give you that. But until then, toodles."

He laughed. "You're a stubborn witch, Cora."

"Bye-bye." She readjusted her shades and scooted up again on the lounge chair, resigned to just ignoring him.

"I take my leave, then," said Orcus.

Please go.

He grabbed the back of her hand, too quick for her to pull away, and pecked it with his lips. "You're welcome for my help finding Gabriel, my dear. May you rot in your own hell with him. You best forget them. They will only cause you more pain. But I will help you. For you—you and I, my love, are destined to meet again and again. Farewell."

Fuck off.

4

LILIES FOR LILLY

"Why didn't you see Dr. Gorsich while I was away?" asked the doctor.

Cora crossed her legs sitting across from her psychiatrist. She reclined on the old brown leather couch and fixed her shades over her nose. He flipped through the pages of his notepad.

"You're the one who disappeared, not me. I just waited ... and, anyways, Dr. Gorsich is a woman."

"So?"

"I don't like woman doctors."

He removed his spectacles and rubbed his eyes, seemingly knowing better than to go there. Then he leaned back in his chair and threw the notepad on his desk. "So, where were we?"

She had never seen him look so awful. His thin hair was unkempt and he wore only a white T-shirt and jeans. His hair seemed grayer and his eyes were sunken in behind drooping wrinkled skin.

This was her third session with the doctor. She had seen him at the time of Danny's death, then once more a week after.

Cora stayed silent. He opened a desk drawer, grabbed a pen,

and picked up his notebook, looking through it again and jotting things down.

Shrugging, she flung her long red hair back and crossed her legs again. The chafing sound she made every time she moved her black latex pant legs over the old worn leather surface grated at her ears. She hated his couch.

She didn't like his office either. It had only one small window covered by an ugly yellow shade. And it was quiet. Somehow the tasteless 1980s brown wood-paneled walls insulated the room.

She removed her dark shades for a moment and looked at him—just looked at him. He usually slouched in his office chair, occasionally leaning on an elbow, and when he was upset, he had this habit of removing his glasses and rubbing his eyes. That was what he kept doing now. When he opened them, he looked guilty, realizing he wasn't paying any attention to her.

"Sorry, I've been away," he said. "How ... how are you dealing with your loss?"

"Huh?"

"Danny died."

"Oh yeah," she said with a nod, suddenly losing her smile. "How pleasant for you to remind me, Doctor."

"That's why you came to me."

"Yes, I know. I've been waiting for you to finish writing in your little book so we can talk about him."

"Sorry, Cora," he repeated with a laugh. Cora laughed too.

"How's your wife, Doctor?" Cora asked.

"What?"

"How's Lilly? Tell me, how is she now? Where is she? Is she still at home or in the hospital?"

"Home. She's been fighting pneumonia and is now in bed. That's why I've missed our appointments for so long." He feigned a smile, then pointed a pen at her. "But I'm here for you."

"Yeah, well, I have a confession to make. When you were gone, I visited her in the hospital. I felt terrible for you two, you're so nice and everything. I wanted to give her some lilies. Lilies are my favorite flowers. I mean, they can be dismal by caskets, but their whiteness is pure. It's calming, you know. I just love lilies. I wish they were more associated with life than death. I thought your wife would want some. Thought it would perk her up a bit. I thought, you know, lilies for Lilly. But she was sleeping and not well enough to talk to. So I just visited her. I should have sent flowers to your home too. Maybe I could have sent them to your office."

"That's very thoughtful of you, Cora, but unnecessary. Thank you."

Cora shrugged again. Then she moved along the couch, making that same swishing and tearing noise again with her rubber outfit.

"Does Lilly like lilies?" she blurted out, almost like a child.

The doctor couldn't help but laugh. "She prefers roses."

"I'll make a note of it next time." She raised a finger pretending to mark the air.

The doctor straightened his glasses and looked at her. "I'm sorry, Cora, I've been away ... why don't you tell me more about Danny?"

"Danny's like your Lilly." The doctor turned from her, looking upset, but Cora went on. "I loved Danny and now he's gone. We were married for thirty years, you know."

"Cora, your husband was much older than you, and you don't look much older than twenty."

"Thanks, Doc, but I'm the goddess Persephone. I already told you that."

He scratched more things in his book.

"Anyway, Doc, I have the power to heal. Only I don't have the power to save." She flashed him a smile that felt more bitter than happy. "Only Nephrea could save anybody. If I had had the power to save, I wouldn't have hesitated for a second to save Danny. In fact, I healed him for thirty years during our marriage. I healed every wound that man ever had. But, you see, I don't have the power to revive terminal wounds. Everyone has a time when their clock stops ticking—when they finally become terminal—and when your time's up, your time's up. There's not a damn thing I can do about it."

He nodded silently, and Cora became solemn.

"You see, just like any pretty girl, I fall for men—Danny, Arthur, David, Nathaniel—so many men that would seem just like a long list of names to you meant something to me. I remember their eyes. I remember the touch of their skin. I remember their hair—curly, long, or soft. Their smell. Their aftershave, their cologne. I can still smell them. I remember the things I liked and the things I hated—usually one and the same. When they pissed and when they chewed, or spat and farted. Their vomit and their shit. Their sweat. Everything."

"You loved these men."

"Yeah. Everything about them. That's what I'm trying to say. But, you know, now they're gone. But I never forget them. They're like permanent scars. Whether you believe me or not, I'm destined to walk this earth for an eternity with the memory of these men. They all leave me and there's nothing I can do about it. They all leave me, so ... how am I supposed to be happy?" She knew there was no answer to that, and that was the reason she'd never cared for therapists. "So, I suppose, sometimes I freak out. And why not? If you had to live the life I have, you'd freak out a bit sometimes too."

"Where are you going with all this, Cora?"

"You asked me about Danny and I was about to tell you. Something happened while you were away ... and it upset me. A lot. I suppose I missed the opportunity to tell anyone 'cause you were gone so long. I've really wanted to tell somebody."

"That's why you're here." Dr. Tenor put his notebook down on his desk. "If you have something to say, get it off your mind, Cora. You'll feel better."

"Yeah, well, it's a little sick ... I don't know."

"It's totally up to you. It's your session. Is it about sex and drugs again?"

"No," she said, chuckling at his sarcasm. Then she bit her lip and looked away. "It's kinda worse."

"How so?"

"Well, it's Halloween, right?"

"It was a couple weeks ago."

"Well, on Hallows' Eve, I did something that even creeps me out." She chuckled. "It wasn't exactly on Hallows' Eve, but I suppose it could have been. I guess I wanted to try to help Danny. Or, no, I wanted to help me. And it wasn't to be festive over the scary fall harvest holidays you humans call Halloween." The therapist looked over his glasses and just waited. Cora laughed. "Shit, it's really sick."

Cora jumped up and walked to the window. It had been a habit when she got tired of sinking into the leather couch.

"You know, I can't get tattoos," she said, looking down.

"That's what's so terrible?"

She shook her head. "I can't get tattoos. I like them, but I can't get them. They're cool, right? I tried. I wanted a long bird along my back. A phoenix. It was going to have rainbow feathers along my shoulders. I had it all planned. It was going to be magnificent. You should have seen what happened with the tattoo artist."

"What?"

"He freaked out." She turned back to him with a sad smile. "He said he had never seen anything like it. My skin heals too fast. I like to take advantage of it, you know, when I sunbathe. I can lie out under the sun for hours and never get a burn. But, with tattoos, the ink washes out within a day.

"So, this guy set the whole thing outlined beautifully in black. Then, a few days later, I returned, but it had already faded. The artist thought I was reacting to the ink or something. I tried it three times, but I've since given up. My immortal skin just can't take it. It's a damn shame 'cause the bird looks beautiful. I have one. Mainax is my pet. He was given to me by my mother, Nephrea." She looked up and chuckled for a moment. "Actually, first by Sara, then lost, and then given back to me by Queen Anna. It's a bit of a family heirloom."

"Is all this what you wanted to tell me? About your pet bird?"

"No," she laughed. "I just find it ridiculous that I can wear all the scars of my past husbands, but I can't wear a fucking tattoo. That's how weird I am. I suppose I'm a bit of a freak, you know."

"You're not a freak."

"But I am."

"Is that what you wanted to tell me?"

"No." She giggled again. "I wish it was that." She jumped back down on the couch. Then she removed her glasses and leaned forward. He always seemed a little uneasy when she removed her sunglasses.

"I ... I ... I can't." She plopped back on the couch, laughing again. "I just can't. God, it's so fucked up."

"It's up to you," he said and shrugged.

"I ... I just can't. I ... I spoke to Danny," she blurted out. She lost her smile the minute she said it. She threw her shades back on and folded her arms.

"What do you mean?"

"I spoke to Danny."

"What do you mean?" Dr. Tenor squinted, lifting his pen, ready to write again. "You spoke at his funeral. He's passed. Did you see a vision of him?"

"No, I went back to the cemetery and I really spoke with him, Doc." She leaned back and laughed nervously again. "I don't think I should tell you. It might creep you out. Just forget it."

"It's up to you."

"Do we have time?"

"Yes. It's your session, Cora."

~

W ell, it was a couple weeks ago. Hashan took me in our limousine at two in the morning. I didn't even tell him what I was doing. He was a little miffed that we left so late. He thought it was just more grief or maybe some late rendezvous with friends. I've been known to do shit like that from time to time, as you well know.

Anyway, he drove me to the parking lot of Danny's cemetery. Then I got out, carrying a handful of white lilies in one hand— beautiful lilies, my favorite flowers, like the ones I gave your wife —and a flashlight. I had to quietly pass a few gates and look over my shoulder for guards, but it was quiet. Then I stood over his tombstone. That damn slab of rock made me so mad. They had just laid it. It was a little too clean and tidy. It made me even more determined. I searched around me again. There was no one.

I was wearing a dark robe with a hood. I would have scared the shit out of anyone walking by. They probably would have mistaken me for an ancient druid or a vampire or something. Anyway, in my other hand I was carrying the shovel. I put the flowers down and went to work.

Dr. Tenor, you won't believe the time it takes to dig a grave. I mean, you've got to dig down over six feet. It's a lot of work. Not to mention I had to do it quietly. Then you've got to loosen all the wood and nails covering the coffin. The mortuary does a fine job and makes it difficult for time to rot through to the body, but even more difficult for grave robbers. Finally, I struck the dark mahogany. Even then, I had to dig around the casket some more to free it. Then, I opened it.

Seeing Danny again was not pleasant. It was absolutely dreadful. It's not that he looked any different. He still had his mustache curled and his beard was real short—you know, he had always tried to look weird, like that painter Salvador Dali. And he had his same bushy eyebrows and short dark cute hair. Thankfully, it had only been a couple months, and worms and mold had not passed through the internment process yet and eaten up his face, as in my fantasy. And he had that fake painted smile that the mortician gave him. And there was a terrible stench.

It was when I looked at him, I mean really fucking looked at him, that I had second thoughts about the whole thing. But I had felt so utterly alone.

For the first couple months after death, I have the power to reanimate any part of the body. After time, the power fades. I knew this because I had done it countless times before.

I think, in some ways, I didn't really want to do it. But I knew that if I didn't do it now, I wouldn't ever be able to do it again. So, what I did was I laid my hand on his icy chest and felt his muscles and tendons, the sinew between the bones. I could see it all in my mind. He may have still looked human, but his organs had coalesced and there was little left but a zombie-like gook and sinew that you could barely recognize as organs. But there was still space in those lungs and fleeting thoughts running through his mind.

I concentrated on his mouth. I wanted to hear him again. I can't recall what I said. It was something about how much I loved him. He was able to move his lips and take in a little air. It was dark and I watched with the flashlight I was carrying. He turned slowly to me and opened his dry dead eye a crack. Then he let out a long growl of a noise, something awful. He was angry. Through my hand, I could feel him shouting at me to leave him alone. It was being shouted through every part of him. I thought in that moment—how typical. How absolutely typical of our time together on earth—on Gaia. Even our last words were a nasty fight. We always fought.

But the fight was wonderful. Even this last contact, with him crying out and hating me, was like heaven to my heart. I wept over him and I swear I think I saw a tear form over his own eye. Then I just lay on top of him and cried for the longest time. All the while, he kept repeating, through his actions and his mind, and his body and soul, for me to just let him go. To just leave. To just let him go. You know, let him rest in peace.

So I did.

~

C ora paused and then looked at the therapist. He was looking at her oddly. She laughed inappropriately behind her sunglasses despite herself.

"It was my last chance, you see," she said with a shrug, shaking out her long red hair.

"Cora ..." She raised an eyebrow. "You really did this?"

"What do you mean?" She smiled a mischievous smile, as if she was messing with him. But she wasn't. The truth seemed weirder as she heard herself tell it than had it actually been a joke.

She moved about and chafed the old leather of the couch. He was stone silent. He couldn't say another word.

"Anyway, Hashan made sure that the cemetery cleaned up my mess, so by now, the tombstone's back and it's as if I was never there. Poof, as good as new ... with a fresh bouquet of lilies."

"Are you serious?" he finally asked.

She was trying hard not to laugh. "Yeah."

"You really went to Danny's grave and dug him up?"

"Yep."

"And then you believe you spoke with him? Or ... he growled?"

"Well, after a few weeks, the decay of your muscles get to the point, Doc, where it's very hard to say anything. The whole thing made me feel a little dirty. But you know, it's either within the first few months or not at all. I mean, I could try to commune with the dead after, but that's ... that's just gross."

"You really think you spoke to him?"

"Yes, Doctor. Actually, I'm quite sure of it."

"Hmm," the doctor said. He scratched something in his note-book and then looked away for a moment, silent. "Have you seen him anywhere else?"

She burst into laughter. "Of course not. He's in a casket."

"Oh," he said and put the notebook down.

"I love him and I miss him," she said, her words slow and very measured. "And I knew that it was the last chance I would ever get to lay eyes on him. As mad as he got, he knew it too."

"All right."

"You don't believe I touched him?"

He shrugged his shoulders.

She laughed again. "What a world we live in, Dr. Tenor. If your wife passed and you had the chance to contact her, wouldn't you dig her up from the grave too? If it was the last chance you'd ever have to contact her again?"

That hit a nerve. He had been more amused than disturbed by her story, which had seemed to distract him, but now that she'd mentioned his wife again, he sank back solemnly in his chair. Then he ran his hand through his thin gray hair and put his glasses down.

"Sorry," Cora said, putting a hand up. "I was just thinking—"

"I'm here for *you*, Cora," he repeated.

"I know."

"Thank you for sharing."

"Really?" she asked. "You don't think I'm a total loon?"

"No. I think you're having a hard time coping with your husband's loss. But you sharing this is progress for you. I've known all along how hard his death has hit you, but you've been denying it. But, let's say you really talked to him, what Danny told you is right. You have to move on. He already told you that with your new name."

"Yeah." She nodded in thought. "Well, don't worry. I won't do it again. It's just too gross." She laughed. "So, what do you think?

You think I'm crazy, Doctor? A real loon? You think I need medicine?"

"I don't know, Cora, do you?" He smiled. "No, I don't think you're crazy. I think you're a young lady with a very active imagination. If that gets you through your grief, then I think it's okay. And, no, you don't need medicine—unless you've got other plans I need to know about?"

"No," she said.

"Okay, Cora."

"But I am crazy, Doctor. You'd be crazy too if you had to live an eternity watching the people you love—who deserve better than you—wither and decay to dust and leave you all alone."

5

SPECIAL DELIVERY

Cora was standing before a very large mirror beside her marble-tiled bathroom, trying on innumerable black dresses to look good for Gabriel.

She had thought of Gabe all month. If he had been single, she would have had her way with him that night, getting the attraction and fucking out of the way and then never seeing him again. That was what she usually did with men. Then she could just watch him from afar, like she had done with Lilly. But this was different. He was married. If she couldn't fuck him, she had to speak to him.

But she wanted to speak to him.

She had finally decided on a black lace dress. Around her neck, she'd draped a rather large and ridiculously gaudy diamond-studded gold necklace, her best, and applied black eye makeup and red lipstick matching her long red hair. She'd slipped into some sexy black stockings and short black boots. She'd had every intention to sit on her raised chair, drinking and smoking, when she heard a revving engine from a car driving into her front circular driveway.

She ran back into her marble bathroom and looked out a tiny

oval window. One large paper-wrapped board was hanging from the passenger seat of a silver convertible Corvette.

Mickey McMullen. He was an art distributor who had sold her husband's paintings to dealers all up and down the West Coast. His weirdness always entertained the hell out of her, but now was not the time for his visit.

Shit! Not now.

True to form, Mickey wore a ridiculous beret and a long green coat. As he hauled the wrapped painting from his sports car, Hashan ran to him in the driveway in his usual black suit to help. Cora ran to the stairway. The two of them were hefting a large painting into the entryway.

"You could have had it sent," said Cora, making her way down the stairs, her voice echoing in her empty house.

"Cora, darling," Mickey said, looking up. He sounded genuinely happy to see her. "Do you think I'm going to trust a delivery truck with this?"

The two men slowly leaned the painting along the base of the stairway. It was dark. Cora had all the lights off downstairs, and although the downstairs was full of windows, night was falling.

Cora walked over and kissed Mickey's cheek. Then he gently took her in his arms for a quick embrace. He pulled back and stared at her.

"Jesus, you look stunning, dear."

"Thanks, Mickey," Cora said with a chuckle.

"Look, I told you" — he walked over and tore at the paper, revealing the painting — "this painting is as lovely as you."

"I didn't even know you still had it."

"Yes. It should have been sold, Ms. Lovely. This painting is worth more than anything he ever did. If only you had let him sell it."

Cora looked at it. She didn't want to. She had once demanded that Danny destroy it.

It was one of Danny's earliest works, before his art had turned more modern and eclectic. The scene was classic Renaissance, with streams, rivers and fields painted in a background—only the fields were blue-green, representing the ancient blue lands of Azure. The center consisted of a polished white marble courtyard surrounded by white Greek columns at the summit of a mountain—Olympus. The sun shone green far over the horizon. There were two figures at the center. A man and woman. The man wasn't Danny. It was some other nude figure, looking more like a model than a simple man. But he wore a painter's hat, and he had Danny's mustache. He was reaching out a hand to a lady climbing the summit under him. The lady wore an elegant white peplos dress and golden sandals. She had Cora's face. The lady reached her hand up to touch his. The lovers looked into each other's eyes in rapture.

As if a picture depicting her ancient beloved home wasn't enough to draw emotion from her, the sight of the two lovers nearly touching was too much. She felt like stumbling, but Mickey wouldn't have even noticed. He was fixated on the artwork.

"It reminds me of the Sistine Chapel," he said with a finger to his cheek. "Like man trying to touch God, only here it's not God. It's certainly the best thing he ever painted."

"You think so?" she asked, surprised.

"Oh yes. It's magnificent."

Mickey turned and faced her. He smiled gently. "I hadn't met you yet, Cora, when he gave me this. He had painted this after you two had first met. I recognized your face in the painting from the pictures he sent me of your trips in Europe to Madrid and Paris. Danny was constantly talking about his new firecracker. How much adventure you gave him. I wanted to ... tell you that at the funeral. How much he loved you and how wonderful you—"

"Enough, Mickey," she said, raising a hand. "Really. But thank you for sending me the painting."

"There's a few more where this came from," he said with a

nod. "But the others are odds and ends, mainly unfinished works. This is the best work he ever did."

"You can have them. Or, send those by delivery truck next time, instead of your Corvette."

"Of course," he said with a chuckle.

When he had finished pulling off all the paper packaging, he addressed Hashan. "My, you look as dreadful as always."

"And you are as colorful as always, sir."

Mickey's small spectacles were teal, and he looked over them at the butler with a smirk.

"Mickey, I'm sorry," Cora said, "but I'm expecting company. If you'd like, Hashan can get you a drink, but I have to get ready."

"Don't worry, dear. I won't be staying." He leaned over and kissed her cheek again. "Just take care of it, okay? You don't know what a pain in the ass it was driving it down the Pacific Coast Highway."

"Okay, Mickey."

"Toodle-oo." He turned to Hashan. "And bye to you, short, dark and dreary."

And that was that.

When the double doors shut and the coast was clear, Cora picked up the painting as if it was as light as a feather—though it likely weighed over fifty pounds—and walked with it through the hallway and living room, opening the sliding door with her other hand, towards the pool.

"If he comes, Hashan," she hollered back to the house, "tell him I'm delayed."

It was evening. The sun was just barely visible over the ocean as a strip of red along the distant horizon. Cora set the painting down beside the fire pit and dug into her pocket for matches. Then she lit the gas and started the fire.

Company or not, she wanted the deed over with. And fast. The faster it was done, the less she'd have to think about it.

She looked at it and then shook a little. She wished she hadn't dismissed Hashan. Perhaps he could do it ... no, she could never convince him.

There it was under twilight, a painting of her face, otherwise no different from the face she had been staring at but a moment ago in the mirror when getting dressed. Her long blond hair—her natural color—and her blue eyes staring into his. It wasn't Danny, but it was his disposition. To her, it was him. He held his hand out to lift her up. Only Danny and she could understand the meaning. With all the depths of her sorrow and pain, it was always Danny that lifted her up. And now, he was gone.

Shit! Tears rushed to her eyes.

She raised the painting up over the flames, but she couldn't drop it.

Past the two figures in the center lay the lands that were drowned under miles of sea, the mythical blue world of Azure. Her true home. How could she destroy this? Danny, being a genius, had taken her verbal descriptions down and copied them to a tee. It really looked like the nymph world of Azure: the streams under Mount Olympus of glowing blue-green, then beyond, the forests of blue and the violet trees. And then further, there was just a small glimmer of emerald crystal from Nephrea's palace. And beyond that, the mythical Strait of Azure separating the nymphs' mythical world from Hellena, Greece, on one side and Aethiopia, or Egypt, on the other.

How could she destroy this? It was the only rendition of Azure left in the world. Her true haven, her true home, since destroyed. He had drafted it, perfected it, and then hidden it from her, knowing she would destroy it. And Mickey was right. It truly was the best painting he had ever painted.

Goddamn you, Danny!

Then she heard another car—her hearing as sharp as her strength. She knew it was Gabriel.

She dropped the painting on the fire and ran back into the house.

6

DINNER DATE

Gabriel was early this time. His flight had left LaGuardia without a hitch. Cora had offered to send a limousine, but he had refused this time. For one reason or another, he didn't want to take anything from her.

His hand shook as he leaned on the beige leather armrest of an Uber sedan. His driver drove up through a thick woodsy hillside and down towards the shore, then circled around the driveway as Gabriel stared at the large white modern structure. The driver couldn't tear his eyes off it either. Now evening, there were elegant antique streetlamps lighting the private driveway. An Audi, Ferrari and BMW were parked beside the grand entrance. The entrance was columned in the same Doric columns he had remembered, before an entryway of white and glass walls. The floor-to-ceiling windows were everywhere, covered by the same burgundy velvet drapes. As a realtor, he had seen thousands of homes, but he had never seen such an eclectic mix of gaudy, artsy, modern, and ancient architecture.

He grabbed his trembling hand.

Damn.

He didn't want to be here ... and yet ...

He thought of his wife and daughter. Last night, Mina had been busy disciplining little Jordan over not doing her homework. Apparently their five-year-old wasn't reading. His wife, a tall, plump woman with very curly black hair and bright green eyes, had taken a moment from her shouting to say goodbye. She'd handed him luggage she had prepared for him and then resumed screaming at Jo Jo, as they called her. That was that.

He'd spent the evening in a hotel not far from the airport.

He didn't see Mina or Jo Jo much anymore. He was too busy. The most recent transaction had involved a commercial motel in Vermont. It was the largest deal before Ms. Aregard's had landed on his desk. The deal had been sealed last week, and he had gotten a promotion over it. Of course, a promotion would also mean more work and more clients.

But all month, he had thought of Cora's home. He'd looked forward to seeing it again.

When he knocked on the door, no one answered. Typical of the weirdness of the manor, there was a huge brass knocker on double wooden doors. It was then that he saw a note addressed to *Mr. Cartwright* attached to the doorknob. It was simple and to the point:

It's unlocked. Meet me upstairs. We'll eat and chat!

He let himself in. This time, the downstairs was very dark. There were only a couple lights on along the walls of the first floor. He looked up again at those grand stairs that climbed up three to four stories in height with a grand vaulted ceiling. There was music, some modern soft jazz, playing upstairs, out of place in the upstairs dark nineteenth-century castle. And an artificial yellow glowed around the handful of candles on the upper floor.

When he reached the top floor, he expected to see Cora sitting atop her throne at the center of the room, looking down on him in a bikini like last time. She wasn't. On the opposite side of the expansive room, she was busy over a candlelit dining table, setting linen cloth napkins and utensils. The drapes were open and a stunning view of the ocean could be seen from the floor-to-ceiling windows.

It smelled like smoke. Not just smoke—pot.

Why is she setting her own table?

He had difficulty swallowing. He had thought she couldn't look more stunning than before, but her formal appearance proved him wrong. Her short black lace dress fit perfectly over her chest and hips. But she looked preoccupied, not aware of his arrival. Somehow, that was arousing too.

She cocked her head.

"Hi." Despite her smile, she didn't seem like she was in a very pleasant mood.

"Mrs. Anastra."

"Hi, Gabe. Did you have a better flight this time?"

She walked over to him, swaying her hips.

"Yeah. No delays."

She walked right up to him, and his heart jumped into his throat. Her dark blue eyes seemed to glow. He felt drawn to her. She put out her hand for a handshake.

"I ... I'm always impressed by your manor, Mrs. Anastra. The house is breathtaking."

"Well," she said, all smiley again, "I do have an eclectic manor, Mr. Cartwright. But I told you last time to address me as Cora."

"Right, Cora," he chuckled.

She grimaced stupidly and then broke the spell, walking over to the bar. "I'm fucking late as always, Gabe. Sorry. Something came up. I had some difficulty with the fire pit outside." He could never get used to her profanity. It was excessive and jarring. Now, with her so formally dressed, it seemed cheap and inappropriate. "But I fixed it. Then, in the rush, I forgot to ask Hashan to prepare the room for our meeting—though he should have known better."

She went behind the counter and lifted a heavy-looking silver platter from under the bar. Gabe jumped up and ran to her to give her a hand. She brushed his hand gently as she handed it to him.

"Such a gentleman. It's a warm evening," she added as she walked beside him to the dining table. "Another thing I'll miss in Canada. If you don't mind, I like opening the window when I eat. It makes me feel like we're outdoors. I just love the outdoors. And I was smoking." She chuckled. "I feel more relaxed now. I ... I hope you don't mind the smell of marijuana. Of course, it's legal out here now."

"You can smoke whatever you like."

"Yeah. Want some?"

"Huh? No. I don't take drugs when I'm with clients."

They both laughed.

"It's a lovely evening," she said. "Truthfully, I really like LA."

Gabe set down the tray on the table and walked over to the window. The view of the sea was stunning. There was a large fire in the fire pit beside the pool. It looked more like a bonfire and, oddly, there was a mound of black ash surrounding it. The pool was lit with green lights.

"You really want to sell this?" he finally asked absent-mindedly.

What are you doing! Aussie would fire you on the spot if he heard you ask her that.

"Thanks," she replied with a laugh. "I told you, I'm building a replica in Toronto. Come on, Gabe. Let's eat."

They sat down across from each other at the dining table. It was a large dark oak table, but they both sat at one end closest to the window.

The meal was good. She told him it was from Tillman's, her new favorite steak house closer to downtown. They ate in silence, staring out at the city lights.

He liked her perfume. It had a floral smell, not too overpowering, but pleasant and relaxing. At first, her smell competed with the scent of marijuana, but beside him by the table, it filled the dining area—that and the smell of their dinner. And it wasn't too dark. The full moon shone down on Cora's deck below them. But even more spectacular was the view of the ocean.

"Oh, fuck!" she said suddenly, throwing her fork down. He jumped. "I forgot the wine."

She ran back to the bar. He laughed.

"It's all right."

"I'm an alcoholic, you know, Gabe," Cora said. "And there's nothing better than sharing my habit with a stranger."

"Alcohol *and* marijuana?"

"No, usually just alcohol, but tonight something necessitated an alteration in my habits. Really, I only took a couple of tokes, though. But, if you'd like, we can partake in more later."

He laughed. She was very serious, and somehow that made her funnier.

"What happened?" he asked.

"Hmm?"

"You said something happened tonight. Is everything all right?"

"Same old shit, Mr. Cartwright. Life."

She took out two glasses and uncorked a bottle of red wine. She was at the far side of the room, a long way off, but he caught her watching him. When she smiled back, he quickly turned away, embarrassed, and looked outside.

She returned to her seat and handed him a glass.

"It's very good," she said. "Try it." Then she raised her own glass with a wink. "To Platinum Properties."

They clinked glasses, and she sipped from hers while staring out at the view with longing.

He spilled a little red wine on his hand. She noticed and jumped up with a white cloth napkin.

"I'm all right."

He felt a tingle in his chest as she wiped the wine from his fingers. Such a small act left him frozen. He felt lost, mesmerized under her touch. She seemed to be hypnotized too from his contact, taking a very long time to carefully wipe each finger. Then she took one of the drops of wine and brought it up to her tongue. His eyes followed, watching her suck her finger. The action probably took seconds, but time seemed to slow before him.

She giggled.

She returned to her chair and cut some of her steak. "Bon appétit, Gabe." Just watching her cut the steak was so sexy. "Just be careful with the wine. It's thirty years old."

"Thirty years old!" He almost spilled it again. "What?"

"Yeah," she said, swallowing some steak. Then she furrowed her brow as if not understanding his shock. The candles on the table flickered along her perfect thin eyebrows and red lips. "It's from Spain. Very valuable. It's my way of thanking you for closing the deal. Do you like it?"

"Of course." But he put it down, losing his taste for it. This was just too much.

"I'm very rich, Gabe. Do you like wine? I like red. A lot of other pretty girls like pinot grigio, but I like red. You like red wine?"

"Yes."

"Refined. Like whiskey? You're refined. Of course you would. And how fitting that you fancy whiskey, and ... Canadian whiskey, right?"

How odd it was that she could talk and act so formally and then change in an instant to a foul-mouthed little girl. He had never met anyone like her.

"But I didn't tell you I like *Canadian* whiskey, Cora," he said. "I do."

"Oh, I thought you said Canadian. You know, Toronto reminds me of you. You're not so far from there in New York, right?"

"Why are you moving there, Cora?"

She shrugged. Oddly, the question seemed to upset her again.

"I really want to thank you," she said formally. "Tell Austin you guys made a really fair deal with the buyers. And you don't know how happy I was when I heard you were permitting me to work on the Toronto property before the deal was sealed. And then to delay escrow. You"—she chewed some meat and continued with her mouth full—"you guys really make me happy."

He found himself staring at her lips as she spoke. It almost made him shake. Her tongue ran across them. The act of licking the dark red wine from her cherry-red lips was irresistible.

"Well," he said, trying to swallow some steak of his own. It was delicious. "The sellers are only allowing you to work on the lake and property at the moment. I know you wanted to remodel inside, but they can't permit that until you sign."

"Still, even the outside is better than nothing, right?" she replied with a big grin. He loved her smile. And her energy. "It makes the move easier."

"Sure."

Oops.

She quickly turned her eyes to the window and looked very upset.

"Sorry, Cora, I forgot."

"No, you didn't ... you just remembered. It's okay. It can't be helped." But she sounded terrible. "The death of a loved one is difficult. And it never goes away, Gabe."

"I'm sorry."

She took a deep breath and then slowly cut some more steak. Only the sound of their silver forks and knives echoed in the room. She was angry now, and she seemed to be attacking her plate.

She ate more steak. Then she ate quicker, as if using it as a distraction from her thoughts.

The simple act of cutting the meat with a steak knife and

chewing it was alluring. She cracked a smile as she caught him looking at her. He couldn't resist. Then she ran her hand along her long red hair.

"I've had thoughts of moving to Toronto too," Gabe blurted out. It felt forced, said in order to just say something.

"Really?"

"Mina and I."

"How is the family, Gabe?" She really didn't seem to care.

"Fine."

Then more uncomfortable silence.

"Cora?" he asked with a cough. "Can I ask you something?"

"Hmm?" she said, shoveling some mixed vegetables onto her plate. "I'm all ears."

"Your husband passed three months ago in the house, right? The buyers have asked for more information on the matter. I've been asked by my boss, Austin, to find out more too. Austin thought you could tell me more when you saw me personally today."

"He dropped dead," she said matter-of-factly. "All they need do is check the police report."

"How did he die?"

"Does it matter?"

"Well ... I'm not trying to reopen old wounds, but people are superstitious. Some people believe in ghosts."

"I'll have you know that ghosts are very real, Gabriel," she said, pointing at him with a fork. "I've seen them." She looked up, brushing a red bang from her forehead. Then she smiled a fake smile. "He was knifed in the chest by my front door." Then she gazed at him as if she was reading a news headline, challenging him to care.

"I know ... but, forgive me, Cora, but was he pronounced dead on the premises? It was unclear on the report."

"Check the police report again. You'll find it is quite clear. He died in my entryway. So, yes, I suppose his soul was taken at the entrance of my home. What the fuck does it matter?"

He shrugged his shoulders uncomfortably.

"Why do the buyers need to know that, Gabe?"

She was smart. He could see it in her eyes as she calculated everything she said to him.

What an amazing woman. Pretty, fun and bright. And when doing business, she seemed as shrewd as any other client he had ever dealt with, if not shrewder. That was sexy too.

She was so hot. He had never met a more attractive woman.

What am I doing?

When he didn't answer, she took a deep breath and said, "People are assholes. One morning I heard sirens from this very room. I ran down and Hashan nearly tackled me by the stairs. He was crying. You met him. He's the iciest man in the world. I adore him, but I don't think he's ever cried before. Can you imagine that man crying? Anyway, when I saw that, I nearly fell in fright. I rushed down the stairs. There I was met by a group of people surrounding a black body bag before the floor vase by the door. My dead husband. Mr. Anastra. That's what happened. That's what you can tell the buyers. Now, please, don't ever ask me again."

She swallowed more steak.

"Of course."

"Never," she insisted, opening her eyes wide for a moment.

"I'm sorry."

"Shut up with the sorry. Now you know. Just don't mention it again."

"*Sur*—I mean, yes. There was ..." He hesitated. But Aussie, who he wanted to kill at the moment, had asked him to find out even more. "There was the assailant. He was shot dead, according to the report."

Gabriel had seen many sides to Cora. She had been playful, childish and alluring when they'd first met. She had been smart and cunning now when being questioned. And she had been sweet when she'd wiped the wine off his fingers. But now, Gabriel saw something he had never before seen in her—fury. She looked menacing.

"Hashan shot the assailant in the back," she snapped. "He was outside the house when he heard the disturbance. My butler has a concealed weapon permit and is known to carry often. Both dead bodies fell beside that same lovely white ceramic vase that welcomed you by the front door of my fucking house. I already told the police everything. Is that enough, Gabriel?"

"No ... I mean, yes, Cora. But, on the report, it wasn't reported how the assailant was killed, and, oddly, it was never investigated. I'm sorry to rehash all—"

"Stop saying sorry!" she snapped and slammed the table with her fists. "Fucking fuckers! Goddamnit!"

She slammed her fist on the table again and rushed to the window.

He almost said sorry again.

"The food is magnificent," he sputtered.

"Yes," she replied with her back turned to him. "Of course it is."

"You've seen ghosts?" he asked, desperately trying to change the conversation. "Where?"

"I wish here," she said, cocking her head back with a sad grin. "But Danny has never visited me in my house since his death."

"Where? Where have you seen ghosts?"

"The River Styx. You know, Gabe, all along the river are vapors, or ghosts, of people who died." She stared out the window as she spoke. "Their hands reach for the wooden raft of the Ferryman, Charon, as he takes his sickle, chopping them off or kicking and tossing them back down into the river. And if you fall in the water, you lose your memory. Hypnos, a tributary, carries with it strange magic. I've seen many lose their memory forever. Many others stand in line before the Ferryman, awaiting admittance. And then Charon appears menacingly before them like a demon with his sunken eyes, thin skeletal arms and legs and glowing red eyes. Few ever pass. It's awful. But, you know, Queen Nephrea did. She offered an elixir prepared by the goddess Persephone herself to Charon in order to cross the water. Most everyone else remains ghosts. Legend says some pass with coins upon the raft. I think that's complete bullshit. Others fall and drown, fall and drown, repeatedly in damnation, never making it to the other side. Yeah, I've seen spirits, Gabe ... in my dreams."

She's so weird.

"In my dreams," she repeated with a nod, turning to him and shrugging, as if guessing his thoughts.

"Sure."

He quickly raised a hand, regretting the word as she clenched her fists and lost her smile.

"Well, now, isn't this depressing," she said. "This is not becoming the night I had hoped for. Not the night I was hoping for at all. It's not your fault, Gabe. I'm the one who should be sorry. I must confess, something came up tonight that reminded me of Danny. It was bad timing because I really had been looking forward to seeing you again."

His heart raced when she said that. She had been looking forward to seeing him! He had looked forward to their meeting too.

"Tell me more about yourself," she said. "Your wife. I bet she's pretty," she preempted him before he could reply. "I'm sure anyone who would marry you must be quite striking."

"Yes, Cora. She is. And I have a daughter."

"How nice."

"I have a peaceful life," he added, looking down at his plate.

"Right. That's why you work for a company in the quiet city of Manhattan."

"You can still live peacefully in Manhattan," he said with a chuckle.

"If you say so."

She leaned her hand on the window. He sipped some wine, almost spilling it again, as she stared at him. "I have a proposal."

His hand holding the wine visibly shook. "Hmm?"

"I would really like it if you'd stay here with me over the next couple days. I don't see any reason for you to get a hotel. There's plenty of room in my guest quarters downstairs. Hashan can ensure you're comfortable." He hesitated for a reply. "I will ensure that you are well taken care of. I can promise you it will be more comfortable here than a local hotel. You won't be disturbed. Think of it as a six-star resort."

"Cora, I have a hotel. You always offer too much. This food and this incredible wine is far and above any other hospitality I can expect. More than any clients have ever given me."

She laughed. "Well, it would be very important to me personally, Gabe, if you stayed here. Just until I sign the deal. Only for the weekend."

He thought: *Absolutely not.* Then he thought: *Yes.*

"You can have a swim," she added with a giggle.

He laughed despite himself.

"Really, Gabe, it would be easier," she said, sitting back down across from him. "I like to keep my clients close."

"All ... right ... Cora. How can I refuse? Thank you."

"Great," she said, lighting up, but she still seemed unable to recover the playfulness he remembered from when he had first seen her. "I just need time. If you're close, it'll be much easier to do business. I only need a couple days. If anything comes up, why, I can just run downstairs, knock on your door and hand you the papers with my signature."

At that moment, her phoenix flew onto her arm. It made him jump. He hadn't seen Mainax the whole meal and had forgotten about the magnificent bird, who seemed to pop out of the shadows. Cora jumped in surprise too, but then she laughed. He liked her laugh.

She petted the bird's head, turning and staring out towards the sea again.

"He's fascinating."

"I'm a fascinating gal."

That was sure true.

"Would you like to pet him?"

7

COME CLEAN

Cora nearly collided with a pickup truck, switching lanes from the far right to the carpool and, fortunately for her, with two inches to spare between her and the truck's bumper. She cursed him for slamming on his brakes, then sped off, only to have to slam on her own brakes yet again when another idiot in a blue Tesla crossed the lane illegally in front of her. She revved up her 200-horsepower silver-and-black bike, flew back in the saddle, and quickly swerved around more metal, nearly hitting the side mirror of a car stopped in the fast lane.

It was then that she first noticed the dreaded flashing red and blue. She searched in front. She had a long open stretch on the carpool lane before the next exit and the next perceived obstacle. So she revved her slick Ducati again and rode as fast as she could between two cars. Behind her in her side mirrors, the flashing lights dimmed in the background, but she still had to move fast. The cop might radio for help. Carefully, she slowed her cycle down and swerved back into traffic, then made for the far-right lane to head down the offramp. She lost the officer, but then the traffic thickened again right off the intersection under the overpass. LA traffic—ubiquitous as smog. That was one thing she wouldn't miss in Canada.

She revved her massive engine once more, rushing from zero to sixty in less than three seconds, turning when the light turned red.

It wasn't like she was in a rush. This was how she always rode. But she was also hungry.

As the traffic went on and on, now in the city streets, she thought of Danny. That burning painting, twisting and turning to ash under the flames, blurry behind her tears. After she had tossed it into the fire, she had run into the house, but she couldn't help looking back down on it from her upstairs windows.

She should never have married him. She should have waited for the true Napean, Gabriel. Marrying Danny made her abandon Lilly and Gabriel. That act helped seal her agreement with Imada not to interfere with their sick plans.

But she had loved Danny.

She had prophesied Danny's death. She'd told him a month before he died. She wouldn't know the exact events, but she knew it would happen within weeks, she had told him. Danny had asked if there was a way out. That broke her heart. She had wept bitterly in his arms that night, shaking her head. And then he had comforted her. *He* had comforted *her* over his death. How typical. That was the sort of man Danny was. She was Persephone, a demon from the depths of hell, burning him and his paintings so that she could move on to the next man while, in all the days Danny had lived, he had cared for her. She had never deserved him.

She had told Gabriel that she had been asleep when Danny died. Of course, that was a lie. She hadn't slept for weeks until the terrible deed had been done.

Cora and Daniel had accepted their fate, but Hashan hadn't. Their butler had loved Danny too much. Hashan had fought with them when they had told him, and then, when it was clear that they planned to do absolutely nothing, he had run from them.

When the fateful shot had echoed through her house on a

rainy morning—it was a Saturday in August, Cora remembered, and, unlike today, stormy—she had whispered goodbye. She'd thought weeks would prepare her. They hadn't. How could it be that after thousands of years of loss, she had never learned to accept the death of a loved one?

The gunshot hadn't been what killed Danny. Danny had been prophesied to die by a knife. The gun had been fired by her butler. Hashan had been roaming around her grounds for weeks, waiting to kill the killer.

After the shot, a terrible tempest had stirred, with wind nearly blowing down all the trees surrounding her grounds. Rain crashed against the windows, threatening to crack them open. But Cora had remained upstairs in bed, weeping. Providence had been done. War had been declared—again—and her husband was dead.

That was when ...

A pearly-white Mercedes didn't see her, coming a foot from colliding with her leg while she was riding the shoulder to turn right at a yellow light.

"Fuck!"

Cora cursed, hit the car window, and then flipped him off.

That was when she had called Orcus. That hadn't been easy. She hadn't spoken to her bastard former husband in twenty years. She had wanted to know Gabriel's whereabouts. In sympathy, the bastard had told her that he lived in Manhattan. Cora had planned her future accordingly and worked on buying a new home in Toronto, for it was close enough and, by prophecy, Gabriel would eventually move there. But she had loved her house in LA for nearly a century.

Cora arrived at Tillman's, pulling her bike into a driveway through an alleyway and parking it in a small valet lot. Brick buildings surrounded her, a few stories high. Tillman's was her new favorite steak house—the same one she had ordered takeout from two nights before for Gabe. She cut the engine, took a deep breath, and dismounted her bike.

Tonight was going to be fun. If she couldn't fuck Gabriel, she'd fuck somebody else.

Wearing her bike jumpsuit—this one was cherry-red—shaking her pretty bright red hair out, adorned in dark black mascara and black boots, she made a valet terribly nervous as she threw him the keys. Then, with a wink and a sway of hips, she strutted into the swanky restaurant.

Tillman's was full of suits—men with slicked-back hair, nicely trimmed eyebrows and manicured fingernails—and waitresses with hair nicely tied back in buns or ponytails and wearing elegant lovely long dresses. It was the sort of place where all the tables had nice ironed white tablecloths. Cora's outfit didn't fit in at all. Apparently, the blond maître d' thought so, too. The hostess had a look of shock mixed with disdain as Cora approached her desk.

She flashed Cora a very fake smile. "May I help you, miss?"

"Table, please."

"Reservations?"

"No."

The maître d' opened her eyes wide and then tried to cover it up with more phoniness. "We're fully booked. I'm sorry." She wasn't sorry.

Cora turned her head, half rolling her eyes. "Be a hun and tell Devon that Mrs. Anastra's here—Cora Anastra."

"Devon?"

"Your manager," Cora answered. The maître d' looked at her stupidly. Cora took a deep breath. "Look, the freeway's a train wreck and I haven't eaten since yesterday. 'Kay? Why don't you be a sweetie and ask Devon for a table?"

The blonde bitch hesitantly turned and lifted a phone.

Cora flashed a fake grin of her own. Then she looked around. She took some red lipstick out of her small bag and applied it. It matched her suit. The lights were very dim. There were few windows—there was nothing much to see outside anyway except the parking lot between brick buildings. Cora looked at the booths. Each booth was private—like a room within itself. She loved that. It was enclosed with a smooth oak finish. She hoped Devon would give her a nice booth or something.

"Devon's not here today, miss."

Goddamnit!

The maître d' spontaneously recoiled back from Cora's look. Cora put her hand over her eyes and ran her other hand over her red hair.

"I'm sorry, Mrs. ... uh ... Anastra."

Cora averted her red eyes.

"Okay." There were a few stools by the bar. "I'll try the bar."

She didn't want this. She wanted to just sit alone at a booth, stare at the fabulous maple leather cushions and get completely inebriated. Then, when drunk enough, she'd stumble to the bar and fuck somebody. Some nights, she would have loved the bar. Not tonight. Not so soon after burning Danny's painting. She really needed a drink. Then a fuck. She wanted to be alone and drink until she was drunk enough not to care anymore about anyone ... like Danny.

The bartender approached her. "What can I get you?"

You. Damn.

He was a super cute tanned hunk with stubble on his chin, but well groomed, with nice dark hair and rough skin. He was strong too. She liked how his sleeveless dress shirt was worn tight over his broad shoulders and chest. There was a tattoo on his left arm. It was some serpent or something. Cora loved tattoos.

"I'd like steak," she said.

"Steak? At the bar?"

"Aha. It is a steak house, isn't it? The place is packed."

"I suppose. Well, it's Saturday—"

"Rare," she said, touching his arm. He smiled. He seemed to

like it when she ran her thin pale fingers against the dark skin of his arm. "Make it rare with some potatoes, 'kay? And a large vodka martini with olives."

"Rare? Okay. You want the drink up?"

"Yeah. Shaken and up. And get me two."

"Oh. Expecting someone else?"

"No, I just want to get drunk."

On her right, two salivating young men were eyeing her. College boys, she guessed. One was blond, tall and lanky, the other fat with an unkempt beard. On her immediate left was a couple holding each other. A date—she guessed. Oh, how she just wanted a booth.

"Sucks they couldn't get you a table," the bartender said as he spread out a white cloth napkin for her meal. *Yeah.* "It's not often that I have to serve steak at the bar."

"Just make it yummy, okay?"

"You bet."

He had a look about him. She couldn't quite place it. His dark eyes and short hair reminded her of someone she had seen before. And his smile was sweet. Maybe he was an actor? He looked like an actor.

He handed her the drink. She smiled and raised the glass to him.

"The other will be ready in a minute," he said with a smile.

"Quicker the better."

Who's that damn actor? I've seen him in so many movies.

"How do you like it?"

Damn, I'd like to fuck you.

"It's very good," she said, raising her glass again. "Thank you."

He stared at her as he shook the contents of her second.

Then the little twerps on her right spoke. "I really like your outfit. Is it comfortable?"

"What?" She leaned back, shocked that the little kids wanted to talk.

"It looks kind of rough." The tall boy laughed with his friend. They thought it was soooo funny.

"Oh, I'm a rough girl."

"Yeah, we figured that."

"Figured what?" she snapped, acting offended. "What kind of a girl do you think I am?"

"Nothing. I just—"

"He just really likes your outfit," said the chubby one with a beard.

"Gentlemen," the bartender interrupted them. She was relieved.

"Here you are, miss. The second," said the bartender.

"I'm gonna need a third," she said, gesturing to the boys.

The bartender chuckled. "Let me know. I've got the steak on the grill."

She really wished he had the steak on a grill. She could just imagine the bartender wearing that shirt in shorts, standing beside her pool on a summer day. She could have it arranged. She could probably even have him wear the ridiculous clothes of her fantasy. She laughed to herself.

"My friend," said the fat one. *You're still here?* He touched her shoulder. She lurched back, looking at his finger in disgust. "He's kind of shy, you know."

"It doesn't sound like you two boys are very shy." She took a large swig of her drink. "Not shy at all."

"Well—"

"We have a party we're going to tonight," said the blond, ignoring her. "If you're interested"—he jotted down an address on a piece of paper and handed it to her—"please come. It's gonna be a lot of fun."

"You college boys?" she asked.

The blond hesitated, but his friend nodded. She squinted, sizing them up. If she was in a different mood, she would have said yes.

For the boys' entertainment, and to give them something to talk to their friends about, she took the note and shoved it between her breasts. Then she blew them a kiss and turned from them.

The bartender came over with some bread.

"Will it be a while to cook the steak rare?" she asked the bartender.

"I'll go check on it, miss."

The two boys got up—thankfully. The blond touched her shoulder again. She drew back. "Come by if you can make it."

"Thanks, but I'm getting plastered tonight." She toasted them with her glass.

Then she looked around the restaurant. A light piano piece was being played by a man in a tailcoat. He sat towards the opposite end of the restaurant, near a window facing the alley parking lot. He played very well. There were a lot of people tonight. Their murmuring filled the hall. She gazed at an old couple. They held hands as they stared into each other's eyes. That was sweet. Then she saw a family of four. They were dressed nicely. The young children, the only ones she saw at the restaurant, were quietly eating dessert. There was another large party towards the opposite side of the establishment at a large open table. The group of maybe ten people were laughing boisterously. Many other couples held hands or spoke to one another privately.

She was people watching—one of her favorite things to do. She could have done it for another hour, had she not been interrupted.

"Here you are—steak, rare, with potatoes," said the hunk.

"Thank you."

She picked up her fork and knife and ravenously shoveled the meat into her mouth.

The bartender laughed. "You're starving."

"Hmm? Yeah. It's good. I haven't eaten since yesterday."

"Where are you from, if you don't mind me asking?"

"I don't mind you asking. Malibu."

"Have you been to Tillman's before?"

"Uh-huh. I like it." She cut some more steak. Then she bit into a potato. There were many potatoes in a metal bowl, still sizzling hot—small ones. They were fantastic. "Mmm. Yummy!"

"I'm glad you like it," he said with a laugh. A customer signaled to him across the bar. "Excuse me, miss. I'll be right back. You just keep enjoying your food."

"Mmm! Yeah."

She looked around and saw a woman sitting all by her lonesome at the other end of the bar—a very pretty young black girl. She was dressed formally in a long, beautiful white dress. She was attractive, shapely, with her dress flowing nicely over her bosom. The girl looked upset. Cora tried to signal to her, but the young lady looked away.

"So, I take it you like it?" asked the bartender returning.

"Uh-huh." She put the drink down and bit into the potatoes again. "Fuck, these are good!" she exclaimed with a full mouth. "What does the cook do to this shit? It's like an elixir of the gods! Like ambrosia."

"Tell me, miss, what's your name?"

"Cora." Cora Harper. Cora Gable. Cora Remington. Cora Nash. Cora Jasper.

"Well, Cora, I'm glad you like the potatoes. How's your drink?"

"Great. Really. Get me another, would you? And ... more of those fucking potatoes."

He laughed, then nodded. "I'll be back with both."

Cora turned and looked at the girl at the end of the bar again. She looked exactly the way Cora felt—sad. She was young, looked like she'd just gotten out of college. Maybe newly dumped or stood up or something. And this was a crime for such a pretty young girl.

She looked at the piano player. He was playing another soft melody. The music seemed better than before. *Probably the drinks,* she thought. She took a few leftover olives from her two drinks and stuffed them in her mouth. *Yeah, it must be the drinks. I'm feeling much too good for it to be the piano.*

"Here's another," said the bartender.

"Cheers!" Cora said raising her glass.

"I ordered another plate of potatoes for you, too. It's on the house. It's worth it to see you get so excited."

"Cheers," she repeated.

Then she watched the poor girl take out some lipstick and apply it to her lips and run her hand along her short black hair. She was pretty.

"What ...?" the bartender said.

He became tongue-tied. Cora turned to him and laughed.

"What what?"

"I was going to say, 'What brings you alone to Tillman's, Cora?' but I didn't want it to sound offensive."

"I told you, I like the food." Then she raised her glass. "Cheers."

"I wouldn't want to be like those two guys you dealt with earlier."

"Who?"

"The two—"

"Oh, the college geeks. You don't know how happy I was when they left."

"Right. Well—"

"Are you," she asked, blinking stupidly, "coming on to me?"

"Hmm?" He laughed and then looked uncomfortable, nervously wiping some spilled drink from the bar in front of her. She giggled and raised a drink to him again.

"I tell you what," he muttered, "I'll get you more potatoes."

"You do that," she said with a large grin and a giggle.

She was feeling tipsy. She was halfway through her third and she caught herself swaying too easily to piano music.

She looked over at the poor soul down the bar, again fiddling with her purse.

Cora quickly signaled to the bartender. "Oh, bartender."

"Potatoes aren't ready yet."

"Never mind. Look"—she pointed to the girl—"go be a dear and serve her a drink. Tell her she can have whatever she wants. Just make sure it's perfect, okay? She looks so damn depressed. I hope she's okay."

The bartender looked hurt. Cora looked at him, confused. Then she chuckled, having totally forgotten about their flirtations. *Shoo, shoo. There's plenty of me for later.*

"Okay," he said, suddenly a bit deflated, "I'll take care of it."

He walked over to the mystery girl. Indeed, she was about to get up and leave. Cora watched as the bartender spoke to her. Then he pointed in her direction. Cora raised her drink and smiled.

Cora turned and stared at the bottles against the wall. They were blurring a bit. She was definitely buzzed.

The void was very comforting. This was what she had rushed through the city for—nice blissful anesthesia for her pain before a night of drunken bliss. She thought of absolutely nothing and she enjoyed that. Nothing except that poor girl from the end of the bar. What the hell was the matter with her? Had she just lost a husband she had known for thirty years too? Or maybe she had just met her soulmate, who turned out to be married?

"Here you are."

Another plate of glorious potatoes.

She smiled. He turned and acted all professional. She couldn't suppress a giggle.

"Excuse me," someone said. Cora turned. Behind her stood the young black woman. She was coy. Then she raised a cocktail glass. "Did you buy me this?"

"Yeah. Tell me it's yummy."

"Yes," she said chuckling. "Thank you."

The two stools to her right were still empty. Cora gestured to them. The stranger sat down. She smiled for a second but then looked away, putting her head in her hand, cursing to herself. She turned and noticed Cora looking at her.

"Sorry," she said.

"Don't be sorry. Look, you seemed so damned depressed. What the hell's the matter?"

"Asshole. He's a total asshole!"

I knew it. He always is.

Cora shrugged and smiled. Then she remembered the phrase of her recently deceased husband. "Sure," Cora said.

"He's a total asshole."

The stranger put her head back down in her hand. Cora put her arm around her and rubbed her back. That didn't go unnoticed by the bartender. At first, the girl pulled away, but then she just nodded, crying into her hands.

"You want to tell me about it?" Cora asked, leaning closer.

"We were supposed to meet here. He said he had a business engagement, so he'd be late. That was an hour ago." She looked up. Tears were running down her face. "He said he'd be done by eight and we could meet. Tillman's is our meeting place. It was where we had our first date."

"He stood you up?"

She nodded.

"Asshole," Cora repeated. She drank down her martini. "Oh, bartender!" she slurred a bit too loudly. The bartender walked over, irritated. His look was suddenly unfriendly. "Can you get me another drink? And for the girl"—she turned to her companion, who was a bit out of focus—"what are you drinking, dear?"

"Rum and coke."

Rum and coke! It's gonna be a fun night after all.

"Martini. Get her a martini, too, would you?"

The girl looked up at Cora strangely. Cora smiled and patted her on the back.

"What's your name, dear?"

"Ayla."

"Ayla ... interesting. I like it. I'm Cora."

"Hi, Cora." Ayla gave her a thin smile.

Cora looked down at the girl's cleavage. "I tell you what," she said, "I have a proposal. Let's forget about assholes tonight. That's why I came here. Let's forget them altogether, whaddya think?"

Ayla chuckled and nodded.

"I've spent a long, long time trying to do that," she added. "You know ... forgetting about assholes."

Nathaniel, Arthur, David, Samson, Victor, Henry, Daniel ... Gabriel.

"Did you come here alone, Cora?" asked the bartender. "I can call you a ride home."

"What?" she asked, jerking back at his sudden interruption. She touched his hard chest with the tip of her fingernail. "Don't worry, sir. I won't be riding my bike drunk. I plan on riding someone else tonight."

Then she burst out laughing. Ayla chuckled too.

"You know something," Cora said, touching his hard chest again, then winking at Ayla, "you're kinda cute."

The bartender shook his head with a smile.

"Look, this girl here was just stood up tonight by ..." Cora turned to her. Ayla opened her eyes wide in humiliation, and Cora put her hand over her mouth. "Shit... I think ... I *am* drunk."

"It's okay," Ayla said with a smile.

Cora looked back at the bartender. "But he is quite handsome, isn't he?"

The bartender shook his head again.

"Try some of these potatoes, Ayla. They're fucking good."

She pushed the plate over. Ayla grabbed her fork and sampled some, then nodded and smiled. "They are good."

"Right? No, not good, *fucking* good."

Ayla laughed.

The bartender handed Ayla a martini. Cora raised hers for a toast. They clinked their glasses. Ayla sipped from the drink and almost spat it out.

"You all right, Ayla?"

"Cora, I must confess, I don't drink often."

"Nah ... I would never have guessed ... Ayla ... Ayla. That's a really pretty name. I haven't heard it before."

"Cora's not so popular either."

"Nuh-uh. Not true. Cora's hysterical ... I mean, historical." *Fuck, I am drunk.* "Cora ... is like *coral reef*. It's Greek. The Olympian goddess Persephone was also known as Kore, God bless her damned piece-of-shit heart."

Ayla furrowed her brow.

"Can I tell you a secret, Ayla?"

Ayla nodded.

Cora put a finger to her lips and whispered, "I'm Persephone."

Ayla just laughed.

"Now, tell me about this asshole. How sure are you that he stood you up? Maybe he's just late." Cora regretted the words the moment they spilled out of her lips. The question stung.

Ayla started gulping down her martini.

"I hate him. I thought we were going to get married. I even met his parents. But two weeks ago, I caught him with another woman—someone from work. He promised he would never see her again. He—"

"They always do."

"Yeah. He—" She finished the martini. Cora opened her eyes wide, loving it. Ayla squinted, looking like she was about to spit out poison. Cora patted her back. "I ... can't trust him."

"Drink's good, right?"

"Yeah." Ayla laughed.

"Would you care for dessert?" asked the bartender. He made sure to barge in between them.

"Not yet, mister." Cora looked up at the bartender, waving her finger. He couldn't help but smile. "Tell me, when are you getting off tonight?"

"Ten," he replied.

"And what time is it now?" Cora asked, squinting.

"Nine thirty."

Cora looked at him, then at Ayla. Ayla looked miserable, staring at the bottles in front of her like she had done earlier. Then she looked back at the bartender.

"I tell you what," she said, "why don't you two come to my place?"

The bartender lifted an eyebrow. Ayla looked terrified.

"Ayla," Cora said. "Forgive me. Just understand I'm talking from four martinis, but you really need to get out. I mean ... fuck him, right? This man screwed you. I'm here because a man screwed me. Why does that have to ruin our lovely evening? Come to my house. I have a house on the beach."

"You planning on riding us on your bike?" asked the bartender.

"What's your name, anyway?" Cora asked, feeling cross-eyed.

"Bryce."

"What a safe name. Bryce. Come with us, Bryce. I have a house overlooking the sea." Then she turned to Ayla. "Neither of you will be disappointed. I promise."

"You planning on riding us there?" he repeated.

She drank the last drops of her drink and smiled slyly. Then she wagged her finger and shook her head. "Come with me in my limo and you won't be disappointed."

"*Limo?*" he asked, raising an eyebrow. "All right."

Cora smiled wide. Then she turned to Ayla. Ayla hesitated, but one martini for her was like four for Cora. She was already drunk.

"Fuck it, right? Let's see—thirty more minutes. Ayla, that means you can have two more martinis."

~

They returned to Cora's late. Cora showed them in, stumbling in her drunkenness. She pointed to her right down a dark hall.

"No one enter that door. That's my one rule, okay?"

They nodded.

"Take your shoes off." But Cora kept her black leather boots on.

Ayla started laughing hysterically at nothing in particular. Bryce helped her walk. They stumbled up the wide stairs. Cora almost missed a step, tripping. She laughed, recovering, and then leapt up faster to the upper level of her bedroom as if being chased by them.

It was dark. Only dim candles around the rails glowed yellow.

She reached for a switch. As the lights lit up the large upper floor, the two of them looked at the room in awe. Ayla ran to the window to look outside. Bryce shook his head in amusement. Then he spotted the bar and chuckled.

"What do you think?" asked Cora.

"It's amazing!" shouted Ayla.

Bryce just nodded, walking towards the bar.

Cora fell over the unmade black silk sheets of her large bed. She slipped off her long black boots. Staring at her friends, she unzipped the top of her red outfit down the side, slowly revealing her naked white breast. She caught the corner of Bryce's eye. He watched her undress. Then she grabbed a remote and put on some soft fuck-jazz. Ayla was still staring out the window, oblivious.

Cora shot Bryce a coy smile. She stared at him and shrugged. Bryce turned away and looked at the bottles along the bar.

"Make yourselves comfortable."

"It's beautiful, Cora," said Ayla, turning to see Cora's top half off. She looked away, embarrassed.

"Sorry," Cora said with a laugh. "I forgot I had company for a second." But she didn't lift her top back up. "I would offer you a drink Ayla, but"—she giggled and fell back on the bed—"I think we've had plenty."

Ayla laughed.

"You can have whatever you'd like, bartender."

Bryce smiled, running his fingers along the tops of a few bottles.

Cora gestured to Ayla to sit beside her by the bed. Ayla hesitantly sat down, looking uncomfortable.

"I'm so sorry, dear," Cora said, running her hand through Ayla's short black hair. "It was wrong what that man did to you."

"Never mind," Ayla said with a nervous smile.

Cora touched Ayla's dark-skinned cheek. "You're very pretty, you know."

"Thanks," she answered, frozen, almost trembling.

"What do you do, Ayla?"

"Hmm?"

"What do you do for a living?"

"I'm an actress—well, at least I'm trying to be an actress."

Cora laughed. She couldn't help herself. But then, she put her hand over her mouth. "I'm sorry, but you wouldn't believe how many people have told me that. At least you didn't say writer." She turned to Bryce. "How 'bout you? You an actor too? Or are you just an amazing bartender?"

"I had dreams."

"Of course."

"This is such an amazing place," Ayla said. "You've been so kind. I loved the ride. And"—she chuckled—"the drinks. But I really should be going."

"Me too," said Bryce.

"But you two just got here."

Ayla nodded and sat up straighter. But then Cora snatched her arm. Ayla turned with surprise. Bryce turned too, staring.

Then Cora put a finger by her lips. She gently pulled Ayla down onto the bed. Ayla said nothing but looked terrified.

"Cora," said Bryce, "you—"

Cora lay beside Ayla and kissed her gently on the cheek, then ran her hand along her short hair. Ayla trembled under Cora's touch. Cora gently pulled her closer. Then Cora giggled. Ayla chuckled too.

"I ..."

Cora put her finger on Ayla's lips. Then she substituted it with her lips.

They kissed. And they kissed some more, Cora licking and sucking Ayla's tongue. Then she reached around Ayla's neck and kissed her ear and ran her nose along the girl's black hair. Ayla closed her eyes. Cora liked her smell. It was vanilla and rose petals.

Then Cora touched Ayla's crotch. That was when Ayla pulled back.

"Cora, I'm drunk. I don't think—"

"Shh. Relax. I promise I won't do anything you don't want me to."

Cora took Ayla's own hand and ran it along Cora's slick red latex hip. Then she kissed her lips again.

"Cora, I've never even"—she pulled away gently—"kissed a woman before."

"It's nice, right? There's always a first time."

Cora moved Ayla's hand up to her chest, rubbing her black palm over her breasts. She closed her eyes as Ayla touched her hard nipple with her fingers. Then she opened one eye and looked over at Bryce. He was staring.

"Ayla," Cora whispered, "peel down the rest of my top. Go ahead."

Ayla's hands trembled. She shook her head, but then Cora reached over and grabbed Ayla's hand, running it over her top again, pulling down the cherry-red latex to completely reveal her breasts. Cora pulled away and looked down, chuckling. Then she ran her own hands along her skin and nipples. She reached over and kissed Ayla again. Ayla closed her eyes. She let Cora embrace her. Cora reached back, untying Ayla's dress from behind. Slowly, Cora pulled it over Ayla's head. Then she removed Ayla's bra. Cora laughed. Ayla laughed too. They caressed each other's breasts and rolled over each other a few times on the bed.

"Feels good, right?" Cora asked.

"Cora, why do you wear this?" She pointed to the red latex jumpsuit now draped along her waist.

"Feels good," was all she said with her eyes closed. Then she opened an eye again. As she kissed her stranger, she looked over at her man. Bryce was leaning on the bar, trying to look nonchalant. Trying not to laugh, Cora freed a finger and gestured for him to join them.

They were breathing heavy, now rubbing their bare tits together. Occasionally Ayla would giggle.

Cora reached her hand inside Ayla's black lace panties. She figured Ayla had worn the sexy garb for the asshole. Well, no need to waste it. Her fingers roamed down over Ayla's pussy, stroking it slowly. Ayla let her inside. There was no more resistance. Ayla rubbed Cora's chest while Cora rubbed Ayla's pussy. Then Cora entered gently with her fingers.

Bryce approached and stood over them. He was no longer a cool hunk. He looked nervous. Cora loved it.

"You're pretty," she whispered in Ayla's ear. "Very pretty." Then she turned to Bryce. "Take off your shirt."

Ayla turned, surprised. She had apparently forgotten all about him.

That was when, as Cora tugged her tight red suit down below her belly button to pull it down her waist, the note that the two boys at the bar had given her landed beside Ayla on the bed. It couldn't have happened at a worse time. It clearly read an address and phone number. Ayla jumped up, looking confused.

"No," Ayla said, covering her chest and shaking her head. "I don't want to—"

"What?" asked Cora angry. She leaned her head on her elbow along the mattress.

"I can't."

"Can't what?" asked Cora. "You're already naked."

Ayla looked down, ashamed. Her dress was on the floor. The only clothes she wore were her black panties. She shook her head. "I'm sorry. I have to go."

"Don't be sorry," Cora said. She jumped up and gently touched Ayla's shoulder and held her hand. She led her back to the bed, and they sat beside each other. Then she ran her hand gently along her hair again. "Shh. I told you, no one's going to do anything you don't want to."

"But I don't think—"

Cora grabbed Ayla hard and threw her back down on the mattress. At first, it shocked Ayla, but then she allowed it. Cora kissed her violently along the neck, running her tongue down her shoulders to her breasts, sucking and squeezing her nipple with her mouth. Cora looked up and pointed Bryce again as she sucked, ordering him to join them.

"Take your shirt off," Cora demanded.

That's when she saw Gabriel from the corner of her eye. She had heard Gabe walk slowly up the stairs from his guestroom even before she had removed Ayla's dress. She knew he had been watching.

She supposed it was a game for her. It was like some kind of twisted vengeance. If she couldn't fuck him, well, then, he couldn't fuck her either. Unless ... he joined her. And if he wanted to join her ...

Gabriel was watching in the shadows down by the top rail, hiding. Cora moved back to Ayla's lips while Ayla kept her eyes firmly shut. Meanwhile, Gabriel's eyes were wide open. She could see his azure blues watching in the darkness. He probably figured she couldn't see him. A normal girl couldn't, but Cora's eyes were sharp. She could peer through the darkness. She looked right at him.

Cora yanked down Ayla's black panties, then her own. They kissed and rolled around a bit naked, giggling. Cora fingered along the curves of Ayla's butt and ran her hand again over and over Ayla's wet pussy, sucking at her lips while touching her. Then Cora wrapped her legs around Ayla's and began to rock back and forth, pleasuring the girl. Cora and Ayla moaned together. Again and again they rocked, and for a moment, Cora forgot all about her peeping tom realtor.

When Ayla climaxed, Cora looked back at Gabriel and smiled. Her smile was enough. Gabriel jumped and ran down her stairs. Cora fought with herself not to burst out laughing.

Then she turned Ayla onto her side, presenting her ass and pussy to Bryce.

"You do have a big cock, right?"

8

THE GOING AWAY PARTY

I t was on the fifth day of Gabriel's imprisonment—at least, that was what his stay felt like—when Hashan approached him to make him feel worse by inviting him to a "soiree" Cora was having. A going-away party. Gabriel nearly threw the door closed on the small crow. He was furious. More delays. This time it was over her name. Apparently, his eccentric client was delaying over her name change, refusing, for one reason or another, to sign papers before officially changing her legal name to Aregard. Cora claimed she had to work it out with her lawyers, but all the company's attorneys back in New York claimed there should have been no reason for the delay.

And now, she was having a party.

Bitch.

Peering through a crack in the red drapes, Gabriel watched as the long circular driveway quickly packed with cars and limos. Excited couples wearing masks and formal clothes, many women in short black skirts and men in dark suits, had been rushing towards the door. Now the walls were filled with the constant banging of bass and the screams and wails of drunken revelers.

In the dark, he looked at the velvet mask lying at the

threshold of the door. He hadn't moved it. Someone, probably Hashan, had slid the mask under. Now, light from outside shone through a crack at just the perfect angle to illuminate it. It seemed to tease him, beckoning him to put it on and join them.

He lay on the bed on top of the sheets in his white underwear, staring at the ceiling, trying to ignore the noise. He had spent the last hour trying to sleep.

Then he jumped, hearing a girl scream.

He got out of bed, pulled his phone out of his jeans, hanging over a nearby chair, and looked through his messages. He had called Mina. He'd also had a chance to talk with little Jo Jo. That was at five o'clock his time, eight o'clock New York time. Now it was ten. He thought of calling his wife again, but then another yell from upstairs knocked some sense into him. Then he thought of getting dressed and leaving. If she didn't want to sign the papers, he could just tell his boss that the deal was off.

No, he couldn't leave. It was too important an account. He fell back on the bed and threw a pillow over his head.

That was when he heard a knock on the door. He picked up the black silk robe draped at the side of the bed—it was Cora's, of course, doubtless a very expensive one—and walked to the door. There was no peephole, so he cracked the door open.

He expected Hashan. His eyes widened when he recognized Cora.

"Hi." She waved, flashing a guilty smile.

She looked completely different than he had ever seen her. She wore a long white dress held by a gold clip on her shoulder. This left bare her pale skin along her arms and shoulders. She had on sandals and her red hair was curled. Her makeup was more ordinary. She wore long diamond earrings. That looked formal. But the formal clothes and curled hair made her appear more mature. This was how he had imagined his client would look.

Her blue eyes shined with her smile.

"Look, I am *so sorry*, Mr. Cartwright." She slurred her words a little, obviously drunk. "It seems my going-away party is getting a little out of hand. The noise must be terrible."

"Where have you been?" he asked in a forced whisper. "I've been looking for you for days."

She smiled slyly and for a moment, in horror, he feared she'd mention seeing him watching her last night. She couldn't have seen him. Could she? It was too dark.

"I'm sorry," she said with a smile. "You know I'm mourning. I'm really having a tough time." It didn't look like she was having a tough time. "It's kinda screwed everything up. I'm really sorry, Gabe. You've been so sweet to stay."

He was angry, and yet he liked her classy get-up and her smile. He hated himself for that.

"I'm really sorry, Gabe," she repeated. "I've been so busy."

"Cora, all you have to do is sign. I can return home with the new contract and we can wait for you to finalize your name later. All the appraisals are redrafted. It's done with your new surname. I amended everything. I just need you to—"

As he was talking, he noticed the colored lights flashing around her and the hip-hop music blaring. Then there was the murmuring, the occasional shouting, the laughter, and the distinct smell of pot from outside the door. A few women ran by Cora. One even tapped her on the neck and winked at him. Cora turned for a moment and giggled.

She put her hand over her mouth and apologized again.

"You're not even listening," said Gabriel.

"Huh? Hey, you want to join us?"

"No."

"Oh." She smiled, touched her neck and seemed to stagger back a little. "I can get Hashan ... to get you a hotel ... for the night, Gabe. You need sleep. I—I can't sign anything right now."

That was true enough.

She laughed. She was carrying a glass of white wine, of

course. He hadn't noticed at first, but then she giggled again and brought the shaky glass up to her lips.

"It's late," he replied. "I'm not so sure I can get a room."

"Hmm ... no worries. Hashan has his ways. He can take care of it. I'm sure—"

"It's okay. Don't worry about it. I'll try to close my eyes and make do as best as I can."

She smiled even more. "You're so sweet, Gabe. You're such a nice man. Are you positive?"

"Yes."

"And ..." She looked at him, blurry-eyed. "Uhh ... umm ... uh ... what were we talking about?"

"Nothing," Gabe said, rolling his eyes. "We can talk tomorrow."

"Tomorrow," she said with a nod. "All right. I would say we'll try to keep it down, but"—she burst out laughing—"I don't want to promise the impossible."

"Just meet me tomorrow, okay?"

She nodded.

Then she looked at his robe. She seemed to stare at his body for a moment with a smile. He wondered if she'd even remember their conversation tomorrow.

She stood there by the door, looking down at his bare legs in thought. Gabe felt uncomfortable again. He was beginning to think that Cora had other reasons for disturbing him.

"Well, good night," he said.

"Oh, good night, Gabriel. Have pleasant dreams."

~

It started as a soft moan, then another, and then yet another. It was worse than voyeurism. The moans and groans and shouts of ecstasy made his mind race. He *heard* sex. And so, he could imagine it. He could lie alone in his underwear listening to it as it echoed around the room.

He had fallen asleep. He wasn't even sure what time it was. It had taken him a couple of hours to finally doze off. Then he awoke to the sound of them. It must have been after midnight. The music had actually quieted. Now he heard groan after groan in the darkness. Gabe turned and put a pillow over his ears, in disbelief at his predicament.

He rolled over and closed his eyes again, but his attempts were futile. There was no possible way to ignore it. There were so many voices that his mind whirled thinking of how many people were fucking outside his door.

One voice in particular was high-pitched and shrieking—a girl in total ecstasy. His mind fell on this one. She was probably young, maybe twenty, maybe a brunette. He thought of her as thin with small tits and a tight ass, riding her man. Her perky breasts bouncing rhythmically up and down with the music while still probably wearing a black velvet mask.

He looked back down towards the door at his own mask. Then he had a terrible nasty thought: he could join them. No one would ever know.

What am I doing?

He pounded his forehead to knock some sense into himself.

He tried to match Cora wearing the elegant dress she'd had on when she had knocked on his door a couple hours ago with the sounds of debasement and debauchery echoing through the walls. Was she partaking in this? Of course she was. She might have looked like a classy princess tonight, but she wasn't fooling him. He remembered the other night.

He had watched her upstairs as she had rolled about on that huge black bed with the black girl. He remembered Cora touching and pleasuring her, and as she did, Gabe stared at Cora's perfect perky pale tits—absolutely perfect. And then, her bright azure eyes. Even if she saw him, she had no shame. It was as if she wanted him to watch her. No ... not watch her. She looked like she wanted him to *join her*. And the way she'd stared at him in the midst of sex was the most alluring of all.

Maybe she had wanted him to catch her all along. After all, she knew he was in the house downstairs. She had hardly been quiet. Was she doing that again now?

He reached into his pants and touched himself.

Bitch.

What sort of a place was this? He regretted not leaving. He had been tortured when he'd called his wife to tell her he wouldn't be coming home yet. And now ... this? The moaning only got louder through the walls. And it was getting faster and heavier.

Bitch!

His mind wandered, and as each voice was matched to an imaginary body in his mind, he began to settle on only one. He remembered again the redheaded vixen goddess, his Cora, that he had watched the other night. Just like tonight, he had heard the sounds, and so he had walked up the stairs to see what was happening. He could do that now. He could take the mask and walk up the stairs to see her having sex. No one would ever know.

He thought he heard her. It sounded like her voice. Her voice was so alluring.

Then he heard a scream. It sounded like her. It sounded like ecstasy.

Bitch! Bitch! Bitch!

A different voice shouted. The yelling was so loud this time that Gabriel jumped in bed. Someone was climaxing, a girl screaming in ecstasy. It sounded like the sound was coming from the ceiling. Gabriel's heart beat fast. His mind wandered again, searching for Cora's voice.

Then it all ended with a loud knock at the door.

Gabe pulled his hand out of his underwear and jumped from the bed.

There was more pounding on the door. Had Cora run down again to talk to him?

He grabbed and pulled on his robe again.

"*Oh, Mr. Cart-wright.*" It sounded like a few girls. He heard giggling, then more banging. "Anybody there? Mr. *Cart-wright?*"

He unlatched the lock and turned the knob, cracking the door open.

Three women, each wearing a velvet mask, stood outside his door. One carried a bottle of liquor; another had a bong under her arm. The third was empty-handed, but when the door opened, she rammed her face inappropriately towards his, laughing hysterically. All wore the same distinctive latex jumpsuit as Cora had the other night, but in different colors. They were about the same build as Cora. One wore cherry red, another navy blue, and another black. But none of them had red hair.

"So," said the one in navy blue, pushing the door further open and looking around the room, "this is what's over here."

Another, the cherry-red one, ran her hand over Gabe's chest as she walked in. He batted her hand away.

"May we come in?" said the last, coming in anyway.

"What is it you girls want?" asked Gabriel.

That made them laugh even more.

The black-skinned one wearing a black jumpsuit turned to the door and locked it behind her. Then she turned on the main lights. They all looked around in awe at the large casita as the room lit up bright. Then she ran her hand along Gabe's short hair. He pushed her away.

"Handsome."

"What do you three want?"

"Why aren't you joining the party?"

The black one picked up his mask by the door and showed it to her friends. They all giggled.

"I'm sleeping."

"How can you sleep with all the noise?" asked a blonde. She

was the one in cherry-red. Then she touched his chest. She managed to fit her pale cold fingers between the folds of the robe. He recoiled. She laughed.

"Don't mind us," said the one in navy blue. She also had blond hair, but she seemed older. Gabe guessed the two young ones were nineteen, maybe twenty. The older one looked maybe thirty. She walked curiously about the room, picking up random stuff—pens, papers, his shirt—whatever was lying around the room. "We're a little drunk." Of course they were—he could smell the liquor on them. She turned towards him and raised the bottle. "Want some yummy 151 rum?"

"No." Gabe took the arms of the one in red and the one in black and pushed them towards the door. "Look, you girls need to go."

"Aww ... but we just got here."

The one wearing red touched Gabe's cheek. He turned from her. She still had the bong under her arm. "And we're doing drugs."

"Get out."

"Maybe that's why Cora didn't want us here, Shirl," said the one in red to the oldest in blue. "He's boring."

They all laughed.

"I kinda like his robe," said the one in black, running her hand along the black cloth. Then she reached along the hairs of his chest. He batted her hand away again.

"You girls need to leave."

A wail came from upstairs then, so loud that everyone froze and looked up. Then they giggled.

"Cora sure knows how to throw a party, eh, Mr. Cartwright?" asked the girl in red.

"How do you know my name?"

"Cora told us all about you," the one in navy blue said with a shrug.

"You're wearing her clothes?"

"Yeah," said the one in red, running a finger down her body, delineating her hip and ass. "Do you like it?"

"Why?"

"It was my idea," said the one in red. "We thought it'd be funny. We think Cora has taken a fancy to you. That's why she keeps you locked up in her home. But"—she walked up to him and grabbed his crotch—"why should she have all the fun?"

Gabe pushed her away and ran for the door. He reached for the latch, but before he could unlock it, he was tackled to the carpet. He was surprised to see the lady in black jump on top of him, straddling him. This was followed by the one in red, who pulled his arms up and pinned them under her knees from behind. The one in navy blue just looked down at him, amused.

"Get off me!" he shouted.

"Just relax," said the one in black, reaching down and kissing his cheeks. She removed her mask. She was a cute black girl. He was surprised at how young she looked.

"I know how to keep him still," said the one in navy blue above him. She reached from behind and began peeling off the blue suit from the side. She was performing a striptease, moving to the thump of hip-hop emanating from the walls outside the room as she slowly stripped off her clothes. Like Cora, she had worn no top under the latex, and her large white breasts were exposed.

Gabriel was now genuinely terrified. He was being pinned by two girls and forced to watch a strip show by the third. And then the one in red reached into his robe and began touching his chest hairs again.

"Get out, girls! I don't want this!"

"Shh," said the one in black, leaning down over his ear. "Shh. You're so uptight. Don't worry. Just relax."

"Maybe he needs a drink from the bottle?" suggested the stripper above him again.

She stripped down to her panties and ran her hand along her

arms, down her chest, around her nipples, and over her privates. Then she took her panties off.

Gabe jumped in a panic, fighting to move underneath the other two girls. The naked older woman turned and spanked her ass over him, then tapped the one in red, quickly switching positions with her. Still wearing her mask, the older woman proceeded to fall over him, fondling him naked beside the black girl while the blonde started to strip down her own red clothes above him.

"Guess I'll be last," said the black girl in his ear with a giggle.

"Get out of here! I don't want this!"

Gabe fought with them. But every time he pushed free, another pinned him back down.

The blonde peeled her red suit off, rolled off her panties and joined the other naked woman with a giggle. They moved about his body, kissing and fondling him. One began sucking and biting his toes while the other held him down, rubbing her breasts along his chest.

Then one of them touched his cock. "Ooh, it's hard."

"Get off me!"

They giggled again.

As he felt his underwear being pulled off, another grabbed his penis. Gabe's heart was bursting in his chest. Any arousal or excitement was now sheer terror. He thought of his wife and kids. Then he began to doubt himself. Perhaps he was letting them do this?

The three, now all stark naked, lay over him, writhing.

He broke free and rolled towards the bed, but two leapt back on him, laughing hysterically. He felt one of them grasp him between her legs and begin gyrating her naked pussy on his leg while another yanked his hands back hard again, leaning over them. He freed a hand and hit her squarely in the jaw. Then he yanked his body free from them again.

"Hey, what's your deal? Just relax, Mr.—"

Then there was a crash. The door to the guesthouse flew open and a woman screamed. The girls jumped just enough for Gabe to finally roll out of their grasp.

"Out! Out! Out! ... Get out of here!"

Gabe looked up. He was dizzy, almost as if he had been drinking with them. The whole thing felt like a dream. He could still hear the music, and now strobe lights flooded in through the door.

"I told you never to enter this room! *Get out!*"

It was Cora. She stood at the threshold, looking angrier than he had ever seen her before. She grabbed each girl and dragged them out the door. The last of them, the eldest, was hurled over fifteen feet out the door as if she weighed only a few pounds. Then, in humiliation, Cora chased the naked girls out of the crowded house and into the cold, dark night. The crowd outside the door roared with laughter.

Cora rushed back. Gabe was still lying on the carpet, stunned.

Cora still wore her formal dress, but the dress was now wrinkled and her red hair was disheveled. And the weirdest thing—Gabe thought perhaps it was from the stress of the evening—was her eyes. It seemed they had changed from blue to a glowing fiery red.

"You should be ashamed of yourself," she said, looking down at him and shaking her head. "Why, you're a married man."

Then she slammed the door on him.

He lay there naked and confused. It had all happened so fast. He wasn't even sure if it had happened.

Then he thought of Cora and her look of disappointment. Apparently, she was blaming him for being raped in her own home.

9

CORA'S CHILDHOOD

"I fucked someone last night."

When she saw the doctor's expression of shock, she burst out laughing.

"I hope it doesn't make you think less of me, Doctor ... I love sex, you know. Danny knew it. It strained our marriage. It always does. I mean, whether I find a husband or not shouldn't stop me from fucking, should it? And I find a man's body is like a good piece of steak—nice and tender, always different, always wonderful."

She was trying to be funny, but she didn't feel funny. She felt dreadful.

"Got a bit of a hangover, though. I can't recall how much wine I had. And my muscles ache really bad—you know, is it from the fucking? The bike accident? Drinking? Or all of the above? How are you, Doc?"

"I'm well, Cora. You were in an accident?"

He was lying. He looked even worse than before. His thin hair seemed thinner and unkempt. His eyes drooped even more behind his spectacles. He probably hadn't slept for days.

"I'm sorry I had to cancel our last appointment."

"That's okay, Doc. Don't worry about it. How's Lilly?"

"I'm here for you," he replied.

But Cora sank into the couch, sighing and staring at him, resigned to keeping her mouth shut until he fessed up. She wouldn't say another damn word.

He looked up and nodded, managing a thin grin.

"They're moving her to the ICU. I'm afraid I'm not sure when we can meet again. They were trying chemo, but her white cells got too low."

"She has to do chemo? How awful. Is she throwing up?"

"Sometimes."

"I hate throwing up," she said, wrinkling her nose. "It's so gross. How long will she be in the intensive care unit?"

"They don't know."

"On a ventilator?"

"Yes."

"On pressors?"

"Cora," he said, looking at her suspiciously, "you're sure curious. I'm here for you, not my wife. But thank you for your concern."

"I know a little about hospitals. They say if you need pressors, to keep the blood pressure and heart up, things could be close to ..."

"Death. Yes, Cora, she's dying." He looked terrible as he said it.

"Did they tell you how long?"

"They don't know," he snapped, taking a deep breath. We're not here for me, Cora."

"Yeah ... how awful. Why does this shit always happen to nice people?"

"They're doing everything they can."

"I hope so. I hope she gets better."

He straightened up in his chair, closed his notepad and

looked straight into her shades. "Why did you make love to someone last night?"

"What?"

"You said you had sex with someone. Are you in a new relationship?"

She burst into laughter. "I'm always having sex with someone. I was trying to be funny. Anyway, last night was just a one-night stand. Maybe it was a way to get even with Danny again. You know how I like doing that. Or maybe this time I'm mad about the other guy."

"Other guy, Cora?"

"Yeah. I've been seeing another man. His name's Gabriel. Really sweet, like you. But things got a little out of hand at my party. I think he's a bit upset with me."

"Do you think you're ready for another relationship?"

"I don't know, Doc, what do you think?"

"Well, Danny wanted you to move on."

"I love him." Cora nodded. She was as surprised by that admission as he was.

Am I? In love? I'm supposed to be.

"Danny?"

"No, Gabriel."

"How long have you been seeing Gabriel?"

"Well," she said, biting her lip. "We're not really seeing each other. I had him stay at my house on the beach for the past week on business. I met him a month ago. See, he's my realtor."

"Oh."

"And he's married."

"*Oh*," he said, opening his eyes wider.

"Right." Cora laughed. "But he's an Ambrosia."

"An Ambrosia?"

"Ambrosia. I told you, Doc. He has the same blood as Nephrea—Nephrea Ambrosia, the nymph queen. My foster mother."

"I see."

"Yeah. I know you don't fucking believe me, but Gabe is a descendant of the nymphs I protect from Azure. I love them. And now, after thousands of years, I finally can really have one of them for myself. A male nymph. A man. It's a bit ironic, being that he's one of the last, but that's the prophecy."

"Well, whatever his ancestry, I think, if you feel ready enough, it might be good to help you move on."

"Really? I'm surprised. Even a married man?"

"You're an attractive young woman," he replied with a shrug. "But I wish it was someone who wasn't married. Does he like you the same?"

"Yes. But he won't admit it. See, he got married before I looked him up."

He didn't understand that, and Cora wasn't about to explain.

"You know, there's something I haven't told anyone," said Cora. "I've been wanting to tell you. I mean, Hashan knows, but he doesn't count." She chuckled. "I would love to get it off my chest."

"That's why you're here, Cora."

"I ..." She hesitated. "I burned Danny's painting." She sank back into the cushions, feeling awful. "See, it was a painting of us. Well, it wasn't actually of Danny, but the man in the painting was supposed to be him. It was him touching me. I was in the painting. You know, it was our love together."

He looked disturbed by this.

"What the hell's the matter?"

"Cora, I know I told you to move on, but I didn't tell you to cut him off. This is like your name change. I didn't agree with your husband when he arranged that either. It was too drastic. You have to learn to live with your loss of Danny, not eliminate him."

"But I had to, Doc. It was a painting of me. He had no right to paint me. I told him never to paint me. Of course, I'm not being vain, but no one should paint me or take pictures of me. I need to avoid pictures and paintings of myself. Otherwise people will find out about my immortality."

"Hmm," he said in thought. "That's interesting. I thought you destroyed his work for very different reasons."

"Really?" she said, amused. "What? Do tell."

"I thought it was your anger over him leaving you."

No, that's why I just crashed my bike into a fucking building.

She gave him a fake grin and felt heat rush to her cheeks and eyes.

"I was really upset after I burned his painting. It didn't make me happy—not happy at all. Then, when I chased Gabe away, well, now I feel alone. Very alone. Absolutely alone."

"Well, Cora, I suppose, your loneliness is good insight."

"Yeah." She sat up straighter on the couch. "I want to kill him. You're right. I'm furious. Danny had no right to leave me. You know, he was too young. Most of my other husbands die a nice old age. Then Gabriel ... well, Gabe's being a dick. I mean, I had a party because I'm leaving—I'm leaving for him, by the way, if you want to know the truth ... but, the point is, Gabe was a total dick. Just because he's married doesn't mean he can't partake in a little fun. He should have joined us. Him not joining ... I suppose ... makes me think that he'll never join me. And that just won't work, being that we're destined to be together. If we're apart, I'll be absolutely miserable. So, I suppose, yeah, I'm angry. I'm really pissed. And, that's why I crashed my bike on my way to San Diego on the 5 freeway."

The doctor wrinkled his brows in confusion.

"You know," she continued, wrinkling her own eyebrows in thought, "I suppose crashing my bike into a wall off the 5 last night was like banging my head against my hand when I have a headache. There's no one I can get mad at, so I just hurt myself in a way I can control. It helps 'cause I felt helpless, Doc. You know? It's not like I could kill my useless fucked-up self, 'cause I'm immortal, but I can bash my head against a wall. You see? You know? Do you understand?"

"No, Cora," he said with a thin smile. "You're veering off on your fantasy again. And you're saying quite a lot. You were angry at Danny for leaving you, and now you're angry at Gabe for not joining you. So, you feel alone. But you're not alone.

"I think you're being too hard on yourself. I see you do this a lot. You make yourself out to be some kind of monster. If you're such a monster, why would good people like you? You're not a monster, Cora."

"But I am."

"I don't think so," he continued. "And as far as these men, is it really their fault? Gabe's married. And Danny didn't take his life, it was taken from him by God."

"By God, Doc?" she asked with an amused smile. "God? Did you just say Danny was taken by God? You really believe that? I didn't know you believed in God, Dr. Tenor."

"I do, Cora."

"That's really surprising considering all you're going through with Lilly," she said, scooting up on the couch again. "Sometimes I think *you're* the one who needs help getting through the death of a loved one."

That shook him. Dr. Tenor tensed up and looked flustered. He put his glasses down on his desk a little too hard and rubbed his eyes.

"I shouldn't have said that," she said. "That was really, really wrong. I'm sorry. It's just that you pissed me off with that God stuff."

He took his pen and wrote something down in his notebook. Times like these, she didn't like it when he was taking notes.

"Anyway, the depth of my shit goes far beyond Danny or Gabriel. I *am* a monster. I keep telling you that. You're very wrong about me."

"You're not a monster, Cora," he said absentmindedly, still jotting down something.

"But I am ... and if you knew about us, you'd hate me too. If you knew Imada, you'd hate me too, Dr. Tenor."

She took a deep breath. She liked the doctor, but she knew she was right. If he knew the threat to him and his family, he would turn and run from her as if ... as if she was a monster.

"You're not a monster," he repeated, but she wondered if he was saying it to convince himself. Her comment about Lilly's death had really shaken him.

But I am.

It began to rain outside. She wouldn't cry. She would shed her tears in the clouds instead. She heard water hit the ceiling and drops drip down the glass behind the window shade.

Dr. Tenor will die tomorrow.

She heard it in the wind and rain. She had felt it weeks ago. She knew it. And when she looked at him—a shell of a man, a skeleton, like her dug-up husband—she knew he was destined to die and there would be nothing she could do about it.

Fool. And he didn't think she was a monster? That enraged her. She and her bastard husband might be outcasts, but they were still Imada. It was Imada that caused his wife's suffering, and it would be Imada that caused his death. And so, it was her fault. She felt guilty—for such a nice man to be a part of her curse and for her to have lied to him to keep tabs on his wife. Dr. Tenor had every right to know before he passed. So she'd tell him. He would never believe her, but she would tell him anyway. Then, later tonight, she would visit his wife in the ICU and kill her.

She leaned forward and smiled a fake grin. "You want to know why I call my husband a bastard?" She was surprised how quietly she spoke.

"You told me. You said he was cruel."

"No. Cruelty isn't half of it. He is the true definition of a bastard. No one could raise such a vile, loathsome snake."

Dr. Tenor put the notepad down.

She fell back in the cushions and grasped a brown corduroy throw pillow tightly in her shaky hand. "I don't like talking about it."

He said nothing, as stubbornly silent and still as she had been about Lilly, waiting for Cora to proceed, so she nodded slowly.

"When I was very young and was taken down to the underworld, he used to do unspeakable things to me. But first, he wooed me with gifts. Gold necklaces, emeralds, diamond bracelets—taken from corpses, of course—and the finest meals of mutton, cakes, and wine from the ancient world. I recall laughing with him into the late evening hours, wearing beautiful jewelry and long gilded gowns once worn by queens. I rarely thanked him, though, for I resented living in a dark, dank cave. But at first, I genuinely mistook him for a caring man. Soon I knew better.

"When he didn't get his way, he'd punish me. The punishments were genius. Pure genius." She threw her red hair back in thought and looked up. "Pain. Humiliation. Torture. As far as the things I loved, he would take each and every one of them to the nearby volcanic fire pits, chain me naked, and force me to watch them turn to ash under my nose. Burn them, as I burned Danny's painting. I soon learned to value nothing. As far as my body, I didn't have that either. He used to whip me, only my skin healed by next morning. In some ways, that was worse, for he knew that no matter how hard he hurt me, it would never leave a mark on his beautiful bitch. He would give me twenty lashes"—she moved her fingers as if counting—"if I lied; thirty if I stole; forty if I healed the sick; fifty if I even looked upon a man."

She paused and squinted, then continued coldly, "If he was really angry, he'd use the scourge to tear pieces of flesh from my back and bleed me. Or he would mark me with burning coals.

But all that wasn't true pain. Although he spoke of me to his sinful demon subjects as his lovely Queen Persephone, he wouldn't bat an eye before using my body. Sexual humiliation was his real weapon—his way to show all others that he possessed me."

She stopped and took a deep breath. She spoke in complete sincerity, as if her words were common knowledge, but the doctor looked worried. That was kind. It made her laugh for a moment, and she shrugged.

"I'm sure you don't believe a word of it, but this is why I call him a bastard." He was about to say something, but she raised a hand. "Humiliation is the best way to make a beauty like me submit, of course. When truly angry, he would take all the horny dead motherfuckers from Tartarus and have them join in a group orgy. Thirty or more would lie in his bed chamber under the damp earth. They'd bend me over or writhe on top of my naked body like snakes, one after another, as if I was the village whore, as if that way I would believe that I truly was the piece of meat that he thought I was, even though I was their queen. And I couldn't do a damn thing about it."

She paused and breathed again, then covered her eyes as she began to shake. "I suppose I learned to take it, but it made me into a deceitful scheming evil bitch. A demon. Something that you would, indeed, find in the depths of your Christian hell. I learned to, instead of turn the other cheek like your God, take both my hands and strike any man's cheek as hard as I could—anyone who dared cross me. All those who screwed me, I assure you, one day were fucked far worse than I was. I made sure to take vengeance on them all."

She jumped up and walked to the window, her back turned to him. Her eyes shone red through her sunglasses. She pulled back a corner of the closed shade and hid her face from the doctor.

"It was ironic. It finally took my mother to come and rescue me. Nephrea, my real mother, was a soul who actually did turn the other cheek like your Christ. It's a lovely teaching, isn't it? Absolutely lovely, if you can truly live in this world and turn the other cheek like Nephrea, like your Christ, your God. But for thousands of years, I have met few who can manage that. You have to be truly selfless. Nephrea was. She forgave me for any wrong I ever did to her. She risked her life in Tartarus for me, willing to die or rot in prison for an eternity under the depths of the earth for me. For me. My own blood mother, Ceres, never gave a shit about me. If anyone could see your God, it was her. She was willing to take any humiliation or pain if it meant the salvation of someone other than herself. And that is where I fail. How could *I* do that? I who was raped and savaged by the shit of the earth. Abandoned by my mother, Ceres, to lose all dignity of my body and soul. To hold no ... no worth of my own for an eternity. I lived hell. Me under my demon husband.

"This is why I am a monster. You who are mortal can count the people who hurt you, but for me, the number was endless. And so, don't judge me. And don't be surprised at the anger that I hold towards Imada, how I used my rage against them in order to hurt my family and that bastard Hades that still walks this earth. How I will continue to hurt them, take both my hands together, and strike them down as they lay hands on the only people I love. I will protect who I can, while I watch helpless as those"—tears flowed from her eyes—"like you, Dr. Tenor, are unjustly taken from this earth. I am allowed to exist forever, while the just and righteous and good, like you, are uprooted and murdered on this planet. That is the justice of our world. And that is why I, unlike you, cannot subscribe to your beliefs in God, Doctor ... I'm sorry."

Dr. Tenor had no idea what to say to all that. Cora simply nodded in the silence. But then she threw her sunglasses on the sofa behind her, leaned her forehead against the glass and wept silently.

"I can't," she said between sobs. "I can't believe in a God who would let such things happen. To my family. To you. To Nephrea's race. I can't. I've spent eons apologizing to Nephrea. She believed in me, but I wasn't the person she wanted me to be."

"I'm sorry, Cora," was all he could say.

"Just like I couldn't take burning that painting," she said, shaking her head. "I felt like I was burning Danny. Danny was like Nephrea. He was so damn nice. Gabriel is like Nephrea. And so are you." She paused and said slowly, "that is why I love you. I cannot live in this world without you, and yet I know that you all leave me. I *am* a monster. I have been defiled, dirty; now I defile everyone else. I am nothing, and so I spread the same to those I love.

"When I was dark and felt nothing for myself, only Nephrea was able to reach deep inside my heart and bring me back. She brought back my self-worth so that I could finally fight that bastard husband of mine."

"She loved you," said the doctor.

"Yes," Cora said, tapping her head against the glass. "Yes, Doctor, she loved me. But she also left me alone."

The rain now splashed against the glass, as if someone threw pails of water at the walls of Dr. Tenor's office. That torrential rain helped drown out the sound of her own sobs. When it finally let up, she continued with her back to him.

"My conceited bitch sister, Minerva, and her Hellenistic civil liberties helped shape your world. She and my family, *gods* as you call them, built your cities. They gave you order and made the State. But they despised Nephrea's descendants. They hated my beloved Ambrosia family, the last nymph monarchs, Queen Anne and King Sol, scheming to bring about their end. It was what Imada did to them that made me commit the greatest sin of all."

She paused with her head down, letting the water drop from her eyes just as it flowed down the cold windowpane beside her face.

"One day, Anne and Sol's daughter, Princess Cassandra, fell in a cave at the foot of Mount Ambitus, descending into my realm.

Can you imagine my joy, Doctor? I hadn't seen an Ambrosia for centuries. She looked like Nephrea. She acted like Nephrea. I cared for her like my own daughter in the depths, and then I painfully helped her escape—I helped her leave me because I could not face watching her come to the same fate as I had under my beastly husband. So, I was left alone again. But that was okay … that was okay because I felt like I was helping Nephrea.

"It was when Casey emerged again that my heinous fucked-up family of gods hurt her. And when Imada hurt her, that was enough to push me out from the depths. It was as if they had hurt Nephrea herself, and whatever happened to me, I couldn't care anymore, for I would do absolutely anything for my beloved mother—my true mother, Nephrea. In vengeance for Imada's act, I killed thousands of souls with the help of an unlikely ally—my bastard husband. My fury was so terrible that I was even willing to side with my abuser, though I shall never forgive him.

"You see, Doctor," she said, pausing for a moment and wiping her tears, still not daring to turn and show her bright red eyes to him, though their reflection glowed in the glass, "Nephrea's love might have brought me out of my bastard husband's imprisonment, but it was my rage, my fury, my hands—fully grasped together, hitting their goddamn cheeks as hard as I could—that finally returned me to the surface of your world. I am a monster, a beast, and you should by all rights fear me."

She turned but kept her eyes covered with her hands, peering at him between her fingers.

He sat frozen in his chair, speechless.

Cora quickly grabbed her shades from the couch, then angrily fell back on the couch, grabbing some Kleenex from the table and wiping her face.

"Don't worry, Doc. No one dares fucking touch me anymore. Instead, for centuries, Imada lurks in the shadows, hurting you. My enemy is your enemy. Imada. They cleanse everything they deem poison. But who are they to judge what is poison and what is not?"

He said nothing.

"I am Persephone, the goddess of the Underworld. Do you understand? As long as I live, I carry destruction. I am a devil. A demon. I *am* a monster. But whatever happens, at least be comforted knowing that I am also *your* monster. Thinking I'm anything else ... is sweet. But I cannot turn the other cheek like you. I ... I'm sorry. I just can't do that. Forgive me."

She leaned her head in her hands and wept bitterly again.

When she finally got control of her sobs, she attempted a laugh. "See why I don't like talking about myself? But I'm a bitch. Here I am flippant about your wife's illness and then ... to make it up to you, I go and make you feel sorry for me."

"I'm here for you, Cora."

"Yeah, well, I'm not here for you."

Tomorrow your wife shall die by my hands. In revenge, they will come for you. I'm ... sorry, Dr. Tenor. If I could, I'd trade my life for yours.

Is that wish enough to save me, Nephrea?

10

THE PRISON BREAK

Cora had not waited long to visit the hospital. She had gone that same night with Hashan in their stretch limo. When they'd arrived late that rainy night, Hashan had stood holding an umbrella, reaching out a hand to help Cora into the hospital parking lot.

The pair was quite a contrast to the white-painted walls of the hospital. She looked a little like an ancient druid, wearing a long black robe with her face completely covered under a hood, while Hashan looked just as macabre in his jet-black suit and shades.

When the sliding glass double doors of the hospital opened, it was dim, as it was nearly past visiting hours.

Cora was not all that surprised at the tall man in a dark cloak greeting them. Orcus.

"Turn around now, Persephone, and go home," Orcus said.

Cora ignored him and headed for the elevator.

"Turn around," he repeated from behind.

"Nice seeing you again, sir," Hashan remarked feebly.

The elevator door opened and Orcus barged in with them. When the doors closed, Orcus said, "If you don't leave, things will get very hard for you. I will stop covering up your mess."

"I did okay without you for centuries, bastard," Cora replied.

Cora was amused at how her butler turned to the wall, as if trying to give them some semblance of privacy.

"If you do this, they will be at your throat," Orcus said. "I already have been informed that the prisoner I had has escaped."

"What prisoner?" Cora asked with a wry smile. "Do tell, husband."

"Never mind."

The elevator door opened and, now three black-cloaked visitors walked down the floor to the ICU.

"I don't know what you're concerned with," Cora said, trying to ditch him. "Lilly is terminal."

"I'm not stupid."

"That's debatable."

Cora stopped for a second and directly faced him. "Whose side are you on, anyway?"

"I'm beginning to think their side is more peaceful."

"Coward again, Hades?" she asked with a smirk.

"You've been warned," he said, nodding his head. "Good luck to the two of you. I'm not helping with this one."

"Bye-bye," she replied with a wave.

Orcus left them.

Cora and Hashan made their way down more dark halls of the hospital. Any nurse or patient walking the hospital floors was likely spooked by the sight of them in their black clothes, thinking perhaps death itself was paying the hospital a visit.

When she was shown the small all-glass room in the ICU, Cora was surprised to see the thin Lilith had become fat as a whale in just a couple months. Her dark hair was just a few strands along a wide circular face with folds. She had wires along her neck and arms and was connected to a respirator. She lay with her eyes closed, struggling with the machine to breathe.

"Why don't you just die?" Cora said quietly, but she gently rubbed Lilly's hand.

Cora looked out the window towards the nursing station. A couple of nurses were watching them suspiciously.

"I need to commune with her, Hashan," Cora said, staring at the nurses. "Can you stand by the door and draw the curtains?"

"Yes, madam."

Hashan walked in front of Cora and drew the yellow drapes over the windowed wall facing the inside of the ICU. The minute the drapes were closed, Cora placed a hand over Lilly's rounded stomach and closed her eyes.

"She's still alive," Cora said, cracking a smile.

"Of course she is, Cora."

Not Lilly, dope.

But Lilly's thoughts were in Cora's mind too. Lilly was suffering, weak and barely conscious. Her pain was exquisite. The cancer was everywhere. Cora had revived many in her lifetime, and rarely if ever had she felt so much suffering. She couldn't understand why Lilly was doing it. Indeed—why didn't she just die? She felt the cancer eating her head. She could feel it pressing in the stomach along the intestines, obstructing and slowing her bowels, causing intense pain. And she could feel it blocking her lungs. Her heart labored as her kidneys failed to cleanse her blood. Even the mask, which provided vital air, controlled her. Lilly desperately wanted to be free of it all. It was as if she was telling Cora one thing—she wanted to be free. Free from her life. She wanted to die.

Why don't you just die?

Cora knew the answer, but she couldn't come to grips with it. She could feel it, a different kind of tumor, growing in Lilly's stomach. Lilly was suffering for her unborn baby. Through all the exquisite pain, she was attempting miracles in order to save her unborn daughter. She was not only sacrificing herself, she was suffering for her child.

This was what Cora's mother, Nephrea, would have done for

Cora. And when Cora realized that, she lost control of herself and broke down in tears.

A nurse ran in just at that moment, upset that they had closed the curtains. But as she entered, she apologized to Cora at the sight of her weeping.

"What is it, Cora?" asked Hashan.

"Is everything all right?" asked the nurse, opening the curtain.

"We're fine," dismissed Hashan.

The nurse took the hint and walked out, but she kept looking suspiciously back towards the room.

"Hashan, we're not going to let this happen." She took a deep breath and wiped more tears from her eyes with her sleeve. "It's time. We're gonna help her."

"She's terminal, madam. You told me. What can you do for her?"

"Not her. The baby."

Hashan looked bewildered. Then Cora stepped back from Lilly and tried to compose herself. "Hashan, I'm sorry, but you're really going to hate me for this."

"What?"

"We need to get Lilly out of here, but I need a distraction."

"Oh," he said, trying to hide his fear. "Well, I can speak to the doctor, then, and somehow get her released."

"No. There's no time. They're never going to let her out alive. And they'll never agree to a transfer. She's too ill. And the baby— if we don't get the baby out now, she'll die too."

Hashan looked down for a moment in thought. "Perhaps we can get Dr. Tenor to take her home to hospice, madam."

But Cora had already started pulling out Lilly's IV. She unplugged the respiratory machine and was about to pull off her mask when—

"Stop!" shouted one of the nurses, running into the room. Cora didn't stop. She reached for the endotracheal tube in her mouth. "Get out of here!" The nurse turned to the nursing station. "Call security! Call security!"

"Cora, what are you doing? We're going to go to prison over this," Hashan said in his usual stoic sort of way. Had she not been so intent on her plan, she might have laughed.

Cora shoved one nurse to the floor, and Hashan pulled another nurse away from her. "Let's go!" he cried.

"No!" With inhuman strength, Cora threw a third nurse across the room, then turned to Hashan with wild burning eyes. "Not without her. Lilly's as good as dead."

And so are you, dear friend.

Hashan jumped back as Cora reached under his own shirt, unfastened his gun from its holster, and grabbed the pistol. More nurses rushed in, desperately trying to stop Cora, but Cora shoved them off again. Hashan fell back against the outside window in horror as his beloved mistress pointed the gun at his head. *Forgive me, Hashan.* Hashan looked as scared and confused as his flat face could ever possibly allow.

Cora pulled the trigger.

And now the chaos was complete. All the nurses in the room stopped pulling at Cora and ran. The impact of the bullet and Hashan's head against the window shattered the glass wide open. Half his body lay hanging from the opening in the room like a limp sack.

"Shit," Cora said, looking at him. She brushed the pieces of glass off his dead body.

Then she turned back to Lilly.

She grabbed a syringe from the bedside and quickly deflated her endotracheal tube, yanking it from her mouth. Then she ripped out the line from her neck. Blood squirted across the bed. She had to press hard on Lilly's neck with a white towel to stop the bleeding.

For a second, Cora glanced through the door at the nursing

station. The ICU had emptied. This was all according to her devious plan. All the lights were off and it was eerily quiet.

But after a minute of silence, an overhead siren went off and a voice came over the hospital intercom:

"CODE SILVER. CODE SILVER."

Cora couldn't stop the blood from squirting from Lilly's neck. She grabbed the bedsheets and bundled them up, adding them to the now-drenched red towel.

Lilly writhed in pain, then opened her eyes for a moment. It was the first time in decades Cora had seen her eyes—those bright azure eyes, the same brilliant blues as her brother Gabriel's—and in the chaos, it almost made her freeze.

"It's me, Persephone," Cora whispered into her ear. "I'm taking you out to save your child, Lilly."

If there could be any peace left for Lilly, that was it.

Cora still had memories of visiting Lilly as the mysterious lady of her childhood. *Persephone.* She had uttered that name to her many times when Lilly was little. *Persephone*, the woman who had visited her like a fairy godmother, appearing before her from time to time over the years—her protector, her guardian. Likely Lilly recognized the voice. She seemed more at peace.

With that, Cora lifted Lilly and laid her near Hashan. Then she pulled Hashan from the window back into the room. Cora looked out and saw red and blue lights along the circular driveway below. She moved a chair under the window to use as a ladder. Lifting Hashan in one arm and Lilly in the other, she stood over the gaping hole that had previously been a window.

"*Stop!*"

Behind her in the ICU was a guard brandishing a gun. Wind and rain hit her face as she looked down at the parking lot two stories below. She jumped, carrying her important cargo.

The guard fired. A bullet hit her in the back. Cora felt the searing pain as the bullet passed through her chest. She gasped for air. Then, amidst the severe pain, she made it worse by landing hard sideways on her right ankle on the cement below, instantly cracking it.

She screamed in pain.

It was pouring. Red and blue flashing lights reflected off the incoming fog.

As Cora rose, three squad cars surrounded her. Guns drawn, the police were using their car doors as shields.

Cora set her precious cargo down with her tattered body for a moment.

"*Stop! Mrs. Anastra! Stop!*"

Cora raised her hands. The police likely thought she was surrendering, but the fog thickened. Then a wind, like a tornado, formed. It touched the ground, contacting the three squad cars and throwing them into the air, rolling them along the asphalt and crashing them into other parked cars. Thunder cracked from above. Mixed with the fog, the odd weather turned the hospital into a dreamscape.

Cora, now with her black hood pulled up, lifted the two bodies and limped down the center of the now-broken police barricade. A couple police fired upon her, but the stray bullets didn't impede her. She walked over to her black stretch limo and put the two bodies in the back.

She raced to the beach. The police cars at the hospital were disabled, but she knew more would come, so she drove as fast as she could, heading to a familiar cliffside. When she reached it, she fought her pain, limping out of the car into the pouring rain and laying the two bodies down, hiding them under cover of bushes and leaves. Then she crouched over Lilly, gently holding her head and running her hand over her cheek. Lilly was still alive, but barely breathing.

"Lilly. Lilly! Oh, Lilith."

Lilly opened her eye a sliver. She winced in pain. Cora touched her stomach. The child still lived.

"Lilly."

Lilly gasped for air again. Cora put her mouth over hers, then touched her chest.

Cora tried to heal her. It was futile, but she thought she owed it to Lilly to try.

"Don't leave me," Cora said, shaking her head. "Don't go."

Lilly smiled. Despite all her pain, she smiled. And as she looked up into Cora's eyes, she seemed to recognize her Persephone. It made Lilly smile more.

"No." Cora touched her again, tears forming in her eyes. "Lilly."

Cora felt the cancer in her blood. She saw it everywhere. She touched her again and hunted after the diseased cells. She searched everywhere to kill it. But it was too late. It was taking over so much of her body that she couldn't destroy it without destroying the rest of Lilith's body.

Let me go.

"I can't," Cora said, shaking her head. "I won't."

Lilith turned her head and opened her eyes wide again for a moment. Her bright dark blue eyes—azure blue. They were the same as the nymphs' and the gods'. The same as Harmonia's and Anna's. The same as Cassandra's. The same as her own. The same as Nephrea's. The same as Gabe's. Cora seemed to exist solely for those azure eyes.

Let me go.

"No! I'm alone. I'm all alone! Why do you all leave me! Why have you always left me here alone!"

Let me go.

Cora fell sobbing onto Lilly's chest.

Then Lilly stopped suffering. She took one last breath and finally rested. But even as her body died, her spirit could be heard in Cora's mind.

Let me go.

Cora felt the words. In her mind's eye, the words were no different than Danny's.

Let me go.

It was no different than Arthur's and David's. No different than any of them had ever been. Yet it hurt just the same.

Then she felt the baby.

She would free the baby like she had freed Lilly from the oxygen mask and the tubes. She would save the child as she killed her mother.

When the baby was born, exhausted but still determined, Cora stripped off her own clothes and her butler's and threw them into the limousine to destroy later. Then she dragged Lilly's dead body in.

She gently laid the baby, crying and confused in the rain, under a bush beside her dead butler.

"Be right back."

To complete her plan, Cora backed the limousine up on the road overlooking the cliff. Then, when she judged the distance adequate, she pressed her foot hard on the gas. When she reached the edge, the stretch limousine hopped over the sidewalk and then sped off the cliff, violently crashing and rolling, dust and sand blowing along a shattering windshield while the walls of the car crushed in around her. The impact was violent enough to ignite the gas tank, and everything lit into a giant fireball. With the searing heat of flames surrounding her, Cora sat there in a flash of extreme pain, waiting for the explosion to consume her. Then her body became incorporeal—like a ghost, a vapor.

She floated back to the top of the cliffside, where she found the baby safe and sound, crying her eyes out, beside Cora's dead naked butler. As Cora's arms grew solid enough, she embraced the baby, rocking her slowly, both of them hidden under the bushes and trees.

~

Orcus watched with a smile as the bright red flames and smoke engulfed the evidence beside the ocean waves. Then he walked along the cliffside, searching for her. He knew he had found her when he heard a baby crying. A naked pale long-haired redhead held a baby hidden behind branches and leaves. Beside her, a body lay on the ground—a dead Indian man. Orcus stood over her.

"Give me the child," he said, stumbling around leaves. "Give her to me, Cora. You can't take care of her."

"I won't." Cora looked down at the baby with a sweet smile. Then she looked up at Orcus. "She belongs to me now."

"Cora, she's not yours."

"She's not yours either. I'm giving her to her uncle."

"This means this much to you? You can't keep them alive."

"Lilly did. She lived as long as she could to save her. Now she's reborn—living on as my baby. One last nymph. One last time."

"And the death of Mrs. Anastra?" Orcus said with a smile. "How convenient."

Cora looked up with a smile. "You will take care of Mrs. Anastra's records, husband?"

There was some silence.

"I told you I'd protect you, not the ones you care about," Orcus finally replied. "Are you aware they've already had their vengeance with the doctor too? The doctor's dead. I'm sorry."

"I foresaw it."

"Of course you would."

11

MINERVA

O rcus stood on the cement patio on the fourth floor of Minerva's beach house, overlooking a stunning view of her private island and the clear Mediterranean. Her small island was about twenty miles from the much livelier island of Ibiza, which he could still see on the far-distant horizon. It was quiet— almost too quiet.

He stood near the edge of an infinity pool. To his right was a private vineyard, and to his left was an old lighthouse. The island was crescent-shaped and encompassed only this small cliff and valley. He was close enough to the water that he could still smell the ocean beside the pool.

The sliding glass door opened behind him. He turned and readjusted his sunglasses.

"Uncle!" yelled Minerva in her Spanish accent. She ran into Orcus's arms and embraced him tight. She rubbed his bald head, chuckled, and then pulled away.

Minerva did not look like a normal woman, no matter how hard she tried. Her immortal youth contrasted uniquely with her older tastes in makeup and jewelry. Her black hair was long and slightly curled. Her sharp blue eyes watched Orcus with distrust but exuded wisdom and intelligence. She was attractive—that much was certain—but where Cora wore plain clothes and seemed to allow herself to look eternally young, Minerva covered herself with gold chains, emeralds and rubies along her neck and wrists and thick eye makeup. Her eyeliner was dark and thick enough to appear as kohl. She had on a white beach cover-up shirt and golden sandals.

"Athena," Orcus said with a genuine smile. "You look as lovely as always."

From the corner of his eye, Orcus saw two guards in blue suits, leaning against a white wall at the other end of the patio near the outside concrete stairs. They stood with their arms folded, watching them.

"Welcome," she said with a smile. "Have you had your *déjeuner*?"

"I've eaten."

She gestured to a set of navy-blue cushioned outdoor chairs overlooking the sea beside the pool, then raised her hands and clapped loudly while still looking at him, flashing a fake smile. "Perhaps some hors d'oeuvres?"

An old gray-haired gentleman in a tuxedo walked over from inside the house with a silver tray. He placed the tray on a small bamboo table between the two blue chairs and poured two glasses of red wine, handing one to Orcus and bowing to him. There was also a dish of *higo*, or figs, that he set out. The servant then excused himself.

"Go ahead," she said, gesturing to the wine. "It's from my local winery." She laughed again. "It's made by me, Uncle."

Orcus nodded. The wine was a little tart, but smooth. As he sipped, she watched him.

Orcus scooted back against the cushion of the chair. The two guards still stood beside the stairs, staring at them. He grabbed a fig. "You've always known how to live in style, Minerva," he said. "Very impressive house. And island."

Minerva could not hide her disgust at his manners as he spoke with his mouth open.

She studied him. Minerva had been studying people all her life. Her entire purpose seemed to be to understand people in order to manipulate them.

She finally turned from him and looked at the sea. "Yes. Yes. I've been happy, Uncle, to stay in one place, unlike the rest of us. But you haven't visited me since the turn of the century. September 2001, it was."

"An interesting time ... I've been very busy."

"Yes."

"But we still do business together."

"Of course," she said, looking a little uncomfortable. "Is that why you're here? Did the US government need more of my services? I just provided you intelligence on Beijing's CSR 412 ramjet. I would think that would put me in a good place with your people."

"There is no concern regarding your place, Minerva," he said, washing some fruit down with more wine. "Washington is always appreciative of your cooperation. But, please"—Orcus pointed at the guards with the hand holding his glass of wine—"keep your voice down regarding foreign affairs."

"My guards know everything," she said dismissively.

Liar. But you always were a liar, weren't you, Athena? The best one.

"Anyway, it's so good to see you." She furrowed her brow. "And so I wonder"—she grabbed a fig herself—"why have you requested an audience with me now?"

Orcus smiled. He saw it make her lips quiver for a moment and she quickly averted her eyes.

"Cora did what Imada forbade her to do. She saved Lilly

Tenor's daughter. She helped the Ambrosia family again. By doing this, she broke the pact. I'm assuming that upsets you."

"You don't have to ask me that."

"I'm assuming you knew?"

He didn't have to ask her that either.

With his superhuman hearing, Orcus heard a sound, very faint, off in the distance and turned. To the human eye, it would be a speck—perhaps confused with a fly—but Orcus discerned copter blades. It was a drone. A drone was watching them and possibly listening to their conversation.

"It would be best if you were honest with me, Minerva. We are at a very delicate point. I can't remember such a tense time since the forties, and though I personally have an affinity for the challenge of world wars, you know I've devoted the last two centuries trying to maintain peace for the human race."

Minerva reached over the table for another fig, her hand shaking.

"I questioned Hermes," Orcus continued. "He was found loitering near Persephone's home at the time of Persephone's husband's death."

"From what I hear," Minerva quipped, "you did more than question him."

"If Persephone hadn't lost one of her husbands by your hand—"

"Not my hand," she corrected him.

"Of course—not *your* hand. Pardon me. Persephone had not lost a husband by our family in centuries. This is quite a provocation. And I'm wondering why. Perhaps you know. I've done everything I can to stay her hand since Daniel Anastra's death. But can you blame her? Why would Hermes do such a thing? When I 'questioned him,' he mentioned your name."

She smiled, challenging him with her own glare. "How unpleasant. I had hoped that you were in town for a social visit." She took a deep breath and said impatiently, "Let me make this clear, Uncle: never once did I order the death of that whore's husband. And, frankly, it surprises me that you care."

"I just told you, Minerva, I care about peace. I believe Danny's death stupidly pushed Cora into helping the Tenors. She ignored Gabriel and Lilith for the last few decades. She honored your agreement. It was only after one of you ordered Daniel's death that Cora came out from hiding."

"So you're blaming Imada for Persephone's newfound interest in Ambrosia's family bloodline?" she asked with a laugh. "It is precisely the opposite, Hades. You need to blame Persephone for destroying our home in the name of the Ambrosia line."

"The minute Daniel died, Minerva, Cora looked up the Tenors. She hadn't seen Lilly since Lilly was a child. She honored the truce. She accepted her place and, I believe, would have let you all complete the extermination—until Hermes stirred the pot again. Then she contacted me. And I helped her. I helped her because she was right. It was reprehensible for Imada to do what they did."

Minerva drank some wine, then abruptly squinted at him. Her expression made her look sinister. Orcus felt like she was finally revealing her true vile self. "What do you want?"

"Who ordered Daniel's death?"

"You still love my sister, don't you? After all she did to us? To you? May I remind you that Persephone killed off more nymphs than we ever did. Perhaps she wants to help them out of guilt."

They fell silent. Orcus used the silence to enjoy the stunning view.

"You still love her, don't you?" she repeated.

"That has nothing to do with it," he replied with a laugh.

"Hmm." He witnessed her phoniness return. It was this phoniness that Orcus despised, a sentiment he shared with Cora. "Well, unlike you, I still speak to our family." She paused and looked out at the shore too, taking a deep breath. "I could tell you, Uncle. I could tell you why the tide is turning so sour, as you said. And perhaps, if you knew, you wouldn't judge us so harshly."

"Tell me."

"Well," she said, raising a finger as if pompously giving the god of the underworld a lesson, "there are only two gods that can tell the future, right?"

"Yes. Cora and her mother."

"Yes. And what do you think the family would do if it was prophesied that the birth of the last Napean nymph would lead to Imada's destruction? And possibly the end of society as we know it? The end of our Western society, something I've spent five millennia protecting and nurturing. Your job has been peace —how noble. My job hasn't, Uncle. My job has been the maintenance of justice. We've worked together most of the time, but sometimes our interests conflict. Wouldn't this prediction be enough to end our truce and make us aggressively want to hurt Cora?"

"Sara gave this foreshadowing?"

"Maybe. Or maybe we heard it from Cora. What if I told you, Uncle—this is hearsay, of course—that one of the three Olympian staffs was found by one of our brothers? Poseidon's trident." She gave a sly grin and stared at Orcus for a moment as if waiting for her words to sink in, then nodded at Orcus's shock. "Yes, that would be quite a weapon, even now. Of course, any of the three staffs would be. But the timing is interesting, isn't it? Finding the trident at the same time as the near completion of Imada's cleansing of the Ambrosia family might just make Imada rather nervous regarding the foreshadowing of our end. It seems to give validity to the horrifying prophecy.

"Imagine, Uncle, if Persephone got her hands on the trident again and wanted to repeat what she did to Olympus. Perhaps this time, instead of causing the great flood, she could sink the whole world." She sipped some wine. "That's if you believe in the power of prophecy, of course."

There were three Olympian staffs at the time of the great migration: Zeus's famed thunderbolt, which held the power of thunder and lightning; Hades' Staff of Azure, which held the power to freeze; and Poseidon's trident, which could shape water and quake the earth. At the time of the great flood, and the end of Mount Olympus, Persephone had stolen the trident from Poseidon and used it to destroy the palace of the gods. The subsequent destruction of Mount Olympus had led to a flood that had spread to nearby Greece, Phoenicia, Assyria and Egypt.

Apparently, Imada now feared that Persephone would do it again. It was such a great irony, and so typical of his family's hypocrisy, that after Imada had murdered people of Napean nymph descent for thousands of years, a genocidal "cleansing," as Minerva called it, they still feared his former wife's fury more than any other god or goddess's.

"And where is Sara now?"

Minerva laughed. "You really don't have much to do with your family anymore, do you?"

He turned from her and looked over the stunning view of her island again. That gave him respite to think.

Imada had attacked Persephone because of this prophecy. But why? The timing of Danny's murder obviously corresponded to Lilly's death and pregnancy. The murder, then, had backfired and made Cora more determined than ever to fight Imada and help Lilly's unborn child and the dying nymph family. Before, deep in her hedonism, she had been perfectly happy ignoring the Napean line, allowing Imada to complete the Ambrosia genocide. The whole thing seemed poorly planned, if it had been planned at all. It certainly didn't fit Minerva's wit. It seemed idiotic.

Or was it? Perhaps there was a member of Imada who wanted Cora to fulfill this prophecy Minerva claimed would lead to the "end times." Or, perhaps Daniel's death had been a mistake. Whatever the case, it was clearly not Minerva's style. At most, she had merely assisted the assassin.

"No." Orcus shook his head as if sharing his thoughts. "I don't think you were directly involved."

"Of course I wasn't."

"But I do think you know who is."

Minerva chuckled, then raised her glass in a toast and placed a finger over her lips.

"To answer you, Minerva, regarding Cora, it is not love. She's an extreme thorn in my ass. I help her for political reasons, not personal."

"Of course, Uncle," she said sarcastically, drinking more wine.

"Since her saving the child," Orcus continued, "I've been very busy modifying and rewriting records to allow her identity as Ms. Aregard to stick. This is the first time she killed herself *after* she changed her name. But apparently, mothers can't rush babies out from their bellies—especially when one is dying of cancer. And that brings me to another question—Lilly was pregnant right around the time she developed terminal cancer. Don't you think this was a remarkable coincidence?"

Minerva stared out at the view of the shore but gestured over her lips again. Of course she wasn't going to tell him a damn thing, but he could tell she was disturbed by that question.

"I know you weren't directly involved, Minerva, but you do know who was," he said, breaking the silence. "Was it Hera?"

"You know Hera lost her senses thousands of years ago, Uncle, with the loss of father ... and her loss of power. I'm not amused by your duplicity. You ask me to be straight and you're playing games."

"Artemis, then?"

"I think you should leave," she said, facing him directly. "It's clear that you're not here to be cordial. I'm at the services of your government, but you have no right to ask me personally about each member of our family you care so little about."

"I know you're not directly involved, niece, but you're

watching her," he said with a sly smile. "If you don't talk, I could implicate you."

"Your estranged wife has been destructive since she was born!" Minerva snapped, finally getting angry. "Don't be so surprised I watch the demon witch. And I have every right!"

The guards by the outdoor stairs were stirring, one of them placing a hand on the handle of his pistol. Orcus looked out at the horizon again, searching for the drone. He found it. Now there were two.

"Once Persephone took your staff and froze your kingdom," Minerva continued, "she doused the flame to the engines that provided you pleasures from above. The fact that you didn't chain her then proves you're completely leashed to her. Then she sank Olympus and buried your realm. Given the chance, she'll destroy the world. I know it. So don't be surprised if I watch her. But I can assure you, I had nothing to do with Daniel Anastra's death—not to say I'm totally unhappy about it."

And that was enough for her. Visibly angry for the first time, she turned from him and folded her arms. Orcus caught the guards moving a little closer at her outburst.

"I could make you tell me."

That got her furious. She spun around, even more pissed, with eyes blazing red. "You've helped me spread democracy. For that, I'm grateful. But, Orcus, I warn you, don't lose it all over Persephone. She no longer loves you."

Orcus said nothing, for the wise witch was right.

"I don't understand." Minerva shook her head and narrowed her flaming eyes. "Why do you care for her and the nymphs she protects? Why? Is it Cora or ... perhaps ... it is Harmonia?"

"What?" Hearing that name angered him. He felt his eyes heat up too. "I told you never to mention her name."

"It's the only way I can make sense of you," she said, shrugging. "Your cold heart only loved two people—Harmonia and Persephone. You gifted Harmony and her nymphs the teachings of Ares, giving them so much power as to threaten man and the very existence of Greece. And so Zeus removed Harmony and gave you Cora. But even after Harmony left the world, you still assisted her daughter, Nephrea. Why? It's clear that you hold an affection for these Ambrosias, not just your estranged wife. The nymphs are mutant aliens on this planet and can only be a poison to our development of the human race. They need to be cleansed. I believe you're not only protecting Cora. I think, just like the last time, so long ago, you still have feelings for the Ambrosia family too, and your heart blinds you."

"With all I've sacrificed!" thundered Orcus. "How dare you!" He jumped up, pointing a finger at her head. He was surprised at his own fury as his words thundered through the valley. "How dare you, Athena, accuse me of acting only out of passion!"

She jumped back in surprise. The two guards rushed forward with guns raised in the air, yelling for him to put his hands over his head and fall to the ground.

"Leave us!" cried Orcus, whirling around to face them. He waved an arm out towards them, still twenty yards from their position, and both men were tossed in the air, crashing against the concrete wall of the stairway and falling, stunned.

Minerva looked like she was about to fall off her chair in surprise, her eyes still blazing red, but her expression full of fear.

"How dare you utter her name!" Orcus cried. "You know full well of my hatred for Zeus after what he did to Harmony. And I had every right! Why do you think Zeus lies chained and buried under the rubble of my kingdom, bound by my own hands! Would you like to lie beside him? Do not disrespect me! I've devoted centuries to sacrificing for peace. Now you and the family have threatened the balance. I honestly don't care about your fucking prejudices and hatred regarding the Ambrosias. I only desire peace. That's why I came here. Not for Cora or anyone else. How dare you twist this as if the problem is me! Cora made peace with you and you broke it. *You*, not her!"

The guards slowly rose. Minerva turned to them and raised a shaking hand. "Go," she said to them.

There were now four drones circling off in the horizon.

"I repeat," Orcus snapped staring at her, "who's responsible? If you don't tell me, I warn you, I'll blame *you*, Minerva. Then I'll consider taking you back with me to America to question you just like I questioned your brother!"

"Sorry," she said. "Please, please, Uncle, sit back down. I'm sorry. How stupid of me. I should never have mentioned her. I meant nothing by it."

Orcus reluctantly sat back down on the chair. He could hear his own panting and still felt the warmth from his burning red eyes. Minerva, too, breathed heavily, trying to maintain her composure.

"Bitch," Orcus said, managing a thin grin. "I can't believe I'm still mad over something so long ago. But ... don't ever mention her name again."

"I'm sorry, Uncle. Please forgive me."

"Persephone and I should have been the ones above ground, not you. And Harmony was the bravest, noblest Amazon nymph, the bravest woman, to have ever lived on earth. How dare my brother take her from me. No, Athena, I don't speak with the family because I can't stand the fatuous, inauthentic fuck-dribble that spews out of your mouths, your superior airs—as if you and your father knew what is proper, judging Persephone and me. Your arrogance is why the family's fallen. Zeus and Imada should have been under the earth for a millennium, not me. Not me! Do you understand?"

"Yes, Uncle."

"Not me!"

He turned to the sea again with hands on hips, taking deep breaths to calm himself.

"I know you weren't directly involved—*directly*," Orcus finally said, shaking his head. "I peeled off your brother's skin until he told me. His final word was 'Dellon.' Now, if you want to be useful to me, Minerva—not to the United States, but to me—tell me where Apollo is. Tell me the whereabouts of Apollo and Ceres. Do it quick, before I choose to force it out of you."

"It was not ordered by me. It was a mistake."

"I believe that. Now tell me, niece, where are they?"

"Do I have a choice?"

"No, you certainly do not."

12

A CASE OF MISTAKEN IDENTITY

C ora died.

She read it on social media, laughing at the gushy sentiments by all the phonies who claimed to care for her. They'd never seemed to care much for her when she was alive. Many didn't even care that she had killed someone. It seemed people figured Lilly was so ill that she was on her deathbed anyway. And, apparently, it was okay to kill Lilith because poor Cora Anastra was grief-stricken over the loss of her beloved husband. They forgave her, now that she was dead, of course.

Then there were the constant visitors to her home and incessant amusing lies by her butler, Hashan, by the front door. Cora had even been taken to the station the day after her disappearance. She still couldn't get over the smell of urine in the back of the police car.

At the station, they had questioned her. She hadn't told them a thing. She had just looked at them through those dark shades with her arms folded, wearing her favorite black jumpsuit. She had told them to call her lawyer, Douglas Hanson. Then she had told them to fuck off. They had let her smoke. Then she had fallen asleep in her chair. Eventually, after a couple days loitering in a cell, some guy named Orcus had bailed her out.

It was all an unfortunate ritual for the immortal goddess. She always had to dispose of her former identity to make way for the new. Everyone accepted the mistaken identity, for it was much easier for people to believe a lie than to actually believe that she was immortal. And now, in the twenty-first century, no matter how ludicrously she embellished the facts, no one was ever going to believe that a redheaded goddess from Ancient Greece lived in Malibu.

Now the only thing left on Cora's mind was her favorite realtor. Well, she had to protect him. Right?

So, shortly after her "death," Cora called Austin. She tried not to laugh at his surprise when he heard her voice.

"It was just a mistake, Austin," she said with a laugh. "Really. You can see I'm very much alive."

"Cora, you just lost your husband," he said. "You told us. The house was clearly under Daniel Anastra's name. And the story mentions Danny's name and how Cora killed a psychiatrist's wife in her grief."

"You hear me now, right? That lunatic wasn't me."

"But Gabriel even had our lawyers rewrite the contract under your new name—Aregard. I remember."

"So, what's the problem, then? The contract for my house in Malibu is under Aregard, right? All the papers are legally under Aregard. There should be no problem finalizing the deal. Forget it."

And why wouldn't he forget it when, ghost or not, he could sell two multimillion-dollar mansions?

"Well," Austin's voice came back after a long sigh, "I'm glad you're okay, Mrs. Anastra or ... Aregard. What is it I can do for you?"

"Well, I've been thinking it would be simply lovely if you could send your illustrious associate, Gabriel Cartwright, back to

Los Angeles to have dinner with me. I'd like to finally sign the contract. Say, seven o'clock?"

"We've been trying to reach you, Cora. The buyers are ready to drop the deal. Why haven't you answered your phone?"

"I've been a little busy."

"It's going to be difficult. The buyers want out."

Cora waited, purposely leaving the line silent for a long time.

"Ms. Aregard? Are you there?"

"Hi."

"Well ... I ... I don't think Gabe wants to meet you. If I can convince the other parties, I can send somebody else. I think Helen Morkey can help you with the sale."

"No one else. Only Gabe. I need Gabriel Cartwright. Send him back to me. I really need to say sorry. I feel so awful about what happened."

"Honestly, Cora, it was all I could do not to fire him on the spot when he told me that he didn't have the contract signed yet. He was in such a state."

"What was wrong with him?"

"He accused you of rape."

Cora bust out laughing. It seemed to disturb the voice on the other end of her cell phone. He muttered something and then said, "He ... he was perfectly willing to walk away from the company after what happened. I've never seen him so upset. In fact, he was talking about consulting a lawyer."

"He's not the suing type."

"Well, you know he's a married man."

"Nobody's perfect."

More silence on the phone. Cora laughed harder. "Send him here, Austin, 'kay? Send him to me so I can sign the papers. That is what you want, isn't it?"

"Of course. But we can just as easily ship the documents."

"I need to apologize," she said earnestly. "Please, I need to see him in person."

"I'll ask, Cora. Actually, he was upset when he heard the news about you and your accident—at least, what we thought was you and your accident. We all were."

"Sweet. You're all sweet. And Gabe is a really terrific guy. Just send him here, Austin, and I'll sign. I promise."

"I'll try."

Cora waited for weeks. Finally, she impatiently left messages on Gabriel's private office voicemail herself to convince him.

13

THEIR SECOND DATE

M r. Gabriel Cartwright traveled in the back seat of someone's banana-smelling white SUV, Ubering through dense downtown LA traffic to a restaurant called Tillman's. He regretted not insisting on a meeting in a conference room or an informal coffee shop. But the secret of all secrets was that he wanted to see her.

He had really been affected by the news that she had died. When Austin told him he had spoken to her, he was overjoyed.

Now he felt confused. He hated her for her antics, but he genuinely missed her.

He wouldn't openly admit it, but he thought of her often— her long deep red hair, matching lipstick, and tight clothes. Her clothes were almost as inviting as if she didn't wear anything at all. But even more attractive was her attitude. She brought a smile to his face with her obvious flirtations and superior conde- scending attitude. Those bright blue eyes that told all who she deigned to gaze upon, *I can do whatever the fuck I want to you.* It was so ridiculous, childish, but strong. She was an enigma. An immature, almost frighteningly powerful woman who he felt like bowing under and becoming her slave more than her friend ... or lover. If he didn't have Mina, he would have her. And somehow he was sure, absolutely sure, she would have him. His hand shook to that.

They were driving through traffic and the sun was nearly down. He gripped his hands together and silently cursed at how stupid he was being. He felt sweat drip down his back, which was odd in the cool air-conditioned car.

"A nice place," commented the driver.

"What?" he snapped, irritated his driver was talking.

The driver was an older Asian gentleman wearing a ridiculous large gray cap. He looked shady, like he could pull out a gun and mug him. Gabriel had found him near LAX. He was beginning to regret not taking Cora up on her offer to hitch a ride from Hashan.

"Tillman's," the driver said. He had a thick Asian accent. "You like restaurant? Tillman's? Is good."

"Never been," Gabriel replied. But now he was relieved. Talking allowed him not to think about Cora. But then, not thinking about her made him think of her again. "You've driven people there before?"

"Once. It's full of money. And strange."

Yep, that's Cora ... shit, I'm thinking of her again.

The car stopped by the valet inside an alleyway, and a sharp-dressed boy in a suit ran over and opened the door for him. Gabriel threw his bag carrying his laptop and papers over his shoulder and walked to the front wooden double door entrance.

There was something unique about Tillman's. It was the sole restaurant in the midst of downtown. The valet parking lot was under three large brick buildings. The restaurant seemed lost among the buildings, but it was new and fresh, with a modern feel. As he got out of the car, he could hear hip music playing in the background. Then, as another sharp-dressed young man in a double-breasted white suit opened the door for him at the entrance, he was struck by how small the place was. It had a series of tables towards the center, a bar at the side and a dozen or so booths built into the walls, and that was it. Its size seemed quaint and private. There was a simplicity to it all—that, too, was Cora. It reminded him of her open, largely unfurnished mansion. There was little lighting, the restaurant being dimly lit by candles on the tables—again, like Cora's house. It was not hard to see why she liked it. There was a nice display of wine bottles along the maître d's counter and a few canvases splashed with paint along the walls. Then there were just the white-clothed tables and windows. Most of the windows were draped and closed with blinds. There wasn't much to see through the glass—just the parking lot.

The maître d' was formally dressed in a long black dress, a line of people waiting before her. He stood in line, his hand shaking nervously again. He squeezed it with his other hand, feeling stupid. Then he straightened his thin black tie, running a hand through his short slicked dark hair. He looked at his phone to check the time and used the reflection to check his face. Then he realized, most uncomfortably, that the place felt romantic.

He thought Cora would be easy to spot. Perhaps, he imagined, she'd be wearing her black lace dress with her fiery hair. Or maybe she'd be dressed like a goddess with her hair curled—like at the party. Or perhaps he'd catch her hitting on some men by the bar. But he couldn't find her. He was a little late and thought perhaps she was already seated.

His impatience got the best of him and he left the line and started walking by each of the booths. Each booth was very quaint, like its own room with a central yellow flickering lantern. He had to peek inside each one. He would never have recognized her had he not been looking. He actually walked right past her.

She was wearing an old-style beige dress that looked like it belonged in a black-and-white movie from the 1920s. Her long hair was tied neatly back and her makeup was conservative. Her fingernails were perfectly manicured with red polish matching her cherry-red lips. Most striking was her hair—blond. She sat alone, staring out at the window to the parking lot, sipping from a hot mug. She had perfect posture, like a royal princess. It was such a striking transformation that he had to turn twice to make sure it was really her. The only thing true to character was that she was wearing a pair of dark sunglasses.

"Hi," she said with a wave when she noticed him. She sipped from her cup.

He came back to the table and she gave him a calm, sweet smile.

"You found me," she said quietly with another gentle smile. She blew on her cup with her red lips. Then she stuck her hand out to shake his.

The touch of her hand was at first sweet. He rubbed his over hers, touching her soft skin and the hard parts of her knuckles. Her touch excited him, and the hand that held hers started to shake a little again. He quickly drew it back, embarrassed.

"Hi, Cora … it's good to see you."

"It's so lovely to see you, Gabriel." She spoke so formally.

He swung his bag over onto the other side of the booth, opened it, still standing, and pulled out her folder. As he thumbed through the papers, Cora ran a hand across her golden-blond hair. Then she embarrassed Gabe again. She removed her glasses.

He had forgotten how strikingly brilliant her blue eyes were. They were a glowing dark azure. They stared at him, as if peering into his soul. Then she smiled gently.

Instead of sitting down like a gentleman, he practically fell over the cushion of the booth.

"Sorry," she said, jumping up to help him, "are you all right?"

That only made it worse. She kept flashing that damn smile. His eyes avoided hers, falling on her pale arms and then her cleavage.

He coughed.

"You look beautiful," he stammered, then repeated under his breath, "simply beautiful."

"Why, thank you," she said, waving her hand along her hair again. "How sweet. I'm so glad. I really did what I could to look nice for you. I so envy men. It takes us forever to get ready."

Ready? Ready for what! Our meeting?

"Your," he said, thumbing through his folders, "your hair's blond?"

"Yes, Gabe. I told you before. This is my natural color."

"Oh ... it looks good. Very good."

"Thanks. I did it for you."

I did it for you?

She sipped some more of her drink. He looked at her and lost himself for a second. She giggled a little. Then he straightened himself over the seat.

"Well," he said with another cough, "I was so relieved, Cora, when I heard you were okay."

"Right as rain," she said, clearing her own throat. She straightened up in the chair and tried to look serious, but she wasn't. He could tell from her smug smile.

"And now we can close the deal," he said.

"Aha. About time, isn't it? Tell me, Mr. Cartwright, would you care for a cup?"

"Hmm?" he asked. Then he finally found the right portfolio, thank the gods, and brought it out in front of him. "Here you are." He pushed it to her.

She completely ignored it.

"Would you like to try some?" she asked again.

"What?"

"It's a bit cold here. The warmth of my cup would do you good. We're starting to lose our winter, but the manager—his name's Devon, by the way—seems to think it would be a great idea to freeze all his fucking customers."

Gabriel frowned. He didn't like her language. "You know, Cora, I really wish you wouldn't cuss."

"Oh, sorry. I'll behave." And then she gave a flash of that smug smile again.

"If you can sign the areas I've marked," Gabriel said, "I think you'll find the deal's fair. The buyer is very anxious to complete the sale."

"It's very good. Try some," she said, pushing the cup towards him.

"What is it? Coffee? I'm surprised you're not drinking."

"I am ... it's sake."

Then she burst out laughing. The ridiculousness of her joke make him chuckle with her—mainly because she laughed so hard.

"Oh, Gabe! Funny, right! Why wouldn't I be drinking? I'm a fucking alcoholic." She covered her mouth. "Shit ... I mean, excuse me, I'm an ... alcoholic. I can get you some if you'd like. *Sake.*" She said *sake* with a sharp Japanese accent. Apparently, she was in a good mood.

"No, thank you."

She shrugged and kept chuckling while sipping her drink.

"Cora," he added, clearing his throat and becoming serious again.

"Yes, Gabe?"

"I've made the adjustments you asked for, accounting for the gold bars along the windows upstairs. I ran some estimations. If you don't approve, we can change it. I figured you fit around three bars of gold per foot. On the current market, a brick of gold is worth about half a million dollars. If you run that all the way across your second floor, which is around seventy-five feet long, it comes to a grand total of a hundred and twenty-five million dollars. So, I added this to the sales price. If you'd like, I can get an adjuster to measure it properly, but the buyer is getting impatient."

"You're so smart, Gabe."

"Well, if you'll just sign the pages I marked, then the deal will be done."

"But then our night would be over," she said, sipping some more.

He sighed and shrugged his shoulders.

"Come on. Relax. It's good to see you. How's the family?"

"You don't care about my family, Cora."

"That's not nice." She looked genuinely hurt.

He regretted saying it. It came out nasty. He wasn't even sure why he'd said it. The effect of his words fell like a hammer, and she fell silent.

The waiter arrived. He was a jolly overweight bald man with a mustache.

"Are you ready now, Ms. Aregard?" the waiter asked.

"Yes, we're definitely ready now, Harold. Get him a steak cooked medium. I'll have it rare. Then get us some of those small irresistible potatoes." She turned to him with a smile. "You've got to try them, Gabe, they're out of this world." Then she turned back. "And we're ready for the champagne—your 2006 Dom Perignon ... and a martini, one for both of us. Make it dirty with blue cheese olives. And ... hmm ... bring us two martinis each."

"Very well, madam."

"Thank you, Harold."

He walked away. Then she looked at Gabe as if considering something. She spoke in a hushed voice. "You know, he's hot, right? There's something about the thin mustache and suit and his large stomach. I'd love to just meet him alone in the kitchen." She laughed. "I mean, the bigger the size, the more to hold. Right? I don't mind the fat, as long as he's got a big cock ... I mean"—she shrugged—"I'd fuck him."

"Why do you talk so dirty, but dress so nice?"

"Why, would you rather I dress dirty and talk nice?"

"You're out of control."

She giggled and shrugged again. Then she passed her cup to him. "Hey, would you like to try it? It's a very nice *sake* imported from Japan."

"What's with the cup?"

"That's my joke. Like I'm not drinking? I thought it would get you to laugh—relax you. You're not really relaxed. I'm funny, right? Fun. Why do you have to be such a goddamn Debbie Downer sometimes? Have some fun."

"Are you expecting more people? Are we to finish two martinis and a glass of champagne?"

"Well, I can always help you with yours."

He shook his head. He took the mug and pressed it to his lips. It was sake—just sake, nothing special. He shrugged, unimpressed.

But that wasn't why she'd handed it to him. She took it back, winked at him, and gestured for him to watch. Then she ran her tongue along the rim of the mug. She put the cup down, raised her head, and slowly licked her lips, closing her eyes. "Ummm. Good, right?"

"Just sign the papers, Ms. Aregard."

She pouted but then laughed again.

"What's this about blonding your hair for me? We're here for business."

"I told you. It's my natural color." He nodded. Then she leaned forward and whispered, "It's blond everywhere, you know."

He slammed his hand on the table. It startled her.

"Why do you insist on bringing sex into everything?"

"What do you mean?"

"Blond everywhere? Why can't you control yourself?"

"I ...," she said with a look of surprise. "I don't know. I like having fun. I like sex. I like to fuck."

That was it. It was just too much. "You're intolerable." He grabbed the papers in front of him and started pushing them violently in his bag. Cora looked around. A few people at other tables looked over, staring at them.

"Are you serious?" she asked in shock. "Just sit down. I was joking."

"You've been playing with me since LA," he snapped as he threw the rest of the papers into his bag. "I'm done. It's not funny. Go call Aussie and deal with him alone."

"Just sit down."

He shook his head.

She grabbed his hand and whispered, "You're being a dick."

He looked at her, surprised by her expression. She wasn't acting funny anymore. She looked genuinely upset. "I *am* playing with you," she said. "I'm trying to have fun, Gabriel. What the hell's the matter with you?"

"It's disgusting. In some ways, it's even worse from your mouth when you're dressed nice."

"Dressed nice—well, at least that's a nice thing to say."

"Just sign the papers," he said with a sigh, standing over her.

"Sit down," she said in a forced whisper, looking around, embarrassed. "I can't very well sign papers you just put away."

She gestured for him to sit again. Then the waiter came by, bringing them her ridiculous order of four drinks, a bottle of champagne, and some bread.

"Well, I suppose fighting with you is better than nothing," she said.

"Cora, I'm here as a business partner."

"Really? Business partner?" She looked at him, amazed. "That's a little presumptuous, don't you think, Mr. Cartwright?" she asked formally. "I'm not your *partner*. I'm trying to do business with your boss, Mr. Kliger. You are simply a newly hired employee—"

"Then why did you beg to see me?"

"Beg to see you?" she asked, laughing. "That's ridiculous. Do I look like someone who would beg to see a realtor? Or anyone, for that matter?"

"Aussie hounded me for weeks after I returned. He wouldn't let up because he knew how important it was to you that I came back. I don't see why. We could have just sent you the papers."

She closed her eyes and took a deep breath. "Just sit down, Gabe. If you'd like, I can just eat and say nothing the rest of our meal if it upsets you so much. We can have a lovely boring dinner together." She looked miserable.

He laughed. He just couldn't take her anger seriously. The laughter caught her off guard. She stared at him, confused.

"You can't be authentic, can you?" he asked. "Everything is a game—even this. Now you want me to feel bad for you?"

"Authentic? I don't know what the hell you're talking about. Just please sit down."

He sat down and pulled out the papers again.

"You're an enigma, Ms. Cora Aregard. I've never met anyone like you. I don't understand you."

She shrugged and nodded. Then she put her sunglasses back on and folded her arms.

"You will sign these? Now that I flew all the way from New York?" *You bitch.*

But she gestured zipping her red lips, shook her head, and turned away from him. Then she looked out the window overlooking the parking lot.

"Hmm?" he asked.

She gestured closing a zipper again, apparently having resolved not to say a damn thing.

He grabbed his martini and drank it down in anger.

She glimpsed him from the corner of her eye and laughed, but quickly put a hand over her mouth.

"What's with you, Cora? Sometimes you act like a little girl."

But she didn't answer him. She shook her head, zipped her lips again, and looked away.

"Even this is a game, isn't it?"

"I don't know what the hell you want from me."

He pushed the papers towards her. She looked down at them with disgust and then turned again.

The silence was long and drawn out. Gabe became impatient, readjusting himself on the cushion of the booth. He ran his hand repeatedly through his short hair, looking at her, exasperated. Finally, he chuckled a little, leaned back, picked up the other martini, and said, "Well, we have dinner. This is what you wanted. I suppose we have time. Why don't you tell me about yourself?"

"What would you like to know, creep?"

"Why do you dress the way you do?"

"What?" She looked down at her clothes. "You don't like this dress?"

"Not now. I mean ... the last time I saw you. That red plastic one."

Heat rose to his face and his hands trembled. He felt like ducking under the table. He was humiliated. He had just referred to her cherry-red jumpsuit, but the only time he had seen her wearing it was when she was peeling it off and fucking two guests in her bedroom.

She giggled. He turned furious, knowing she knew their unspoken secret.

"I like to look sexy," she said with a shrug. "What's wrong with that?"

"You only like *looking* sexy, Cora?"

"That sounds offensive."

"Judging by your parties, I don't think it's a look."

"Are you referring to the party I invited you to, but you didn't attend?"

"No"—he leaned forward—"I'm referring to the party where three of your friends attempted to rape me."

She surprised him by removing her shades again and grabbing his hand. He quickly tried to pull away, but she wouldn't let him go.

"I'm so sorry, Gabe. I really am. That's why I wanted you to come. I really wanted to personally apologize for what happened. I tried to give you peace that night. I didn't mean for any of it to happen."

She was earnest. He yanked his hand away. He wasn't nervous anymore. He was angry, remembering the night again.

"I don't think this dinner has anything to do with that," he said, shaking his head.

Then their meals arrived.

They ate uncomfortably, not saying a word. It was no longer a joke for Cora to keep quiet. Gabe didn't say anything either.

But the food was amazing.

"How are those potatoes?" she finally asked with a smile.

"Good."

"Fucking good, right?" She didn't wait for his response, just stabbed a bunch of them and ate them. "Thanks for coming, Gabe," she said with her mouth full. "I understand you didn't want to."

"It's not that I didn't want to. It's just ... I'm a married man. It seems that you're forgetting that."

"Whatever gave you that idea?" she asked, blinking and feigning surprise. She smiled wide. Her look was so contrived that it forced him to laugh.

"I think you're just a rich girl who doesn't know what to do with her money," he said after grabbing some potatoes of his own. "Life's just a joke to you." He was satisfied with that, for the moment anyway.

"Oh?" she asked, chewing on some raw steak. "You believe that, do you?"

"I don't know what else to believe."

"And where do you think this rich girl—girl sounds a little offensive, by the way, Gabe—got her money?"

"Is that a riddle?" he asked, squinting.

She merely shrugged and grabbed the contracts, thumbing through the small stack of papers for the first time. She picked up the pen.

He watched as she looked through the paperwork. He was fascinated with her. Now she looked professional and mature, not like the debutante she was acting like only a minute before. She was a complete mystery to him, and he was intrigued. She looked as if she was the CEO of a company as she perused the documents. He wanted to reconcile these two Coras. Which one was she?

"Parents were rich?" he asked.

She just shook her head. There was silence. She signed some more.

"You struck it rich in Vegas?"

"Nuh-uh. No one ever strikes it rich in Vegas anymore." She looked at him as if he was stupid. "It's fixed. Everyone knows that. It's not the way it once was, anyway."

"Vegas would be a good town for you."

"There you go insulting me again," she said, hitting the table with her fists. "What the hell does that mean?"

He shrugged.

"Anyway, I don't gamble. Gambling implies a possibility of losing. I never lose."

"All right. Tell me, then. How did you get your money?"

He finished his second drink and leaned back again, staring at her.

"What?"

"Tell me how you got all your money."

She smiled and seemed to consider it, but then she wagged a finger at him.

"Oh no. Nuh-uh. That's a bit personal for a realtor, mister."

"Why? Think of it as important information to seal the deal."

She began signing the last paper. As she read, she sucked on the pen. It was a little thing, something sensual that he realized she didn't intend. That made it sexier. He watched her red lips and white teeth probing around the end. Her tongue rolled around the edges. Then she tapped it against her chin. When he realized what he was doing, he ran his hand nervously over his hair again and quickly looked away. She didn't seem to notice. Then she put the pen down for a moment and considered his question.

"You really want to know?"

"Yes, Cora."

"You sure? It might ... freak you out a little."

"Try me."

"You won't believe me."

He waited. She looked around the restaurant, searching each table carefully as if she had lost something. For a moment, she looked nervous. Anxiety was something he rarely saw in her. Then she turned back to him with a big grin and a nod.

"Okay"—she pushed the signed papers to the side for a moment—"one question, Gabe. Answer one question. If you answer it, you'll understand me."

"All right. What?"

"What would you do if you could live forever?"

"Huh?"

"What would you do if you could live forever?"

"I don't know. Travel with the wife and kids. Tour the world."

"That would take a lifetime. Then what?"

"The world's a large place."

"Fair enough—a few lifetimes. Then what? What would you do then?"

"I don't know. Would I be rich?"

"Oh yes, very."

"I think I would be very happy, Cora."

"No. You wouldn't be happy," she said, shaking her head and losing her smile. "You wouldn't be happy at all. What would you do after your wife died? And then your friends?" He shrugged. "All the buildings around you crumbled to dust? Or the city and lands you once loved flooded and buried under the sea? What would you do then, Gabe? Would you be happy?"

"It's an interesting question. It doesn't sound like it."

It was more than an interesting question. She looked suddenly sad.

He looked at her, perplexed. Then he felt cruel. Maybe it was the alcohol, but he figured she deserved it. "This is the real you, isn't it? Sad and depressing."

She looked away from him and nodded. She just stared out the window—at the cars being valeted. "Yes. Sad and depressed. That is me. But you asked about me."

"I'm sorry, Cora. I ..."

"Humans ..." She hesitated for a moment, looking around the restaurant again. He felt his skin crawl. Then she spoke quieter. "Humans think that they would be happy with money and immortality. Perhaps for a short while, they would. But it is actually the worst curse, Gabriel." She threw her hair over her shoulder and shook her head, as if she could shake away her thoughts. Then she cupped her lips and whispered, "I'm immortal, Gabe."

Gabriel must have looked the way he felt. She giggled.

Is she completely mad?

"That is the answer to your riddle," she continued quietly with a shrug. "You might think I'm insane, but that is what I am. That is why I am filthy rich. That is why I do whatever I want with whoever I want. That is why I enjoy the rush, however fleeting, of—pardon my French—fucking. I enjoy what I like. That's how I tick. Just like those lovely potatoes. I order them because they taste good. Just like you—I requested you for a dinner date because I like you. You're a good man, Gabe."

"Are you insane?"

Of course she is.

"You want *authentic*? Well, here I am." She took a deep breath and sighed. "Gabe, you heard of the crash by the beach. I had my lawyer prepare papers to your company attesting that I wasn't the woman who died that night. That it was a case of mistaken identity. That I never knew Danny Anastra and that the house had always been under my name, Aregard. This was matched with the county records. But you know that isn't true. You know how much I cared for Danny. How much I loved him. How could I not be Cora Anastra? I saw to it that any pictures related to me as Cora Anastra, on the internet, by TV, or any other means, were destroyed. How could the woman who went to the hospital and crashed on the beach not have been me? I told you of my love for Danny. I told you how terrible I felt when he died. I still do. And you knew that I changed my name."

"What are you getting at, Cora? Are you telling me you lied to us?"

"I'm telling you—*you*, mister—that both Coras are one and the same. I'm telling you, Gabe, that I faked Anastra's death, not for Platinum Properties, but for all the people who knew her, so that I could continue and start a new life as Cora Aregard. Your company could give a shit about who I really am, if they get the deal. I probably could have forged the paperwork myself for Austin. I'm telling you because I care about you and I want you to know the truth. Authenticity is as important to me as it is to you. Changing my identity is what I've always done to fit in with your world. I've had to do it time and time again because *I am* immortal."

She grabbed her champagne glass, toasted to him, and drank from it. Then she turned back and threw her sunglasses down on the table. She had an amused, almost mocking look.

"But you won't believe me, will you? Because the truth would mean you would have to accept something you can't possibly accept. And you can't, can you?"

"I don't know, Cora."

She nodded. "Cherish your family, Gabe. That little girl of yours. Only those that die find true salvation. I never will. We immortal are cursed forever."

She pushed the papers back to him, and now she looked miserable.

"Sorry ... Cora," he said, confused.

"Forget it, Gabe. Forget everything I said. I'm just so happy to have had the chance to see you again."

But then he realized that their night was over. He didn't want it to be.

He stared at her, trying to comprehend all the words she had just thrown at him. He tried to reconcile the madness. She could play with him like a teenager, do business like a CEO, strut around like a whore, then show glimmers of brilliance with her mind. Now she was certifiably insane.

"Thank you for coming," she said sadly. "After you have dessert with me, I think you should leave. It would be best now. Go return to your family."

That's it?

"Okay, Cora," he said, coughing nervously. But for a second, he thought he saw a glimmer of a playful smile from her again. "Thank you for ..."

"Of course."

"They have good dessert here?"

"Yes, Gabe. Very good. I'll show you what I like."

14

DISTURBANCE ON DEPARTURE

Gabriel's flight to LaGuardia was delayed, so he had to wait at the airport terminal, Gate 9, sitting on a bench and staring out into the darkness at the lights from the departing planes. That was when Mina called. He listened to her talk about their daughter, Jordan, and how she needed to be enrolled in a summer preschool reading program. Gabe said it was expensive and unnecessary. There was a long silence on the phone.

"Look, I don't want to fight," she said.

"Who's fighting?" Gabe had asked. "I just don't think we need to put Jo Jo through this right now."

"You don't want to because we don't have the money."

"No. She's doing fine."

"You're always thinking she's fine, but we can't let her get behind ... Well, I'm enrolling her anyway."

"The hell you are," Gabe said. "And yes, we don't have money to tutor a five-year-old."

"It's not tutoring and she's six."

"She turns six in June, Mina."

"Look, I don't want to fight," she said with a sigh.

"We're not fighting. Just don't waste our money on—"

"I don't want to fight."

This was precisely why he had booked a hotel in New York for an extra night. He liked business trips. It helped free him—free him from everything. And her.

He also felt distracted and upset. His visit with his client had gone well. Too well. She was gracious and polite. She was a complete pleasure. He would have loved to see her again.

That was what he could do. Maybe he could tell Mina his flight was delayed again?

"We have to ready her for kindergarten," his wife said. "You don't know how hard it is for her to adjust."

"Come on, Mina! This is ridiculous. Look, I have to —"

And that was when it happened. Gabriel heard two loud pops and then an explosion before passengers jumped up and started scrambling down the large walkway to the exits. His terminal was close to the TSA baggage metal detector and exit, and the noise had come from there. He watched as black smoke rose and then heard a skirmish erupt with some shouting. Then Gabriel clearly saw two officers grabbing a man and hauling him from the walkway into one of the duty-free shops. Few others noticed in their panic. Stupidly, Gabriel hadn't left his bench. He was looking for his phone, which had flown out of his hand from the shock of the explosion.

Gabriel crouched down to grab it from under the bench.

Airport guards started shouting for everyone to evacuate. Over the airport intercom, a voice asked everyone to calmly exit the airport.

Through the smoke, he saw officers throw the man in the shop violently against a wall. Then another man—a very large, tall bald man in a dark suit with a goatee—lifted him up by his neck. They exchanged a few yells—and blows—and there was a flash of light from something metallic—maybe a knife. A knife— yes, it was a knife. And he could swear the tall bald man took the knife and thrust it into the man's chest.

Gabriel was stunned. He quickly gathered up his bag and ran with the other bodies towards the exit.

As he passed the smoke-filled room, he saw something that really creeped him out: the bald man with the goatee stood over the man they had detained. His eyes, which looked over his sunglasses, were blue—the same bright blue as Cora's and his own. He looked directly at Gabe, smiling. The man under him lay lifeless on the floor—was he dead?

Gabe's phone vibrated in his pocket as a few police rushed in the opposite direction, towards the smoke. He looked down at his cell phone—the number was Cora's.

"Are you all right?" Cora sounded very worried.

"Fine."

"I'm so relieved," Cora said with a sigh.

He liked hearing her voice and her breathing through the phone.

But then he thought, it had just happened. How did she even know?

"Why don't you wait there, Gabe, and I'll have Hashan drive you to Long Beach Airport? I have a private jet there. Or, I can arrange for you to stay in LA one more night."

"No. No, that's all right, Cora. I'm fine. You've done so much for me already."

"I'm just glad you're okay. Listen, Gabe, I'll take care of this, okay?"

"What? What do you mean?"

"I'll take care of it. Don't worry. There's something ... something I need to tell you."

"Cora, I have to go. My wife is calling."

"All right. Listen, I had a really good time. Thanks so much again for seeing me this evening."

"The pleasure was mine, Ms. Aregard."

"Be careful, Gabe."

Outside, he waited to cross the street into a parking lot and was almost hit by racing police cars, their flashing lights lighting up the darkness of night.

Finally, he answered his wife's call. "Where the fuck have you been! Why did you hang up on me!"

He thought of Cora's call. He had liked hearing Cora's voice.

15

ABSOLUTELY DREADFULLY DEPRESSING

Cora stood by the sidewalk, waiting for Hashan. She looked like quite a diva that morning. She wore a black dress with a matching wide-brimmed hat, black gloves and sunglasses, carrying a large black umbrella in one hand and dragging a small wheeled cart with the other. She watched as Hashan ran through the rain from their limo, across a grassy field, and around the tombstones, carefully carrying her martini in one hand and a baby wrapped in a blanket in the other. He desperately tried to shelter the baby by tucking him tight in his arms and covering the baby's head with the hand holding Cora's drink. He didn't have an umbrella.

You're such a bitch, Cora, she thought.

She looked down at her wagon. She had three beautiful bouquets in it, but they were getting drenched in the pouring rain.

"Here you are, madam," Hashan panted, handing her the martini. The baby cried more.

"Extra wet. Thank you, Hashan."

"Of course."

Then she looked at the bundle of noise in Hashan's arms.

"Take Baby back to the car," she said.

"I can't leave her in the car, Cora," he said, shaking his head. "We won't be leaving for another hour."

"Nothing will happen to her in the limo."

"Sorry, madam, I won't do it."

"Grace couldn't care for her today?"

"No, madam."

"Let's get this over with," Cora said after rolling her eyes and sighing.

They walked down a grassy hillside, following a sidewalk. She dragged the small cart behind her as Hashan carried the fussy baby, doing his best to calm the infant under the shelter of Cora's umbrella. Cora searched the grounds, having trouble finding what she was looking for.

"Damn."

"What's the matter?"

"I can't find the place. Do you remember the section?"

She looked down the hill and caught a family grieving over a freshly dug mound. They too wore black. She figured a service had just ended. A young boy in a small dark tux and a woman in a matching black dress—probably his mother—stood over the grave. The mother had one arm wrapped around the boy, the other carrying a large black umbrella.

Cora turned away, disgusted. "God, I hope it wasn't his father."

Hashan simply nodded.

"How terrible. I really hate this place, Hashan. Let's find them and get out of here."

She looked down at the soggy flowers again, then gazed back over at the boy and his mother. She couldn't help but stare.

She stopped and raised a hand, stopping the small cart. Then she lifted the martini glass as if toasting the mother and son.

"To life," she said, raising her glass towards them, "and all its fucked-up glory. Ummm..." She spun around, looking at Hashan and sipping her drink. "Ummm! Yummy. That's really good. You're getting so good at this. That's a very good mix of vermouth. Or maybe it's the extra water?"

"I get a lot of practice."

"That you do," she said, chuckling. "That you do. I'm sure the rain gave it the perfect touch. It's like God rained down tears and made it perfect, right?"

"Yes, Cora."

She downed the drink and handed the empty glass to him. She really wanted to smash it on the ground.

"I can't believe this. Look at the flowers. I'm going to be laying fishbowls."

"May I suggest that we drive to another location? Perhaps we can return here later. Perhaps we can visit Art's site first."

She looked at his drenched hair and face and imagined that she looked just as dreadful.

"There were no other umbrellas in the car?" she asked.

"No."

"Of course not. How absolutely dreadfully depressing. Fits the mood."

"Yes, Cora."

They walked together for some time, huddling closer under the shelter of her umbrella. After some time, the rain stopped and the baby finally quieted.

The other tombstones were not hard to find. She laid the large bouquets over them and kissed the stones. Hashan looked away, giving her privacy. Then they headed back towards the missing one.

Cora returned whence they came when first entering the cemetery. She pulled the cart across the grass close near tombstones, carefully looking at each one for the right name.

"It's not fair," she said, shaking her head.

"We can check the office, Cora," Hashan said, laying a hand on her shoulder. "They'll know where David is."

"Shit." She shook her head again, fighting back tears. "I don't fucking care."

It was bad enough visiting the dreary place, but not finding one of the graves was unbearable. She hadn't cried visiting her other loved ones, but a missing tombstone was far worse.

She jumped and grabbed the last bouquet from the cart, throwing the umbrella on the ground and then hurling each flower into the air, one at a time.

"They can all have them! They can share. Like their dead bodies really give a shit."

She turned from him and started to cry into her hands. Hashan draped his coat over her head to give her shelter.

"It's all right, Cora." She leaned into his arms and cried like a child. When the tears stopped, she looked up at him and shook her head in confusion. "Why do you stay with me? Why haven't you left me like everybody else?"

"Perhaps I'm bewitched by your beauty, madam."

She chuckled. Then they walked slowly, arm in arm, back to their car.

"How long has it been, Hashan? How long have you been in my service?"

"Thirty years. Danny was a good man. Only my grandfather knew Arthur, though."

"They were all good men. Wonderful men. And they're all like Gabe."

Hashan nodded.

"Kind hearts and souls. I don't deserve any of them."

"Don't talk like that, Cora."

"It's true ... you know Gabe even says *sure*. The same way. The same word. It's all the same thing all over again."

"I like him, madam."

"I don't know why he would like me."

"Few are as wicked and lovely as you, Cora."

"Ahh. You always have the right thing to say to me at the

wrong time. Are you really going to follow me to Toronto? Are you ready to leave LA?"

"I will stay with you until I die, Cora."

"You had to say *that*, Hashan. How dreadful. You had to say *that*, here."

She stopped for a moment. Hashan placed his palm on her cheek and then wiped some of the tears from her eyes with his handkerchief. He was such a kind man. Hashan—the only one who cared about her.

"You look like shit, madam."

She laughed.

He wiped some more tears. When she was ready, he picked up the baby, who he had left in the wagon while comforting her. Then they resumed walking.

"Let's check with the office," he said. "They'll know where to find David's grave."

"Forget it. I'd rather find Gabe's." Hashan raised an eyebrow behind his sunglasses. "That is all he will one day be. Like the others. Like you. It's absolutely dreadful."

"It's not like you to be this morbid, Cora."

They took the empty cart and walked back to the paved sidewalk. The rain dwindled to a gentle drizzle. They headed to their stretch limousine.

"The question is—are *you* ready to leave LA?" Hashan asked.

"Sure, Hashan. There's no one left here that I care about." She looked down at the baby in his arms.

16

THE NECKLACE

"Y ou never told me about her," said Mina. "What's this Ms. Aregard like?"

Gabe violently stuffed some T-shirts and jeans into his bag. It looked like he was trying to hurt someone inside the luggage. She furrowed her brow. Then she helped stuff a few more things—some of Jordan's toys.

"You packed my brush and shaver?" he asked.

"Yes."

"And you have the passports?"

"Yes," she said with a smile.

"She's eccentric, Mina," he finally answered. "A very odd woman. A very rich one—one of the richest. But very odd."

"Nice? Is she nice?"

"Sure." He smiled at the irony of uttering the word Cora hated.

"How rich?"

"Very. We're not sure where she gets her money. She's got properties all over the world. She did our entire transaction in gold. That was ridiculous. It was as if she made her money off drugs or something. I ran a search through government records to make sure she was legit. Everything was fine. Her credit's outstanding. She's clean. But how she got all her money is confusing. She's unemployed and was married to a painter."

"Was? Divorced?"

"No. Her husband died."

"Oh my. What happened?"

"He was murdered."

"God! You're kidding."

"No. That's why I can't be too hard on her. She can be a real pain in the ass, hon. But sometimes, I wonder if her weirdness is because of his death."

"Maybe she's mafia or something," she said playfully. "Maybe we should stay away."

"Don't be stupid. This is the biggest deal we've ever landed."

"I know." She hugged his arm and laughed. "What about *her*, hon?" she asked playfully. "Is she pretty?"

He quickly yanked the bag away from her, zipping it up. That was when little Jordan ran into the room, racing a toy train on the carpet. She rammed it right into Gabriel's foot.

"You got all your bags packed, Jo Jo?" he asked. He looked down at his little girl and smiled.

Mina surprised him by grabbing him from behind with a laugh. She touched Gabriel's cheek as she held him in her arms. He had shaved his cheeks clean. She ran her hand along his face and kissed his cheek.

"Can't wait to meet her. Thanks for the trip, babe. It's way overdue. I'm really excited."

He looked down at her and kissed her lips.

"Sure," he said, with the naughty satisfaction of uttering Cora's dreaded word.

Mina was already dressed. She had on a long white shirt that went down to her hips, covering the top of her jeans. Her long curly hair was kempt and her face was nicely made up. She looked pretty. Little Jo Jo looked like a complete mess. Jordan had just eaten and was still munching on a cookie. The chocolate was all over her face.

"We haven't gone on a vacation since she was born," Mina said. "You remember? And now Niagara. I've never seen Niagara Falls." She looked at Jordan and rubbed her hand over the girl's messy curly brown hair. "You excited, Jo Jo? We're going to Canada. Toronto! We're gonna see a really beautiful waterfall. Niagara Falls."

"Ah-ha," said Jordan with a big grin. "Canda ... Tonto, right?"

"Canada, baby," said Mina. Then she turned to Gabe.

Gabe went back to attacking the suitcase.

"Did you check the reservations at the hotel?" she asked.

"Yes!" he barked. She jumped at his anger. Then he reached out a hand and stood silent for a moment, trying to collect himself. He ran his hand through his short hair. Mina stared at him, confused.

"Sorry. I'll feel better when all this packing is over."

"Okay ... I'll get Jo Jo dressed."

They drove his 5-series Bimmer up north to Buffalo. By nightfall, they crossed the Rainbow Bridge into Canada. They planned to stay at a resort in Niagara Falls, on the Canada side, for two days, then travel up to Toronto and meet up at Aregard's chateau by the afternoon.

It was hot and humid. It was turning summer.

They had a great time in Niagara. Their room was upgraded by a "friend." Mina thought it was his boss, but Gabriel knew better. The suite was magnificent. The food was good. The view was priceless.

On both days, Jordan had a great time running up and down the outlook over the falls. Gabe and Mina walked behind their hyper child, holding hands and staring at the scenery. It was crowded, but they had nothing planned except visiting the falls. The highlight was the outlook at the top of the tower.

On the morning of checkout, when all their bags were packed, they heard a knock on the door. Mina let in a man wheeling a baggage cart. She went to grab their stuff, thinking he was going to carry their luggage, but the man gestured to three bags. He laid them out on the bed before her. She looked inside. In one was a black tux, in another a black dress, and in the third was a cute small version of the black dress. Then he handed her a wooden chest.

"What is all this?"

"Compliments of Ms. Aregard," said the gentleman. Then he left.

She read a note. When she opened the wooden chest, she screamed.

Gabriel ran out of the bathroom. He had never seen her so excited. She removed a very large diamond necklace from the chest. It was studded with the kind of diamonds people wear on their wedding bands—only oodles of them. She seemed like she was about to faint. They were encrusted on a yellow gold band. Gabriel had seen it before—Cora had worn it on their second "meeting." Then Mina removed more, two long matching earrings with three diamonds apiece. She was speechless.

"We can't take this," he said.

"I ... I can't believe this. This is worth"—she examined the stones—"thousands ... maybe millions."

"You can't wear it. It's ridiculous."

"Huh? Is it real?" she asked, looking up at him.

"If it's from Ms. Aregard, then yes." He reached for it, but she pulled it from him. "You can't accept this."

"The hell I can't!"

"Mamma," Jordan said, tugging at Mina's pants. "Mamma."

"Wait a minute!" she snapped. Jordan nearly fell over. The child struggled not to cry.

Gabriel looked at the note. It was written formally and eloquently, but it had Cora's flair. It asked them if they would do her the *favor* of wearing these special gifts as a thank-you for the sale of her lovely chateau. Then it spoke of how excited she was to see them at her housewarming party. It was handwritten. He liked that, thinking how she had used her pretty pale dainty hand to write the note. It reminded him of the note she had left for him by the front door when he had met her that second time at her house. She had probably sucked on the tip of the pen like she had at Tillman's, thinking of the right things to say.

Jesus, what am I thinking!

"We ... we can wear it just for the day, babe, right?" asked Mina. "Just for the party. Then we can return it to her. It's so beautiful. What will it hurt for one day?"

Bitch!

Why was it that a gift pissed him off so much? It was like Cora. So lovely. So incredible. So unattainable. And now Cora was waving that in front of his wife, all soon to be taken away.

Bitch.

"Can we, hon? Just one day? *Please!* We'll return it tonight when we see her."

Gabe was staring at his suit on the bed. He said nothing.

"Well," she said with a big grin. She chuckled. Then she turned her back to him and handed him the priceless necklace. It was heavy. "Put it on me, won't you, dear? Let's see how it looks."

He reluctantly obeyed. He moved some of her curly hair from her neck and clasped it on. In her skirt, it looked a bit ridiculous. She ran to a mirror.

"What do you think? Hmm?" She twirled around like a little girl.

"It's beautiful, babe."

"Nice, Mamma," said little Jordan.

"I'm just gonna wear it tonight. Tonight. Just tonight." And she laughed.

"I don't think—"

"Come on, babe! It's not going to hurt for one day."

"It's not proper. We can't—"

"I'm going to wear it," she said, turning back to the mirror with a nod. "And that's that. Don't be dull. You're so boring sometimes. You can return it to her tomorrow."

And that was that.

Then they were off, back on Queen Elizabeth Way north to Toronto.

~

G abriel was a complete mess. He habitually tapped hard on the steering wheel as he drove in order to hide his tremor. His wife caught it a few times and looked at him oddly. It got worse the closer they got to Toronto.

And he hated the tux. It was stuffy. The fact that it was charming wasn't even a part of his consideration. Then there was the sweating. He didn't want to drive in the tux, but he realized that there might not be anywhere to change before the party. And then there was the fact that it was a gift from Cora. He felt Cora's spirit haunting him, as if she was laughing at his discomfort over the tux, the drive, the necklace, and their eventual reunion.

Perhaps the gifts were charms. Perhaps Cora was a witch, and by having his family wear these items, she could curse him and his entire family. Then seduce him. That was obviously what she was doing.

Why was he so afraid of her? Was he afraid? Or was it something else ...?

He felt his heart beating faster.

They had reservations late at a hotel in downtown Toronto. They would return there after visiting Cora's place. For the sake of time, they would go to her party first and then check in late at night at their hotel. But no matter what Cora offered, he would not be staying at her house this time.

"I'm going to rest for a while, babe," she said to him, closing her eyes.

"Okay."

Gabe looked behind him. Jordan was thumbing through a picture book. She looked up and smiled. It made him chuckle. She looked like an adult browsing a magazine.

"You doing okay back there?"

"Yeah. When will we be there, Daddy?"

"Soon. It's not much further."

He brushed the sweat off his forehead. Then he moved about on the seat, uncomfortable, trying to shift the sticky pants and shirt off his back. He had the AC blaring, but it didn't seem to be working well enough.

As his wife slept, he looked at her dress and necklace. It was a little gauche. The diamonds seemed too flashy. Somehow the necklace on such a lovely dress was too much. Cora had worn the necklace, but not with a long flowing dress. It seemed too much. Too showy on his wife.

That made him wonder what Cora would be wearing. Had she given them clothes in order to be certain to top them? No, that wasn't her style. Or were they entering a trap and the whole party was actually an alcohol-crazed sex show? Perhaps she wanted to mock them by having them be the only ones dressed up. Anything was possible with Cora. That was why he was sweating bullets and shaking along the steering wheel. He thought of warning Mina, but he didn't know how to put it. It would mean he would have to unveil the events in LA, and unveiling that, now, as he drove to her party was ridiculous. But Cora wouldn't humiliate them. She was too thoughtful to do something like that. Or was she?

He wondered what she was wearing. Would she also be in a fancy dress with rich jewels? Or would she wear her cherry-red bikini? Or that elegant '20s short dress? Or one of her jumpsuits? What surprise did she have in store for him? Would she be dressing for him? For *him*? He hoped so.

He glanced over at his wife sleeping beside him and felt awful. Then he nervously tapped his fingers on the steering wheel more violently than ever.

17

THE REUNION

Cora's property was in the rural outlying regions of Toronto in Prince Edward County. After leaving in the morning, it took another two hours to get to her manor.

The land was stunning. Gabriel had forgotten how picturesque Canada was, with its farms, fields and forests beside the highway. He enjoyed driving the long, sparsely populated stretches as he left Toronto. And it only got prettier the closer he got to Cora's address.

He spotted her property a couple miles out along the water as the road turned sharply near a sandy embankment close to the shore. The house was on a peninsula not far from a lighthouse. Few other buildings were in sight. By the side of the road, he spotted dirt paths descending to a sandy shore, but there were few people on the beaches. It was quiet. Her Malibu home was secluded by thick trees, but here, her home was secluded by a sparse population. And Lake Ontario was beautiful, spreading out beyond sight as if opening into the sea.

He turned on a dirt road and drove up a slight grassy incline into Cora's driveway. The dirt road turned into freshly paved asphalt.

The mansion was a huge lodge built along the lake. Cora undoubtedly hated the exterior. It was an old three-story mansion painted reddish brown with wooden-slab walls and small windows overlooking the lake. A large wooden deck stretched along the property, and Gabe already spotted people packed along the wooden rails, staring out at the gorgeous lake. Pity. Cora intended to bulldoze the structure. She had purchased it for the land. And, indeed, the driveway was already paved in the same manner as the house in front of her LA mansion. In fact, Gabriel found everything similar outside, from front yard gardens and marble statues of Greek gods around the house to white Doric columns with the same antique 1920 streetlamps surrounding the road. Even the view was similar—this time Lake Ontario instead of the Pacific Ocean.

They had planned on arriving a little after two. They were late. The sun was dipping down low over the horizon. There already were a lot of cars lined up in the driveway—expensive ones. Gabriel parked behind a line of them. Many people were walking up to the entrance. They all wore formal clothes— *thank God.*

"It's breathtaking," said Mina as she got out of the car. She took a deep breath, enjoying the fresh clean air. The evening was still humid, but much cooler than it had been. She opened the door for Jordan. Even little Jordan looked around at the property in awe. She looked cute in her matching dress.

Gabe grabbed Mina's hand, Jordan took Mom's, and the three followed another couple in front of them towards the entrance.

Hashan was at the door greeting guests. Gabe's heart raced at the sight of the crow. The short black stiff wore the same black suit he had on when he had first met him. Gabriel began to doubt he could survive this. His hands were sweaty and Mina pulled away, noticing.

"You okay?" she asked, looking at him, bewildered.

"Yeah."

Hashan handed each guest a small board. It was a menu. Each guest perused it as they walked in. When it was their turn to arrive by the threshold, Hashan made sure to personally shake Gabe's hand and welcome him. That wasn't missed by his wife. There was even a hint of a smile from Hashan behind his shades.

The home was cozy. A large entryway greeted them, but then it opened up into two stairwells and multiple small rooms. It lacked the grandeur of her LA abode. Doubtless that would change. The inside was decorated like a cabin. Dark wood lined all the walls. There was even a moose's head by the entrance. He smiled, imagining Cora's opinion of a moose head.

It was busy. He had to carefully maneuver around many young men wearing tuxedos and women in long elegant dresses. A few servers in matching blue suits walked around, offering hors d'oeuvres, cocktails or champagne. And the rooms were full of the murmuring of the guests mixed with the blaring of music—some sort of techno music. It didn't fit the black-tie affair at all. It fit Cora, though. There were absolutely no children—except little Jo Jo. That was the only thing that seemed to make his wife uncomfortable. There was an awful lot of wine, beer and champagne, though.

They headed to the far end of the house, beyond the two stairwells, to the outer deck. Here there were a series of smaller rooms, each one with windows as walls looking out towards the lake. Gabriel grabbed some meat on a stick from a silver tray and opened a sliding door for his wife and daughter. He stood with his wife on the long outdoor wooden deck. Jo Jo stood under him, uncharacteristically quiet, likely intimidated by the crowd.

Mina leaned over the wooden rail and took another deep, relaxed breath.

Gabriel still sweated, no longer from heat, but now with excitement. He felt like a fool. Or a love-sick schoolboy. He couldn't control it and he felt ashamed. But his wife seemed to have no idea. She kept staring out at the water with their daughter.

He searched the guests, looking for her. Part of him hoped she would never show up.

He caught more laughter and shouting from inside the house. That was when he spotted her through a window. She stood sipping a martini, talking to guests in one of the adjoining rooms. Typical to character, she was the life of the party, laughing and probably cracking jokes. She blended in well. Perhaps this was why he hadn't at first noticed her.

She wore an elegant long black dress. It was nothing like the classy one she had given his wife. It was formal and simple, but a bit too tight along the legs and waist. It showed off her curves as it tapered down all the way to the floor. Part of it dragged on the ground. It was sharp along her chest. Her hair was straight and red again. She held hands with a blonde girl. Gabriel's heart jumped into his throat when he recognized the blonde, who wore the exact same clothes as Cora. The two laughed together, telling secrets in each other's ears. Occasionally, Cora ran her hand down her friend's yellow hair. This was the same blonde who had worn the cherry-red latex suit at the going-away party in LA. His heart thumped harder. She had touched him and run her breasts across his chest. She had tried to rape him! This was her best friend? He felt sick.

Then he felt worse. Cora looked over and recognized him. She smiled, but turned away and continued to talk. But as she spoke, she kept flashing an occasional glance towards him.

I shouldn't have come.

She kept looking over. He turned away. Then he patted Jordan on the head and looked out at the water as the sun set. He rubbed his hand along his wife's back and she turned and smiled. They watched as the sun fell below the horizon.

"I'm so glad you could make it," said a quiet voice behind

them. His heart felt like it was going to explode in his chest. He heard that voice even in his dreams.

Gabriel spun around. Cora and her matching partner stood behind them, holding hands.

"Oh, hello," said Mina. "And you are...?"

Mina looked at Cora, her eyes traveling from her red hair down to her sandals. She was visibly shaken by her looks. Then she looked suspiciously at Gabriel. Apparently, she had been expecting someone ... older—much older—or at least less attractive.

"Cora Aregard," Cora said calmly but sincerely, putting out a hand. "And you must be Mina? I've been wanting to meet you."

"Yes."

"I see you like the view?" Cora said, leaning on the wooden rail and looking out too.

"It's beautiful."

"This is my partner, Grace," Cora said and gestured to the blonde. Grace smiled, then smiled more at Gabe.

Gabe squinted. Cora flashed another smile at him, this one playful.

Partner? What are you up to?

"A pleasure." A pleasure, indeed. Mina seemed very relieved.

"Gabe," Cora said, putting out her hand. "It's been a long time."

Gabe.

Gabriel shook her hand coldly, but Cora held it for a long time. Then Grace turned, trying not to laugh.

"And you must be little Jordan," said Cora, kneeling down to the child, who looked completely terrified. Cora quickly turned back to Mina.

"You look very pretty, Mrs. Cartwright. Thank you for wearing the dress I sent you."

"Thank *you*, Ms. Aregard. And thank you for the necklace. It is simply gorgeous."

"It looks so lovely on you. Your dark skin matches the gold. I knew it would."

"You knew I'd have dark skin?" she asked, amused.

"Yes. Well, Gabe told me your mother was from India."

"Oh."

They stood uncomfortably. Then Grace made things worse by staring at Gabriel. Jordan started shuffling around, bored. Cora stood next to Mina and leaned along the wooden rail again.

"I should say," Cora said, still talking too formally to Mina, "that I owe all this to your husband. He is a remarkable agent. A very valuable asset to his company and to my organization."

Cora sipped her martini. Then she looked at the others and realized they were empty-handed. She snapped her fingers at one of the servers carrying wineglasses. The woman handed two to them. Mina sipped it and smiled with a nod.

"Your organization, Ms. Aregard? What exactly do you do?"

Cora smiled a fake smile, then squinted, looking dangerous for a brief moment. Gabe knew her well enough to know that the question bothered her.

"Trading, Mrs. Cartwright."

"What sort of trading?"

Cora lost her smile. Grace reached over and kissed her cheek, then whispered something in her ear and walked away.

"Rare metals and property, Mrs. Cartwright ... I hear you work on a magazine?"

"Yes," Mina said, looking at her suspiciously. "Something else my husband told you about? My husband has apparently told you quite a bit about me."

Cora nodded. "After he mentioned it, I ordered a subscription. I really like your articles on breeding. Fascinating. But, forgive me, I don't care much for bitches." She covered her mouth, looking down at little Jordan. She chuckled a little. "Sorry, I forgot the little one. What I meant to say is, I'm not a fan of dogs."

"Not a fan of animals?"

"No. I didn't say that. I fancy animals, I just don't like dogs. But you clearly have a broad knowledge on the subject. That's what I was impressed with. I suppose if I did like them, I'd consult with you first, my dear."

She laughed. Mina chuckled uncomfortably too.

"If you don't like dogs, why'd you buy my magazine?"

"Because you're Gabriel's wife, and Gabriel is responsible for all this." She gave an expansive gesture at the lake. "I owe him a lot, and helping out by subscribing to your little magazine was my pleasure, Mrs. Cartwright."

Mina didn't like that.

Gabe looked at Cora crossly. He caught a hint of a grin again from her.

"Thank you," Mina said. "Your property is stunning."

"Aha."

They all stood there, very uncomfortable. Cora turned and started swaying to the music. It turned more melodic than cacophonous. Gabriel looked out at the water, then up at the full moon. Then he looked back at Cora, and he nearly dropped his glass. She was the only one not enjoying the view. She was staring at him.

Finally, someone ran up to Cora and pulled her away. She laughed and said farewell. And that was it.

Gabriel stood on the balcony feeling abandoned. Alone. Empty-handed. Disappointed. He watched Mina wipe Jordan's mouth and help the girl with a breadstick.

That's it?

For months since the invitation, he had lived a fantasy, imagining that one day he would see her again. His heart slowed and he suddenly felt a profound fatigue. He felt sick again.

"It's so beautiful, isn't it, babe?" Mina asked.

"Sure, Mina." His voice sounded terribly depressing.

Gabe gently pinched his daughter's cheek. Then he looked

around at all the guests. They were getting a little more rowdy—likely from drinking. It was getting dark.

"Makes me want to get a house in the country," replied Mina. "Your client is very bright. She has her own little forest to herself."

"Yeah." Gabe leaned over the rail, nervously fidgeting with his bow tie. "I'm gonna ... look around a little. I want to ... see the property again. I haven't seen it since we made the deal."

"Okay, hon, but not too long, all right? We can't stay late. Jo Jo needs to sleep."

"But we haven't had dinner yet."

"I know," Mina replied, looking at her cell phone, "but it's getting late. I know a restaurant by the hotel. If Jo Jo doesn't eat soon, she'll get cranky."

Ridiculous! They had just driven hundreds of miles from New York to be here, and now she wanted to leave fifteen minutes after arriving so that Jordan wouldn't get cranky?

He walked off irritably.

He really needed to breathe—the fresh outdoor air was stifling. At least, that was what he kept telling himself. His heart began to pound again. And then he felt guilty. He had lied to Mina. He didn't care at all about the property. The deep secret was his desire for Cora.

He wandered around the house, dodging shoulders and saying "pardon me" and "excuse me" every few feet. The home was becoming even more packed. He wandered into the kitchen, the only room that was quiet. It was a small room with a rustic farmhouse look, painted bright white with two revolving doors. Because it was full of food and plates and meant for business for the guests, the stampede of people largely avoided this part of the house. It was even quieter than the bathroom, which had a long line across the hallway. Only occasionally would a server walk in and nod to him and grab a plate; otherwise, it was empty. He leaned against a wooden cabinet and ran his hand along his short hair and just stood there for what seemed like a very long time. He wasn't sure what he was waiting for, but he knew he didn't want to return to the outside patio.

He stood there in silence until the door swung open again. This time it wasn't a server; it was Cora. She smiled coyly as she walked in. He practically fell to the floor.

"Oh ... hi, Gabe. I'm so glad you came."

"Thanks ... Cora."

"I was just looking for a silver tray of cookies. It wasn't for the cookies, you know. It's a bit of an heirloom, sterling silver, lasting many generations. I wanted to show it to a collector."

The lie was so obvious that even Cora couldn't help but smile at her own words. She looked around. Then she whispered to him, "But the real secret is—this is the only room in the house where I can get a second of quiet."

He nodded, and she nodded too.

She walked closer to him, touching his arm gently and smiling. She was going to say something, but he backed away nervously. She shrugged, then walked back across the room, looking through some cabinets.

"Why is the party so formal, Cora? Why a black-tie affair?"

She shrugged again, then stopped rummaging and walked back to his side. She threw her hair back and cocked her head.

"For you. You seemed to think of me once as a tramp. I wanted to prove to you that I could roll in style. But I must tell you"—she whispered again—"all these highbrow people, when they drink enough of their fancy of wine and cocktails, they'll be peeing and fucking the same as us common people."

He laughed in spite of himself.

"Was that vulgar, Gabe?"

He nodded, and she laughed too.

"I like your wife. She's very pretty."

"I see," he said, looking at her.

She remained by his side, fidgeting with her fingers. She

looked down and only turned when speaking to him. She was acting coy, which seemed ridiculous to him.

"I ...," stammered Gabriel, "perhaps you can court her instead of me now that you've switched your tastes to women."

"Gabriel"—she turned, surprised, with a smile—"I've always liked women. I told you that."

He suddenly felt a little angry. He was remembering her "partner."

"Cora, Grace was one of the ones who stripped and attacked me. Is she your friend?"

"Yes." She looked away again. "All the people at my going-away party were my friends. And Grace is a good person, when you get to know her." Cora bit her lower lip. "Well ... she does like sex."

"So, you're seeing her now?"

"No," she said, laughing. "I'm not *seeing* her. I'm actually quite available at the moment."

Suddenly a server barged into the room and saved him. She apologized when she saw the two of them, with their gazes directed towards the white wall—which probably made them look more intimate than if they were facing each other. Quickly the waitress grabbed her tray and walked out.

"Is she your girlfriend?"

"She's a friend, Gabe."

"Why put on this show, then?"

Cora put her head in her hand for a moment. Then she turned to him and touched his shoulder once more.

"Seriously? Gabriel, how can I please you? Did you want me to strut into the home instead wearing lingerie and kiss you on the cheek? Don't you think this relaxes your wife a bit more?"

"You don't have to relax my wife. I only met you for a little while—on a business trip."

"Aha. Right, Gabe." Cora nodded with a grin, but then she stared up at him with her glowing blue eyes. He was mesmerized.

He looked at her mouth. He wanted to touch her. Kiss her. He wanted to touch her red lips more than he had ever wanted anything before. She seemed to sense it and want it too. He heard her calm breathing. She reached up a little closer.

He quickly turned away. "Perhaps I should go."

"Yeah," she said, losing her playfulness. "Perhaps you should."

"Thank you so much for the invitation," he said with a nod. "We enjoyed the falls."

"Did you? You stopped by the falls? I'm so glad. I want you to be happy. That's all I ever wanted." She smiled at him a sweet smile. This made his heart race again. He looked down. "Gabe, it's ... it's okay. I understand. I just wanted to see you again ... to thank you."

But he shook his head. And then he opened up to her in a way he had not opened to anyone before.

"I ... I've thought a lot about you since I left."

This caught her by surprise. She looked up into his eyes as if she was examining them.

"Sweet. That's sweet, Gabriel. But it's lust. That's all. After all ..."

His lips met hers. The touch of her lips was greater than he could have imagined. It sent tingles down his spine. He grasped her hard and pushed her towards the counter, exploring her tongue. She gasped a little, and it only made him hungrier.

He had convinced himself it was an experiment. Perhaps she was nothing, only a fantasy. He could just kiss her for a moment, verify his hypothesis, then simply leave. Now he was devastated. He hungered for her more than ever.

"You're a married man," she said hesitantly, pulling away. But her voice was breathless, and that made him draw a little closer again.

"I ... I'm sorry. I—"

She put a finger on his lips, then came closer to him again

and took his fingers between hers. His hands trembled terribly for a moment, but hers did too. And *her* tremor was irresistible.

Did she care about him? It seemed she was always messing with him, but her hand shook and her body tightened with the same hunger as his own.

She brought his hand to her lips and kissed it gently.

"What are you?" he asked, looking into her eyes. "I *am* a married man. You said it yourself. But I can't bear to be away from you. Have you bewitched me?"

"I'm holding your hand, that's all."

"No, what ... what are you?"

"I already told you." She moved his hand between her fingers. This was painful. She was close to him—close enough for him to kiss her again. He did everything he could not to, but ... he wanted to. When he looked into her eyes, she seemed to want him again too. "You can have me, Gabriel, if you so choose." She shrugged. "And everything I have—all my money—all my things. Some would take it. But you—you're a good man. You won't. You're married. That is why you are who you are. And so, we can suffer instead ... for now. I will never do anything you don't want me to do. It's all up to you, Gabe."

"Am I another one of your flings?"

"No."

She reached up and pecked his cheek gently. But then he pushed hard against her, closer to the counter again.

She waited with her head cradled near his neck. He could feel her breath again by his cheek. He could smell her hair. Her smell. He could smell her flowery perfume, and even that smell had haunted his dreams too. She was intoxicating. But she didn't move anymore without him. She seemed to have gone as far as she had dared. They stood like this for a moment, but it seemed like many minutes. He didn't mind. It was wonderful. Finally, he pulled away from her hands.

He felt crushed. She seemed to be too.

She nodded in disappointment.

"I have to go," he said.

"I know."

"I ..." He finally moved away from her. "I think I preferred you as the sex-crazed Cora. Not this one."

"I'm still that," she said with a smile and a wink. He chuckled. "Have a safe journey. Enjoy your family. Truly, Gabriel, I wish the best for you."

"Thank you, Cora, ... Cora ... best of ... luck to you."

He hesitated for a moment but then quickly darted out of the room.

18

THE BAD CUT

Cora was pissed. She wasn't just a little angry, she was seriously pissed. Gabriel wasn't the only one dreaming of their reunion. She had planned the whole party just to bring back the well-mannered Midwestern man from Manhattan. She had known that if she made the party respectable and invited his wife and daughter, he would come. She had been right about that. Then she'd figured the rest would be easy. It hadn't been.

All they'd had to do was drink a little. You know, have a few too many cocktails. Then, being that they were in the middle of the woods late at night with a young child, Mina and Gabriel would undoubtedly be willing to accept her invitation to spend the evening at her house instead of driving drunk and risking a DUI or accident on the way back to their hotel. And, judging from the chemistry in the kitchen, it wouldn't have been difficult for her to get into his pants sometime by, say, one in the morning. They could meet in the guesthouse and have at it. Or maybe in the kitchen again. Instead, he'd left at seven thirty.

She watched the family leave from the driveway. Grace stood beside her with eyes wide open in amazement.

Well, the harder the hunt, the greater the reward. Right?

WRONG. You fucking dick! FUCK YOU!

Whenever Cora didn't get her way, she would either plan a grand party or go solo and get shitfaced. She'd already had the party, so the evening would be filled with the latter. An hour after Gabe left, she left too.

She got into her stretch limousine with Hashan and Grace, and they headed to a club in downtown Toronto—a strip club. Grace had a friend who worked there. Her friend used to be a stripper herself back in LA and had coincidentally moved East also. Cora had promised she'd visit. Now, they had hoped they could meet up.

In the car, Grace watched Cora with worry as Cora mixed her fourth martini before they even arrived at the hole-in-the-wall establishment.

They walked inside together, holding hands. Cora was a bit unsteady. They had on the most risqué outfits in her wardrobe. Cora had a short white tight skirt, and Grace wore a matching black one. The outfit barely covered their butt cracks and breasts. In fact, it wouldn't be hard for someone to catch a curve or two from their chest from the bottom or the top. Well, the evening was warm enough. The two girls were so shapely and hot that, when they walked into the dark entrance of the strip joint, the bouncer simply stepped aside.

Inside, the air was full of smoke and colored laser lights. It was a small club. Chairs and tables surrounded only one long stage. An attractive young blonde girl was strutting her stuff on stage, stripping off a police uniform, already touching her small perky tits. The two girls walked over to one of the tables right under the stage.

The club had a no-alcohol policy, but she had snuck her fourth drink by the front desk. She sipped the martini as the dancer slid up and down a pole.

The dancer was a bit blurry.

Cora reached down, fumbling in her tight pockets for a thin

money clip. She took out some nice crisp one-hundred-dollar bills. Grace saw it and tried to grab it from her, but Cora swatted her hands away.

"Hey, don't screw with me tonight, Grace!"

"That's too much!"

"Don't fuck with me, girl!"

"Well, if you're going to give her those, give me a few too."

"All right," Cora said, laughing with a shrug.

The stripper stood over the two friends. She fondled her breasts and unzipped her shorts. Then she yanked them down her legs and dipped her hand slowly along the blond tuft of hairs over her pussy. Cora waved the hundred-dollar bill unsteadily before her. The girl on stage opened her eyes wide and winked at her, coming closer. Cora brushed the bill near her crotch, and the stripper leaned down, nearly straddling Cora's head between her legs. Cora laughed hysterically. Grace stood up and took another hundred and rubbed it along the stripper's ass.

The money got the attention of the bouncer, a large, muscular black man who rushed over to them.

"Girls, that's a lot of money. Perhaps we can interest you in a private show in one of the booths."

"No, thanks," said Cora, staring at the stripper's ass. "I just like to watch."

Grace whispered in Cora's ear. She said something about how black men tended to be well endowed and she'd like to see if this one lived up to the reputation. Cora turned and examined the man. He was very handsome, hairless and bald, but with a tank top revealing huge arms. He was tall, with dark eyes and thick eyebrows, and a long thin scar ran along his thick forehead and cheekbone. He kind of reminded Cora of a pirate, and he even had an earring in one of his ears. She reached back to Grace's ear and told her that he definitely had a large cock.

"You're cute," Cora said, turning to him and running her hand over his thick arm.

"And," the bouncer continued, taking Cora's martini glass, "I'm afraid drinks aren't allowed."

Cora frowned, but she was finished with it anyway. "All right. Would you be a dear and get me coke, then?"

"No." But the man smiled and Grace snickered.

"Have you been with a black man?" Grace whispered in Cora's ear.

"Are you crazy?" Cora shouted. "Why, just last month! Honestly, his cock was too big!"

Grace tried to quiet her. Cora looked at her friend as if it was the dumbest question she had ever heard. She was starting to have difficulty balancing on her chair. She turned to the bouncer, who still stood above them, now uncomfortable at Grace's constant staring.

"Would you care to sit with us, handsome?"

"No."

He walked away, but he looked back at Grace, who couldn't keep her eyes off him. He smiled back at them.

Meanwhile, some boys not much older than twenty were staring at Cora on her left. She turned sleepily and lifted her top and bra, revealing one of her nipples. Grace quickly grabbed her and fixed her shirt. The boys looked over in shock.

"Cora, no more martinis, okay?"

"Don't mess with me tonight, Gracie," she repeated, this time slurring her words and wagging a finger. "Remember?"

The stripper was done. She got a towel and walked off the stage, gladly gathering her hundred-dollar bills.

The two women stared out at the pink-and-purple-lit empty stage, waiting patiently for the next act. Cora swayed to the music, which was some pop tune. She didn't talk, and Grace knew her well enough not to say anything.

Cora closed her eyes, about to lean her arms on the stage and rest her head on them until the next act, when she was touched from behind. It was the stripper, now dressed in red lingerie.

"Thanks for the tip, girls. It was the most generous one I've gotten all night."

"We like to recognize *talent*," said Cora.

"Well," replied the stripper, "you know, it's only twenty for a lap dance tonight. I'd love to offer you two a free show for what you just gave me."

Cora drifted in and out of consciousness, feeling miserable, but Grace looked thrilled over the offer. Grace loved women. When Cora had introduced Grace as her partner to her friends at the party, it was only a half-lie—Grace would have been Cora's partner any day.

"Do you know if Shirl's working here tonight?" asked Grace.

"No. She's only here on Fridays."

"Where are you going?" Cora asked Grace.

"Come with us."

"I thought you wanted to see if black men had big dicks!" Cora asked, so loudly that she embarrassed Grace, who put a hand over Cora's mouth.

"Shut up, Cora!"

"You go, Grace," Cora said, laughing. "I'll wait."

And Cora waited. She had gone to the club for her friend in the first place.

Cora hated strip clubs. She felt like the whole thing was a sham. That was why she gave hundred-dollar bills. It was a message: F-U to the whole thing. They were all about getting hot and bothered over nothing. It was just like her meeting with Gabriel. It was a tease. She wanted the real thing. There was nothing worse than watching a really hot girl strip her clothes off, touch her perky tits and clit, move her sumptuous ass, but then wag her finger at you when you started to come too close. *Nuh-uh-uh.* Then there were those who got off on private dances. The sorry chumps who chose to mess up their jeans under a gyrating hot chick—just as long as you didn't touch. Don't touch. *Nuh-uh-uh.* What total bullshit. What a lie. What a tease. Cora hated lies.

The only time she ever had fun was when she managed to take one of the lovelies home. Now that was a challenge. There was a hunt. But the whole thing of sticking dollar bills into someone's butt crack was overrated and a bit distasteful. Tonight, in her present mood, she would have preferred to watch a fucking porno at home instead. It would hardly have been much different.

Then again, she was with Grace, and Grace never disappointed.

They returned to the limo by two in the morning. Hashan ran and grabbed Cora as she stumbled to the car door. Grace walked behind with two new friends—the stripper and the bouncer.

The long stretch Hummer limousine was dimly lit with neon teal lights along the ceiling. There were long white leather seats along both sides of the limo with a sofa at the back. Towards the front was one white leather swivel chair, a refrigerator, a small bar (of course), a big-screen TV and a small tinted window connecting to the front of the car. Oldie '90s Seattle grunge music played in the background. Hashan was told to drive aimlessly along the highways.

Grace sat on the sofa in the back with her young blonde stripper on one end and the bouncer on the other. Cora sprawled on the floor under a side couch nearby. On the odd occasion when Cora opened her eyes, she laughed, watching her friend. Grace looked over and laughed too. They both knew the main reason for bringing the bouncer on board was to see his cock.

Both girls removed the bouncer's shirt first and ran their tongues along his perfect well-built chest. He had rock-hard abs, and Grace giggled as she brushed her hand along each ridge. Then Grace pulled her shirt over her head. Cora raised her own shirt too and stripped down naked. Grace brushed her hands along his chest again, then straddled him. She ran her chest over his pecs. He reached back and removed her black lace bra. Then she stood up over him and impatiently pulled off her shorts and panties. She leapt back on top of him and pressed herself against his legs, closing her eyes and slowly dry-humping him. The stripper beside them did what she did best: performed a show beside them.

Then it was the moment of truth. Grace took the stripper's hand, and the two of them reached down and unzipped the bouncer's zipper. All to unveil *THE COCK.*

Grace almost squealed in excitement. Indeed, it was huge.

She looked back behind her at Cora, winking and gesturing with a finger for her to join them. Cora laughed and shook her head. Instead, she crawled naked over to the refrigerator at the front of the car and pulled out a bunch of vials and syringes. She sat beside the refrigerator with an unsteady hand, preparing a concoction of Brown Sugar to shoot up.

"What you got over there, Cora?" asked Grace.

"Nothing. Go back to your dick."

And indeed, Grace did. She excitedly pulled off the man's pants and threw them to the side. Then Cora saw her friend dip her long hair over the man's legs while the stripper, naked, began touching herself while watching. Grace bobbed up and down, sucking the man's cock.

Cora carefully set out four vials on the carpeted floor. The floor was steady. They were, doubtless, in the middle of nowhere, driving on a flat highway. She prepared the needles by cooking up a batch large enough for all four syringes, adding just the right mixture and heating the brown base with a lighter. Then she took out a blue band and tied her arm, making her fist and looking for a vein. Her veins were easy to find. They healed fast, never scarring.

She looked back. Grace had her back to Cora now, her ass and tits silhouetted over the bouncer as she straddled him, fucking him. Cora heard her friend moaning while the stripper beside them leaned back on the couch, pleasuring herself.

She stuck a needle into her arm, and her euphoria was

instant. It was exactly what she needed to take away the pain. She fell back against the leg of the white leather swivel chair, seeming to sink to the floor. A deep calm came over her. For a moment, she forgot Gabriel. And she forgot Grace and the stripper. Then she forgot Cora.

Her eyes were now more closed than open. She slouched against the leg of the chair, occasionally looking up at the blurred neon-blue-lit ceiling. She looked over at her friend again. Grace continued to bob up and down, though she too was blurring. The whole car seemed to be circling round and round. Cora felt dizzy, but at peace.

Then she reached for another.

"You sure that's a good cut, Cora?" asked Grace, apparently taking a break.

The naked stripper traded places with Grace. It was her turn to sit atop *THE COCK*.

Sweet. Sweet Grace.

Why the fuck do you care? Why does anyone fucking care about me?

Cora said nothing, just closed her eyes. She wanted to feel the rush again. She wanted to close off from everything and just relax. Stop all thought. Rest. Perhaps sleep. Hopefully never wake. Die. Just die.

If Cora was alive, that was what she would do tonight—die. That was what her new lover had done to her. He had killed her already. Her heart was dead without him, and she couldn't take being away from him. Decades alone? After Danny had left her? How could she take that?

But she had to stay away because ... because ...

Why did she have to stay away?

What was she even thinking?

She heard a scream and then a giggle. The ceiling seemed to come in waves like water. The blue ran over her, pinning her harder to the floor. *Gabriel. For Gabriel. Cheers. Bye. Bye-bye. Can't live with you and I can't ...* What was the reason for living? She had planned the party for him. It hadn't been a housewarming party; it had been a fucking Gabriel-fishing party. She'd even moved to Toronto for him. She hated snow. What was worse, he was an Ambrosia—Nephrea's. She'd go insane if she couldn't have him. She wanted him. And if she couldn't have him ... then, she could die. She could die *RIGHT NOW!*

And then, she thought, even if she didn't die ... maybe if she died, the well-mannered Missourian from Manhattan might come back to save her?

She shot another dose of heroin into her arm and slumped lower to the floor. She felt wonderful. Then she reached for the third, but she could barely move. She felt around the carpet with her eyes closed. There it was. She took the last two needles. Her eyes occasionally fell on a blurry vision of three people fondling and fucking each other in the background. She could no longer hear music. She felt the void, but she wanted to feel even less. Deader. She wanted to be deader, and she hoped the dope would kill her.

Two more injections. Then ...

"*Cora!*"

∾

G race leaned down and shook her, then she slapped her face.

"Cora! Cora! Wake up!"

Nothing. Grace felt her pale skin, even paler than usual. She lifted an eyelid. There was no movement. Cora lay on the floor of the limo like a lifeless doll. Grace leaned close to her mouth.

"She's not breathing! My God! She's not breathing!"

Grace looked over at the stripper and the bouncer. They were sitting on their knees by the other side of the cabin, staring blankly at her—still naked; still embracing each other.

"She's not breathing!" Grace yelled.

The bouncer grabbed a sheet from the sofa to cover himself and darted over. He looked down at her. Grace had a brief flash of hope that the man could do something, but then he gave her that same blank stare again.

"Looks like a bad cut," he said stupidly.

"Bad cut! She looks fucking dead, you fucking moron!"

"My God! What the hell was she doing with all those needles!" yelled the stripper. "Maybe we need to check her pulse or something."

"You fucking idiots!" yelled Grace. "Yeah, a pulse! Or maybe a goddamn doctor? You have no idea what—"

Before Grace could finish disciplining her guests, the car shot forward with enough force to knock her off balance, sending her careening over Cora's body. Poor Cora's body rolled under her. The stripper flew back onto the couch, and the bouncer grabbed hold of one of the side couches.

Grace crawled to a window and looked outside. The sun was starting to come out. She hadn't paid any attention to where she was until now. They were on a two-lane highway driving past thick woods. Grace reached over to get a better look and spotted a dock and some boats that she had seen before on her way up to Cora's house. Then she jumped to the other side. She searched the lake under the rising sun and saw no sign of the CN Tower. A small car whizzed by; it didn't drive in front of them but quickly disappeared *behind* them. Judging by the speed at which the small car was overtaken, Hashan had his foot firmly on the gas.

"Hey! What's going on in there?" cried the bouncer. He banged his fist on the tinted privacy screen that separated their cabin from the driver. Then he pressed a switch to drop the tinted glass. Though the tint dropped down, it seemed he couldn't get the second layer of glass to lower. Grace tried the switch too but to no avail. Behind the glass, Hashan was completely ignoring them. The bouncer lost his footing and fell again as the limo suddenly shifted its direction. A bunch of plastic glasses and two liquor bottles flew off the bar.

"Slow down!" shouted the bouncer.

Grace looked down at Cora again. The bitch had a smile on her blank dead face.

The stripper crawled over and grabbed Grace's wrist. "I think she's dead," she finally said, squatting down and running her hand along Cora's face. She shook her, but Cora didn't move. Then she shook her more violently. Cora's lifeless head moved like a rag doll. It was too much for Grace.

"Stop it!" said Grace. "Just stop it!"

The bouncer began to panic. He took one of the bottles of whiskey now lying on the floor and rammed it like a hammer into the privacy window, trying to get the driver's attention, until it shattered in pieces. Glass exploded all over the front of the limousine. Some of the shards hit Grace. When Grace saw the pieces hit Cora, she became livid.

"Stop it! Damn you, stop it!"

"What else can we do?" he said. "That little shit is going to kill us!"

"You got glass on her! Just sit down and put your seat belt on!"

But he stood up straighter. Then the limo took another dangerous curve and he had to hold on tight to the swivel chair. The turn made him only angrier, but Grace beat him to it.

"Hashan!" Grace shouted, pressing a button on the intercom. She looked through the glass and saw the familiar small man wearing sunglasses, a small hat and a black suit. He didn't look back, just kept calmly driving like a maniac, swerving around cars on the highway as if they were obstacles. Only occasionally, when he turned the car violently, would he look agitated like the rest of them.

"Hashan! Stop the car! What are you doing?"

He was doing about a hundred and ten in a stretch Humvee.

The bouncer wasn't done. Running around in a small white

sheet that barely covered his crotch, he searched for something to break the window, turning over everything in the cabinets and on the tables. He found a corkscrew—and threw it, judging it to be too small. Then he picked up a butter knife—long, but useless against thick tempered glass. Grace looked at his face. He seemed to want to kill the driver. She didn't care if he succeeded in breaking the glass or not, but either circumstance put their lives in danger.

Meanwhile, with some kind of sick irony that only Cora could have wickedly planned, a grunge band blared on the speakers throughout the cabin, something about grandmothers. The music only made the pandemonium worse.

"Stop the fucking car!" the bouncer yelled through the intercom.

"Oh, Cora," Grace said, looking down at her and shaking her head. She held on to the swivel chair as she looked down on the lifeless body, ignoring her own advice about fastening a seat belt and instead kneeling over her friend, swaying back and forth nervously.

The stripper buckled in, and the bouncer kept rolling around the car, pounding the window like a madman.

And then, the music stopped. The car pulled up a long, newly paved road. As they ascended, Grace realized they were in Cora's driveway.

The car slammed to a halt beside the front door. The bouncer was thrown into the front window. All three of them looked out towards the house. The huge driveway was empty with the exception of a 5-series BMW. Hashan had parked right near the entrance. The side door opened, and the bouncer leapt at Hashan.

Hashan was a small man, but Grace knew that one of his many jobs in Ms. Aregard's service was as her bodyguard. She had once seen Hashan pin a huge drunk man's arms behind his back and throw him to the ground before he could toss a drink at

Cora. Now, with the bouncer about to slug him, Hashan pulled out a pistol and pointed it at his head.

"Jesus! What the hell—"

"Step back, sir," said Hashan calmly, gesturing for the bouncer to climb back to the sofa at the opposite end of the limo. He complied with his hands up. The other passengers put their hands up as well. Grace stared at him, confused. Then Hashan smiled at her.

Hashan kneeled over Cora and pulled out a small penlight. He lifted her eyelids and examined them. Then he touched her neck.

"Is she okay?" asked Grace.

Hashan nodded. Grace stepped back and started crying again.

"She's fucking dead!" cried the bouncer.

"I'm going to need some help," Hashan said, looking at the bouncer. "Sorry about that, sir, but it appeared you were about to rush me."

"What kind of bullshit is this?"

"There's a camera by the far end of the cabin," Hashan said, pointing. "I saw Cora inject herself. I have Narcan in the house."

"Have you ever heard of a hospital, dickhead?"

"No hospitals," Hashan said with a thin grin. "That was why I rushed. Cora is very insistent that she is never to be taken to a hospital." He turned to Grace and placed a hand on her, then removed his coat and placed it over her shoulders. She had been so frantic that she hadn't realized she was still completely naked. He grabbed a white sheet from one of the couches and wrapped it around Cora before turning back to the bouncer.

"I could use some help with Ms. Aregard, sir. If you would, the two of us can carry her into the house."

The bouncer squinted at Hashan, who placed his gun back into his belt. The bouncer seemed to consider the proposition and then just nodded.

19

HER CONVALESCENCE

About halfway back to their hotel, Gabriel realized Mina was still wearing Cora's necklace. He slammed on the brakes and quickly did a U-turn. Then the two proceeded to scream at each other at the top of their lungs, with poor little Jo Jo crying in the back of the car. Gabriel eventually gave in and stopped the car by the roadside. His wife got out of the car and screamed some more.

They made an agreement. They would return to their hotel so Jordan could get some sleep, then, early in the morning, Gabe would drive back to the house alone and return Cora's necklace. But the fight continued as Mina suggested he just mail the jewels back when they returned to New York. Gabriel retorted that they were much too valuable to send by mail. He wanted to personally return them and thank her for them.

"Fine! Just make sure you go real early. I don't want Jo Jo to miss school."

It was preschool, of course.

Gabriel arrived back at Cora's house before sunrise. He drove up the dirt road to the circular driveway and parked near the front door, walking nervously up the stairs with the wooden chest under his arm. The house was completely transformed. Whereas there had been a couple hundred people wandering the grounds previously, now it was vacant. Quiet.

He knocked. No one opened the door. He knocked again. Still no one.

He laid the chest down by the door, then ran back to his car and started the engine, driving a few feet before realizing that he was stuck. He couldn't possibly leave millions of dollars' worth of diamonds by the front door. He slammed his fists against the steering wheel a few times, got out and grabbed the chest, and sat back in his car.

He sat for hours. Occasionally he looked down at the chest on the passenger seat, occasionally hitting the steering wheel hard again, occasionally looking out at the lovely property, abhorring it.

He fell asleep.

Gabriel woke up as his car shook. He heard the screech of a car's brakes. He opened his weary eyes and then witnessed the craziest display of madness he had ever seen in his life. He thought perhaps he was dreaming. Hashan and a giant half-naked black man draped in a white sheet carried a body towards the house. The pale white girl's arms flailed by her sides as they ran her towards the house. Then two naked women with long blond hair jumped out of the limo and ran, crouching forward and covering themselves from behind. Gabriel caught a glimpse of the naked ladies' faces and jumped when he recognized one—their mascara was running, but he clearly saw the face of Grace on the one wearing only a long black coat. A shiver ran down Gabriel's spine. Then the shiver turned to horror. He looked at the corpse again as they reached the steps to the house. The dead body had long, deep red hair. Gabriel leapt out of his car and ran after them.

G abriel held saffron drapes in one hand, a glass of whiskey in the other—something he sorely needed. He sipped his drink as he enjoyed the view. The bedroom was faintly lit and contrasted strongly with the light from outside. It was a clear day. As he looked out the window, he had to squint his eyes. A ship sailed far in the distance, and by the rocky shore, a few boys carried fishing poles, heading to a small rowboat. The room was surrounded on three sides by windows. When the drapes were open, it felt a little like the bow of a ship. He had seen it open when he had brought Cora's unconscious body inside. He touched the chipped brown paint along the wooden window frame and shook his head. It was a nice lodge. Pity Cora was bent on destroying it.

Cora stirred behind him in bed. He turned. The bedroom was sparsely furnished with her in her large black bed, a nightstand beside her, and a chair and a desk. There were paintings on the brown-painted walls of trees and docks from the lake. It gave it a rustic impression. Gabe smiled, knowing Cora hated it.

He could only see her silhouette faintly lit from a dim lamp. He turned back and looked outside again.

Grace had thought for sure Cora had died. Gabriel remembered looking down at her blue lips and white face, her body motionless, her eyelids half-closed—lifeless. He could still hear Grace's wailing as he helped Hashan lower her naked body down on the wood floor in the entryway. But after the medicine had been administered, she'd quickly opened her eyes and come to.

The three men had taken turns watching over her for the first few hours. Now it was Gabriel's turn, and he was alone.

Alone in her bedroom.

She stirred again.

Alone with Ms. Cora Aregard in her bedroom—the one place in the whole world he didn't want to be. His phone buzzed. He looked down. He had a train of texts from his wife. He had ignored his phone, telling her it was an emergency. Her texts were getting more and more obnoxious:

7:45 a.m.: I need you back here

7:57 a.m.: Answer your phone

8:15 a.m.: Answer your phone NOW

8:30 a.m.: Where are you? Just text me back

8:45 a.m.: I think Jo Jo's coming down with a cold. I really need you here for her

9:00 a.m.: We're going to breakfast. We'll see you downstairs. If not here yet, TEXT ME

9:45 a.m.: Where are you? What's happening?

And on and on ...

10:02 a.m.: ANSWER YOUR PHONE

10:04 a.m.: ANSWER YOUR PHONE

11:10 a.m.: Leave her! I need you back NOW

He shook his head. He finally sent a message back, telling her he was still delayed. He got an instant text back:

WHY ARE YOU STILL AT HER HOUSE, FUCKER? TAKE HER TO A DOCTOR AND COME BACK NOW!

He had told her the truth. He had said Ms. Aregard was suffering a drug overdose and they were there to check on her and make sure she recovered.

Gabriel put away his phone and looked up at Cora. She was lying over black silk sheets in a thin red satin robe. She wore nothing underneath. He knew because he had helped dress her. She still had her dark mascara on—though a little runny from all the chaos—and her red hair was a bit curly and unkempt. But she still had those perfectly groomed eyebrows and her cute, slightly pointy nose and soft cheeks. Then he stared at those red lips—the same lipstick she'd worn when he'd first met her in LA. Her chest rose up and down rhythmically. She looked so peaceful. He hated her for that. Gabe felt anything but peaceful.

Then he ran his hand through his thin hair and finished his

drink. The glass had been nearly full with little ice. Hashan must have thought he needed it. He did.

What the hell am I doing here?

It was definitely too late for checkout at the hotel. Mina was beyond the point of killing him, yet he clung on to his lie that he was helping Cora.

He pulled the drapes open again and stared outside. The view was truly breathtaking. This was nature. Cora had chosen the property wisely—he wondered how. His company was good, but it was Cora who had discovered personally the land.

Then he heard Cora stir again. She was rolling about, stretching her arms over the silk sheets. She opened those gorgeous blue eyes and flashed a nice angelic cherry-red smile.

"Hi."

"How are you feeling?"

She rubbed her forehead and started to get up but collapsed back in her pillows.

Gabe ran to her and sat beside her on the mattress, leaning over and holding her hand. She looked dizzy.

"Just rest."

"My head is exploding. What time is it?"

"A little after eleven. Why did you do this?"

"What?" she asked with a yawn, stretching out her arms again. She pushed herself up against the head of the bed and pulled up her robe, which was slipping down over her cleavage. She shivered a little.

"It smells like shit in here. Open the drapes, would you? And some windows."

"You don't want to rest?" But Gabe walked over and started opening them.

She shook her head.

As Gabe drew open some curtains, Cora squinted and put her hands in front of her eyes. Under sunlight, she seemed paler than usual, but still gorgeous.

"Jeez, it's bright. Never mind. Close it."

He shrugged and closed them again.

"But do open some windows."

It smelled fine to him. She smelled good. She had vomited once, but there was no sign of it—only the intoxicating allure of her perfume. He had remembered her floral-sweet smell. He had missed it for months. He had thought of it since his stay in LA. The slivers of light on her body from the open drapes made her perfect—somehow, even in illness, simply perfect.

She sat herself up and tried to straighten her robe. "Why are you here?" she asked drowsily.

"Hmm?"

She didn't repeat herself; she just smiled.

"Oh. I needed to return your necklace."

She had this amused smile on her face. Then she seemed to remember her headache and clasped her head.

"Never mix heroin with alcohol, Gabe. Remember that."

He nodded, standing by the window. He had spent the last few hours trying not to stare at her. Now, as she waited for his replies, he was forced to look at her. He blushed a little, his heart racing again as he thought she might have noticed.

"So," she said after a long pause. "Where is it?"

The necklace? He had no idea. He had brought it in his car. He remembered leaving it in the passenger side as he waited for someone to return home.

She started laughing. She couldn't stop, and the act only seemed to be making her head feel worse. Between laughs, she rubbed her temples.

"Oh fuck!" she said, laughing, "you're so funny, Gabe. It hurts, but it's worth it."

"It must be in the car."

"You came all the way back to my house to return the necklace and now you don't even remember where you put it?"

"I'm sure it's in the car."

"A four-million-dollar necklace? I hope you didn't leave it lying out on the seat."

"Uh ... it's fine. I'll go check—" He was so nervous that he nearly tripped over the bed while heading for the door.

"Wait," Cora interrupted, laughing some more. "Forget it. Damn, that's funny! Come back here."

He stood there and looked down. She tried to get a hold of herself.

"Let me get this straight—you drove in the middle of the night from downtown Toronto all the way to my home in order to hand-deliver the necklace I gave your wife. Right? Why didn't you just mail it?" Now *he* was tongue-tied. "Or leave it at the door? And now ... you're not even sure where you left it?"

"I thought you were dead. I ran in to help. I forgot the—"

"You're funny, Gabe."

She turned away from him and lay there clutching her head.

"You okay?"

"It's just a hangover. Unfortunately, I have to feel the bad effects of drugs along with the good."

"You drink too much."

She just nodded.

"Cora, I ... I felt your wrist. My father was a doctor. I know how to check a pulse."

"So?"

"You didn't have one. I'm not sure why you're alive."

She had her back turned to him. All she did was shrug.

"Your father was a doctor?" she asked, still with her back turned.

"Yeah."

"That explains it."

"What?"

"How you care about others. Empathy. Your care over me. Perhaps you should have been one too."

Then there was silence. Cora clutched her head. Gabe stood

uncomfortably huddling over her. And yet, in his heart, he loved standing there. Even if it meant not saying a word, he loved being there. He could stand there forever.

"So," said Cora finally, "why'd you become a realtor? You said nursing. Or doctor. Why didn't you become one of them?"

"It's lucrative."

She laughed again. She still had her back turned to him.

"Funny. You're really funny, Gabe. I wish it didn't hurt so much to laugh. So, you went into it for the money?"

"I don't know. I like teasing out what things are worth."

She turned to him. His body seemed to spontaneously reel back. She was still immensely amused.

"Really? Tease things out, eh? Hmm ... how much do you think I'm worth, Gabriel?"

"What?"

"Tease out what I'm worth. How much do you think Ms. Aregard costs?"

"I don't think people are worth money."

She wagged a finger at him. "No, that's where you're wrong. Everyone is worth something. Not just things, but people. I'd bet your wife is worth a few million. I bet she can be bought for the right price."

"Excuse me? My wife?"

For the first time, he was offended and wanted to walk out of the room. But she didn't join his anger. She just smiled.

"Your wife. I'd bet you I could make her happy for the rest of her life by simply giving her a few million dollars."

"You don't know Mina, then."

"I met her. I know your bitch very well."

"Cora, you're—"

"Just for conversation's sake, I bet if I offered to let your wife keep the necklace, she would be perfectly happy to leave you."

She forced herself to sit up, clutching her head tighter, then raised a hand for him to calm down. She still had a jovial look on her face—as if she was playing a game.

Gabe shook his head. He was ready to leave. "I asked you to be real with me," he said. "You're playing games again."

Then she infuriated him by simply shrugging, turning her body, and lying back down. She didn't say anything else.

He glared at her, wanting to flip her around and throw her off the bed, slap her in the face and punch her. He was furious. He wanted to take all his frustration and unleash it on her. And she would take the blows. He wanted to just ... touch her.

He nearly fell to the floor when he realized what he truly wanted. His hands started shaking again. He wanted to touch her. He wanted to pull off her robe. He wanted to touch the softness of her pale skin. He wanted to run his hands along her naked chest —the soft rounded breasts—the perky tits and nipples he had seen when she lay downstairs getting the Narcan shot. He wanted to kiss her cherry-red lips. With all her sarcastic nastiness, her scheming, her omnipotent arrogance, he wanted to take her, tear off that robe, and fuck her. He wanted her more than anyone he had ever wanted before—more than his wife—more than Mina.

The guilt made his hands shake. But his belief in honoring his marriage only made the desire for her even stronger. His heart pounded. His teeth clenched. All the while, she just lay there. She said nothing, but there was something about her silence. She seemed to know.

"Why are you still here?" she asked.

"Do you want me to leave?"

"No."

"How could you be revived? You went minutes without a pulse and without breathing."

"More talk, huh? Well, it hardly seems to matter. You'll be leaving and returning to your bitch wife soon anyway."

"She's not a bitch."

"Sure."

Sure—apparently, the word didn't affect her anymore.

As if Mina was listening, at that exact moment, Gabe's phone buzzed. He didn't pick it up.

Cora kept her back turned. It didn't stop him from staring at her.

He could smell her. That same intoxicating floral smell. He could see her waist and her rounded butt and imagine the robe falling from her smooth white ass.

"You going to get that?" Cora asked.

Gabe ignored his phone and walked back to the window. He opened the drapes and looked outside.

"You want straight?" she asked. "*Au-then-tic?* Okay, now's your chance, Gabe. This is your final chance to go. Go now. Run from my house as quick as you can and don't look back. Go join your wife and your little daughter. Do it before you do something you regret. As much as I want you, I wouldn't wish my life on anyone."

"What are you talking about?" he asked. This time, he didn't turn. He stared at the same ship far out on the lake.

"You asked why I did what I did. Sometimes, I want to die. Last night, I wanted to die. But I can't die. And I knew that too. But I dreamed you would come to me. Somehow, I didn't predict it this time, but I just knew my knight in shining armor would come and rescue me if I shot up more. I don't know why. And so I did. And so you did. But ... but, now that you're here, you can go. Just leave, Gabe. The deal's done. You gave me one last look at you. Now go before you do something you're gonna regret. Soon, there'll be no turning back. This is your last chance to escape, mister."

"You're so sure of yourself," he said with a chuckle. But he didn't dare turn and face her. "What makes you think I want you so badly? I came here to return your necklace, that's all. It could have been lost in the mail."

"That's why you're still here, right? I thought you wanted to be straight. I thought you wanted us to be honest with each other. *Au-then-tic*."

"Oh, and by the way," she added, "I never said you wanted me badly. *You* said that. I don't think you're being very authentic to yourself."

"You're so conceited. Yes … you're ravishing, but you're only a woman. And, as you said, I'm a married man."

He kept looking outside. He dared not turn. But he could feel her looking at him.

"*Ravishing*," she laughed. "That's a nice word. Am I *ravishing*, Gabe? That's a really nice choice of words."

"Stop playing games. Anyone meeting you would be attracted."

"I'm not playing games. And that's not true. I'll give you one last chance," she said finally. "Leave now or there's no turning back. You want to know how Hashan revived me, I'll tell you. If you stay in this room, I'll answer you. I'll put an end to all the mystery and answer you. But if you stay in my bedroom one more moment, mister, then I'll confide in you—and then I will take you and there will be no turning back."

He should have left. He needed to return to the hotel, but he didn't want to. He didn't want to see Mina. He wanted to stand in the dark room and see Cora.

"Confide in me, Cora," he said, dropping his head down solemnly.

He heard the movement of sheets over her bed and turned, startled. She was standing only a couple steps from him, blinking her blue eyes. He stared at them—almost hypnotic. Oddly, they seemed to flicker a dark red. She touched his hair and ran her hand gently along his cheek.

But then she shook her head and laughed.

"No. I don't think so. Go home. Get out of here. Go back to your family."

She walked back to the bed and lay down, this time pulling the sheets over her. His phone vibrated again.

"Why don't you get that?" she asked under the covers.

"You want me to?"

"I don't want to hurt you," she said. Her words seemed sincere.

"Confide in me, Cora," he said.

"Careful, Gabe."

"It's okay. I'm already here. Tell me."

"Time's up." Sighing, she pulled back the covers and pointed towards the window. "Go open the drapes and tell me what you see."

He looked at her funny. Was this her madness? Obeying, he opened the drapes, shocked to see it was pouring rain outside. It had been completely clear only a minute before, not a cloud in the sky. Gabe turned and looked at Cora, who was staring at the window. As the now-dim light from outside fell upon her, he was startled to see her eyes had turned a bright glowing red. A shiver ran down Gabe's back. Cora simply nodded gently.

"I don't understand," he said, shaking his head.

She smiled. "Now turn around again." The minute she said it, a flash of light came over Cora and flooded the room. Her eyes were red in her pale white face, and she squinted from the light outside. Gabe whirled around to look out the window. It was a bright sunny day again.

"What the hell?" he asked, staring outside.

"Now I've confided in you, lover."

He turned back to her once more. Suddenly, she was standing close to him again. Her robe had fallen by the bedside. She was stark naked. The bright light from outside shone along her skin. She reached over and touched his hair, then gave him a gentle kiss on the cheek.

He closed his eyes. It was what he had desired for hours. No, not hours. Days. Weeks. Months. He turned and their lips met.

She embraced him gently. He felt her breasts against his chest and ran his hand down along the curve of her back, tracing her body to her waist while touching her smooth deep red hair. Her hair was so soft. He touched the crack of her ass. Then he explored her mouth with his tongue as he cupped her buttocks, bringing her body closer to him. She giggled.

But he quickly pulled away, throwing the drapes closed. He was surprised at how fast everything was happening. She smiled in the darkness next to him, her eyes now glowing red. She smiled, genuinely looking happy.

"What—what are you?" he asked, stepping back.

"I'm Cora. Don't be afraid." It was dark again in the room, but she still stood stark naked before him. "Don't be afraid, Gabriel."

"What? Who are you?" He shook his head angrily. "Who are you, Cora?"

"Persephone of the Spring." She walked back to the bed, swaying her naked hips, and she sat down cross-legged in front of him. "Go ahead, open the drapes again."

He was afraid to reach for the window. His hand wouldn't stop shaking as he opened all the drapes, fearing another storm. He thought perhaps he was losing his mind. His hands shook terribly, this time out of genuine fear and not lust. When he finished with the drapes, he turned to her.

She looked strangely vulnerable under the bright light. She sat on the bed naked, not only in body, but in heart. She looked afraid, which was weird. Could anything frighten her?

"Persephone?" he sputtered.

"Yeah," she said with a shrug, then turned from him and looked down. "Pleasure to meet you, Gabriel."

"Are you sad?"

"I am." She nodded with a smile. "Yes, and you're a good enough man to know it. I am very sad. I'm always sad. But now, I'm also a little happy that I found you."

"Cora ... I ..."

She put her finger by her lips and blew him a kiss. She looked indecent sitting there naked, but she didn't move, nor even try to cover herself.

"I think it's enough. Enough talking ... maybe we can just forget about our troubles. Sometimes there are just too many."

"I don't know what to say."

"Don't say a thing."

"I'm a married man."

She nodded and smiled. "Perhaps," she said in thought, "you should leave her." She wasn't trying to be mean. Her look was considerate, not judgmental.

At this point, Cora could have said anything. Nothing would have sunk into Gabriel's head. He was in complete shock and barely listening.

So many thoughts ran through his mind. He was so disturbed that his hands didn't even shake anymore. He just stood there staring blankly at her. He relished the vision of her beauty and hated it all the same. He said nothing. She just smiled.

He walked to her and reached for her hand.

Then he fell. He fell into her arms on the bed, again kissing and meeting her tongue with his. It didn't take long for Cora to help unbutton his shirt, pull his T-shirt over his head and take off his pants. A couple buttons popped off, but that couldn't be helped. Then came his underwear.

Stark naked, the two of them rolled around on the black silk sheets. He ran his hand along her perfect ass while pinching her nipple. Then he reached down and licked and sucked her breasts, her red nipples erect over her pale firm skin. He flicked his tongue along them as she giggled while she reached down and rubbed his erect cock. Then she pulled his head back up and kissed him hard in rapture, sucking and playing with his tongue and lips. They embraced lying on their side and he looked at her eyes, her eyes now wide, now gorgeous dark blues again, staring at him, waiting for him to make love to her.

"I'm so wet," she said. "Make love to me, Gabe. Fuck me. Please."

"I ... I don't have a condom."

"I'm infertile. Just fuck me, Gabe. Enter me, now."

He obliged, entering her. They moved slow at first but quickened with each movement. He looked down upon her, at her perfect face and bright blue eyes, which opened wide again, staring into his eyes; her lips pursed and opened as she quickly came in ecstasy beneath him.

The light was indecent, showing every perfect curve of her soft body. He had never seen such beauty, and in order to last, he had to close his eyes as he began thrusting again, deeper inside her.

He ran his hand along her neck and then through her perfect long red hair. Then he held her as he continued to thrust into her. He felt her breath along his ear. And then he ran a finger along her eyebrows—those perfect thin brows. Then the tufts of his facial hair ran against her soft cheeks. Their lips touched again. She licked and entered his mouth again, while rubbing his back with her long fingernails. He felt her hands probe down along the line of his ass and then grasp his waist on both sides, pulling into him harder with his thrusts. He could not last much longer. He pressed his chest against her soft breasts and leaned his face over hers, feeling her eyelids brush against his. Then their soft mouths touched yet again, with her bestially sucking him. He looked away from her. A hint of pleasure from those eyes nearly took him over the edge.

"Fuck me," came her soothing voice. "Inside. Just fuck ... me. Oh God, Gabe ... oh God, I love you. I love you so fucking much!"

He felt her relax under him. Then he sank on top of her.

It was then that Hashan barged through the door, backing up, ashamed, as he saw the two of them naked by the bed.

"Hashan," she said, turning as if nothing at all was the matter.

"Cora ... I see ... you are feeling better, madam."

"I'm feeling much better now, Hashan," she said with a chuckle.

"Can I do anything for you, or ... him, madam?"

"You certainly can. Get me a martini. A real dry sharp one. And get our guest here one too. Then get the fuck out of my room."

"Very well, madam."

Hashan nodded his head uncomfortably towards Gabe, then ran out of the room.

They laughed together.

"Do you like my room?" Cora asked, waving her hand about it. She scooted out from under him.

"Yes, Cora. But I think I would like it better if we got dressed."

"Of course, lover," she said with a smile.

20

BURGERS

Cora was not very happy with herself. She felt guilty. The plan was to protect, not fuck. That was what she had been telling herself for months. She knew now that wasn't possible. But she had wooed him. Perhaps he didn't love her. Perhaps she was simply a vixen goddess who'd bewitched him. She had predicted their love, but had they fallen in love because of her guile? Or was it real? She was obsessed with Nephrea's family, having loved Nephrea more than any other who had ever walked the earth. Now she had a direct descendant. A boy. The first boy nymph. According to prophecy, the first boy nymph would signal the last. Nephrea's family would die with him. The first and last boy nymph. How could she not love him?

Isn't fucking the best way to protect him?

Then she thought of his cute little daughter, Jordan. And his wife.

You bitch, Cora!

She needed Dr. Tenor.

She felt conflicted. And so, it was ironic that the married man in her room didn't seem nervous at all. With no secrets, it seemed he had completely forgotten about his wife and daughter. He looked thrilled sitting beside her in her bed naked. Their love-making and the shock of her miracles seemed to have finally broken the wall between them.

He reminded her so much of Danny. That hurt too. All her men for thousands of years were always similar. She couldn't help but pick the same men through the centuries. That was a strange providence.

They sat in bed, sipping martinis and looking out on the lake. She noticed his fingers no longer twitched. His eyes no longer wandered. He sat comfortable, naked, drinking his cocktail while she leaned on her elbow, baring her breast.

She used her convalescence as an excuse to remain in bed. Then she told him the drink would help her with her hangover—and her tortuous thoughts.

She gazed at his dark black hair. How it twirled beside his ears. He was so well manicured, so well mannered. He had hard cheekbones and a bit of a receding hairline, but he was muscular and fit and tall. His chest was cut and well developed. He was a nervous, twitchy, handsome man. Very handsome. And his eyes. Those irresistible eyes. Nephrea's eyes. His eyes shone azure blue like her own.

She supposed she was content. Desperate last night to do stupid things to impossibly destroy herself, now in ecstasy over finally being saved by him. Even her headache faded.

Then the phone rang. It made him jump. He grabbed it from his jeans on the floor and put a finger up. She smiled and waited.

His lie was delicious. He told his wife that they still held a close watch. Cora could hear the bitch on the other end of the phone, shouting at the top of her lungs. Then Gabe's hand began shaking again.

She could be bought, Cora thought. Everyone could be bought. The look Mina had given her when she'd thanked her for the necklace revealed all. *Is that why I gave it to her?*

Gabe, why do you stay with her?

Anyway, even if she wasn't courting him, doubtless someone else would. He was a very handsome young man. His short hair and those half-grown whiskers on his cheeks and chin made him look unkempt and clean at the same time. That was Gabe—unclean and clean at the same time—shiny and tarnished. His quietness was adorable. She could buff out his shine. His nervousness was delightful. She adored his neuroses. Danny had had neuroses. She could ease his anxiety ... or stoke it, and be entertained as hell by it.

She'd fuck him again, when the time was right. But after fucking him, she would love him. She would care for him, protect him, and live with him as she had with Danny. She was disturbed by this, for it would lead to pain. One day he would die too. But without him? That was absolutely unthinkable.

"Anything the matter, Gabe?" Cora asked coyly.

He sighed and shoved his phone back into his pocket. Then he ran a hand through his short hair, sat down by the edge of the bed and nodded.

"She's pissed," he said, "and she has every right to be. It's late. They've been waiting in the lobby of our hotel for two hours."

"You were helping a friend in need. She should understand that."

"No, Cora, she doesn't understand that. And I think I did more than help a friend in need."

"It helped," she quipped with a giggle. She placed a hand on his shoulder, looking as if she had a solution. "I'm hungry. Would you like to grab something for lunch?"

"I can't," he said, shaking his head, but he hardly looked like he wanted to refuse. "I've got to head back. It's nearly two."

"That's why I'm starving. I tell you what, I know the perfect place. It's downtown. We can go there, grab a bite, then you can go on your way. I owe you for all your kindness. Besides, it's already late. It wouldn't hurt for her to wait a little longer."

She stared into his eyes. They were jumpy, but they settled on hers. Then he leaned his forehead on hers and laughed.

"What are you up to, Cora?"

"What's that supposed to mean? I want to eat. With a friend."

"You think we can just be friends after this afternoon?"

"Stop being such a prude," she said, hitting his hand. "It's sex, that's all. It's nothing. Humor me and come eat with me. I'll miss you so much when you're gone. Have lunch. I never forgot our dinner a few months ago. I think of it a lot. Since you must go and re-join that *bi*—" He quickly turned away in anger. "Sorry—your wife. If you must go back and join her, at least have lunch with me. I'm a very lonely woman, you know."

He shook his head at that, but then laughed.

"Why are you interested in me?" he asked. "You could have anyone you want—why me?"

She backed away, feigning ignorance. "What are you talking about? We're just friends. I just want—"

"You want to fuck me. You've wanted to since we met. Now it's done. Why me?"

"*Fuck you?*" She laughed hysterically. "*Fuck you?* What language. I love it! How vulgar, Gabe. But please, don't be embarrassed when I tell you, I wasn't talking about fucking you. I was asking you out for a lunch date between *friends*—"

"You said you confided in me," he said, shaking his head. "You wanted to be authentic. Stop acting. If we're really *friends*, tell me straight what you want."

"Okay, you're right." She sat up straight in the bed, her breasts still not covered and her red hair running down her shoulders. Then she blinked her lovely azure eyes and looked straight into his. He didn't turn away, but he looked nervous. "Gabriel, I will be absolutely straight with you—*since we're friends*. I'll be *au-then-tic* and stop playing games. I want to eat lunch. I'm very hungry. Would you care to join me?"

He laughed again. They both did.

"And one more thing," she added, raising a finger, "as your *friend*. I will tell you in all honesty, you are a very handsome, attractive man." He averted his eyes but still smiled. She raised her hand again. "So, I don't know what the fuck you're talking about when you're asking why I like you. There are a lot of girls who would like you. If you have one problem, young man, it's your confidence. But there are no games here. I'm simply hungry."

"Quick?" he asked with a deep sigh and a roll of his eyes. "Something close to my hotel?"

"Yeah. And real speedy. I promise."

"All right, Cora."

After she pulled on her cherry-red jumpsuit, Gabe accompanied her to the garage. As they walked down the halls, they passed the living room, where the bouncer slouched on a couch, watching TV. Grace walked by, wearing tight shorts and a short white T-shirt that showed her belly button. Her blond hair was tied in a ponytail behind her. Grace leaned over Cora's face as they walked by and gave her a kiss on the cheek. Then she winked at Gabriel. Hashan was there too. She caught him in the kitchen, feeding a bottle to the baby. They acted like nothing had happened the night before—and they all acted like it was their home. She loved that.

Cora opened a side door to the garage and touched a button, and the garage door rose up. The only vehicle there was a small black sports car—a McLaren. It was clean and in pristine condition. She winked at Gabe. She loved the look on his face. Reaching in her purse, she pulled out her keys and sunglasses. Gabe walked around the car, touching the dark metal curves in awe.

"I can't believe it," he said.

"Yeah. Nice, huh? It's a McLar-something or other."

"McLaren."

"Right, Gabe. A McLaren."

"I'll follow you."

"Oh no," she said, giggling. She reached over and hooked his arm. "You're coming with me, mister."

"Cora, my car's outside. I need to get back to the hotel."

"Don't worry, Hashan will follow us in your car. Just leave the key on the table near the door."

Gabe took one more tour around the car. He touched the black metal with his fingernail. It was his dream car. He shook his head.

"Come on!" she said "Jump in."

Gabe opened the passenger side, still shaking his head. Giggling some more, Cora jumped in the driver's seat. She ran her hand down the steering wheel. It took Gabe longer to recline in the bucket seats.

"It'll be fun, right?" she asked.

He just nodded.

She turned on the ignition and revved the engine, letting it roar. She got giddy, repeatedly pressing on the gas pedal. He laughed. Then she reached over and touched his shoulder.

"I'll take good care of you. I'm a really good driver. Don't worry. Just ... put your seat belt on."

And then they were off.

Had Gabe known the kind of driver Cora was, perhaps he would have run out of the house in terror and driven himself back to Toronto. He was a good sport, but the minute Cora performed a U-turn and hit the gas, he looked terrified. Cora loved it.

"The funny thing is," she shouted, competing with the car's engine, "I've never driven it. I just had it shipped yesterday."

"It's new?"

"Bumpy as hell, though, right?" she yelled. "Maybe I should

let you drive ... I could pop just vibrating from these fucking seats!"

"You could get a ticket."

She looked over at him, then simply pressed the gas harder. Spinning onto the highway, she sped up to way over a hundred miles per hour. She swerved around a few cars, playing with the car's responsiveness. She liked to slow down below the speed limit, then accelerate hard past other cars, pretending that she was on a racetrack. She was having a great time. They drove halfway there in half the time.

As soon as they approached the city limits, she slowed the car down and pulled onto an offramp, stopping at a gas station. She walked around the car, opened the passenger door, and dropped the keys on his lap.

"I'm being awfully selfish. You want to drive?"

She chuckled at how fast he ran over to the driver's seat.

"Do you like fast cars?" she asked, nearly shouting again over the roar of the engine as they got back on the road.

He nodded. "You just got this?"

"Yeah. I got it for you."

He looked a little disturbed by that. The car slowed. She ran a hand down her long hair, looking out the window. Taking some lipstick out of her purse, she pulled down the window visor and busied herself with her makeup.

"I got it for you." How diabolical, Cora. How terribly sneaky and sweet, and, at the same time ... sad.

It was a joke, but it brought both their moods down.

"I got it for you."

It actually upset her. He wasn't looking too happy about it either.

What game *was* she playing?

What was she going to do after lunch? Truth or a game, it brought home the point that that they were on their way to a lunch date after which they would never see each other again.

Shit.

He never asked her to clarify it. She knew he wouldn't. What would she say? Had she bought it for him? Maybe. The timing was sure interesting. She had known it would arrive the day of her party.

She spent the rest of the ride looking morosely out the window.

Clouds formed above them and it looked like it was going to rain. That was for him. She willed it, for that was her new mood.

Gabe turned to Cora and asked where they were heading.

"Turn right at the light," she said plainly. "There's a hamburger joint about a mile and a half down. They've got the best damn burgers in all of Toronto."

He burst out laughing. "Hamburgers?" he asked, shaking his head. "Only you, Cora."

They waited at the light. She started humming and finally turned to him, touching his arm again.

"You know, Mr. Cartwright, we're gonna be there in a minute. You're at the front of traffic. Now's your chance to really hit the gas when the light turns green."

He turned to her. She looked above her dark sunglasses with a sly grin. Then he obliged her. The car flew forward. She cried out in surprise with the engine and they laughed together again.

They almost shot by the hamburger joint. It was a little shop at the corner of the city street. Cora pointed to a nearby parking garage, and they parked.

Gabe seemed very amused at her choice. It was a casual chain restaurant with plastic chairs and tables lining the windows. It was busy, with a long line before the cashier. Gabe ran to get in line. Cora knew exactly what to order, and Gabe read off her order while Cora claimed a small table. She brushed the table off with a few napkins, cleaning the surface compulsively. He looked over at her from the line, even more amused. Then he walked back with two burgers, a large plate of fries and two cups of soda.

"Umm, yummy," she said after a bite of her burger. She looked at him. He still had an amused expression.

"Something funny?"

"You. I was expecting French cuisine. It's not often I get to ride in a McLaren with an eccentric billionaire to a fast-food restaurant."

"It's not fast food," she said with her mouth full. Then she raised a finger. "This shit is amazing. You can't get stuff like this in a highbrow restaurant."

He shrugged, then took a bite of his burger.

"Good, right?" she asked.

"Yeah."

"So, Cora," he said picking up a fry, "after all this, Hashan will meet me and—"

"Yeah," she said, scarfing down more food, "he'll bring over your car and—"

"I'm free to go."

"Free? Why wouldn't you be free?" she asked, trying to look hurt. He gave her a suspicious look, and she looked down at his plate. "You want your pickle?"

He chuckled and gestured for her to take it.

"Thanks. Hey, wasn't that drive fun, Gabe?"

"Yes, Cora."

She nodded, then looked outside, finishing her burger.

"Since I'll be leaving," he said with a cough, "maybe you can tell me more about what happened in your room."

"I fell in love with someone."

He didn't seem to be amused. "I was talking about the weather."

"I already told you."

"Sorry," he said, grabbing more fries. "You don't have to tell me if you don't want to. It's just that I'm leaving after this. I'm trying to figure you out, Cora Aregard."

She felt awful again at the reminder that he was leaving again.

"You okay?" he asked, biting into his burger. "Did I say something?"

"You told me you were leaving," she said with a shrug. "Anyway, I already told you about me, but you don't believe me. When you don't believe, it doesn't matter what miracles I show you."

"Why are you always sad?" he asked. "If you want to get to know me, want to be my friend, then tell me. Why tell me that you got the car for me? Why come on to me, only to pull away?"

"I've never pulled away," she said, shaking her head. "I've only waited for you to come to me."

"Why?"

She searched his face for a shred of intelligence. "Don't be stupid, Gabe. You're not dumb." She grabbed a handful of fries and turned away from him again.

They finished their lunch in silence.

He wasn't dumb. He was only stupid to himself. She sensed his intentions. She knew better than him that he was about to bolt back to his fucking wife.

"Go home and return to the bitch," she said suddenly.

"What? What's the matter?"

"Why don't you try to be authentic with me for once, Gabe? Or at least to yourself."

He gazed at her in shock. His act of ignorance only infuriated her more.

"You're gonna have to make a decision. I told you I didn't want to take you away from your family, but the truth is we are in love with each other, whether you admit it or not."

He just kept staring.

"Think of your time with me. Think about Cora and ask yourself why she has done so much to be near you. And then ask yourself why you chose to drive all the way back to my house to personally hand me my necklace. And then"—she started getting choked up—"ask yourself why you looked so forward to seeing me. Ask yourself why, when you aren't worrying about your fucking wife, you enjoy my company. Ask yourself why your hand shakes when you're forced to weigh your life in Manhattan on one hand with time spent with me on the other. And know, Gabe, that I will still be here. I won't leave Toronto until you return. And if you never return, know that Cora Aregard still spends every day thinking of you and will think of you until you no longer walk this earth."

"You're absolutely crazy," he said, almost in a whisper.

"Am I? Wish I was." She struggled not to cry. If she cried, he'd care for her again. He needed to go, and she needed to let him.

He got up.

The whole day was probably too fantastic for him. It was too much. He shook his head as if he was shaking her off.

"You'll be fine, Cora. Tomorrow you'll get drunk, maybe shoot up again. Maybe you'll show another poor soul your new joy car."

"That's mean," she replied, forcing a smile. "You're not 'another poor soul.' I know the value of pleasure, but I also know the power of love."

"Like your husband? He just passed."

Cora took a deep breath and covered her eyes. Despite the glasses, she was worried the red would show through. But she nodded, understanding that the only way for them to part was to fight. She had loved too many others to expect anything different. "If the one I love doesn't love me, I spend my life alone. This is what I've done for centuries. Married or not, when the spark is there, I don't let it go. If you leave, I'll be alone."

"Oh, fuck you, Cora! Give me a break on all this goddess bullshit."

Her eyes flickered redder, shining through the glasses and scaring Gabe. But anger was another thing she had spent millennia learning to control. The light faded.

"I have to go," he said. She reached over, but he quickly batted her hand away. "I'm not stupid. I know what you've been doing ever since you met me in LA. I think it gives you sick pleasure to chase a married man. You can sin all you'd like, but I believe in the sanctity of marriage. You talk of love, what of my love for my wife?"

She simply nodded under him. That seemed to make him angrier.

But then a tear rolled down her cheek under her sunglasses. If the tear had been a part of his perceived deception, it would have been a stroke of pure genius by the best manipulator of all time. But it wasn't fake. It was very real. And the authenticity of that was heartbreaking. It tore at Cora's heart and moved Gabriel too.

"Goodbye," she said simply.

"Where's my car?" he snapped.

"It's by the McLaren in the parking lot. Hashan's instructions were to leave it there."

"The keys?"

"Hashan will be there to hand them to you."

"Good ... then I'll be seeing you."

"Yeah. Goodbye, Gabe."

He looked down at her. She must have looked terrible. All the joy from all her antics was gone.

"Why did you shoot up last night? I suppose that was for me too?"

She looked up. She could see he cared, but he still clenched his fists and clenched his teeth in rage.

"Very good, Gabe. Yeah, I did that for you too."

Her sarcasm was intentional. She wanted to hurt him.

"I can't do this anymore. Goodbye."

He ran out.

She watched him through the window as he made his way all the way back towards the parking garage down the street. Then she sank her head in her arms and wept bitterly.

21

THE BOARD MEETING

C ora sat on her raised chair in the center of her second-story mansion with her finger to her chin, thinking—thinking and waiting. She was expecting guests—associates from Platinum Properties.

Her second story was now like the second floor of her beach house in Malibu. She had torn down the house, as she had planned, and replaced it with an exact replica. It had taken half a year, which was very fast—the original structure in Los Angeles had taken nearly two years. It sat atop the hillside, overlooking the picturesque grounds of Ontario Lake. It was lovely.

Her promiscuous tastes had turned the manor on Ontario Lake into a kind of brothel—one with no charge for admission and run by Madam Grace. The other leader was the bouncer—his name was Reginald. Reggie had become more and more at home as a part of her family. Cora loved him. He was a fun, mellow guy. Officially his job had been their security guard. But Hashan already held that title. Unofficially, he was their chief party animal. He and Grace became Cora's closest friends. The two of them together were diabolical. They ran the show, organizing wild parties and orgies while Cora stepped back and watched. Meanwhile, Hashan shook his head and did his best to look the other way.

The house developed a reputation. People from all over the Eastern Seaboard came to Madam Grace's house in order to party and fuck the morning away. The second floor was perfect, like the cherry on top, with its floor-to-ceiling glass wall and Cora's giant bed. The manor was openly despised by many and adored behind closed doors by many more. She received fines and threats by the police, but Cora had enough money and connections to deal with them.

It was a change for her. In LA, she was classy and underground. Here, the organization of daily social affairs was open and in her face. It was Grace. Grace loved Cora. If Cora was a lesbian, she would have found paradise in Grace. Being a hypersocial girl who loved company, and also Cora's best friend, the girl arranged "soirees" at their home almost every night.

But what of Gabriel? Despite wanting him and losing him, she still had the infernal job of protecting him. With the help of her bastard "husband" Orcus, she kept tabs on him, occasionally even visiting and watching him from afar in New York. The visits were absolute torture. She had to watch a man she was desperately in love with, but never go near. Like Lilly, she became his guardian angel.

Once, Gabriel was involved in a car accident off I-95—a really bad one. During the middle of the night, a strange woman in a black cloak visited him in the hospital. The next day, the doctors were shocked by completely healed fractures along his tibia, ribs and pelvis.

Cora couldn't stay away. She tried. It worked for a few months; then she started calling him. Austin had given her his private office number. Gabriel only spoke with her for a minute the first time, but then she called again a week later and they spoke for five. She started calling weekly. She made sure to play it safe and simply act like a friend. Initially he was anxious and uptight, but he eventually became very comfortable. And even just talking to him was better than nothing. He seemed to start to enjoy her calls. But neither seemed to want to meet in person again. They could talk, she could watch, but there would be no more touching. Not with a married man.

Then there was a problem.

The move from LA to Toronto had been a great challenge logistically. A lot of valuable possessions—paintings, furniture, and valuables—needed to be transported. Initially, everything had gone smoothly. But then the buyer ended up not wanting the gold bars under the glass windowpanes on the second floor, asking for them to be removed for monetary compensation. Apparently, it was too much of a liability. In order to seal the deal, Cora was forced to do what she didn't want to do—she had to break down the windows and remove the bars. She'd had them shipped from the US to Canada by train, but something didn't end up quite right in the transfer. She was assured by her realtor company and the movers that there was simply a delay in transport. But one day, Helen Morkey from Platinum Properties called her and told her the bars had actually been stolen; Cora was out seventy feet worth of gold bars, or, as Gabe had calculated, one hundred and twelve million dollars. She knew it was Imada, but Orcus wouldn't fess up.

The day it was discovered, Cora did something she had never done to Gabe before—she screamed at him over the phone. This time it was not in the name of love; it was over business. He reminded her that she almost sold the house with the gold bars included and unappraised anyway. She got crazier, even accusing him of stealing the gold himself.

Then she hung up on him.

Platinum Properties responded by sending associates.

And that was where she was now.

Platinum Properties sent three employees. Those were the

guests she was waiting for atop her raised throne chair as she sat thinking.

When the doorbell rang, midafternoon, she smiled, imagining their impression of her house, still in complete disarray following one of her bordello's typical soirees last night.

She heard Reggie meet them at the door. As they approached the top of the stairs, she examined them. One was an older gray-haired gentleman, the other two much younger—likely his employees.

She was pissed. It wasn't over the gold; there was something infuriating about the fact that Platinum Properties was paying her a visit, but not Gabriel. That just wasn't right. It made her seethe.

Like Gabe a year before in LA, the three stood under her elevated chair as if approaching a queen on a throne. She wore sunglasses and a tight jumpsuit—this time the navy-blue one. Her long high-heeled leather boots were crossed, and in one hand she held a martini, in the other a long-stemmed cigarette. She looked down upon them with disdain, brushing back her long red hair.

One of the younger associates physically shook under her. He was a young nervous blond man not much older than twenty. The other younger gentleman was a chubby bald dark-skinned man. He was cheerier and had a smile on his face. He seemed amused by her show. That made her angrier. The older man seemed impatient and rude.

"Ms. Cora Aregard?" asked the gray-haired man.

"Who the fuck do you think I am?"

"My name's Orpist. This is my associate, Hans, and our trainee, Anthony. We came as soon as we could regarding the transaction."

"You lost me over a hundred million dollars, Orpist." She turned and sipped her martini, sitting very straight. Occasionally, she would flash a glance down at them, then drink some more.

She got up and walked down three steps from her grand central chair behind the steps of her dais. All three looked to see what she was grabbing. She took out another cocktail glass that had been hiding behind the three marble stairs and climbed back into her chair. It was another martini. "Are you three thirsty?"

"Sure," said the young one. Cora lost her smile.

"Hashan can get you martinis, if you'd like. Or"—she waved her hand through the air—"we have wine. Very old wine. Worth a few hundred dollars. But not a hundred and twelve million."

"Fine, Ms. Aregard," said Orpist.

"Is Orpist your first name or your last name?"

"My last."

"What's your first?"

"Stewart."

"Call me Cora. You helped me move into this place, after all. It is lovely, isn't it? Call me by my first name. Call me Cora."

"All right, Cora."

Hashan entered from behind the three men, carrying a tray of drinks over his shoulder. He wore his familiar black suit with sunglasses.

"Ah, Hashan. Thank you," Cora said.

He looked at her suspiciously and disapprovingly, passing a martini to each of the men and two more to Cora. She set the two drinks down beneath her on the steps.

"I'd like to take this time to apologize over all of this," said Stewart. "I'm sure we'll get to the bottom of it." Cora stared at him over her sunglasses. Her naked eyes seemed to make him uncomfortable. "It seems it has to do with the moving service. We ordered an armed security guard. It's possible they were robbed. Well, anyway, your gold was insured, Cora. I'm sure we can get you cash."

"What makes you think I want cash? Cash is confining. I want gold. That was the deal I signed with your company."

"Well, I'm sure we can agree on something. But, Cora, the

authorities are looking into it. We may find the thieves and get you the bars back."

"I've already spoken with the authorities, Stewart. I'm quite sure they have no idea where my gold is." She stood and descended the steps, her hips swaying as she approached the three of them. She seemed to examine them. "Then I spoke with my friends in America. I can assure you ..." She ran a finger down the older man's suit and tie and touched his fluffy white beard, simply adoring it. Then she looked at his hooked nose and glasses. He was cute. She wasn't averse to older people. After all, they were really young next to her. "You won't find the gold. Just consider it stolen."

"Well, we're investigating—"

"Shh." She touched a finger to his lips. "Shh, I already told you. I have friends. Friends you wouldn't even dream of. I've already looked into it."

"All right," he said with a cough.

She removed her shades and looked into his eyes. He backed up. Then she moved on and looked at the fat one—Hans. Then there was the delicious boy—Anthony. The young one was delightful. He was so nervous in front of her that she reminded her of Gabe.

Gabriel. You dick! Where are you hiding?

"Get me replacement bars, Stewart," she said, leaping back up the stairs and slouching deep in her chair.

"Um ... I'll try, Cora. But we'll have to see what the insurance will cover. It may not reimburse the full cost of bars. If it doesn't, we may not be able to give you the exact same amount."

She wagged her finger and chuckled. "Nuh-uh-uh. You get me the full amount. Your company got quite a deal from my sale. Don't fuck with me. I asked for Gabriel Cartwright to come here, not you. Your company has already disappointed me. He could have given me my full reimbursement if he had come, I'm certain. I expect you to do the same."

Stewart looked at her funny. "Gabriel? I think he has other properties at the moment."

"Oh, yes, I'm sure he does."

She should have never mentioned him. She knew it was because of him that she had been in a foul mood. Last night, she'd barely even partaken in the activities at her party. She had just sulked. And it wasn't the gold. It was Gabe. How long did he expect her to wait? He couldn't even come to her when she was in need? It was his fucking job!

"We'll try to get you compensated, Cora," said the chubby one.

She downed the martini while staring at Hans, the fat one. Then she startled them by throwing her glass on the floor. It shattered near their feet along the marble tile.

"I know exactly what you gentlemen can do to compensate me."

She flashed each of them a smile. It seemed to make them more uncomfortable.

"Yes, Cora?" asked Orpist. "Well, that's why we're here. What would you like us to do?"

She ran a fingernail along one of the legs of her raised chair, then pressed her fingers down, slow and careful, over the dark shiny oak as if she was intent on comforting the swivel chair.

She rose up and sat down on the steps under it, folding her hands on her lap.

"How loyal are you three to your company and ... *Ms.* Cora Aregard?"

They looked at her, then at each other. The younger blond man started shaking. It was delightful. *Yes, just like Gabe.*

"We'll try to—"

"Don't try. Don't try. Never try. *Fucking do it!*"

They nodded hesitantly and stepped back.

"I promise I won't do anything you don't want me to do," Cora said with a smile. She picked up a remote by the chair and opened the red drapes covering the glass windows behind her. The sun shone bright on the three of them. They stared in awe at the beautiful vista—the sun's rays reflected along the lake and across the clear blue sky. Then she stood up and walked over to them again.

"First ... kneel."

"What?"

"Kneel before me and look up at me. Think of it as"—she waved her hand in the air again—"an apology. An apology for fucking up."

"Cora," Orpist said, "I don't think—"

"*Kneel!* Get on your knees. It's no big deal. Just do it!"

They looked at each other oddly again, but then Hans humored her. The rest followed, sinking down, slightly, before her. She loved it. They jumped as she reached into a pocket and brought out a curved knife. It was a long sharp one. She ran the dull side along her fingers and then gave the tip a kiss.

"You fuckers hurt me," she said, wagging the knife at them. At this point the older gentleman and the heavyset one looked about ready to bolt. "There was a time when sacrificing knights for the fucked-up actions of their kings helped reconcile mistakes. Now your king fucked up. The question is, how loyal are you? First you took my possessions, then you refused my man. It all puts me in a very, very pissy mood."

Stewart jumped up with his hand in front of him. "We're just going to leave. This is all too ... weird, Ms. Aregard, for us."

"You leave and you won't have an office to return to." And she meant it. "I suggest you wait for my proposal. But I told you ... I won't do anything you don't want me to do. It's all up to you. Of course, it's only your job. Go if you want to."

Stewart looked at her as if she was mad. She seemed to vindicate his suspicions by laughing. Then she got up and walked beside them. She ran a finger over Stewart's lips and spoke quietly, almost in a whisper. "Shh ... Stay." She spoke kindly.

"Don't go. I told you I wouldn't do anything to you that you don't want me to. I certainly won't slice your throat. Just relax."

They looked at each other again. Then Cora giggled. She touched the old man's gray whiskers and walked a few steps back, then turned her back to them and crouched close to the floor.

She took the knife and used it to slice the latex of her outfit. They didn't run. Apparently, they were transfixed by the truly, utterly bizarre act. She slowly cut through the latex, starting from her chest, then peeling it down like a banana all the way down to her waist. The sound of the cloth being cut echoed through the room as her guests stared in silence. She cut, sliced, and peeled until the suit was torn, revealing her pale naked skin underneath. Then she tore pieces of her outfit off her arm, her leg and her waist. She cut some more until every piece was removed from her naked body and thrown to the floor before them. Then she stood up straight, turned, and faced them with a wicked smile. The three were immobile, in complete shock. She threw the dagger to the side and it bounced along the marble floor, echoing across the hall.

She walked up close to them. First, she approached the older gentleman, violently grabbing his head and kissing him on the lips. He moved back at first, surprised, but then let her push her tongue into his mouth. The other two stared as she made out with the man who looked twice her age.

"Yummy," she said with a giggle.

Then she turned to the heavier one. She did the same to him. Last, most deliciously, she approached the young blond. He shook under her as she embraced him tight and enjoyed him the longest.

"Cora," stammered Stewart. "We're here—"

"Shhhhh," she said, turning to him. "If you'd prefer, I can grab the knife and cut you. Either way, I will have my sacrifice. It's just a business trip, right? A business meeting. I know what all you boys do on your business meetings. Maybe, just maybe, I might accept your apology when you three pat my back ...and ass ... and I"—she laughed, closing her eyes and rubbing her breasts before them—"pat yours."

They looked at her. She was likely the most beautiful woman they had ever seen—and she knew it. She quickly turned and walked back to her chair, swinging her naked hips as she walked. She knew they couldn't avert their eyes from her hips and the curves of her chest. She leaned slowly over to the floor and grabbed the other martini, then walked back in front of them. She poured some of the drink over her naked chest, slowly running her free hand over her breasts, nipples, and then down to her privates. Stewart turned away, but he didn't run. The other two stood motionless. She took a sip from the remnants of her martini and examined the three of them.

"Now, kneel before your Persephone. Show me your allegiance."

All three kneeled before her. She shattered another martini glass on the floor beside them and burst into laughter.

"Excellent, boys. Very loyal. Now, stand up and drop your pants."

22

DUSK

Cora jumped awake to the sound of a vacuum by the foot of her bed. She opened her eyes and looked around. A few candles were still lit, but most of the light came from outside under and around the red curtains by the window. By the foot of the bed, Hashan busily moved back and forth with the vacuum, holding the baby in one arm and moving the vacuum with the other. The baby was crying. She wasn't sure what was louder—the baby or the vacuum.

"What time is it?" she asked with a yawn.

"Three."

More crying grated Cora's ears.

"Three in the morning?"

"No, madam. Three in the afternoon."

He looked at her. He wore his usual black suit, but his sunglasses were tucked in a shirt pocket. He wouldn't have seen a thing had he been wearing them.

He turned off the vacuum, walked over to the central raised chair and pressed a button on a remote. The curtains opened. Hashan put on his shades and turned back to Cora. Cora yawned again and stretched out her arms. As she stretched, the soft black silk sheets fell from her naked body and exposed her breasts.

"Please don't forget, madam, that I am a man."

"Oh," she said quickly, pulling the sheets back up.

He took out a milk bottle from his pocket and tried to calm the child. It perked Cora up. Watching the stiff Hashan caring for a baby was hilarious.

After the baby calmed with the bottle in her mouth, Hashan sat the baby down on the marble floor and went over to the bar.

"Have they gone?" she asked loudly over the vacuum.

"Yes," he replied. "They left before sunrise."

"A fun night, Hashan. You wouldn't have expected it from their polished black suits. But my jaw is hurting. An awful lot."

She touched her jaw with a chuckle. He shook his head in disapproval and grabbed a few stray glasses and began washing them.

"We didn't mean to wake you, but it is getting late."

"Don't lie, Hashan," she replied. She squinted outside, admiring the view. "Sometimes you act like the father I never had."

She got up from the bed. She was still naked. For Hashan's sake, she walked over to a nearby nightstand and quickly grabbed a white cloth robe. Then she made her way over to the window and looked out along the lake.

A few ships were sailing out into the distance. There were also a few people walking along the shore. It was Saturday, and her property was always covered by visitors on the weekend. She didn't mind. Sometimes she enjoyed people watching from the comfort of her home. She watched fathers and sons fishing or families picnicking. It was nice. Then she stared along the trees and bushes lining the rocky shore.

"Did you have a nice night, madam?" Hashan asked sarcastically, running a towel over a glass. Cora mused that he looked like a bartender.

The baby was lying on the ground, sucking on her bottle and playing with a beer bottle cap with her feet.

"Always fun to be above ground."

"Indeed." He turned on a faucet and started washing more glasses. "Madam, I noticed, when I welcomed the three gentlemen, that one had a ring on his finger. The other was young enough to still be in high school."

Is he being a little shit this morning?

"Can you get me a cup of coffee?"

"Of course."

"Or perhaps a martini? It is, after all, late."

She stared outside. She didn't like her butler's tone, and she was beginning to get sore over being woken up.

"I'll make you coffee."

He's definitely being a shit.

Hashan stopped cleaning and turned on the coffeemaker. When it was ready, he put just the right amount of sugar and cream for Cora's tastes. He walked over and handed it to her. She didn't look at him; she just stared outside.

"Perhaps an ice pack too," she said, grabbing the cup as she stared outside. She opened and closed her mouth, wincing in pain. "My jaw is just killing me." She laughed again.

"Cora," he blurted out in irritation, "I'm not one of your guests to mess with. I'm your friend. That's not funny."

She turned to him. "What's up with you? Why are you being such an asshole this morning?"

"Perhaps because it's not the morning. It's three o'clock."

She squinted at him. Then he turned coldly and walked back to the bar. She shook her head and sipped the cup.

The truth was, she couldn't recall much. She had pleasured the prim and proper associates from Platinum Properties with her mouth and then partied the rest of the night away. Her bar was left open until early the next morning, and then she'd vomited and collapsed. That was all she remembered—until Hashan had woken her up.

"Sorry, Hashan." He simply nodded and went back to cleaning the glasses. "But ... why are you being such a prick?"

He looked at her, considering her question. Then he put the glass lightly down and walked to her. And then, he did something she loved. He took his glasses off. His small bird eyes and his bushy eyebrows just looked at her. She really loved him.

"Honestly?" he asked.

"Of course. Always."

"I'm worried about you. Partying all night is one thing, but sleeping till sunset is another. It's not like you, Cora."

She didn't answer him for a while, just sipped her coffee.

"I think I need to see him again." She was surprised at how sad she sounded.

"Yes," he replied solemnly.

"I ... I've tried to do what's right. Now I'm only doing what's wrong." She cocked her head. He was staring out at the water too. "I noticed the ring and the kid, too, Hashan ... only, you know I don't have a fucking soul to worry much about, anyway."

"But they do."

"Hmm. You always know the wrong thing to say at the wrong time," she said with a nod. She blew a thin mist from her cup and then took a deep breath. "You know, it will be winter soon. Then this lovely view won't be so bright and cheery. Everywhere will be snow. Then, perhaps I can find a way to just die. To fall asleep and never wake under the ice. That's what I really want. That is what would make me happy. Instead of these fleeting moments. Even if I finally see Gabriel, he will only live for so long. If there is a way to destroy me—you know, burn me to cinders and watch me never breathe again—it would make me very happy. If you ever find a way, Hashan, never hesitate. Just destroy me. Blot me out. So that I don't have to keep waking up in shit ... and hurting others."

"I know, Cora."

"No, you don't." She kept staring outside. "You're a mortal man who's done his duty. You've followed in your grandfather's footsteps all in order to take care of a crazy woman who can drink and fuck while you pretend that you're your grandfather. You don't understand the world because it is only measured in decades for you, not millennia. You can accept these fleeting images." She sipped from her coffee. Now she was being the *shit*. "I can't."

"I've accepted my life with you."

"Then you're an idiot. You should leave and enjoy your life instead of hanging around a fossil like me."

She walked away from him and climbed up onto her elevated chair, angrily pulling out cigarettes and a lighter from her robe and lighting one.

"Would you like me to leave you alone, madam?"

"No, it's too late. You've already fucked up my day."

He shrugged and returned to the bar, cleaning glasses.

He had cleaned everything. She marveled at how spotless everything was. She searched for any remaining mementos from the evening, but her butler had removed every trace of last night's chaos.

Or so she thought, until her eyes fell on the baby again. Oddly, the baby was jerking up and down on the floor.

She dropped her cigarette and leapt off her chair.

Hashan ran beside her. "What's the matter?"

"Baby's not breathing!"

Cora picked up the baby and looked at her head, then opened her mouth. "She's got something in her throat! Damn it, can't you watch her for one second, Hashan! What is so hard about that!"

Cora reached in but couldn't snag the object. She turned the baby over and gave her a few forceful blows on the back with the heel of her hand.

Finally a bottle cap flew out of the baby's mouth—the cap from a beer bottle.

Cora lifted the baby and hugged her tight.

"Don't do that, Baby! Don't you ever do that to Mommy, 'kay? Are you all right, Baby? You okay?"

The baby started crying terribly. Cora held her tight and focused her mind on the baby's body, healing any wounds in the baby's mouth and throat.

"Why can't you keep an eye on her!" Cora snapped at Hashan, looking up.

"She looks better in your arms, madam."

"What? What did you just say?"

Cora looked down. She hadn't even realized she was rocking the child, who was now healed and finally quite content, quiet and totally at peace in Cora's arms.

"Don't do that, baby! Baby, don't you ever do that again."

Hashan reached for the baby, but then she started crying again. "She'd rather be with you, madam."

"Take her," she said, pushing the baby to him again. "Shut up, Hashan, and take Baby downstairs to Grace."

"All right, madam. As you wish. But ... you know, Cora, I really wish we would give her a name, instead of calling her Baby."

"Fuck off, Hashan. I don't like your attitude today. Call her whatever the hell you want. And don't wake me up ever again."

Hashan took the baby. Cora looked down at the infant and couldn't resist a smile. "She's cute, though, isn't she? Just ... just get her away from me. I'll only hurt her more. A baby shouldn't be around a beast."

"You're not a beast."

"Yeah, Hashan?" she said, heading back to her window. "Well, I'm no mom."

"You should see Gabriel," Hashan said without turning as he walked to the stairs. "See him. I know it will make you feel better."

"Maybe," she said. "Yes, I suppose that's why I was so upset. I was an idiot."

"Yes, madam," Hashan said, standing by the stairs.

She laughed at his formal speech.

"I'll visit him in New York. Maybe I'll cheat again. Why did he have to get married?"

"As you wish, madam."

She laughed again. "Yeah. Anyway, maybe you're right. Maybe I should be getting up early and enjoying the morning while it's still sunny and nice outside."

"I think so, Cora."

Cora stood before the view of the lake. She leaned her forehead on the glass, watching a family below meandering down a dirt trail to the water.

The baby started crying.

"Downstairs, Hashan," Cora said, cocking her head back at Hashan. "Baby's crying again. Go see if Grace can take care of her."

Hashan looked down at the child in his arms and shook his head in frustration. He headed to the stairs, but then stopped and walked back to Cora offering her to hold the baby again.

Cora furrowed her brow and reluctantly grabbed Baby. She looked down at the baby's bright blue eyes. "When you grow up, nymph, you'll learn to hate me like I hated my mother. Just like that. Just like how I hate Sara. That's what happens to us little girls when we grow into big ladies. Right, cutie?"

Cora could swear she saw the baby frown. Cora giggled and held the baby close to her chest. She felt a glow holding her. Then she kissed her head and rocked her in her arms while staring out at the lake.

"I'm sorry," she whispered in the baby's ear.

23

CONFIDENTIALLY, I AM

Cora rode with purpose astride her new black Ducati, weaving through the streets and alleyways of Manhattan, swerving around the iconic yellow taxis and sandwiching herself between the lines and lines of cars. She tried her best to pretend there were no people, ignoring the blaring horns and the shouts of passersby. The crowds were a bit of a shock after living for months in the quiet suburbs of Toronto, but she liked the energy. Blasting music in her helmet, she nearly ran over a pedestrian, ran a few red lights and then ignored the endless honks and shouts.

She passed the building where Platinum Properties resided, thinking about her planned rendezvous. She wondered if Gabriel was still working hard behind his desk somewhere high up above her in the tower. They had finally agreed to meet. She had asked him to visit her again in Toronto. When he had refused, she'd tricked him into a short meeting near his office. At first, Gabe had suggested the morning. She'd refused. Then he'd suggested lunch. But that would never do. Finally, she'd told him to meet her after work. There had been a long silence on the phone and then a laugh.

The sun dipped down the horizon below the surrounding walls of concrete and glass. It was getting dark along the narrow streets. And it was cold. There were clouds above her, and the wind cut through her thin coat like ice.

Her date was scheduled for seven. It was nearly six. She cursed and rode a little harder. She was late. Her plan was to go to a nearby hotel, make herself irresistible, then walk across the street to the restaurant. She had already arranged for her dress to be delivered to her room at the adjacent hotel. She knew it would take her longer than an hour to get ready. By seven thirty, she had to send a text to Mr. Cartwright, telling him she was running late. Gabriel sent a sweet text telling her not to worry about it.

When finally pretty, she jaywalked across the street, avoiding the long trek to the intersection on the far end. Then it began to lightly snow. The cold bit into her skimpy dark blue skirt, bare arms and lower legs. She shivered a little and then tripped, nearly ruining all of her hard work by landing in a pothole. Cursing, she jumped at the sudden blaring of car horns and then ran as quickly as she could. She ran a hand along her blond hair, grateful to feel no new kinks, then checked her ears for her long gold-and-diamond earrings, readjusted her infamous diamond-studded necklace around her neck, lifted and adjusted the dress over her bosom and darted the rest of the way across the street.

Her destination was a rooftop restaurant at the top of the skyscraper. The elevator ride up over fifty stories seemed endless. She averted her eyes from strangers—they all gazed at her. One even tried to flirt with her, but she uncharacteristically ignored him.

The restaurant took up much of the upper level of the skyscraper. It was a very swanky place with nice white tablecloths and dressed-up waiters and waitresses, the guests dressed more in black-tie attire than casual—not much different than Tillman's, but a little chicer. On one side were floor-to-ceiling windows looking over the Manhattan skyline. Cora looked at the dark blue carpet and the stylish décor along the walls. The large room was lit by candles and faint yellow lamps. The white-and-black walls separated by white columns were decorated with modern paintings—more blocks of color than anything of substance. It was very tasteful. She smiled and nodded at her friend's choice.

The maître d' welcomed her. Cora was amused by her expression. Cora must have looked like a young princess dressed like a queen. It was a strange combination, but perfect for her. *Well, Gabe, you wanted au-then-ticity. Here I am.*

She spotted Gabriel sitting at a table at the far corner between two large windows. He was sipping wine with one hand and checking his phone with another. She thought perhaps he was checking the time or answering one of his wife's annoying texts. He wore glasses—that was new. She had never seen him wear glasses. Maybe reading glasses? It made him look older. She could see pieces of a breadstick by his plate and a glass of water half-full. He was dressed formally in a nice dark blue suit, slightly unshaven, but his hair was short and neatly combed to one side.

He turned and saw her carefully walk down the hallway in her tall high-heeled shoes, swaying her hips. He nearly dropped his glass of wine. Cora smiled at his gaping mouth. She ran her hand across her long hair to make the moment perfect. Then she smiled again, this time a genuine smile. It worked. All her preparation was worth it. To finish him off, she stood over him and bent down, lightly kissing his cheek. She giggled as he blushed.

"Cora ... you look stunning."

"It's good to see you, Gabriel," she said. "It's been a long time."

She sat across from him at the small table and looked out the window. She flashed a smile as he turned back. He looked at her. Then he gestured to the table. Sitting in front of her was a martini. She laughed, took out the olives, and delicately sipped it.

"Yummy," she said with a smile. "Thank you. I told them you were the only man who knew just how to treat your clients."

"Who?"

"Your associates."

"Oh," he said, looking disturbed for a moment. Then he noticed the necklace and pointed at it. "It looks lovely on you."

"Thanks, Gabe. I'm happy to have it back."

"Your hair ... it's blond again."

"Yeah. It's natural. You seemed to like it the last time we had dinner—remember? You said then you wanted me to be *au-then-tic*." She smiled coyly, giggled a little, and raised her glass to him.

He laughed.

"You look quite handsome and distinguished yourself, Mr. Cartwright."

He put his phone back in his pocket and took out some papers from under his chair. She lost her smile. He noticed, but he nervously rustled through them anyway. "Look ... I have good news."

"Yes, Gabe?"

"I can get your gold back. I had it arranged—you know, spoke with Aussie. I can't believe this happened. The sale of your LA home meant a lot to our company and—"

"The future sales of my offshore sites."

"Yeah. You mean a lot to the company. So much that I wasn't afraid of meeting with you this time."

"*Afraid?* Why on earth would you be afraid of meeting with me?" she asked. Then she reached out a hand for him to hold. He hesitated but then smiled and held her fingers. His hand shook a little. "Friends, right?"

He quickly pulled his hand away, raising his eyebrow. "Sure ... I mean, yeah. Look, I'm really sorry, Cora, about the last time we met. Things were happening so fast, it overwhelmed me."

"We've been through this on the phone."

"I know, but now you're here in person. This time we're meeting over *my* apology."

"Apology accepted," she said sweetly.

He chuckled.

There was an uncomfortable silence, but Cora was giddy inside. She knew this "business" meeting was a complete sham. His nervousness gave away his true intentions. He still cared for her. Maybe this time, there would be no more hesitation ... or pain.

Then her impatience got the better of her. She wanted to play with him—toy with him a little—just have fun. He looked away, seeming to sense it. She took a breadstick and rolled it around her tongue, making sure to stick out the tip of her tongue so he could see it. She stared outside, pretending to be oblivious to him.

"Anyway, we can fully compensate you the money lost from insurance, Ms. Aregard," he said stiffening himself in his chair. "Then, if you so choose, we can buy back its full weight in gold. I heard about your deal with Orpist. I can draw up the papers and you can sign for the transaction now. It's a very fair deal. Platinum Properties will lose a little over it, but Austin's confident that you're worth it as our client."

He took out a pen and pushed some papers to her.

"I expect full compensation, Mr. Cartwright," she replied, just as professional and cold. She threw the breadstick down on the plate and took a long swig of her drink.

He chuckled. Surprised, she turned and met his gaze. "What?"

"I've missed you. I've forgotten how much funnier you are in person."

"Hmm. Well, you can be a little dick," she said, but she smiled. "And a liar. What you say you want and what you do or don't do are completely different. When you reach out, then pull away and act like we're friends, that's a bunch of *in-au-then-tic* bullshit."

"We haven't seen each other for months and we're already fighting?"

"We're not fighting, Gabe."

He raised an eyebrow again. Then he sipped some wine.

"Cora, do you have any idea what it looks like for a lady dressed like you to swear like that?"

"No. Tell me, Gabe, what the fuck does it look like?" She paused, making sure to smile a sly, wicked sexy grin. "Tell me, Gabriel, how should I talk when I dress *like this*?"

He rolled his eyes and smiled, looking away from her.

"Where the fuck is the waiter?" she asked.

As if summoned by her comment, the waiter rescued them.

"Good evening," the waiter said. He was a jolly short gentleman dressed in a tux, his long black hair slicked back and a distinct tattoo of roses along his neck. He looked polished and professional. "Welcome. Have you had a chance to look at the menu?"

"No," Cora said. "But we're ready to order." They both looked at her funny. "I'll have a steak—rare—a baked potato, and something really fucking spicy." Then she gestured to him. "Get him a steak too, but make it medium. He doesn't like his shit as wild and gamey, you see—unlike me. And get me another fucking drink."

"Very well, madam," the waiter said, looking at her oddly.

"Will you stop it?" Gabe asked with a smile.

"What? What the fuck did I say?"

"I can be a real trashy bitch, you know," she whispered. "Or" —she shrugged and blew him a kiss—"someone real cultured and sweet."

Then he spoiled her fun. He just shrugged and drank more. "Whatever. It's good to see you again."

She looked out the window at the city lights for a long while, just enjoying the view.

"It's very beautiful," she said. "Thank you. I haven't been up in the clouds like this in a very long time."

Then she turned to him and squinted, examining him. "Can I tell you something? I enjoy our little talks. You know, sometimes it's very boring in Toronto, and having the chance to talk with you on the phone is very special to me. I value our friendship."

His eyes met hers and seemed to get lost for a moment. She could feel it inside. She was mesmerized too. Hypnotized.

"You can't help but be what you are," he finally said, shrugging again.

"I'm trying to say something nice," she said, hitting the table. "What the hell does that mean?"

"It's just you're addicted," he replied with a shrug, sipping some wine. "All you do is swear and think of sex."

"I've done little of it since ..." She thought for a moment, then she stopped before telling him any more.

"Cora, you're addicted. I heard what happened to my associates. At least, there are a lot of rumors."

"That was fun," she admitted with a nod.

"We're friends," he said with a sigh. "You don't have to come on to me."

"Yeah, friends. Of course." *Do friends dress like this for business meetings?*

He took her hand. The act seemed so weird after his statement that she couldn't help but look at him as if he was crazy.

"I've valued our moments too." He chuckled. "My life is ... plain. You give me a little spice. I like that. I like your calls, Cora."

She nodded with a smile but pulled her hand away gently. That was sweet.

She wondered if it still snowed outside. It was hard to tell, being so high up from the ground in the dark. There were remnants of ice along the borders of the glass. She reached over and touched a pane. It certainly was cold.

"How are you doing?" he asked. "Is everything well up there in Toronto? Hashan?"

"Just fine."

Their food arrived. The steak was nice and rare and the baked potato looked lovely. She liked the presentation. The steak had garnishes rising above it like pillars of a thin green statue, and the sauce covered half the meat over half the plate. Even the baked potato wasn't simple—it was cut inside in pieces with a sauce running over and along the border. The plate had a modern feel to it. She always liked the presentation of food. It was like a kind of primal art. The chef cooked it; you looked at it, savored it and then you ate it. It was like sex. You looked at a man's body, you touched his hard chest and the hardness around arms, legs, and ass, then you ran your cheek along the stubble of his cheek, you licked and sucked each other, then fucked. If done slow and measured, it was art too. Like the iconic statue of David. You admired the hard form and edges of his body, then you touched him with your eyes. She loved that. She looked at Gabe. She touched him with her eyes. She remembered seeing him naked, now so long ago. Then she examined his white shirt and short thin black tie, his small vest and his long black slacks. He had the same body under there. He wasn't an Adonis ... she had had much more handsome men. But he had confided in her with care. That made her wet. Dates were like sex. Meals shared were like sex between two lovers—you shared a meal, then, if all went well, you shared your bodies. Either way, it was the act of sharing, touching and fucking that made life—touching and fucking the right stuff, anyway.

She laughed at her dirty thoughts, then put a hand over her mouth, realizing she'd laughed out loud.

"Something funny, Cora? You've been real quiet. You okay over there?"

"Aha," she said, munching on some potato. "The food's really good here, Gabe."

"Not as good as burgers?"

"No," she said with a chuckle, "those burgers are amazing."

"I ...," Gabe said hesitantly.

"What?"

She picked up two chili peppers from the edge of her plate

and looked at them. These were the spicy parts of her dish. She shrugged and threw them in her mouth. Then her eyes widened.

"*Fucking hot!*" Cora yelled.

"Quiet, Cora!"

"Jesus! Fucking hot!" she repeated, waving a hand before her mouth and searching the room. "Where's some water!"

Gabe burst out laughing.

"It's not funny!"

"Hold on." He jumped up and dabbed his mouth with a napkin, then ran over to find a waiter. The waiters were nowhere to be found. Cora grabbed the only liquid near her—Gabe's glass of wine. Her martini glass was empty. She guzzled down the rest of his glass. She watched Gabe searching the room for a waiter. He finally gave up looking. He grabbed the nearest glass from an empty table and ran back over. He handed it to her, but she refused.

"You don't know where that's been."

"Oh, come on! Just drink it."

"No," she said, running her hand over her forehead. Her skin was beet red. Gabe couldn't stop laughing. Now people were turning from his laughter. "I'm not touching a dirty glass of water. Stop laughing. It's not funny. Just get me some water—*fresh* water."

"It's just two chilis. I thought you liked spicy food?"

"No, not really. I'm Greek, not Spanish. Hey"—she looked at his plate—"why didn't you get peppers? That's not fair."

"I didn't ask for them. Rather, you didn't order them for me."

"*Fuck!*" she yelled. "Get me some water, Gabe. Right now! I mean it, mister. Get me some fucking water!"

The waiter was flagged by Gabe. He ran over.

"Yes?"

"Some water for her, and hurry."

"But?" He looked at the glass.

"Just a fresh one."

"Okay."

"Hurry!" she said.

"Sorry. I'll be right back."

Then Gabe laughed again. "Some goddess." His phone buzzed. He glanced at it, then stuck it back in his pocket. Finally, the waiter brought over a fresh glass of water. She downed the whole glass. Then it was the waiter's turn to laugh.

"So sorry, miss. You requested spice and the chef added chilies. There was also chili in the sauce."

"No problem. Get me another four, would you? And I finished his glass of wine—get him another."

"No," objected Gabe. "I'm all right."

"Nonsense, Gabe. We're celebrating. I'm about to get my money back." Then she turned to the waiter again. "Another glass for the gentleman. And get him a few peppers too. It's just not fair."

"Very well, madam."

"Cora, I've already had two glasses."

"So? You driving? It's New York. You can get a cab or something." She looked around for more water. Then she grabbed the so-called dirty one. "Fuck it," she said under her breath and drank it down.

"Tell me, how is it that a so-called goddess can't eat spicy chili peppers?" Gabe asked with a smile. The attack of spice seemed to lighten him up. It was catching and she laughed.

At first, she shrugged, but he stared and waited for an answer, so she answered him straight. "What your race once called gods are not the gods you know of today."

"Really? How so?" He seemed genuinely interested. He didn't look like he believed her, but he was curious.

She looked at him for a moment, debating whether he could take it. She didn't want to push him away again, but he was in good spirits. She drank the rest of the "dirty" water and nodded at him.

"I'm not a *god*. I'm a being that's immortal. I'm not Jesus or Buddha. You can think of me more like ... an alien, I suppose." She paused for a moment, looking for the waiter. She wanted more alcohol. "Anyway, forget it. You're already looking at me like I'm crazy."

"No. Go on. It's fascinating."

He had a grin on his face. He was really amused at her words. It upset her a little. She was confiding in him and he was acting like it was all a joke.

She took the papers and quickly glanced through them and then asked him with a gesture where to sign. Then she said, "Maybe you should answer your bitch wife who just messaged you instead."

"Nice try. You're trying to piss me off to change the subject and fight again."

"I've already showed you, but you don't believe me. Wasn't changing the weather enough?"

"I can see with my own eyes," he replied, looking her over. "Anyone seeing you right now would not doubt your divinity."

"That's sweet." She smiled. "Very kind. Thank you."

"You are," he continued, "the most beautiful woman I've ever seen. I don't doubt you are different. You also look young. If I were to pick you out on the streets, I would guess you're twenty-two."

Older than twenty-two.

The waiter rescued her again by handing her another glass of water and Gabe a glass of wine.

"You're becoming a bit transparent." He lifted his wine. "This is the oldest trick in the book—drugging me with wine."

"If I wanted to drug you, Gabe, I wouldn't have used wine," she said with a wink.

He laughed, then shrugged and drank down half the glass. She raised an eyebrow at him and he laughed again.

"So, you're Greek?"

"I'm Persephone, Gabriel. Persephone, the goddess of the underworld and the goddess of spring."

"Go on."

"You want more?"

"Oh, yes."

"I'm one of the twelve Olympians from Hellena," she said. "Or Greece ... Persephone ... once abducted as a teenager and taken down into the depths by the god Hades. He took me from my fields in Azure with his flying chariot and dropped me down into his underworld. He tricked me into partaking of the pomegranate. Then he did terrible things. I lived for many millennia in the wretched city of Tartarus—a forsaken land as close as you can get to your hell. But, then, in time ..."

She abruptly stopped.

Something was wrong. Someone was listening to her tale, and it wasn't just the mild-mannered realtor from Platinum Properties. With her keen hearing, good enough to hear ten floors down, she heard something unnatural in the air when she started explaining her secret past. That worried her. It was forbidden for Imada to reveal themselves publicly. When she looked back at Gabe, he looked worried too.

"Is everything all right?" he asked.

"Yeah." She feigned a smile. "I ... I made my way above ground," she continued, much quieter. "*Greek myth*," she emphasized, "said that the abduction created the seasons. Have you heard this story? Indeed, there was little snow and ice before my abduction. It is said my return above ground represents the beginning of spring. Then, every year, the earth repeats the abduction by turning frigid cold to mark the anniversary—winter —and then warm again in spring. It's a beautiful myth, really.

"It's myth. I ..." She paused for a moment, listening again. "Persephone ... did live for a millennium under the earth, then rose above ground and stayed up here with man as a lady. Rising as Proserpina with man in Rome and living all the way through the conversion of Rome by Constantine to Christianity—up to the modern day. Under Constantine, Persephone converted."

"You're Christian?" he asked, very amused.

"Yeah. Got a problem with that?" she snapped.

"Have you read the Bible?"

"Yes. Cover to cover."

"Did you skip over the parts about sin?"

"I've asked for forgiveness. I've gone to confession ... I used to be a lot worse."

Gabe laughed and so did she.

"Anyway," she said, shrugging, "Persephone witnessed the destruction and pillage of the Roman empire by the barbarians of the north. For many decades, she was forced to live in caves, avoiding man. The times were apocalyptic, and if you were Christian, you would indeed have thought it was the end times. Then she lived through the Dark Ages, through the plague—many of them. Hundreds of years of poverty and shit, watching more people die ..." She stopped for a moment, looking to the window with a shrug. "Well, you asked why I'm sad."

"Then the Renaissance?" he asked with a smile.

"Yep," she said after a long pause. "The Magna Carta, then Leonardo da Vinci—yes, the Renaissance. The Spanish Armada, the rise of France, the rise of England, American independence ... all of it, at least the stories you've heard—many are half-truths."

"I'm fascinated." He didn't say it to be cruel. He almost said it just to say something.

"Then the United States and then Los Angeles."

"Persephone?"

"Persephone," she said with conviction. He removed his spectacles and stared at her. "There's not much more to tell."

"No, I think there's a lot more."

"You can google the rest."

"I am googling the rest."

"Cute, Gabe." She chuckled. "I—I learned how to conceal

myself ... or to fit in. I also learned how to make money. I had a lot of time. And, yes, I've sinned. But I've done what I can to make amends to God. I am—"

He put his glasses in his pocket and pulled the papers back to him, checking to make sure all the spaces were signed.

"Thank you, Persephone."

She smiled at his use of her ancient name. "You asked. Now you can think me mad if you wish."

"It certainly fits. But it does sound completely and utterly crazy."

She looked down at his plate. There were two peppers there.

"Your turn," she said, gesturing to the chilies.

He took both of them and threw them in his mouth. She giggled, taking two more from a separate plate and joining him. They stared at each other. It didn't take long for them to grab their waters. This time, the waiter had made sure to be prepared by bringing them two glasses.

"Jesus, those are hot!" he said. "What sort of chilies are these?"

"Pot primo, I'm guessing," she said.

"How do you know?"

"I've been around."

"And you're ... Greek?" he asked, coughing, his face flushing red.

"Originally."

She looked at him. His disbelief was annoying. She had already shown him miracles. What more did he need?

But then, she thought of the perfect thing. She nodded at him and said a few words in fluent Greek—Ancient Greek. The sentences translated into how true love cannot ever be avoided, and how she loved him.

Upon her utterance of the ancient tongue, she heard a disturbance again. This time, she was sure of it. It was muffled but sounded like a shout. As if someone objected to what she had said. She looked carefully around the restaurant. If they wanted a fight, she'd oblige them. But they never showed themselves to her. Imada feared her.

When she turned back, Gabriel's smile had vanished and he looked spooked.

"Sorry, I don't mean to frighten you," she said.

"What did you just say?"

"Ancient Greek," she answered. "What language would you like it to be?"

"How 'bout Spanish?"

"*El verdadero amor nunca puede ser evitado. Te amo, Gabriel.*"

"How many languages do you know?"

"Most of them. Pretty good for a twenty-two-year-old, eh, Gabe?" She drank the rest of her water.

"Did you want something more to drink?" he asked.

"Of course."

He flagged the waiter. His mood seemed somber, but that was okay with her because she was spending time with him.

But something felt wrong. She felt a premonition that something very bad was about to happen. The restaurant no longer felt safe, and she worried for Gabriel and everyone else.

He reached in a pocket and checked his phone. Then he sighed.

"I know you're a wonderful person, Cora. I've always known."

"I think we should go," she said.

"What?" he asked, confused.

The waiter walked over. Gabriel held her hand, looking at her, bewildered.

"Umm," Cora muttered, turning to the waiter. "How about dessert? Do you have any chocolaty things?"

"Yes, madam. We have a lava cake. The chef can make it very spicy for you."

"Thanks."

The waiter left. Then Gabriel leaned towards her. "What's wrong?"

"What do you mean?" Cora asked with a feigned smile.

"You just said we should leave. And you look nervous. That makes me *very* nervous, Cora."

She tried to force a laugh. "I'm not sure ... maybe nothing."

He nodded dismissively, acting as if it was probably more of her eccentricities, and then asked, "So, you're leaving tomorrow?"

"Huh?"

"You're leaving tomorrow?"

"Why do you always have to ask when I'm leaving?"

He chuckled.

"I guess. I don't even have a hotel."

"You drove here straight from Toronto?"

She nodded.

"I can get you something."

"That would be nice." She laughed a little. She was feeling the drinks. "Look, just forget all the shit I told you ... let's talk about you. How's the family? How's Mina and little Jordan?"

"Fine." He drank down the rest of his wine. Then the waiter brought him another.

"Good. I hope you're happy. You deserve it."

"Mina is ..." He looked pained.

"Hmm?" She reached over, then searched his face. "Everything okay?"

"Forget it." He leaned back in his chair. "I ... actually, the fact is, things are not good between us. You were right. She's a complete bitch."

"I know," she said. "I'm a very good judge of character."

"We're getting a divorce."

"TMI." Cora put her hand up. "That's enough, Gabe. You don't have to tell me anything more."

"Bullshit. You've been coming on to me for months. It was because of you that I had second thoughts about her. The fact is, our trip to Canada was a complete disaster. She's obsessed with Jo Jo. Understand, Persephone"—she smiled—"that I adore my daughter. I love her more than anything in the world. And part of me still loves Mina. But, everything is so fucked up. She's in another world half the time. And work is only getting more difficult."

"You don't have to confide in me."

"Why? You confided in me. You've discussed all your hallucinations and delusions of grandeur."

"That's unfair."

"I know." He turned to the window. "It's the wine talking. The fact is, I looked forward to seeing you. But I can't understand why you chased after me. You. Why?"

"Gabe, that's your biggest problem. You're a great man."

She looked at him. He seemed happy. He was finally relaxing in her company. But it was sad to her, in a way. She wondered if their divorce was her fault. That hurt her. She had done everything she could for it not to be.

"I'm sorry," she said.

"For what?"

"About your wife. I never wanted to hurt your family. I've done everything I could not to do that."

"No, Persephone." His words slurred a little, and he was getting a bit too relaxed with his drink. "You planted that necklace."

She raised an eyebrow.

"You knew full well what you were doing."

"No, I never meant to hurt you."

"Forget it. Just forget it." The waiter came over and handed him another glass. He took it and nearly spilled it. He chuckled a little. "I'm only worried about Jo Jo. I only care about her now."

Then he gently took her hand and rubbed her fingers. She let him. It was cute. "You've been here for centuries?"

She nodded.

"Ever married?"

"Yes. Many times ... remember Danny?"

"Sorry."

"It's okay."

"Then you've been through a lot of pain?"

"Oh yes."

"Did you ever hurt anyone? Did you ever hurt your man?"

"Yes. I've hurt a lot of people, Gabe. A great many men. Even those I've loved."

Now she felt miserable. And she must have looked it. He had confided in her drinking. It was risky, and she didn't think he would have told her sober. The whole evening seemed wrong.

Everything was always wrong for her. Why? All of it. It wasn't fair. She had promised herself she would only move on him if he was free. Now he was—because of her? She didn't believe in taking him married—not out of morality, but because she simply didn't want to hurt his family. Now they were hurt. And they would only be more hurt after he left.

"Why have you been chasing after me?" he asked.

"Gabe, why wouldn't I? You're a wonderful man."

"No. Sorry, Cora, I don't believe that. You could have any man in this room."

"That's true."

He laughed.

"Tell me," he said, rubbing her fingers again.

"What?"

"Tell me why."

"I've told you enough already."

She felt her eyes starting to heat up and glow red. When he looked at her, he reeled back in his chair, looking startled. She saw his look and quickly covered her eyes with her free hand.

She was getting upset, but she wasn't sure why. Was it Gabe? No, he was merely opening up to her and trying to get closer. What was wrong with that? Unless her guilt made her feel angry.

No, it seemed to be something else. Something or *someone* else. Someone was listening in on them, and now she sensed it. And her eyes reacted, not to what was happening but what was about to happen. She felt it but couldn't understand it. All she knew was that they needed to leave. And leave *now*.

"We need to go," she said again.

"Go?" he asked. "Now?"

"Yes."

"All right," he said with a laugh, pulling her hand up to his lips for a kiss. "I believe you, Persephone. You bewitched me. Take me. Take me, Cora, I'm yours."

Oh no.

A flash of light and an explosion filled her ears. She still held his hand, touching his fingers. Had she not, she would have lost him forever.

The flash, though probably lasting a millisecond, seemed to go on for an hour. The sound was louder than any normal audible sound, causing her ears to ring. She felt a sting, and a blast of air knocked down everything around her. Then complete darkness.

She screamed, but no one heard her—her body was gone. But she could still feel Gabriel. His body was gone too. Just the core of him remained at the tip of her phantom fingers. He lived only there, perhaps a handful of cells left surrounding hers and a life force barely palpable. But it would be enough. She'd done it before. She could revive him. Thank God he had touched her!

Who had done this? Who had tried to take him and ruin her life once more?

The flames grew furious, covering everything with an unbearable heat. The smoke made her choke. She coughed, but she couldn't hear it. Her body was incorporeal. She was like a ghost or a shade. Her body would regenerate soon, but it would take time.

Her head, burning like molten lava, fell into her wafts resembling a hand. She wept like a child, then she wailed, her cries filling the room as the fire began to rise, echoing through the floor of the demolished building. Everything around her was burning up in flames.

Then the smoke started to clear. From above the room, her spirit looked down on the carnage. Shattered wooden tables were tossed now into tinder, pieces of torn clothing dashed in crimson and everything was surrounded in fire.

That was when she heard screams. Those still alive were sobbing near the exit. The remnants of the charred restaurant now looked more like a demolition site.

Her vision sharpened. She could make out the window, now with a large gaping hole in the glass, over fifty floors into the night sky.

When her body formed enough for her to stand, she ran to the exit.

People were huddling, trying to help one another, some holding lost limbs, others bleeding profusely, others simply in shock, holding their ears—their eardrums likely blown from the explosion. Her spirit, still partially incorporeal, rushed to their side and began healing everyone she could touch. People saw her, likely as a blur.

First she healed an arm. She made it whole, and the shocked little girl, who lay against the wall sobbing, looked down at her naked healed arm in even greater shock. Then she moved on to the others. A man who was on the verge of death. Half his torso lay across the room, with his guts strewn across the carpet under a cracked dining table. She healed him whole too.

Then she heard Gabriel's voice. She held on to him tight, still feeling his spirit.

She went to every body still salvageable.

Then came the first responders—the firefighters and the police.

She wailed again. Many of the rescuers who attended the

wounded, though few needed much assistance anymore, heard her scream. It was like a banshee's cry through the wind, making their hair stand on end. She cried out at the injustice. She cried for God above.

She cried for vengeance.

Why keep her on this earth? Why couldn't they have finished her too?

She felt Gabriel cry again in fear. She held on to him tight.

Then she heard her own words from five thousand years before, carried by the wind. Only Imada would know the words, for she had uttered them on the shores of Aigai. It was her cry for vengeance before she had destroyed their home. Through the air, a voice mocked her. He spoke her vow:

I will make you cry tears of longing, beasts of Ida. Man and nymph would have done better if you had all been feasted on by Cronos! Take and devour me now if you want peace, for behold, I come to destroy all under your power, Zeus, false god of Gaia.

Now she knew she had been watched. She had broken Imada's sacred law and told a mortal of her race in public, a grievous crime. But she cared little for their law. And, anyway, this wasn't the real reason for their violence. The war had already begun with the death of Danny. Again. A war being waged now to kill Gabriel and his niece to complete their genocide of Nephrea Ambrosia's beloved race.

In rage, this time Cora's own, the building shook, and a sudden torrent of wind and rain, torn from her heart, rushed into the building like a tempest. The first responders crouched in shock against walls, drenched by the rain. It rushed in from outside, dousing all remaining flames.

If only she could see him. If only the perpetrator had enough courage to show himself. She would tear him apart.

Then she felt Gabriel again. His voice was gone, but she could feel him, a life force without form, like a child desperate for help.

She would care for him. And she would make him whole again. And she would love him.

24

THE TRIDENT

Five thousand years ago, the Greek hero Theseus Aegeus, accompanied by six other Athenians, was blindfolded and taken by boat to the labyrinth of Crete. The labyrinth was built by Daedalus under the orders of King Minos, but its precise where-abouts were kept secret in order to protect the king's mutant son, Minofus the Minotaur. It is said that even the builders under Daedalus were blindfolded as they sailed to the cave dwelling. The only mortals who knew how to reach the labyrinth were three sailors, King Minos, and his daughter Ariadne—and of course Theseus, after he managed to defeat the Minotaur. When Theseus took his rightful place as Athens's first king, he told the goddess Athena of the secret lair.

Minerva had kept secret the location. Even when Orcus had visited her at her home in Spain after the death of Daniel Anas-tra, she had told Orcus that Dellon, or Apollo, presided in Greece, but she'd left it to the god of the underworld to search for the exact location. Just as Ariadne had once protected her brother Minofus, Minerva protected Apollo. But after the restaurant explosion in Manhattan, Orcus had threatened to blow Minerva's private little island to bits if she did not reveal the precise coordinates.

First came the airstrike. Bunker-buster bombs completely flattened an empty hillside along the shore in Crete. Then Orcus flew personally from London to a secret compound in Rota, Spain, and from there traveled by helicopter to the island of Crete with a group of specially trained marines.

When hovering over the exploded shoreline, the tall bald god wearing a black cloak leapt from the military transport helicopter into the shallow waters. A minute later, his army landed behind him.

The god of the underworld ran swiftly through the smoke and debris and climbed down a crater created by the destruction until he found an opening into the tunnels.

He coughed and struggled to breathe in the thick smoke. Most of the light from his flashlight shone back at him. He had to feel his way along the walls for part of the way.

Then the pathway lit up with the flashes of gunfire. Two or three stray bullets hit his arm and flank, but he was undeterred. He ran down the hall and grabbed two men—stunned by his brazen charge—crushing one's trachea and then reaching for the other's neck, but the remaining man frantically pushed away. It became clear to Orcus that these men were not attacking him; they were running. He let them.

He soon found two large doors of gilded wood and threw them open. It was pitch black inside here too. He looked inside along a muddy wall, water still trickling down from damage from the bombing, and his flashlight landed on a light switch. Orcus switched the light on and squinted at the sudden brilliant light reflecting off walls of gold.

He instantly recognized the chamber. Doric columns surrounded the walls—six on one end, and fifteen on the other. The columns were designed in the exact fashion as those in Apollo's famous Temple at Delphi—the Temple of Alcmaeonidae. Close to the Doric columns were white marble statues. He recognized the most prominent figures: Athena, old ragged Hephaestus, Hera, Artemis, Ares, Poseidon, and finally Zeus. Zeus stood tall in the center of the room, wielding his mighty lightning bolt. The statues were old, damaged—cracked, some missing limbs— and quite possibly originals from the Temple in Greece above. Towards the far end—the adyton—was a dais raised on marble steps, not unlike Cora's "throne." And above the dais was the largest statue in the room—a white marble rendition of Apollo wearing a chiton, with a bow and arrow in one hand and a lyre in the other. At the floor under the throne coiled a large onyx python with a stone arrow lodged in its forehead.

Orcus had always been amused by Apollo's myth, which claimed that Apollo had conquered the python in vengeance for Hera's persecution of his mother, Leto. His victory gifted him the famous sight of Delphi. But Orcus knew the true identity of the "snake." The python symbolized Cora, and the pompous young god imagined himself finally avenging Persephone, standing over her as if she were a defeated trophy while stealing her power of prophesy.

Orcus still squinted, his eyes adjusting to the bright light as he walked down the long, wet hall. He stepped over rocks and stone that had fallen from the violent explosions above and splashed along a wet floor.

He had thought the throne was empty, but as he moved closer to the adyton, he noticed a body sprawled underneath Apollo's statue and over the marble throne. Then he saw blood. Everywhere. Crimson flowed like a stream all the way down the chamber along the floor to the entry doors. Orcus had thought he was walking on water from damage to the pipes above, but when he finally looked down, he realized it was blood.

The lanky man on the throne lay impaled by a gold staff,

thrust erect into the center of his body. It was here, at the entry of this gold staff, where the blood flowed like a trickling waterfall from his chest. He looked like a sacrifice.

"I have a message for you, Hades," echoed a pained voice.

Orcus approached the dais. The ground was wetter here, the crimson stream flowing deeper over his boots. Then he looked at the impaled man—Hermes. Apparently, Hermes had been pinned a long time ago, so long that blood from his immortal body had been magically renewed as it filled the entire chamber floor. The gold staff branched off into three blades near the god's torn wet shirt, and so Orcus understood the staff to be not a single golden staff but Poseidon's trident.

"The message is clear enough," Orcus responded with his eyes wide open. "I don't believe it." He shook his head.

"I suffer for your message! I … I am your message, Uncle."

"I understand their message. They sentence you. They punish you after you murdered Daniel by mistake, inciting Cora to break the family's treaty and save Lilith's daughter."

"I'm glad for her pain."

"Then you failed in killing Gabriel twice—the first time in the airport, thwarted by me, the second in the restaurant. They sentence you because you have failed, old friend."

"I am witness to the damage your wife wrought to our family! This trident destroyed everything. Persephone destroyed everything. Now, after you free me, she will simply destroy everything again!"

"Poor nephew," Orcus said, shaking his head sadly.

He laughed. "Do not pretend to care! You … you hurt me much worse than Dellon did." He laughed, spewing blood from his mouth and nose. "Your brother. Your brother, the great sea god, shall rise to retake the world. He has found passage, Hades, finally freed from the sea by Dellon. Be warned! He shall use your wife's fury again to flood the earth. So says Sara. Then we shall take back everything. Imada shall rule Gaia from Amphitrite. There … there is nothing you can do about it."

"Poseidon is gone, Hermes. And so is his sea kingdom. No, they scorn you. They treat you worse than I ever did."

And then the madness of his nephew became manifest. Hermes burst out in maddening laughter, grimacing with wild red eyes that turned white as they rolled up into his head. He gnashed his teeth and his face twisted in excruciating pain from his movement on the trident that still pinned him. He coughed up a torrent of blood.

"I am your message," cried Hermes, coughing out blood. "Your brother rises! Persephone shall sink the earth, and then Imada shall come and rule the remaining sea. All of Gaia shall be as water, so says Sara. And Amphitrite will rise as a new Atlantis and we shall rule the world once more."

Amphitrite was the undersea palace of Poseidon. But since the flood, it had long been forgotten. Had Amphitrite not been destroyed? Orcus had seen no evidence over the millennia that the underwater kingdom still existed. The idea that it wasn't buried was too incredible, but Hermes's diseased mind seemed so convinced that, for a moment, Orcus thought it possible.

Oh, how Imada had fallen. This underground chamber was all that was left of Apollo's temple, his power buried under the ground. So many of his family had either lost their senses, scurried into holes to hide or been buried into nonexistence.

His family had once ruled with the most powerful monarchs —the Caesars, Charlemagne and up to the Spanish Empire. It was Spain where their power had waned when, in a similar age, he and Cora had helped prop up a little insignificant island, England, against the Spanish Armada, changing the world. In the sixteenth century, just as now, Cora and Orcus had sided against Imada genocide—the Inquisition—which had murdered nearly the entire Ambrosia race. Minerva had never left Spain—she was the last remnant of power still above ground.

Orcus looked down at the impaled messenger god. This act was a show of Imada's rage at Persephone and himself for what he had done to them—their visual representation of the damage Persephone had wrought on her family wielding Poseidon's golden trident.

"You are made a fool," Orcus addressed the fallen god. "They promised you freedom, knowing you'd never get it."

Hermes looked up, confused.

"How easy it would be to pull this staff," Orcus said, running his palm along the cold metal and even feeling a surge of power. Indeed, he would have loved to wield such power again. "If I pull it, I save you and the staff. But then Cora, or any one of us, can use its power and fulfill Sara's prophesy.

"So you see, there really is no choice. I will never allow Cora or anyone else such destruction again. I have spent hundreds of years trying to keep peace. Therefore, this trident must be buried.

"Then there is you," Orcus said, turning from the trident to look into the god's red eyes. Hermes remained quiet, in a silent but seemingly agitated panic. "The message manifests Athena's warped sense of justice. Cora and I may be snakes, but her justice is far more terrible.

"This is not a plan of Apollo's. I think it is Minerva's. It is an action worthy only of Athena's great guile and wisdom. She knew exactly what I would do. And my forced action allows her both greater security and, at the same time, the benefit of getting rid of you.

"I'm afraid they have sacrificed you. They have sentenced you to an eternity of drowning in your own blood. In a short time, your blood will fill the entire chamber. It will coalesce and congeal until it encases you in a prison for all eternity. But this is the only way to stop you. I can't allow you to continue to harass Persephone and kill thousands of people in the wake of your madness. Nor can I allow the trident to see the light ever again.

I'm sorry." Orcus looked down and shook his head. "I am truly sorry, old friend."

Orcus turned his back on Hermes and walked back towards the exit of the chamber.

"Wait!" cried Hermes. "Take it out of me. Release me, Uncle!"

Orcus could hear the sudden desperation in Hermes's voice. The messenger god seemed to finally understand his predicament.

Hermes raged with screams of agony.

Finally Orcus's army arrived in the chamber. He watched as the marines ran inside, squinting at the brilliant light.

"Do we have Dellon, General?" a young officer asked Orcus.

"No, he ran," Orcus replied.

The soldiers looked around. A few picked up various objects of great value—gold chalices studded with rubies, a pitcher of solid gold, silver cups, shattered crystal, ancient coins of Spain, and countless other objects reflecting more of the sun god's buried light.

"Help me, Uncle!" cried Hermes, laughing nervously. "Do you have any idea the sentence you give me? You have no choice."

The soldiers looked over at the throne, surprised. They too had not noticed the man and the pole affixed to the marble chair.

Orcus cocked his head. "I understand the message."

Hermes cried out incomprehensible words. There was no madness; it was complete terror.

Then Orcus addressed the soldiers as he approached the exit. "Set charges and bury the chamber."

"Sir?" the soldiers asked. Orcus looked back at Hermes as the blood flowed like a stream from the god's body, a flowing crimson making its way over golden goblets beside the coiled python statue. "What about the gold?" one of the soldier's asked. "And that ... man?"

"Bury him."

"Uncle! Uncle! How could you! How could even *you* do this!

Take it out of me! Have mercy! Please! At least ... at least carry me down to the depths. If you are to leave me for an eternity, take me to Tartarus and chain me to the fiery rocks like you did Cronos and Zeus. At least that's a better fate! Please!"

"The passage to the underworld was lost long ago, Mr. Horace."

25

PROPHECY

Cora leaned on the rail of her deck, gazing out at the water. A fog had rolled in, which wasn't too unpleasant, as it left a moist calmness in the air. But it was getting cold—frigid cold. She wore a rather unsexy heavy red raincoat, with her hair tied back in a ponytail. And she shivered. She mused that, not too long from now, she would have to weather more snow. She hated snow.

She was alone. Terribly alone. Never in Los Angeles had she felt so alone. The colder it got, the fewer guests visited the shore of her lake. But, of course, it wasn't just strangers—it was Gabe.

A single tear ran down her eye. She leaned over the rail, looking down at the trees below her on her property.

It was drizzling. She caught a squirrel scurrying to take shelter. Then, with her sharp eye, she caught a deer watching her a mile off, further under the branches and leaves. The deer was eating grass but stood frozen, keeping his eyes on her. The deer feared her. He reminded her of them. Imada—sniveling cowards crouching behind trees while manipulating man. They feared her too. Oh how wrong Dr. Tenor had been. She was a monster.

And now, in battle, she would become exactly what they feared her to be.

"You called, wife?"

She had heard his footsteps but didn't turn. Her instructions to Hashan had been to just let him in. It was the first time in centuries that she actually welcomed him.

"I need your help."

He laughed, which made her cringe. She hated that laugh, full of derision and mockery.

"That's nothing unexpected," he said. "It would be nice, however, being that I just traveled over a thousand miles to see you, if you did me the honor of turning your pretty head and saying hello."

She cocked her head and said, "Hi." Then she wiped her eyes.

Orcus smiled and nodded. He looked remarkably plain. He was bald, wearing a long black coat, black slacks and loafers. The formal wear made his goatee more distinctive. His expression showed concern. That was sweet.

"What can I do for you, my lovely wife?"

"I need to know where they live."

"Jesus, Cora," he said, shaking his head and draping his arms over the rail. He looked out on the lake too. "You know how I love you. I helped you once in their destruction. Wasn't that enough?"

"Their addresses," she snapped. "Only then can I stop them."

"No."

"I was touching Gabriel." She was surprised to hear her voice choke up. She hated that, knowing that her bastard husband would only draw strength from her weakness. He was such a bastard. "I felt him and held him. Had I not been holding him, Gabe would have been gone forever ... I need their information to protect him and the baby."

"I know of your pain, and I'm sorry. Truly. But they're the last of the family. That means Imada is more determined than ever to finish them. And your protection is only causing you more pain. Leave them, Cora. Honor your agreement. Let them die, mourn, then move on. You can't keep protecting them."

"You know I can't do that. Their addresses, please."

"What are gonna do? Rain on them?"

Cora laughed and shook her head.

"Cora," he said, wagging a finger, "I told you before, I've helped you for *you*, never for the Ambrosias. For *your* happiness, not these nymphs'. I could give a shit about them and this new sex toy of yours. And as far as that little maggot, that baby would be better off being killed than being raised by the likes of you, and you know it."

"Give them to me. I can protect Gabriel a little better knowing where they hide."

"I won't do it," he said, shaking his head. "You see what your 'protection' did for you."

"Give me what I ask. It will make me happy."

He laughed.

"Who was responsible anyway?" She turned and examined him carefully.

"The bombing was the work of a terrorist organization from Turkey. Homeland Security is dealing with the government in Turkey to determine the source. Over fifty people were killed with—"

"Cut the shit. It was Imada. I'm asking who. Which one from our family?"

"Stop it," he said, shaking his head. Then he wagged that infernal finger of his again. "Do not forget that they still want to get even with you. Don't you act like you're the victim."

"I think it was Hermes. I thought I recognized his voice. It certainly couldn't be Father. Maybe Mother?"

"Your mother is the only one, other than me, not trying to destroy you—believe it or not, Cora."

"Thanks for that," she said in triumph. She had just tricked him into giving her information. "I just need to know where they're hiding. I'll take care of the rest. I'll never tell the source."

"No."

"What do you want? What can I give you in order for you to tell me?"

He smiled, a very sly smile at that, and ran his hand through her hair.

"You fucking pervert. That's the one thing you can't have."

And that was when Hashan walked outside.

"I brought you two drinks," he said, carrying a small silver tray. He laid it down on a tiny wooden table beside two lounge chairs. "I remember the last time you visited, sir, you liked our martinis."

"Indeed, I did," Orcus said, turning. Then he picked up a glass and looked at it. The contents in the martini glass were not clear this time; they were red. It made him laugh. "Ah, Persephone. Red. How fitting. A cosmo?"

"Pomegranate martini," Cora said, shaking her head and sipping her own glass.

"Cute." And Orcus laughed even more.

"You owe me, Hades."

Then Cora turned to Hashan. "Thank you." That was enough. He understood and left.

"This is quite good," Orcus said, sipping some more. "A little too sweet, but good. But, Cora, after thousands of years, I would think you would have finally forgiven me."

"Well, I haven't," she said, turning back to the lake. "But maybe you can make it up to me by giving me what I ask for."

"And," Orcus said, "where is your new lover? Is his body lying in your bed?"

"He's back at home with his family."

"Good. Wise. This is a very dangerous time. Stay away from him, for his own safety."

"Can you help me?" Cora said, touching his arm. He pulled it away. "I'd very much like to pay them a visit. And, if you tell me who did it, I can avoid punishing the wrong one."

"No."

"Why?" She didn't like the tone of her voice. It almost sounded desperate.

"I've told you before. Unlike you, I care about the human race. Unfortunately, your interests do not align with ours."

"Then leave the information with me. You can stay out of it."

"There's one of you and ten of them. Don't be an idiot. And what if the culprit happens to be your mother?"

"You just said it wasn't," she said, looking up at him. "And you took care of Father, so you said. That leaves eight."

"Cora, you did enough already."

"In one year, they knifed my husband, murdered Lilith and her husband, and now attempted to kill Gabriel. Tell me! If you love me, as you annoyingly say, do this. It won't affect you. Your precious USA will go untouched. Let me have my vengeance. If they hunted you, you would ask for the same."

He groaned and leaned over the rail, rubbing his eyes. It was almost amusing to watch this giant man weaken before her.

He was an attractive brute. His strength and arrogance had once thrilled her. Once, she had even loved him.

"You took their power," he said with his head in hands. "Now you want to hunt them. Leave them to me."

"I can't trust you anymore. I've left too much to you. Gabriel nearly died."

"Good day, Cora," he said, straightening and then bowing once more. He began a hasty exit. "I'm truly sorry for what happened. I came to tell you that. And to say that I'm doing everything I can to make sure it doesn't happen again."

"Wait ... perhaps a trade, husband?"

He made his way to the sliding door.

"You asked for prophecy."

That stopped him. He turned and slowly walked back, then leaned on the rail, facing her with a large grimace. "Say that again, Cora? I'm not sure I heard you right. What did you just say?"

"You will consider it for my sight?"

"Why, of course, my love," he said, lighting up with an open gesture of his hands.

"Don't call me that. I don't see a choice. But I have conditions."

"Yes?"

"I can be a source, like an oracle ... like the Oracle at Delphi. I can give you pieces of the future, but you will have to put the puzzle together yourselves."

"Why?"

"Because you will have no need of me if I tell you everything." He raised an eyebrow. "And anyway, you know how this works—things are not always clear. I never could have guessed the fuckers would blow up my boyfriend."

Orcus grinned a sardonic grin. Cora wished she could wipe the smile off his face. She hated him again.

"You could have guessed it. I warned you." Then he gestured for more. "Well, Cora, you have my attention. Go on."

"I offer my services," she said with a nod. "You hand over the information regarding Imada and I'll help your governments."

"They're your governments, too," he said. He placed a finger over his chin in thought, then said, "You know, despite how much I still love you, we could very well get a lot more from working with them than you. Why should I betray Imada again? I'm happier staying out of it."

"Prophecy is better than anything they can give you. And this isn't about love, dick, it's business. Anyway, I want their information to watch them, not to disturb them. I will not sink down to the level—"

"Don't lie to me, Cora. I've known you for thousands of years. You have blood in your eyes, ready to strike. I don't need to be handed a bloody drink to know that."

"Wouldn't you?" And indeed, at that moment she felt the warmth in her eyes.

"Maybe."

"Just give me their contacts."

"And you'll come to Langley?"

"Fuck no! I'm not asking for a job. I have no interest in your business. You come to me and ask me questions and I'll provide you what you need."

"You will promise never to mislead us?"

"I'll try, but the future is always up for interpretation."

Orcus looked out to the water once more, rubbing his goatee in thought, then turned back with a jovial grin. "I will trust you, for I need to keep an eye on you. It seems our enemies think you will destroy the world."

"You can trust me," she said with a smirk.

He laughed. "No," he said shaking his head. "No, I can't."

"You have to—if you want my gift."

"Apparently." He put his hand out to shake. She kept her hands firmly on the rail. "I'll get you their whereabouts and you'll fill me in on our future."

"You'll wish you didn't know."

"But," he said, raising a finger once more. She wished she could chop it off. "Even though you're offering me an offer I can't refuse, I warn you, as your dear friend and husband, you should simply get rid of the two of them."

"You don't know the future."

He examined her face, wrinkling his eyebrows and smiling a sardonic nasty grin again, then chuckled jovially. He cocked his head and nodded, immensely pleased at their new wicked arrangement.

"Would you like to go inside for caviar?" she asked. "You said you liked it."

"Oh, have I finally risen in status as a true guest, Ms. Aregard?"

"No, it's just getting cold. I hate the cold. It reminds me of you."

26

THE EYE

Having lost Gabriel again, knowing that he now loved her, sent Cora into the deepest depression she had been in eons. Now she mourned for Danny *and* Gabriel.

She had returned him home after making him whole again. Then she had abandoned him. She wanted him to sort things out with his family, keep him away from *her* family, and just let time pass before he decided whether to accept a life with her. A life with her would not be easy. If he was crazy enough to still want her, now that he knew exactly what she truly was, for all her innumerable faults, she'd take him. If not, she'd just watch him.

He did in fact call, but she never answered the phone. Phone calls were too painful now. A call meant brief contact followed by days of longing. If she was going to talk again, he would have to come to her for good or stay away. She didn't want to play games anymore. Of course, her friends, Grace, Reggie and Hashan, begged her to just answer the phone.

To get her mind off him, she decided she would take her friends to London, England. They had been at a pub in Toronto one evening when Reggie had confessed that he had always wanted to go to London. His mother—Cora had joked and called her "mum"—was over there. So, she surprised the gang one morning and told them they were all heading to England. Hashan would gladly stay behind and care for the baby.

And now it was nearly midnight. Reggie had rescued Cora twice from nearly toppling over their balcony and plummeting a hundred feet into the dark water below. There was a brass rail, but it was short and easy to jump or fall over. She probably could have swum, but then she would have missed the rest of her party. She adored the view and kept swinging dangerously over the brass railing to the blaring music. She had actually succeeded in losing a glass of wine. She hadn't stopped laughing as it had clinked and clanged and then shattered against the brick wall. Then she'd asked Reggie for another. The trio partied all night together on the balcony while a larger group went wild inside. Others came and went from inside, carrying paper cups of beer or glasses of wine. Reggie stood like a sentinel, making sure no one was stupid enough to fall over the edge. Cora kept staring at him and laughing hysterically at his calm, stern face. He would just raise an eyebrow with a thin grin, making her explode even more. Grace was nearly completely gone. She mimicked her friend, dangling her body over the precipice and scaring the hell out of both of them.

Cora eventually got so plastered that she stopped dancing and just sprawled on the patio couch, staring at the ships off on the horizon. They could just see the Eye and Parliament lit yellow off in the distance. But it was the lights reflecting over the river that were most magnificent.

Grace didn't stop. She kept swaying and leaning dangerously over the unprotected cliffside. Cora chuckled but got nervous a few times at her friend's antics.

It was cold. She wore a thick white cotton sweater and jeans. She tied her blond hair back and had to frequently blow air into her hands. But the cold was worth the view. The outfit made her look formal—she had remarked: *cultured*. She wanted to look like a proper British girl. But then she figured she ruined the whole thing by exaggerating her makeup. Of course, Grace copied her. The two looked like sisters.

It was far after midnight. Many of her guests had gone home and it was becoming quiet. The music was even dying down.

"Hey, Cora," Grace said, jumping onto the couch beside her. "Having fun?"

"Yeah."

"I met two businessmen inside. They gave me their cards." She laughed. "You should see them. They're wearing frickin' white suits. It's hilarious ... I told them I was starting college on a foreign exchange program. They think I'm an innocent young American."

"Aren't you?"

"Yeah." She had a really big smile. It made Cora laugh. "Come on. They're pretty cool guys. I think they think I'm a virgin. I want to surprise them, you know, show them what's underneath. The lace under our sweaters will turn them wild."

"I wanna see the sunrise."

"That's another couple hours yet, Cora," said Reggie, stone-faced, having overheard them.

"Reggie, fuck you. Just do your job and make sure I don't jump off the edge, 'kay?"

"That's what I'm doing."

"How come he's not drinking?" Cora asked Grace.

"I have him watching you, bitch," Grace said. "I love you." And Grace nuzzled into her.

Cora laughed. "Okay. Just get off me."

"No, I mean, I *really* love you, Cora."

"She *really* does," Reggie said.

Cora sat up straight and ran her hand down Grace's hair. Then she looked at them and said in her best British accent, "Are you two having a jolly good time?"

Grace laughed—a little too much. Cora lost her smile. It

wasn't really that funny. The fact Grace laughed so hard showed how screwed up she really was. So, Cora grabbed Grace's drink from her hand.

"Hey!" Grace exclaimed.

"You've had enough."

"You think you're my mom or something!"

"Yeah, I do."

"Look, come with me and fuck the suits!"

"Listen to you. You sound ridiculous."

"Hey, what's with all the business guys, anyway, Cora?" asked Reggie.

"It was a London Law Expo. I invited them." He looked at her strangely. "I wanted a party. You both wanted to party. It couldn't just be us dancing, right?"

"I want to pick the two still wearing suits," said Grace. "It's just so wrong, it's right, you know? Then again there were two others offering candy."

"Go do that, Grace—or whatever. Just leave me alone. I want to watch the sunrise on the Thames. Just be careful. There's a reason I dressed us up. It was to keep you clean tonight."

"You're one to talk, Cora," Reggie remarked.

"You're still thinking of him, aren't you?" asked Grace, opening her eyes a little too wide in understanding. She still leaned her head under her elbow. Her moment of epiphany was not amusing to Cora, who gently pushed her off and crawled back towards the rail. Reggie jumped, thinking she was being stupid again.

"It is beautiful," Cora said, looking at the view.

"A little cold, girls," said Reggie. "Why don't you two go inside?"

"Because it's beautiful," Cora said. "And then your watch would be over ... then I might have to watch you."

"You know, I've got an idea," said Reggie, cocking his head with a sly smile.

Cora ignored him and leaned over the railing. She had no intention of jumping. Rather, she was debating whether she should vomit over the edge. The idea was more out of interest in watching it trickle down along the brick and stones into the dark water than out of actual nausea, though she was feeling a little sick. She spat a little just to see how the wind would move it. Then she started to feel dizzy. She closed her eyes, which made it a little worse. Then she closed her fists and concentrated on keeping control of her stomach.

"What did you say, Reg? You always have crazy ideas."

"Call him."

"Who? Call who?"

"*Him.*"

"Yeah!" yelled Grace, jumping over to her all giddy, close to the ledge. Reggie ran over to catch her.

"What?" Cora turned and looked at him as if he was insane. "What are you talking about?"

"It's been months. Why don't you call him? As a *friend*?"

"Who?" Cora asked, pretending not to know.

"Gabe."

"Are you crazy?"

"Yeah," said Grace, embracing her arm. "Just call him!"

"I'm in London to forget him, you dope! What a stupid—"

"It could be fun, Cora," said Grace.

"No." But Cora loved Grace's sneaky expression. "I don't even have his number," she added, finally shaking her head.

"Give me your phone," Grace said. "You have it. I'll find it for you."

Cora shook her head and turned back to the water, deciding to wait for the sun to come up instead. She intended to stand like a soldier with Reggie for another couple of hours. But then, she felt someone reach down into her tight pant leg. Grace pulled out the phone, laughing hysterically at herself. She ran a few steps away and jumped up in triumph.

"Give me that!"

Grace lifted her index finger and walked towards the rail. Then she leaned far towards the edge. Cora opened her eyes wide, and Reggie darted over to grab her.

"Get away from there!"

"Let's see," Grace said, thumbing through the phone, ignoring her. Reggie jumped towards her, but Grace threatened him by dangling one leg over the rail. "There's Hashan. He's having a jolly good time by himself at home with the baby. Then there's ... God, Cora, there's a lot of men here. Let's see where the well-mannered Mr. Cartwright is."

"Stop it, Grace!" cried Cora. "Get away from there! It's not funny!"

"Oh, but it will be when I call him."

Reggie was hovering over her, but she wouldn't let him get close enough. Every time he approached, she threatened to pull the other leg over.

"Here it is! The sweet employee from Platinum Properties— Mr. Cartwright." Grace pressed a button and placed the phone to her ear, waiting. "Hello? Yes? Is Gabe Cartwright there?" Cora gestured to Grace desperately to give her the phone. "Hello? I have someone—"

"Give me the damn phone!"

Grace started laughing so hard that she bent over. It was just enough for Reggie to finally catch her and pull her from the rail. Cora grabbed her phone.

"Hello?"

Cora recognized his voice immediately. Her heart raced. "Gabe?"

"Hello? Cora?" said the voice on the other line. It was clearly Gabe's voice, but he was out of breath.

"Aha. Cora Aregard."

Cora knew she sounded wasted. Half of her regretted it, the other half wanted to burst out laughing in his ear.

"Cora? What's going on? Do you know what time it is?"

"Late here, or early." Cora laughed. Grace laughed even harder. "So, what're you doing now, Gabe?"

"Running."

Cora covered the phone and turned to Grace. "He's running."

"That's *fucking hot*," Grace said. Cora laughed. Reggie rolled his eyes.

"Running? I didn't know you ran."

"Yes. I exercise every night, Cora. What's this all about?"

"I thought this was a good place. I'm—"

"Drunk. You're drunk, Cora."

She didn't say anything.

"I've called and left messages with you for months. Now you call me wasted? There's a lot of noise. You at a party? Of course you're at a party. Yours? Where are you?"

"Hmm? What?"

"Where are you? Do you even know where you are?"

Cora turned to Reggie and covered the phone. "Where am I?"

"England."

"Oh," she said with a nod. Then she uncovered the phone and spoke in her best British accent, "*London, England.*"

"England? What the hell are you doing in England? What time is it over there?"

"Huh? I don't know." She covered the phone and turned to Grace and said, "He's out of breath."

Grace whispered back, "*Fucking hot!*"

"Why are you in England, Cora?" he asked, exasperated, but with a hint of amusement.

"Well, it's my birthday." Grace fell to the floor in a ball in complete hysteria. She was so loud that Cora tried to shush her.

Then after some uncomfortable silence, Gabe said wryly, "Happy birthday, Cora."

"Thanks, Gabe. That's sweet."

"I didn't know you had one ... listen, I want to talk to you."

"You want to talk to me?"

"Yes. I told you, I've been trying to reach you since our dinner. I was so worried about you. But now ... I don't even know if you know who you're talking to."

"How's the family? The bitch?"

"Fuck you, Cora. I answered your call. I told you we're separated."

She laughed.

"Why are you in England?"

"Well, we're visiting Reggie's mum." Grace lost control again. Reggie grabbed her by the arm and pulled her quickly inside.

Then something strange happened. It was fun to talk to him drunk with friends, but alone on the balcony—that was something entirely different. She remembered why she hadn't been talking to him.

What am I doing?

"Anyway, *you* left me last time, Gabe," she said.

"What?"

"In New York, you left me. I understand."

"What? What are you talking about? We're lucky to be alive. I didn't leave you. I've done everything to get a hold of you. I was just happy to find out you were all right."

There was silence on the other end; doubtless Gabe had stopped running.

"Cora, we need to talk. But not now. Hold on a minute."

She was dizzy. She walked towards the edge of the rail. Her guardian was gone. She could jump.

"Cora? Are you there?"

"Hi."

"The divorce—"

"I'm sorry," Cora interrupted. "I shouldn't have called. It was just a stupid joke my—"

"Wait. The divorce will be final in six more months, Cora. There's another few mediation sessions, but I'm sure you know how lawyers drag things out. It's all about Jo Jo and custody. My wife's telling all these lies about time spent with her. She wants Jo Jo all to herself. No one seems to understand that I worked day and night. Now the bitch wants to take my girl from me. She's accused..." He kept going on, but Cora stopped listening. She just looked out at the river. A tear rolled down her cheek. Her hand holding the phone dropped to her waist—she almost dropped it over the edge.

She hated him. She hated him more than anyone in the world because she knew he was the one for her. She didn't want to be the one for him. She didn't want to live only to see him die. She was tired of seeing them die. So tired of it. And him being an Ambrosia ... she knew she couldn't take seeing an Ambrosia die. Not if one lived with her. She couldn't take that.

She thought of Lilly. She remembered begging her not to leave her. Why did they leave her? Why did everyone leave her? But she had watched Lilly from afar. Had Lilly lived with her, intimately in love, her loss would have made Cora lose her mind.

That was what Gabe was—Danny *and* Lilly put together.

But she loved him. She didn't want to love him.

In the past, before their date in New York, they'd talked and confided in each other like this frequently. They'd confided so easily on the phone because ... because they were meant for each other—because they loved each other. But now, it was different. She could hear it in his voice. He wanted to be with her. Why? Why would anyone want to be with a monster? Why would anyone want *her*?

Why had they called him? Could she be any lower?

She brought the phone to her ear again. He was still rambling on and on about his troubles that she really didn't care much about.

"I just don't know what to do," he said. "You were right about Mina. You were right. I—I just want you to know that you helped me see what I should have known all along. Thank you, Cora."

That was the nail in the coffin. He was actually thanking her for ruining his marriage.

Cora stayed silent. Gabe finally stopped ranting.

"Maybe you're too drunk to answer. Forget it. I just know that I want to talk to you again."

"I have to go, Gabe." The phone shook in her hand. He was silent for a minute on the other end.

"Hmm? Sure."

What? What did he just say? SURE? FUCKING SURE!

She took her phone and hurled it over the edge of the balcony. Then she shouted as loud as she could into the night. She didn't yell at anyone in particular. She just yelled. She hurled obscenities in the air and cursed like a madwoman. Once, perhaps, there would have been someone or something to yell at. Now she just screamed.

Reggie ran out and grabbed her, but she pushed out of his grasp and threw him down to the ground. He jumped up, thinking she was going to leap off the ledge. Instead, she leaned her head in her hands and wept bitterly. Reggie laid a hand on her shoulder, and Cora fell into his arms, crying.

27

PERSEPHONE

G abriel was miserable. He did what a fileted fish carcass does after being caught and disposed of on the deck of a fishing boat. He spent all day sitting in his car in the driveway of Cora Aregard's house, waiting for the fisherman to finish him. He knocked every few hours. There was no answer. Not even the creepy butler Hashan answered the door. And so, he waited some more. He also called her. He left a few messages on her voicemail. Then he yelled at himself out loud in his 5-series BMW like a lunatic, wondering what madness had come over him.

Eventually he realized that Cora might close the door on him even if she was home. He was breaking every rule in the courtship book that he had learned since grade school. He was making a complete ass of himself and he didn't even know why.

Was this another power of the "*goddess*" Persephone? Had she bewitched him with some kind of love potion from Aphrodite? Or was he just desperate after losing his wife? Or both?

Absolutely miserable.

Part of him wanted to completely fail and never see her again. She was a perverted narcissistic cruel debutante acting like a spoiled teenager older than his great-greatest-grandmother. How in the world could he live with that? The other part wanted to spend every waking moment with her. He was so stricken that he would have accepted one last meal of burgers with the vixen bitch.

He loved her. Now she knew it. Maybe that was why she'd hung up on him. Of course it was.

By evening, on a cold, clear early-winter evening along Ontario Lake, he tried another desperate attempt to reach her. He had eaten granola bars and drunk water all day. His back ached. But he would try one more time. He got out of his car once more and walked to the grand entrance, ringing the doorbell.

He turned at the sound of a car. It was a stretch limousine. He squinted as the car pulled beside his. Then three people got out and walked slowly towards him. He knew all three of them—Hashan, Reginald and Grace. But there was no Cora.

"Look who's here," said Reggie with a smile. The man towered over him.

Hashan looked simply depressed. Grace seemed to be in forlorn spirits too.

"I ..." Now he didn't even know what to say.

"She's inside, Mr. Cartwright," said Hashan.

The weird butler actually still wore his sunglasses in the twilight. He smiled a not-so-kind smile, then nodded and gestured for him to step aside. Then he brought out a chain of keys and opened the door.

"Inside? I've been knocking."

"Perhaps she doesn't want to see you," Hashan said coldly.

Grace looked at Gabe with a pitiful smile.

"Come on in," Grace said and gestured for him to enter.

The house was dark. If Cora was there, she was in darkness. None of the lights were on downstairs or upstairs in the mansion. Only candles were lit and dispersed throughout the home. Reginald and Grace said goodbye to him. Then they did something very strange—Reggie shook his hand and Grace touched his shoulder and smiled sweetly. Grace gestured for him to walk upstairs. Then the three of them watched him by the entryway as he climbed the stairs alone. He looked back and shook his head at them—everything, as odd and weird as always.

Gabe walked up the wide stairs—the same stairs as in Los Angeles. If he hadn't seen the outside, he could have been fooled into thinking he was back in LA.

His hands shook a little, and he felt a shiver along his back. When he reached the top, it was dimly lit by candlelight. In the middle of the room he was startled to see Cora sprawled in her elevated chair in darkness and silence.

She was stark naked, a martini in one hand and a cigarette in a long-stemmed holder in the other. It was like when he had first met her, but this time she sat in the nude. Her only clothes were two very large black leather boots. And it was deathly quiet. Gabe tried to control his shock. She had the same long red-dyed hair and cherry-red lips she had had when they'd first met too.

She gazed down on him.

"Hi."

Then she looked away, inhaling her cigarette smoke. She turned back to him, seeming to examine him. She smiled after another deep drag from her cigarette. "You messaged that you wanted to talk?" He didn't say anything. She stared down at him. "This is what you wanted, isn't it? This is why you've been sitting outside my house all day? To fuck me? Isn't that it?"

"This isn't exactly what I had in mind."

She squinted at him as if not totally believing him, then picked up her remote and opened the red velvet drapes. The moonlight was bright enough to light up the room, making her even more indecent. It was a full moon outside. Her pale, perfectly curved breasts and hips glowed under the brighter light. He turned from her, embarrassed by her nakedness. She chuckled and walked, swaying her naked hips, down the three marble steps to him.

"What did you want to ... *talk* about?" she said in a sultry voice as she stood close to him.

He forced himself to look into her eyes. "Stop it."

"Stop ..." She puckered her lips. "What?"

"Stop what you're doing."

"You wanted to talk," she said, feigning surprise. "Or..." She walked close to him, ran a finger along his chest and whispered in his ear. "*Fuck?*"

He avoided her bright blue eyes and walked to the dining room table, sitting down.

"I wanted to talk, not fuck."

She chuckled and shrugged. Then she climbed up on her chair again and swiveled it towards the dining room table.

"Well, why don't you come closer? Otherwise, you'll have to yell to hear me."

That was when her bird, Mainax, fluttered its majestic wings over her and then perched on her arm. She petted him.

Somehow, though naked, her majesty intimidated him. As he picked up the heavy wooden dining chair and carried it under her, he felt small. He sat and looked up at her.

"I think, Cora, perhaps—"

"I'm Cora Ambrosia," she said, waving a hand in the air. "My husbands have always known my real name. So should you. It was given to me by a nymph with azure-tinted skin a few thousand years ago. She adopted and raised me. My mother's name was Nephrea. She and her husband, Akhenaten, had a daughter in Egypt who carried on generation after generation to eventually have you. If all this is too fucking weird for you, Gabe, then perhaps you should leave. You really don't want a life with me."

"Ms. Ambrosia—"

"I haven't heard it said like that before," she said with a giggle.

"Cora, I ..."

"Spit it out, Gabe."

"I have thought of you constantly since I met you."

"Liar. You thought of me after I seduced you. You did not think of me constantly when you first met me in LA. You were too busy being attacked by Grace and her friends."

"No, even then I was enticed by your beauty."

"What delicious language, Gabriel," she said with laughter. "*Enticed.*"

"Cora, it would be much easier if you put something on."

"Don't ever tell me what to wear!"

Gabe jumped. Mainax fluttered away, landing on the bar across the room.

She stood on the three steps above him suddenly furious. Her eyes glowed red. She was menacing under the light of the full moon with her red fiery eyes and naked figure, as if she was some kind of demon.

"Why don't you just kill me?" he said quietly under her.

"Why don't you just kill *me!*" she screamed back. "Just get out! Get out of my house! You sit outside in my driveway begging for me! You want me? A monster? Fucking moron! I'll destroy you! I took your family, then my family tried to take your life! They blew up that restaurant to kill you."

He didn't say anything. He just stared up at her, dumbfounded.

"You want a girl who lives on the edge, eh?" she asked. "What do you think I am? You think I'm a fucking doe like you? What kind of a man are you? I'm a tiger. And that's what your filthy fucked-up heart likes, right? You want to be around that?" She laughed cruelly.

"Stop it, Cora," was all he said.

He walked under her. Then he took her hand. At first she jumped, but then she froze. He touched her naked arm, then he stepped up a step and reached up for her shoulder. He simply touched her back. Then he touched her cheek with his palm.

She softened and leaned into his palm, closing her eyes. "Get out," she said softly.

"You got naked to fuck me?" he asked. "Screw me as a final one-night stand so you could forget about me?"

"I can never forget you," she said softly, shaking her head. "You are my soulmate. And you are an Ambrosia. You and your blood have haunted me for thousands of years. Whether you"— she looked down with a mix of derision and contempt—"*fuck me* or not, Gabriel, I will protect you. This is why you didn't die at the restaurant."

"I don't want to fuck you," he said. "I want to love you."

She looked at him as if he was crazy. Then she laughed. "I need a drink."

She jumped out of his grasp and pressed another button on the remote on her chair. Lights switched on, nearly blinding him. Then, naked and sultry as always, Cora Ambrosia walked to the marble bar and reached underneath it for two cocktail glasses. She filled them with ice and poured whiskey into them. Then she returned. He stared at her perfect perky breasts as they swayed along her hips. She smiled, seemingly knowing he was watching her. He gazed at her soft skin, her full cherry lips, red nails, legs and red hair.

"Have some Canadian whiskey," she said, walking back and handing him a glass, raising her own. "To two totally fucked-up people."

They clinked glasses and drank, gazing and becoming lost in each other's eyes.

"Why did you look for me?"

"Hmm?" She seemed to be in as much of a trance as him.

"Aussie told me you asked for me personally even before we had met. Why? Tell me, Cora. You could have used any realtor for the sale. You could have used anybody with your money and property. Why me? It's like you looked me up."

She nodded with a smile. "Yes, I looked you up, Gabe."

She sighed, walking over to sit on the bottom step below her chair, patting it for him to join her. He sat beside her. He could feel her, even without touch—he could feel her beside him. It was hypnotizing.

"I had to," she continued. "I should have looked you up sooner. I couldn't because of my love for Danny. You see, I have the power of providence. I knew one day we'd be together. But the death of my husband forced me to find you. Lilly's life was almost at an end. I knew my family of gods, Imada, would move on you next, so I had to act quickly and find out where you lived. I asked another friend to give me your address and then I—" she gestured to the room—"made this so I'd be near you."

"Providence?"

"Yeah. I can tell the future. I knew about us before you were born. I merely had to find you. But I loved Danny so much that I lost you." She looked sad for a moment. "Then I was too late ... I never wanted to break you and Mina up. I feel so—"

"It's okay," Gabriel said and took her hand. She looked down at his hand.

"My desire got the best of me," she said with a nod. "You were right to hate me for the necklace. Even subconsciously, I suppose, I scheme. I'm a very wicked girl, Gabe."

"I don't care, Cora."

She stared at his hand holding hers and seemed to struggle even more. Her hand shook like his once had. She lifted the glass and drank some more, as if to stop the tremor.

"You see, in a lifetime, one will find their soulmate. I think many find them but lose them, mistaking them for someone else. But, in my case, I must find one ad infinitum, every lifetime. Forever. It is the most painful curse of joy God has given me. You're a lot like Danny. Sometimes, that hurts too. My men are always similar.

"See, if you lived forever, you would always—" she hesitated and gave him a sad smile—"choose the same kind of person. People think they have free will, but life is about chance mixed with tastes. My tastes are you, Gabriel, and I foresaw it. But this time, you were pure. You were as close a direct descendant as I will ever come to my beloved Nephrea. To my family."

She lifted his hand and kissed it. It wasn't a sexual kiss. It was just a kiss. That melted his heart more.

"But what would make these other men in the past that you like," he said, shaking his head, "necessarily want you?"

She smiled and gestured at her body. It was crude, but it made the point.

"My men are always a little different," she continued. "That is why it's always painful when I lose them. But they love me ... even me."

"It's crazy," he said, finishing his drink. He jumped up for a moment.

"I'm crazy. If you don't like it, leave me." Then she smiled at him. "But you won't, will you? You never will. There's something between us that attracts us. Through thick and thin, eh, Gabe?"

He nodded.

She finished her glass.

He got up and walked over to the window and stared out at the lake. He could just see it under the full moon. He was happy. He was happy to be in the same room with her.

"So, now what, Persephone?" he asked with his back turned.

"I'm telling you the truth, Gabriel. I'm being *au-then-tic*."

"I know. But what now?"

They were interrupted by a baby's cry. He laughed when he saw her disgusted expression. Pointing with the same hand that held her glass, Cora said, "That's the other thing I forgot to tell you about."

Hashan ran up the stairs, carrying a sobbing child. The fussy infant sounded inconsolable.

"I don't know what to do!" Hashan said. "She won't stop crying. I tried to take her for a drive in the car, but—" He stopped when he saw her sitting stark naked. "It seems I always come at the wrong time with you two."

"Forget it, Hashan," she said with a laugh.

"I'll try to rock her again to sleep, madam," he hollered, rushing back down the stairs.

"The baby's yours?" Gabe asked.

"Fuck no," Cora said, bursting out into laughter. "I can't stand babies. They're filthy and noisy. And they cry and cry."

"Whose is it, then?"

"Your niece. Dr. Tenor's. Dr. Tenor died a year ago. He was murdered like Danny. Killed by Imada. Dr. Tenor was married to—"

"Lilly? *My* Lilly?"

"Yes. *Your* Lilly. Your sister. She had a daughter. Do you know what that means? Poor daughter's parents have passed away. And ... maybe it's another thing you need to consider if you decide to stay with me." She bit her upper lip and spoke quieter, as if telling him a secret. "I'm actually kinda nervous, Gabe. Living on this earth for thousands of years, I never really cared for one of those things. I've had Hashan doing all the work, but he's terrible too. I was ... kinda hoping you would help us."

He burst into laughter. "So, my sister was also—"

"Nephrea's descendant." Cora nodded.

Gabe looked out at the calm glistening moonlit water, and then back down at his drink. He'd needed a lot of them over the past year. Everything was so tumultuous. The rough ride wasn't only Cora, though. He sort of enjoyed her sharp turns.

"A life with you?" he asked, more to himself. "On your terms? You can be a real crazy bitch."

"Okay. Leave, then."

He turned from the window. He half expected she'd be right behind him. She wasn't. She had walked back up and sat on her elevated chair.

"I'm here," he said. "I love you."

"I know," she said, looking down at him. "Dreadful, isn't it?"

They both laughed.

"I will never have children," she said. "I'm barren. All I can promise you is that I can take good care of you and that child. I will keep you two healthy and safe until you die."

"That sounds awful."

She chuckled and nodded.

He walked back to her and ascended the first step, taking her hand again under her. She looked down at him, looking sad. She shrugged and brought his hand up, kissing the back of it.

"You scared?" she asked.

He looked at her, confused. He didn't understand.

"I am," she said, looking down at him.

He stepped up one more step and kissed her gently on the lips. He leaned his head on her forehead, enjoying the sound of her breath for the longest time.

"I love you too, Gabriel," she whispered.

It melted his heart.

But then he gently pushed back.

"What's the matter?" she asked with an amused smile.

"If you foresaw us together, why look me up? I don't understand. If you knew we'd be together, why seek me out? Why didn't you just wait for me to eventually appear? Why find me?"

She shrugged and put her arms around him. Then she looked deep into his eyes and giggled. "I wanted to fuck you."

THE END

Cora continues Greek mythological mayhem in the 21st century in the "Furies" series:

- MY EVIL EYE
- THE GUARDIAN, a novella
- NECTAR OF AMBROSIA , a novella

ALSO BY A.L. HAWKE

PARANORMAL ROMANCE

- MY EVIL EYE
- THE GUARDIAN
- NECTAR OF AMBROSIA

- ALONDRA
- THE HAWTHORNE UNIVERSITY WITCH SERIES I-III
- THE HAWTHORNE UNIVERSITY WITCH SERIES 4-6
- THE HAWTHORNE UNIVERSITY WITCH HOLIDAY COLLECTION

- SHADES
- HAUNTING JOY
- PHANTOM MASQUERADE

FANTASY: THE AZURE SERIES

- HARMONIA
- CORA: RISE OF THE FALLEN GODDESS
- AZURE BLUE
- CORAL RED
- PRINCESS SOJOURN

SCIENCE FICTION

- CANDY SAVANT SERIES

Books available at https://alhawke.com/books

PARTING WORDS

What did you think of *CORA*? By placing a book review, you can inform others of your thoughts and help spread the word about my book.

Want more? Periodically I like to send news regarding current or new projects. If you'd like to be privy, I encourage you to sign up to my email newsletter. Your information will remain private and you can cancel any time.

Sign up at www.alhawke.com or scan the following QR code:

ACKNOWLEDGMENTS

I want to thank the following beta readers who stuck through four years of permutations in order to bring about this completed work: Rob C. and John P. And to Monique S. who reviewed the final draft providing key insight.

Thank you to my editor Maya Rock for her support in early developmental editing. The original story was an epic fantasy frame story, if you can believe. I hung on to all her valuable critiques and recommendations.

Huge thanks to my editor Eliza Dee of Clio Editing Services who line edited, proofread and tweaked everything in between in order to polish my book. She made tough suggestions that made for a richer, more exciting, and just plain fun novel.

Finally, thank you to Regina Wamba of Mae I Design for creating a cover that looks more like a painting (*right?!*).

You've all enhanced my art. I am deeply grateful.

ABOUT THE AUTHOR

A.L. Hawke is the author of the bestselling Hawthorne University Witch series. The author lives in Southern California torching the midnight candle over lovers against a backdrop of machines, nymphs, magic, spice and mayhem. A.L. Hawke writes fantasy and romance spanning four thousand years, from pre-civilization to contemporary and beyond.

Visit A.L. Hawke at www.alhawke.com

Email: contact@alhawke.com